JIGSAW PART II

Ted Miller Brogden

ISBN:0692889434
ISBN-13:
978-0-692-88943-5

Jigsaw Part II

M E Publishing
Beaufort, SC

ACKNOWLEDGMENTS

I offer sincere thanks to the following people who have assisted me in the production of this book: **Linda Whitney Hobson**: Editor; **Kymbra L. L. Bryan**: Secondary Editing/Proofreader; **Kim F. Goff**: Technical advisor; and **Beta Readers**: Penni Bland, Diane Chatman Byrd, Tracy Draughon, Maria Herring, Donna Littleton Koelsch, Ray McDonald, Bobby Stevens, Lisa Ward Thompson, and Bonnie Wise.

Ted Miller Brogden
Goldsboro, NC
May 1, 2017

Dedicated to my son Gabe and his beautiful wife Lisa—living the Good Life in Charleston, S.C.

CHAPTER ONE

Old ending...New Beginning

Jigsaw Part II

An innocent clicking sound precedes the hammer-slam into the firing pin of Gustavo Jobim's single-six Ruger. Hot lead and gases scorch my skin, boil my blood, and shatter my cranium. Quiet folds in, and for a moment I'm at peace.

In the distance a Siren beckons in a childhood tune: *"Hush, little baby, don't say a word, Mama's gonna buy you a mockingbird."* Unlike the Argonauts' moment of crisis, though, no Orpheus comes to drown out the lilting enchantment. Intense heat burning into my brain drives me diving headlong into cold blackness, only to surface into a fog thicker than I've ever seen. A few yards away, now, the sweet voice comes in to serenade and soothe me. Guided only by my sense of hearing, I paddle like crazy toward the alluring songbird: *"And if that mockingbird don't sing, mama's gonna buy you a diamond ring."*

Like a storied biblical miracle, fog breaks and rolls to either side of me. A vision? No, the woman who gave me life, my mother, Catherine Thomas stands before me. She hasn't changed, but I'm a kid again and want my mother to hold me. She smiles, beckons me to sit at her side, and sings: *"And if that diamond ring turns to brass, Mama's gonna buy you a looking glass."*

Loud frantic voices cut into her sweet melody. "Call 911. Elevate his feet. He's going into shock!" Dr. Eva Benson, straddles me and pumps my chest with two handed compressions. A distant call for towels is followed by a closer voice: "Stop the bleeding or he'll die!"

"Ambulance is here!"

Someone yells, "We have a pulse. Faint, but he's alive!"

"No, we're losing him!"

A familiar face floats across the mist. For a second I'm certain the Wizard of Oz is here, and I'm honored until I hear my grandfather say: "Get back down there and finish what you started. There is always a solution, Cape, never forget that!"

Decorative ceilings of the Fisher Mansion fly above me as I'm rolled toward a waiting ambulance. An EMT trotting along side me squeezes a clear plastic bag forcing oxygen into my lungs: "Stay with me! Stay with me!" He yells.

Never a good listener, I leave this annoying madness for a bucolic dreamscape. In front of me is a rolling lawn that stretching for miles. High on a hill sits a whitewashed mansion, in stark contrast to the tropical-blue sky above. My bare-feet and spirit are refreshed in a fast-flowing but narrow stream dotted with white rocks and stones half out of the water. Each stone makes a bubbling eddy, yet curiously holds its position strong in the rushing water. I study the potential stepping-stones and lay plans to reach the other side.

But before I leap from the shore, a man dressed in a robe of light signals me to stop. "Ask and it shall be given you; seek, and ye shall find; knock, and it shall be opened unto you."

His words, are quoted and often preached on by my grandfather from *Matthew 7: 7*. I'm not a church-going-man, never have been, and not much of a believer in God. The Scripture is familiar only because it was pounded into me, Sunday after Sunday against my will.

Despite my unbelief, I have no doubt He is omniscient. As was my grandfather. Above the lush, green lawn the Siren's words rain down on me again and quiet the waters: *And if that looking glass gets broke, Mama's going buy you a billy goat.*

Before I can leap across the stream, darkness closes around me and my mother's voice fades away.

"Wait mama! Take me with you. I love you, mama." I yell and curse the man in light who's pushing me away from the stream. He turns, floats away, but my mother's sweet voice is gone, too.

"I want my Mama. You took her from me when I needed her most!"

"And that moment begat this moment." The man in light says.

Like a feather on the wind I float alone in a sky given to me by Miss Minnie. A dainty hand interlaces fingers with mine and guides me back to earth. I turn to smile at my mother, but Laura Fisher is at my side.

"Laura," I tell her, "now that I've found you, I'm never going to let you go!" Laura smiles and we kiss. Our hearts are awash in pure love. A thousand thoughts I want to share rush into my mind. She presses her finger to my lips and suppresses my words.

"I love you, Cape Thomas. Go back and save our little girl."

I'm alone again floating above Slick Rock Memorial Hospital, looking down at my body lying surrounded by a trauma team intent on bringing me back. Then I see Jana kneeling in a small room near the ER with tears running down her cheeks. I awaken staring into calm, clear, blue eyes. I can't tell whether the eyes belong to a male or female. Even more confusing, an androgynous voice says, "Welcome back."

"Are you, Jesus?" I ask.

"No, but if he's with you." Dr. Jake Draughon says. "I'd love to meet him."

What I perceive as "yesterday" turns out to be three long years for the medical staff of the Brain Trauma Unit-Slick Rock General Hospital. Much has changed since I awakened from my semi-vegetative state. Staff and my therapist, over the last year, have covered a lot of ground to bring me back.

My daughter, Jana, married the friend of her oncologist, a fellow named, Dr. Jake Draughon. The head of the Brain Trauma Unit here. Some people think he's a great guy. Jana and Jake have two children, making me their grandfather. Each day I get better, thanks to my intense combination of mental and physical therapy.

Late in the evening, when other patients are sleeping, I practice mental exercises I devised to help me heal sooner. I know exactly how many tiles comprise my room floor, including the half and quarter sized ones around the border of the room. And I've committed to memory the perforated patterns of the ceiling tiles above my bed. My auditory skills are so refined I have no trouble identifying staff members when they pass by in the corridor outside my room. Some of the female nurses jokingly refer to my newfound talent as my *"Wo-man-nar."*

Even with my extra efforts, though, some days I forget familiar people and events. Or I have dreams that seem so real I commit them to memory, too.

Most of my dreams are of my mother, father, and grandfather. They are the only family I've ever known despite the fact that my parents died when I was five. To help me keep things straight, my therapist refers to them as my *dreamworld* family. I'm supposed to refer to Jana, Jake, and my grand kids, Cape T and Laura—as my *reality* family. I don't see the benefit, but my cooperation pleases her and that may get me discharged sooner.

Whether it is my faux cooperation, luck of the draw, or my complete recovery, I am finally being discharged, and going "home" to a place I've never called home, the Fisher mansion, Jana's home now.

It's not unusual for long-term patients to be sent off in style by hospital staff, and today I am the honored recipient. Like the grand marshal of a parade I bask in the glory of my achievements and offer humble thanks to those who made them possible. As expected, practically all of the day shift stops by to say good-bye and express their well-wishes. I'll miss them, but not this place.

My Final-Day-Stay activities, of parties, gag gifts, pranks and a few heart felt good-byes have worn me out. Awaking from a nap, the darkness of the room tells me I've slept into the night.

A shaft of florescent light, squeezes through the gap in the door left ajar by the duty nurse. Faint laughter, exchanges of pleasantries, and a rustling of coats confirm that the graveyard shift is arriving on the fourth floor. One more round of good-byes from this shift and I'm out of here!

As usual, padded steps start and stop in the corridor as the night nurse begins her rounds. My *Wo-man-nar* is on full alert, but I don't recognize the cadence of this person's steps. She shuffles to a stop at my door to read my prognosis chart. Though, I'm due no medications, I see four fingers slide along the edge of the door, barely widening the gap. In one sweeping motion the door opens and closes without making a sound. Standing with her back pressed against the door is a night nurse wearing the familiar scrubs of the Brain Trauma Unit, but I'm sure we've never met. "You must be new, my Wo-man-nar didn't pick you up?" I wait for some acknowledgment that staff has told the new-hire about my uncanny sensory ability. The nurse nods, but says nothing. First day jitters, nothing odd about that I think.

Other than the soft hues cast by digital monitors marking my vitals, the room is dark. In front of an LED the nurse presses a syringe plunger until liquid drips from the needle, her movements as fluid as the contents of the syringe. In one adept motion she plunges the needle into my thigh muscle and empties the barrel. I struggle to move but am no match for the raw strength of this much smaller person penning me to the bed. I open my mouth to yell only to be dosed with an aerosol spray thick as DDT. My eyes and ears function normally, but everything else shuts down.

My attacker moves back to the door and cracks it just enough to see a few feet down the corridor. Satisfied we are alone, she opens the door. Quick before she's out the door, ambient light from the corridor illuminates a sinister grin. She dons a surgical mask, moves back beside my bed and takes a selfie of us! What the——?

Breathing is difficult. I concentrate to inhale. Nothing is right about this. I struggle to get my hands around her throat, but my muscles don't even twitch. I'm completely helpless, paralyzed.

Frozen by the drug, I cannot turn away as her coppery eyes peer at me from the slit between the mask and surgical garb covering her head. She nuzzles her mouth close to my ear and whispers, "All you hold dear will soon belong to me and this time there is nothing you can do about it. Now I'm going to kill you."

Adrenalin fuels my lunge, but she is gone, like vapor into thin air. Bells, whistles, alarms and flashing lights fill the room. A cadre of medical personnel appear as quickly as the nurse has vanished. Hands like serpents from the head of Medusa come from every direction and force me flat onto the bed.

A penlight temporarily blinds me and I fight with everything I have. The light, as before, consumes me. I am drawn to it because I've been here before, in the re-occurring dream I've had a thousand times. From somewhere in the mansion, my mother sings, but I can't visit with her because Jesus won't let me in until I knock on a door I can't find.

"Calm down, Mr. Thomas!"

"The nurse! The night nurse! Where is she?" I fight to look past the mob surrounding me. She couldn't have gotten far.

But now another nurse with a syringe is headed for me. I kick and fight even harder than before. The mass of bodies piled on me moves away as an NFL-size-attendant pins me to the mattress. "No, stop her! She has a syringe—she's going to kill me." *En masse* the others turn and look at the nurse. She holds the syringe in the air and with the phoniest sweet voice I've ever heard, declares, "It's only a sedative."

"She's lying! She's in on this with that other nurse. They're going to kill me!"

A soothing voice rises above the cacophony. "What other nurse, Cape?"

"The one who tried to kill me!"

"When?"

"Just now! You had to see her. It was only seconds ago! She was covered up except for her coppery eyes."

"Who is the duty nurse?" the soothing voice said.

A slightly overweight woman with gray hair steps forward. "I am,

Doctor."

"Who else is working the floor with you?"

"No one. It's third shift."

I struggle to sit up. "Her eyes, her eyes…I'd know her eyes—amber, tigerish, coppery eyes."

Every person in the room faces me, but none of them resembles my attacker. Obviously the night nurse has changed her looks, easy enough for a woman to do with the right make up. I repeat slowly what my attacker said, "All you hold dear will soon belong to me and this time there is nothing you can do about it. Now I'm going to kill you." I look at the nurse who is checking my pulse and scream, "Say it!"

The nurses look at the doctor. "It's fine. Just say it for him."

Each nurse repeats the phrase but none of them have the accent or tone of the night nurse. The doctor moves in front of me blocking my view of the others and shines a penlight in each eye.

"You were dreaming, Cape. Nothing you saw is real," the doctor says, turning to the floor nurse. "Monitor him closely and let's forgo the sedative for now. Call me if there're any changes."

"Very well, Dr. Draughon."

"Thank you, Jake," I whisper, "and can you leave my door open?"

"Sure, Cape."

"Does this mean I'm not going home?"

Jake moves to the head of my bed, "That depends on how you answer my next question."

"OK, shoot."

"Cape, do you really think a nurse tried to kill you, or do you think you had a nightmare?"

I know the response he wants, even tough the antiseptic scent of the nurse who tried to kill me lingers in the air. I can't take another day in this place. "I must have dozed off. It seemed so real…just another freaky nightmare, that's all."

"Did you see, You-know-who again?"

"You know I don't believe in that holy-roller-crap, Jake."

Jake scribbles something on my chart and hangs the clipboard at the foot of my bed. I look around the room to make sure the others have left.

"Jake, there is something I need to tell you."

"What's that?"

"A tribe in Africa won't let you take a picture of them—"

"Because they are afraid the picture takes their soul. I've heard of them, Cape."

"That nurse, in my dream, took a selfie with me after she shot my thigh muscle full of some liquid that paralyzed me."

"The one who tried to kill you?"

"Yes."

"Well, I hope you smiled."

"But it felt like she took more than a picture."

"Like she stole your soul?" Jake smiles.

"No, like she was documenting her presence?" I said.

Jake walks back to the door and turns to face me. "No, Jesus, right?"

"Nope"

"Too bad."

"Why?"

Jake gives me a big grin. "I'd like to get his opinion on the theory of evolution."

Dawn breaks as a cap of magenta sitting squarely on the rising sun, and not a cloud on the horizon. My eyes burn from lack of sleep, but I see I made it through the night without being killed by a crazy-selfie taking nurse or seeing Jesus.

My send off from the Brain Trauma Unit is epic since after my behavior last night I'm sure staff hopes I never return. In spite of my, episode, I'm feeling good until my wheelchair ride stops at the pick up zone in front of the hospital. A limo with a lone driver holding a *Mr. Thomas* sign is there to greet me. Not exactly the warm welcome I'm expecting from my *reality family*."

"I'm Thomas," I say, and stand to greet the driver. He tucks his sign into the car trunk and opens my door.

"It's a short ride, sir. We should be there in twenty minutes or so."

"Nobody else riding with us?"

"No sir. If you're expecting someone I'll be glad to wait?"

I look across the parking lot, then back at the hospital hoping to see Jana and the kids, or at least Jana—but nothing.

"I guess not."

"Very well, sir. Enjoy your ride."

We exchange mutual nods and I take in the spacious interior of the Limo. A display of assorted booze sitting atop a minibar midway of the car gets my attention. I eye the bourbon, but instead grab a bottle of Fiji water to drown my misery.

"Back in the day someone would have been waiting for me," I mumble to myself. Less than a minute into our ride a Pitt/Greenville airport sign flashes by my window.

My status as a former AeroMax captain will get me a jump-seat on any major airline. But where would I go? That's easy, to see Linda Jessup, the doctor's wife, and my former girlfriend. Sure, Linda's happily married, but she'd never turn me down. Why is it women you treat like crap are always the ones who step up when you need a friend the most?

Though Linda is dependable, she isn't who I want to see. Allison Moore Kress fills that bill. She also abandoned me in my time of need. Oh, she sent a card every now and then, or a text pretending to care about my rehabilitation progress. But Ally is a socialite, so doing things like that comes easy to her. Despite her good manners, the fact remains, she dumped me for someone else and never looked back. I languished away in a hospital, fighting for my life, and she thrived in her high-society-Charlotte life.

Thinking of Ally makes my heart ache. Before Gustavo Jobim shot me, Ally and I were well on our way to falling in love. It's no secret why she dumped me, though— Allison Moore Kress isn't about to settle for damaged goods. If I cared enough to Google her, I'm sure I'd find hundreds of articles documenting her fabulous life style. If I cared to— but I don't. To prove I couldn't care less, I stopped answering her texts or responding to her cards. I should send my self-involved *reality family* the same message. I hit the intercom button.

"Yes, sir, how may I help you?"

"Take me to the airport."

"Why is that sir? My instructions are to drop you off at the Fisher mansion."

"There's been a change of plans. Damn, if I'm going to a place I'm not wanted."

The driver eyes me through the rearview mirror and makes a turn toward the airport. "Sir, you know it's not like your family sent a taxi to pick you up. Most times when folks spring for a Limo, it's because they want the very best for you."

"That may be, but if they don't care enough to meet me at the hospital with smiles and hugs, they don't want me in their house either."

The driver shakes his head. "Be all right with you if I put this privacy glass up? I need to make a call to my dispatcher."

"Fine by me."

"My GPS shows there's a little traffic between here and the airport. The trip may take a little longer than normal?"

"Frankly, I don't care how long it takes." I said. "As long as it takes me far away from here."

When we arrive at the airport the person opening my door, is none other than, Dr. Jake Draughon.

"What kind of stunt are you trying to pull?" Jake asked.

"I'm going some place where I'm wanted, that's all."

Jake's face turns red and I'm not certain steam isn't coming out of his ears. "And how were you going to get—"

"Jump-seat! A courtesy airlines extend to their family!"

"And what were you going to use for money?"

I pat my wallet-less backside. "I was going to borrow some money from the driver and pay him back when I settled in my new place."

The driver puts up both hands like I'm robbing him at gun point. "Now sir, that's the first I've heard of this."

"No doubt," Jake said. "Thank you for calling me. I'll handle things from here."

Jake grits his teeth and points to his car. "Do you have any idea how much time Jana put into this little surprise party she planned for you?"

"Surprise party. For me?"

"Yes, she wanted you to know how special this day is for her and the kids. If it wouldn't break her heart, I'd send you right back to the hospital!"

"I...I thought no one cared. I didn't know—"

"It's not always about you, Cape! This ordeal has been hard on Jana, too. First she thought you were going to die. Then she thought you might be a vegetable. And right now I'm thinking that comparison is an insult to vegetables!" Jake snatches his phone in my face. "You see how many texts I have from her?" I read the first text: *Something is wrong. Dad's missing!* Second text: I *told you I should have picked him up from the hospital!* Third text: *"Check the ER and see if there has been a wreck, please!"*

"I'm sorry—"

"It's OK. I gave her a sedative before I left to search for you. Thank goodness the driver had enough sense to call the hospital and let me know what was going on."

"Why did the driver call the hospital?"

Jake rolls his eyes. "Because he thought you'd gone crazy!"

"What's so crazy about asking a limo driver to drop you off at the airport!"

"You're still in your pajamas!"

Hmm. Good point...

The ride home is anything but pleasant. I stare out the window and pretend to enjoy the scenery whizzing by. Jake drums his fingers on the steering wheel. I guess it's his way of keeping them from tightening around my neck.

Happy face signs line the driveway and party decorations cover the front doors. A big banner stretched across the balcony read: *Welcome home Captain Cape Thomas, best of the best! We Love you!!!!* The banner is signed in crayons by Jana, the kids, Jake and Mr. Fisher—then too many x's and o's to count.

"Do you think it would be OK if I saw them?"

"Jana is sedated." Jake said. "I sent the kids to the park with their *au pair*."

"When she wakes will you tell Jana I love her?"

Jake shakes his head. "Go get some rest, Cape. You can tell her yourself tomorrow. Your room is on the third floor, second door on the left." I look up the winding stair case and back at Jake. "I didn't mean—"

"I have to get back to the hospital. If you need anything press the intercom button marked, Staff." Jake hands me an envelope. "This is some information you should know about the mansion. Mr Fisher, is a real gun-nut and he wants you to know there's a gun-safe behind that mirror. I've never bothered to check. I don't think much of guns."

"Jake, I'm really sorry—"

"You've been through a lot." Jake puts his hand on my shoulder. "I know the battles you've fought and I'm proud of you. What you don't know is the pressure Jana's been under. The kids are a handful, my crazy hours are hard to endure, and she's worried you may relapse. What you did today only strengthens her fears. No more crazy stunts, OK?"

I sit on the steps and look up at the banner. *Best of the best.*

My room at the Fisher Mansion is in a part of the house I didn't see on my previous visits to the estate. Everything about my room is antebellum. Luxurious furniture, bedding, and draperies in abundance, clearly costing much more than my $200,000 a year salary when I worked for AeroMax. As impressive as my room is, it doesn't get my mind off ruining things for Jana and the kids. I vow to do a better job fitting into my new family, but that's hard to do when you've never been part of a family. Not a real family, with fathers, mothers and grandfathers. Heck, I've never really been a father. Now I'm expected to be a father and grandfather. Parenting is definitely a subject I'll have to research. But the excitement of the day is catching up to me. I lie down for what turns out to be a 21 hour nap.

A knock on my door wakes me, and I get my first lesson in how the wealthy are far different from us commoners. I scramble toward the door rubbing sleep from my eyes and almost get bowled over by a fireball of a woman named Louise. "Lawd, have mercy! Did I wake you up Mr. Thomas? They said you was an early riser."

Before I answer, she sets a sterling silver coffee pot and tray on a coffee table near the balcony door. "Weather's perfect for dining outside, if you prefer?" Louise's question sounds more like a command. I nod my head and move out of her way. "I apologize for not finding out in advance, but what you want for breakfast, Mr. Thomas?"

"Ahh, coffee?"

"Yes, sir, on the balcony…and for breakfast?"

I stayed in many motels and hotels during my years with AeroMax, but never have I stayed at a place with this kind of service. "Is there a menu or something I can order from?"

"Haha, now we got ourselves a comedian here!" Louise sits down on the small bench at the foot of my bed and pretends to open a diner order pad. "Yes, sir we do have a menu. It's titled, 'What Ever in the World Your Little Heart Desires'. Now, what'll it be?"

"Bacon, eggs, and grits?" I said.

"Want orange juice with that?"

I decide to test the waters. "Grape juice with a splash of lime?"

"This ain't Starbucks! How 'bout I put you a slice of lime on the side?" Louise said.

"I guess, but how—"

"How extensive is the menu?" Louise puts her index finger against her cheek. "Well, let me help you out with that. If your li'l heart desires filet mignon and an omelet with truffles…we can make that happen. If you want a fried bologna sandwich with beluga caviar on the side, we can make that happen, too. What I'm saying, Mr. Thomas, is that no matter how you think you can stretch our capacity to please, you can't. This is the home of Mr. Nathan Hale Fisher and there is no lengths that he will not go to for his guest. We may have to overnight it in here, but if there is something you desire in this world, we can make that happen." Louise makes a circle in the air with her finger and mimics a ticking clock. "Ding! If you will allow us a little time."

"I apologize for not understanding the capacity of your hospitality. I'm not accustomed to this kind of service. I was raised in a small town— we didn't have much domestic service there," I said.

"Really?"

"Yep. If you wanted something there," I say, "well, you pretty much got it yourself, or did without."

"That's the way I was raised, too."

I step out on the balcony to get a cup of coffee and Louise follows me. "Guess you're right, this isn't Starbucks…this place is more like…Disney."

"Why you say that?" Louise said.

"Disney. You know…'Happiest Place on Earth.' I mean there's nothing you won't do to satisfy a guest, right?"

Louise looks up at the security camera sweeping the grounds out in front of us. "Mister, this place is a lot of things, but bein' the happiest place on earth, ain't one of 'em."

"What, do you mean?"

The security camera makes an abrupt turn, zeroing in on us . "OK, Mister Thomas." Louise says with broad smile. "I'll get right on your breakfast. You let me know if there's anything else you need. Mister Fisher, said to take extra special care of you." Louise backs into the privacy of my room and mouths in a low whispers "Around this place, Mr. Thomas it's a good idea not to believe everything you hear, and only half of what you see."

"Come again?"

Louise puts her finger to her lips and hustles away...

CHAPTER TWO

Back in a New Place

Shadows cast by the majestic oaks on the grounds stretch to the foot of my chaise lounge on the balcony. My morning nap, oddly, has again turned into another long sleep event. Instead of the rising morning sun I dozed off under, I see the sun is now setting atop the western tree line.

A hangover-grogginess in my head leaves me wondering if Louise slipped a mickey into my coffee. Before I chase that rabbit, though, hunger pangs force me to see to my immediate needs. I'm hungry again and I want food, now. In spite of my best efforts I have not found a button marked Staff as Jake mentioned. A quick glance around my lavish surrounding suggests proper attire may be required, even to forage for a light snack.

Finding suitable attire from the dated clothes in my bag is likely an effort in futility. Loud growling noises in my gut are making one heck of an argument for boxers and t-shirts being proper attire.

My knees pop and I groan when I check under the bed to see if Louise stored my bag there. Unlike the under-bed at my house there are no dust bunnies here. The floor is spic-n-span except for a length of coiled rope. No way someone who cleans immaculately missed this anomaly. I put my finger in the center of the circle and pull it out— dangling in front of me is a noose. Thirteen loops, too, good job! Exactly like the ones I tied as a boy. Snugging the noose around my finger, I continue searching for my bag.

The only place left to search is the walk-in closet. A light pops on when I open the door. Long rows of clothes run down either side of the closet. On one side are men's casual clothes, on the other side is an array of bespoke suits, blazers, dress shirts and slacks. A merchandise display like those found at high-end department stores covers the back wall. Shoes and belts for every occasion are stacked on top of shelves that run from floor to ceiling. A note pinned to one of the jackets explains the packed closet: *Dad hope you like them, Love Jana.*

My fingers trace along the luxurious jacket material, high quality cashmere. No telling what Jana spent to make sure I'm dressed in appropriate attire. Without Laura and Jana, my life would be so different. There are those, including Jake, who insist Laura's presence, in my search for Jana, was only a figment of my imagination. I hold the jacket, still on its wooden hanger, up to my chest and observe my image in the full-length mirror. I put my finger adorned with the noose on the scar that runs along the side of my face. This is real and Laura was no figment of my imagination. I'm looking at the proof.

I read the note again. The writing reminds me of the banner Jana and the kids made for my fiasco homecoming party. I imagine the hurt looks on their faces and pain rips my heart. No wonder Jana hasn't been by to check on me. She's probably checking on other things, like finding me accommodations at a long-term care unit somewhere in Slick Rock. I don't blame her. Jana doesn't deserve the burden I am. I unpin the note so I can keep it with my other important documents. Opening a Bible lying on my nightstand, I place the note inside.

Poor Jana! No one deserves the suffering she's endured. I only know bits and pieces of her life before I found her, but I know she had a rough time of it. How many times was she subjected to people like Tate Harris, the slime ball music producer in Nashville…or others even worse than him. I grab the Bible off the nightstand and shake it toward the heavens. "Her rotten life wasn't enough? You had to zap her with cancer, too!"

I throw the Bible on the bed and go back into the closet to get dressed. I've got to find Jana and make things right for screwing up her homecoming party. I slip on a pair of khakis, blue polo shirt, and tan driving mocs, then hurry out.

A plastic Do-not-disturb sign grazes my hand as I close the door. My earlier flippant thought returns—did Louise slip me a mickey? I'm not a heavy sleeper, only 4 or 5 hours of sleep a night suits me fine, so for me to sleep hours on end is certainly unusual…but why would a maid drug me? Reversing direction, I go back in the room. Is it possible I ate the breakfast I ordered yet don't remember it?

The only thing on the serving tray is a coffee pot and small silver bell that I shove in my pocket. If Louise had plans to knock me out for a day, why bother making such a big deal about my breakfast choices? A good question, and one I promise to ask Louise…if I ever see *her* again.

Even though I had visited the mansion before Gustavo Jobim shot me, I was never afforded a guided tour of the place. Without a clue how to find the kitchen, I take matters into my own hand, literally. "Hello!

Starving patient in the house." No one answers so I pull the bell from my pocket and work it like a Red Kettle pro in front of Wal-Mart on Christmas Eve. "Brain-damaged invalid, here, starving to death. Need a little service, staff!" I yell between flurries of bell ringing. Nothing but silence.

"*Well, it appears I have indeed stretched the capacity of your hospitality, Ms. Louise,*" I mumble and head for the stairs. A sweeping staircase leading to the main entrance is like something out of *Gone With The Wind*. At any moment I half-expect to see a gaggle of dainty ladies in hoop-skirts sporting parasols as they sashay past me. Once I reach the foyer I'm drawn again to the portraits of Laura and Bianca in the ballroom.

Laura's eyes shower benevolence, but Bianca's glare disapproval on me. I've never really appreciated the skills of a talented artist, but I do now. I look at Laura's smiling face. "I wish we could have gotten to know one another," I tell her, but as expected, Laura says nothing and I move down the hall toward the rear of the house.

Unlike those in modern houses the kitchen is closed off from the other rooms. One step inside and I understand why. This is a commercial kitchen, much like the ones found in fine hotels. No wonder Louise's options for entertaining are so vast—such a pity she squandered her time but left me starving. I open what I think is a pantry. A bitter cold blanket of air envelopes me. I'm not familiar with them, but there is no doubt this is a walk-in freezer. Bulk items in unopened cases line the walls and shelves of the freezer. A lone fudge popsicle atop one of the cases catches my eye and I down it in three bites. Not a proper meal by any means, but something to tide me over until I figure out what's going on.

Though I don't know it, the refrigerator I'm looking for is camouflaged to resemble a section of built-in cabinets. Once I solve the kitchen designer's evil deceptions, I graze like a water buffalo on the savanna.

Finally sated, I explore the Fisher Mansion dressed in proper attire. I walk down a hallway separating the kitchen from a dry goods storage area. At the end of the hallway is a long corridor that leaves me empty and cold. I head back to the friendlier confines of the ballroom and the portrait of Laura.

There she is, and I'm giddy as a new teen at the high school after scoring a date with the prettiest girl there. I stand on the hearth and tiptoe to get closer. All I focus on is her eyes. "You don't know me...well you do, but we were never formally introduced. I'm, Cape Thomas" I step down from the hearth, and as before, her eyes follow my every move. "You wouldn't believe what I went through to find, Jana. If I wrote a book about it, Laura, it would be a best-seller." The further I move back, the more she smiles. Genius, who ever painted this portrait is a genius! "I wish you could have met, Jana. She's a carbon copy of you."

My thoughts return to the night Laura and I sat in front of the outside fireplace at my grandfather's house. "You stole my heart, Laura. You ruined any chance of me finding true love after we met. I hurt a lot of good women, for no other reason than they weren't you." Her smile fades, I sense her disappointment, so I change the subject.

"They say I died when I was shot. I've always thought death was the end, but you where there and so was my family. Was it real Laura or just a lack of oxygen to my brain? I'm not religious but I'm pretty sure I saw, Jesus. He made me go back and you told me to go back and save our little girl." I look around the room to make sure we are alone. I move to the divan and have a seat, and again Laura's attentive eyes follow me. "I'm confused about that. Didn't I already save, Jana? Or wasn't that good enough— is more danger ahead?"

"Dad, who are you talking to?"

I turn to face the most beautiful woman in the world, my daughter, Jana Draughon. "No one. I was just thinking out loud."

"You were talking *to* her." Jana gazes at Laura's portrait. "Weren't you?"

I don't think Jana will rat me out, but if Jake thinks I'm having conversations with portraits of dead people there's a good chance I'm going back to the hospital, or maybe to that long-term-care-facility Jana's probably found by now.

"Of course not!"

"Don't lie, Dad."

"There is something about that portrait that looks so life-like... but I know it's just a painting, Jana. I'm not crazy." I stand and move in front of Jana. "Don't tell, Jake. Please—I can't do anymore hospital time."

Jana smiles and grabs my hand, "Dad, you're not going back there. And you're right." Jana looks at the portrait. "It's life-like. I talk to her everyday."

"You do?"

"Yep, everyday."

I guess Jana shares that special family gene of ours. "She ever talk back?"

"No, Dad. Why would you think that, she's dead."

"Just checking. Wouldn't want ole, Jake to sneak up behind during one of your conversations. Might give him a reason to put *you* in a straitjacket—he gets kind of ornery, you know."

"Jake is not ornery and we're not crazy for talking to her."

"Half your statement is true, Honey, Jake *can* be ornery."

"Do you think we're crazy, Dad, for talking to her portrait?"

"No, I have it on good authority; we're *special*. But to be on the safe side, I wouldn't get in the habit of conversing with her when other people are around."

"Funny!"

I recall the day my grandmother went to a mental hospital and never came back. "I'm serious. Back in the day they sent people away for a lot less."

"I never know when to believe you."

"Good, Jana—keeps you on your toes." Jana reaches for my hand and we both regard the portrait again.

"Do you think Laura knows we found each other?"

"I guess, only Jesus knows for sure."

"I didn't think you believed in that stuff?"

"That would be, Jake. I see answered prayers every time I look at my family." Jana said, smiling up at me. "I never told you this. The day you were shot—I prayed over you in Jesus' name. Maybe that's why you keep having your dream? Sorry."

"Don't feel too bad, you come by it honestly. My granddaddy, your great-grandaddy, was a praying person, too. Man, the prayers he prayed over me! Sadly, unlike yours, his were never answered."

I look at Jana and back at the portrait, Laura and Jana really could be identical twins a generation apart. "I always wonder how things would have turned out if I had called her, or if she had told me her name? Do you ever think about that?"

"No, I believe our story played out just as it was supposed to."

"We could have been a family, though— that would have been nice."

Jana hugs me tight. "We *are* a family. Because of you, we *are* a family." Big tears stream down her face. "You could have died saving me and you've been in a living hell ever since—"

"Hold on, kiddo! Whatever I've been through is not your fault. A man named Gustavo Jobim bears that burden. Not you, and not me. Jobim, may have nicked me up a little bit, but we're going to be just fine. You got that?"

Jana wipes away her tears and gives me one of those quick smiles strong women keep at the ready. "I almost forgot why I came home. I need to change because, Jake and the kids are coming for me. Grandad is out front waiting for you. Go with him, he has a surprise for you at the

17

graveyard."

"The *graveyard?*"

"Just go, Dad. I have to hurry."

Mr. Fisher appears to be deep in thought. Like me, he's probably thinking about Jana and how she manages our band of misfits.

"Did you rest well, Cape," Mr Fisher asks. "I trust Louise took good care of you?"

So there is a Louise! "She did, but she came up a little short on my breakfast."

"I apologize. Louise, took ill and I sent her home."

"Nothing serious, I hope."

"Oh, probably a 24 hour bug."

Now I know people die suddenly, and there is a 24 hour bug that can take any one of us down with little warning, but Louise looked in perfect health. I suspect her time-off has more to do with her warning to me that was caught on surveillance equipment. Turning my first bit of shared family time into a sticky wicket doesn't seem like a good idea, however—unless Mr. Fisher cares to expand on the subject. "I hope she recovers quickly." I said. "I enjoyed chatting with her."

Mr. Fisher, nods but speaks no more on our ride to the cemetery. The old guardhouse I remember from my previous visits is gone. I'm tempted to ask Mr. Fisher about the pot-smoking guard, but what are the chances a man like Nathan Hale Fisher knew the guard?

On the walk to the mausoleum, I meander around looking at interesting markers and monuments along the path to the family plot. Mr. Fisher marches straight ahead as if like he's on a mission. When I catch up to him, he's staring at a fresh etching.

"Doesn't bother you, does it, Cape?"

I look at the mausoleum in front of me and read *Captain Cape Thomas Loving Father.* The hairs on my neck prickle against my collar and my mouth goes drier than powered cement. Opposite of my final resting place is an addition I've never seen before: *Bianca Jenkins Loving Daughter.* My past visits here, for some strange reason, always put me at peace. Today I'm not feeling it. Maybe it's seeing Bianca's tomb for the first time, or more likely, having my tomb ceded to me and engraved now, this moment, with no prior notice?

"The lettering, Cape? What do you think?"

I can't bring myself to look at my own name again, so I avert my eyes to the sepulcher above mine: *Laura Fisher Loving Mother.* Everything I hold dear in this world I owe to this women. I press my palm against the cool stone she lies behind. Same as I did my first time here.

Mr. Fisher, clears his throat. Is that his way of letting me know I've pondered his question long enough? "Well, does it bother you or not?"

"It's a little unsettling." Together we turn and regard my name. "I mean, it's nice, but a definite reminder of my mortality."

The old man nods, "I know, same thing I thought when my name was put there." I follow his finger as he traces his tomb's lettering: *Nathan Hale Fisher Loving Father.*

Mr. Fisher lifts his finger from the engraving and rests his hand on my shoulder. For a second I'm uneasy, not used to people touching me; after three years of suspension between life and death. I'm not sure whether I belong with the living or the dead. Seems like I've always been conflicted about the living and the dead—and my place among them.

"You know you're part of the family now." Mr. Fisher assures me. "That's why I had the engraving done. I want you never to have any doubts about belonging here."

I get it and I appreciate his gesture, but there're other ways to celebrate a new family member. Pointing at my sepulcher, I assure him in return that, "I thank you, sir, but I hope it's a while before I need your gift. They say I should make a full recovery. You know that, right?" I don't want to be rude, but if my next surprise is coffin shopping. I'm putting the kibosh on that idea, right here and right now.

"Yes, Cape, I'm counting on you getting well, and even stronger." Mr Fisher looks around the graveyard. "I have something to show you." With the agility of a much younger man he snaps a small box from his coat pocket and presents it upon his outstretched palm. "Have a look at this."

At first glance, the box appears to be a novelty item, but the intricate detail, weight, and burled walnut finish say otherwise. Mr. Fisher hands me what looks like a scale model of a nineteenth-century coffin, narrow at the bottom and wide across the top. A latch with the patina of 24 karat gold holds the flip lid closed.

"It came about a month before you were deemed well enough to be discharged from the hospital. I didn't want to worry you with it until you were, you know…more stable," Mr. Fisher says. "I wouldn't have opened the package, but it was addressed to me. Only after I opened it did I realize it had been repackaged after your name was written on the box."

"That's OK, no problem," I rush my answer because I don't want Mr. Fisher to feel that he invaded my privacy.

He turns the box until the lid faces me. With a flick of the latch the spring-loaded lid folds back revealing five circular photographs. Each picture is cut-to-size and glued to a silver dollar size coin. I pluck one of the coins up and let in rest in my palm, then pick up another. One has the weight and feel of pure silver, yet the other weighs practically nothing. "Why are the weights so different?" I ask.

"Some are real and others are plugs. I have no idea what it means, but that's not all." With trembling fingers Mr. Fisher plucks three more coins from the box and another photograph appears. This picture is rectangular and is glued to a gold ingot. The scene is a selfie of me lying comatose in my hospital bed with the night nurse who tried to kill me. "You're sure this came a month ago?"

"Yes, indeed, why do you ask?"

"Where did you keep it?"

"In my private gunsafe. No one else has seen it."

"Or had access to it?"

"No, why?"

If Mr. Fisher is being truthful, it's obvious the night nurse visited me more than once. Then again, he could be lying.

"No, reason."

The other pictures, like this one, are unposed, and candid; each could belong in my family album—if I possessed such a treasure. "What does it means?" I ask him.

"Read the bottom." Before Mr. Fisher secures the ingot I flip the box over and read the fancy script.

All you hold dear will soon belong to me and this time there is nothing you can do about it. And now I'm going to kill you.

I read the phrase again, and the minty essence of the night nurse smothers me again. A terror of being paralyzed and vulnerable shuts me down. What happened to me in the hospital , then, was no nightmare!

I inhale a deep breath, close my eyes, and slowly exhale to clear my mind. Exercises like this are part of my routine that keep me from slipping back into a dark hole I've teetered over for three years. I won't go back there. I can't. I prize reality—as annoying and frustrating as it often is.

"Mr. Fisher, I was discharged from room 416 at Slick Rock General Hospital because there is no night nurse, just as there is no Jesus! It's all a dream." I wave the coffin at Mr. Fisher. "This isn't real, you're not real!" I reach out and touch Mr. Fisher. He grabs my arm.

Oh no—I can feel him clutching my arm, so if I'm dreaming, I've taken dreaming to a whole new somatic level.

Mr. Fisher waves frantically at a young couple walking along hand in hand with a set of twins in tow. They scoop up the twins and run toward us as fast as they can.

"What's wrong!" Jana yells.

"It's Cape. He's having a relapse. Let's help him, Jake."

Dr. Jake Draughon sits me down on a concrete bench in front of the mausoleum. "Cape, what's wrong?"

Good, Jake's here. Everything will be OK, now.

"Cape, can you hear me. Tell me what's wrong."

"No nurse is trying to kill me and there is no, Jesus. That's right isn't it, Jake?"

"Jana, call 911. He has to go back to the hospital, now!"

Just exactly the words I don't want to hear. I shove the box into Jake's hand, writing side down.

"Is this real?"

"Hell, Cape I don't know if its real. I don't follow antiques—"

"The writing on the bottom, damn it! Is it *real*?"

Jake scans the writing and the photo glued to the gold ingot. He grabs the phone from Jana's hand. "Hello, this is Dr. Jake Draughon. I thought we had an emergency, but the patient is fine now. We don't need an ambulance."

The twins are crying—all the yelling scared the crap out of them. Jana cradles the two in her arms and swings them around. "It's OK, it's OK, my sweet ones. We're all just playing." She faces us and hisses, "Laugh! Laugh loud!"

I may be brain-damaged, but I'm not stupid. We all begin to fake laugh and the twins giggle back at us. Jana takes two toys out of her knapsack, gives one to each kid, and we are forgotten by the twins.

Jana pushes us away from the kids and behind the mausoleum.

"What's going on?"

Jake hands Jana the box. "Do you remember the episode your dad had just before I released him?"

"The dream? He has it all the time."

"Yeah, but remembe his last dream was different."

"Right, he dreamed a nurse tried to kill him."

"Remember what she said to him?" Jake asks, and turns to look me in the eye.

"Yes, I do. Dad made all the nurses repeat what she said to identify who it was."

"Right." Jake says. "Read the writing on the box."

Jana reads the writing aloud. "This doesn't prove she was in the room with Dad. It only proves that some sick person engraved what Dad dreamed onto this box. Probably something to do with that damn Fisher Fortune! This proves nothing, Jake."

Jake hands Jana the ingot with attached selfie. "This does."

Mr. Fisher hands Jana all the coins and pictures. Jana and Jake scan the ingot, coins, and pictures over and over. Jana finally breaks the silence. "All of these pictures are recent, but none that we've taken."

Jake, hands the picture on the ingot over to me. "Is this the woman you saw in your room?"

"Yes, Jake, but that's not the selfie taken during that attack. Look, my eyes are closed and Mr. Fisher has had it in his possession for a month."

"She had unfettered access to you?" Jake asks.

"I guess, but why didn't she kill me when I was in a coma? I was awake when she stuck me with a syringe, and it was full of fluid. I saw some of it drip out before she injected me. She could have injected me with poison anytime."

Jana puts her arm around my shoulder, "Thank God she didn't, Dad."

"But, why didn't she when she easily could? She had multiple chances?" Jake said. "Why wait until your last night in the trauma ward to attack you?"

I absent-mindedly take the noose out of my pocket and twirl it around my finger. Cape T sees it, drops his toy and claims the noose. I drop it in his little chubby hand and tousle his hair.

Jana snatches it out of his hand and yells, "What is this, pray tell?"

"I found it this afternoon under my bed. I thought is was something one of the kids dropped. I used to tie nooses myself back in the day."

"Why didn't you mention this noose to me when we talked in the drawing room? I mean *seriously*, it's a noose, not a ribbon bow!" Jana yells.

"I figured maybe one of you guys tied it for the twins—it's sort of like— a toy," I say.

"A *toy*! Toys don't kill!"

"Well, they used to!" I say. "Sling shots, pea shooters, air rifles, cherry bombs. Now, if a kid gnaws a pop tart into the shape of a pistol they're sent to reform school!"

"There is no such thing as a reform school." Jana says. "A noose is not a child's toy. Do you understand?"

"I didn't see it as a big deal, honey—sorry."

Jana's jaw muscles tightens and she speaks through clenched teeth. "You don't see where a potential deadly weapon in my child's hand is a problem!"

"It's a, *simple noose!*" I said.

"Don't say that again!"

"Why? Because it isn't politically correct? That's why I don't tell you guys anything. Even if I'd mentioned the noose, I'd be wrong and I'd be right back in the hospital. I'm like a parolee around here waiting for the gavel to drop!"

"Cape's right," Jake points to the kids who are staring at us big-eyed as if we're a circus attraction. "Let's calm down."

I nod.

"So what's the significance of 13 loops?" Jake asks, taking the noose from Jana.

"It's not an official hangman's noose, if it doesn't have 13 knots." I explain.

"Now, just how do you know that?" Jake says smiling.

"When I was a kid, back in the most dangerous times children ever lived, we knew things like that. There were 13 steps to the gallows and the axes used to behead royalty were 13 inches across."

"You're serious?" Jana said.

"Well, I wouldn't bet my life on it. Those may well be urban legends, but back when boys watched westerns and adventure movies, things like that came up."

"I wonder if the box and coins are somehow connected to the noose," Mr. Fisher says.

Jana and Jake look at the twins. "We, have to call the police." Jana says. "If the noose and coins are related, then Dad's attacker was in my house!"

"I'm way ahead of you," Mr. Fisher interjects. "I called RH, the moment I found the box. He'll be here in the morning"

"RH?" I said.

"Jana's uncle, RH Carter."

"And donor. Don't forget that part." Jana adds. "I told you about that, Dad."

It's hard to forget, RH Carter, and it's hard to forget how slimy he made me feel the day MarKay died. I know he was a perfect donor match for Jana. I'm grateful for that, but Carter is not one of my favorite people.

"Why can't our local cops handle this?"

"RH is FBI, Cape. Local cops will be involved, but RH is coming to stay for a while to help with security around the house."

"Fantastic, I'm *so* glad he can come." Jana says.

My thoughts of RH Carter distract me and I forget the location of

23

the concrete bench. My lapse of awareness skins up both shins and sends me sprawling across the grass where the twins are playing. Luckily I didn't fall on them or I'd have gotten a death sentence—instead I'm confined to bed rest until Jake deems otherwise.

Damn bench! *Damn RH!*

CHAPTER THREE

RH Carter...Again!

Before the plane stops at the terminal Robert Hale Carter grabs his carry-on and heads for the door. From behind him a flight attendant streaks toward the exit. "Sir, please go back to your seat," The flight attendant grabs RH by the shoulder but he bolts through the now open door leading to the jet-way.

"I'm a cop, lady." Carter said. "I got important business here."

The disagreement continues up the jetway and spills over into the concourse area. Frustrated with being ignored, the flight attendant flags down a nearby TSA officer close to where Mr. Fisher and I stand. "Sir, sir!" She calls out. "We have a situation!"

"I told you, I'm a cop, lady!"

"I don't believe he's a police officer." The flight attendant blurts out, "And he disobeyed my instructions."

Carter flashes his badge at the TSA officer who turns to the flight attendant. "He's FBI, ma'am, it's all good." As quickly as she burst from the plane, the flight attendant turns, shame-faced, and fades back into the horde of deplaning passengers.

"Damn, who died and left the airlines in charge?" RH says to no one in particular and splits a slow walking elderly couple in front of him to get over to us. "Sorry you had to see that, Chief." RH said. "These airline jerks get on my nerves." RH sees me only after he wraps Mr. Fisher in a bear hug. "Whataya' been up to, Cape?"

"Oh, just being a jerk. Like the rest of my airline colleagues."

"Colleagues, *really?*" RH stuffs his badge back into his blazer pocket. "Hadn't heard you were back on the line…"

Before I can reply, Mr. Fisher reads the expression on my face and jumps in. "RH, why don't you move up here? North Carolina is a lot closer to Washington than Florida."

Though, RH, has never lived in Greenville, the bustling Eastern

Carolina town has always been part of his roots. Each fall, his family journeyed from Florida to the Carter Family Reunion in Kinston. After the reunion, other branches of the far-flung Carter Clan headed to nearby beaches on the Crystal Coast and Outer Banks to enjoy the still-warm Atlantic waters.

Unlike the pleasure seeking Carters, RH's sect then made a side trip to Greenville to pay homage to his birth mother, Calis Fisher, wife of Nathan Hale Fisher and mother of RH's twin sister, Laura Fisher. After the visitation with Calis at Forest Lawn, RH and his parents also stopped by to visit Nathan Hale Fisher. The annual visitation was more than a reinforcement of the close-knit bonds between the two families. It also affirmed that their decision to try an unorthodox, adulterous sperm donation, among friends, was the right one.

At an early age, RH's adoptive mother insisted that her son know the truth of the emotional sacrifices four young friends made to give life to two beautiful children. It was her way of acknowledging that she and Nathan Hale Fisher were more than innocent bystanders in what many considered an unholy union.

Their defiance of religious and social doctrine of the times resulted in Jana's having a wealthy, if not puritanical, bloodline. Even though I'm pleased with the foursome's unorthodox decision and my fatherhood, I often wonder how Mr. Fisher came to terms with his decision to let RH's dad impregnate his wife, Calis Fisher. Jana, on the other hand, expresses no such inhibitions and participates in the annual Carter-Fisher reunion with the zeal of a Hatfield or McCoy.

Though I am thankful RH was a bone-marrow match for Jana, I'm also thankful none of his other traits survived the procedure to affect Jana.

"You know, Chief I'm glad you brought up the idea of me moving." RH says, starting to salivate like Pavlov's dog then spit out what he perceives to be good news. "I was saving this for a surprise. I *am* moving here, or have moved here in a way. My fiancée is already here. She's been looking at a house for us."

"What about your career?" Mr. Fisher asks.

"Federal agencies are downsizing. I figure it's a good time to get out. I opted for early retirement. And let's face it, you're not getting any younger. I feel like I need to be here for Jana, too. She's got a lot on her with the kids—and, Cape." RH preens like a peacock at a wet-setting-hen's beauty contest. "Yeah, with my, pension and some *very* solid investments." RH pauses and looks straight at me, "we'll do just fine. I've got my eye on a nice house in that swanky new subdivision on Culbertson

Avenue."

"That's wonderful, son." Mr. Fisher pats RH on the back, then adds, "But you can stop your house search. You and your wife will live in the mansion with us."

"You sure that won't be a problem?" RH jerks his head in my direction. "I mean, doesn't Cape put a lot of demand on staff already? Two more people might strain their capacity, don't you think?"

"Cape shouldn't tie up staff, he doesn't require any special needs, that I'm aware of. And I understand his physical therapy will be done at the hospital." As soon as Mr. Fisher and I make eye contact, he adds, "Isn't that right, Cape?" I nod, not really sure if I'm a party to this conversation or a subject of it.

"Besides," Mr Fisher continues, "That old house can accommodate another ten people and the existing staff could handle them with no problem."

"Hey, I didn't mean that you're needy. Cape. That was just a little jet-lagged conversation that didn't come out right, I suppose." RH gives me a stupid grin.

I mirror his stupidity. *Jet-lagged from an hour's flight from Orlando—really RH?* For the life of me, I can't figure out why science hasn't yet declared this cellar-dweller from the shallow end of the Neanderthal gene pool the Missing-Link. Rather than move up here, RH and Pebbles, or whoever his fiancée is, should find a cave and set up house keeping there.

"You know my fiancée, Salome, is a psychiatrist. I bet she can get your head straightened out in no time, Cape."

"I don't know about that. Doesn't seem like she's had much luck treating your babbling idiocy."

"Hear that, Chief? I can't even be nice to him that he doesn't insult me." RH says.

Mr. Fisher ignores RH, and me, too, for that matter.

I find myself fantasizing about killing RH and decide to follow Jake's advice when I have negative thoughts. I move on to a more reasonable topic. "I've been thinking about the coins and the—"

"Cape, I don't mean to cut you off." RH says, looking at Mr. Fisher. "We've decided you don't need to stress over what's been going on. I understand you didn't handle the pressure too well in the graveyard."

"I TRIPPED!"

"Not what I heard, but don't worry. I'll handle everything. That's why Mr. Fisher asked me to come." RH puts his hand on my shoulder. "You just concentrate on getting well."

We? It's obvious Mr. Fisher is all-in with RH's thinking. They've probably spent hours on the phone together speculating on how to solve my problem! No doubt, that Jana and Jake are in on this, too.

First this jerk-off has the nerve to insult my fellow airline professionals, and now he's turning my own blood against me? I inhale and begin my breathing control exercises. The last thing I need to do is draw more attention to myself. If I do Jake will have my butt in the hospital and drugged to the max within thirty minutes.

"It's for the best, you'll see." RH says, and gives me a pitying smirk.

I smirk right back. "Well, that's fine by me Mr. FBI-man. There's just one little old problem."

"What's that?"

"Whether I'm sitting, standing, or lying in a hospital bed... someone keeps trying to kill me! So I can't exactly rest, got it? And who the hell gave you the authority to come up here and take-over any part of my life!"

"What are you talking about?"

"I'll tell you what I'm talking about—"

Mr. Fisher holds up both hands and making a plea for my silence. But I've been quiet long enough. I get nose to nose with RH and look him square in the eyes. "While I'm laid up like a sack of potatoes for 3 years, you're up here trying to take over my family—and my life. And if you're open to suggestions of places to move. I've got one for you...why don't you move straight to hell!"

"What is it with you? I busted your chops in Florida years ago and you can't move past that?" Then RH plays his trump card, "It's not just me. I'm speaking for the family—we're all worried about you. Stop fighting us and let us help, will ya?"

Again, it's clear that I've been the topic of some covert family discussions. Or knuckle-dragging RH may be lying, certainly something he's comfortable doing.

"Cape, it's just that RH has a law enforcement background and—"

"You didn't feel that way at the mausoleum," I say. "You showed me the coffin, and the coins—and you took me into your confidence."

"And the stress got to you, whether you want to admit it or not. My God, son, don't you see we're doing this because we love you. Even RH, does so there's no need for you to be mad at him. He's gracious enough to volunteer for this. Please respect him for that, if for nothing else."

"I TRIPPED, that's all. I didn't have a relapse!"

"Cape, please control yourself. We'll talk about this when we get home —you're getting loud."

Fine, they can all side with RH, but let's not forget the real reason

Robert Hale Carter doesn't want me involved in this investigation, and it sure as heck has nothing to do with him being concerned about my health! It's because he's never gotten over me, a non-lawman, exposing the Kress-Johnston money laundering scam. One of the largest and most profitable bank money-laundering, counterfeiting rings in the world. I understand Ally's, Jim Rogers' and my little accomplishment is taught at the FBI Academy to encourage agents to work more closely with civilians. Truth be told, RH's real reason for retiring early is so he won't get fired for incompetence!

"Cape...Cape?" Mr. Fisher calls to me. "The car is this way. Hourly parking, remember?"

Of course I remember. There is nothing wrong with my memory. Where the hell *is* hourly parking anyway? Before I can orient myself RH taps me on the shoulder and points to the Hourly Parking sign over my head. "This way, Chief."

"Don't call me, Chief. Damn it, I'm a Captain!"

RH shrugs his shoulders and steers Mr. Fisher toward our car, then turns to me. "Do you mind sitting sit in the back, Cape? I thought Mr. Fisher and I could go over the latest evidence on the ride home."

From the third-row seat in the Yukon I observe Mr. Fisher and RH ignore me again, becoming even more mutually fascinated with one another, if that's possible!

Who cares. I'm tired and doze off into a deep slumber.

Rain pinging against my bedroom windows and distant lightning wake me. I don't have a clue how I got from the airport to my bedroom. Jake dosing me with the same concoction Louise used in her *mickey*, if I had to guess. Or, maybe I'm overtaxing my brain and blacking out? It takes a lot of brain power to outwit, RH, that phony. I could relax, kick it in neutral, and let RH run the show?

No way!

I look down the driveway at the Tar River overflowing its banks. Water is already crossing the road and easing up to the mailbox. I flip on the light and dress like I'm late for work. Halfway down the stairs I bump into Jana. "Dad what's the rush?"

"The river rising, must have fell a flood since we left the airport?"

"It's been raining for two days, Dad! They're predicting some minor flooding, but it should be warm and sunny tomorrow."

Furrowed lines are etched across Jana's forehead and concern gathers in her eyes. "Dad, we went to church this morning,   you don't remember?"

I have to fake until I make it, or it's back to the hospital for me. "Yeah, jeez. You think I'm stupid?" I smile big. "And the kids, how cute were they in their little rain suits, huh?"

Jana sits down on the steps and pats the spot beside her. I take the seat I'm offered like a kid reporting to the principal's office.

"And what were the twins wearing? A hint: *not* rain suits."

"Why, their church clothes of course."

"Want to be more specific?"

"No—not necessary. They're kids and I'm not good at describing kids' things. You know that, Honey."

"How was the sermon?" she continues.

"Sooo boring."

"You don't remember going to church, do you?"

"Well, if Jake will stop pumping me full of those shitty—"

"Dad, your language! You already have Cape T and Laura swearing like pilots."

"It *sailors*...swearing like sailors. I do remember that!" I beam.

"Well, that may hold true for other households, but for this one." Jana wags her finger in my face. "And another thing—stop being mean to RH."

"RH Carter's been after me since long before I got this damaged head —and why is everyone in this house against me?"

"We're not against you, and neither is RH. He and Grandad went to the police with the coffin and noose."

"Nice to know I wasn't invited, even though I found some of the evidence!"

"Dad, calm down."

Jana massages her temples with her fingers and sighs.

"I'm calm, see." I cross my eyes and stare at Jana.

"That is not funny."

"You're laughing, though!"

"OK, it was a little funny, but don't do it around the kids. There could be a kid out there who has crossed eyes."

"What's that got to do with me?"

"The kids may think you're making fun—"

"How can I make fun of someone I don't even know?"

"You have to be more sensitive, Dad, children notice things adults do."

"If I get any more sensitive—I'll be squatting to pee."

"Dad!"

"What?"

"Now, you're making fun of women."

"I am?"

"Yes, stop it! I don't want the kids to—."

"Be like me?"

"I didn't say that."

"You were thinking it."

"Dad."

"Fine, you weren't…What did the cops say?"

Jana stands to leave. I grab her hand. "What did they say?"

"This will lead only to another argument."

"We're discussing, not arguing. What did they say?"

"They said it could be anything from an elaborate prank to a mass murder plot. They've put their best people on it."

"Prank?" I said. "She threatened to kill me—in writing!"

"We don't know if it's a *she*. And you weren't killed."

That much is true. *She* didn't kill me, but the attack at the hospital was no prank.

"So when was someone going to tell me about this?" I said.

Jana looks up at the ceiling, like the answer's hidden there. "Dad, you've got enough to worry about…I've got enough to worry about! Just concentrate on getting well, please?" She kisses me on my cheek and whispers, "I love you, but you're wearing me out."

She owns me and she knows it. I'd go through everything I've gone through again and again, even the shooting, just to hear her say, she loves me.

"Honey, I'm trying. I really am."

"I know you are, and I'm proud of you." Jana pats my arm, takes two steps down and turns back. "But try being nicer to, RH. OK? Your constant sniping is causing problems, and Lord knows we have too many as it is."

I don't see me *causing problems* but, as they say in poker, if you can't spot the sucker in the game, it's probably you.

I turn off the alarm system and slip into my raincoat.

"Where do you think you're going?"

"To pick up the mail. Daily exercise—that Jake prescribed."

"Dad, it's raining."

"And," as I shake my raincoat in her face, "I'm prepared!"

My favorite part of the long walk down the driveway is the solitude. The peace and quiet clears my head and gives me time to think. I'd heal quicker, if Jake would quit pumping me full of drugs. I gripe about it every time he writes more scrip. Sometimes, I think he actually listens. Jake's big into natural remedies and holistic methods. Unlike most doctors, he's not a fan of Big-Pharma. And I appreciate his prescribed nature walks. I am suspicious, however, that my walks are his way of ensuring the household gets a break from me.

Our mailbox has to be overflowing. Due to lost days caused by my naps becoming long sleep events. I haven't checked the mail for at least three days, maybe four. No doubt only junk mail and soggy newspapers await me, but the exercise feels great. Steady rains have beaten most of the changing leaves from the trees. A brown and orange carpet of spent foliage squishes under my feet.

Halfway down the hill I look back at the mansion. Pale yellow light from the banker's light on Mr. Fisher's desk silhouettes RH, Mr. Fisher and Jana against the library walls. I cut across the lawn and settle in behind the box hedges bordering the library's bay window. Not that I'll overhear anything. Rainwater gurgling in the downspouts drowns out their voices, but I can see them well.

RH is pacing turning the miniature coffin over in his hands. Jana flails her arms like she's practicing judo. Mr. Fisher is setting back taking it all in. Cops may consider this to be a sophisticated prank. The group in front of me certainly don't—good.

I slip back across the yard toward the circles of light cast by widely spaced yard lamps lining the driveway. Less than thirty yards to the mailbox, sounds of a snapping branch stop me cold. The noise seems beyond the penumbra of the last yard light.

Like most places in the state, over-populated deer herds find easy pickings in the succulent landscapes of suburbia and Slick Rock is no different. Deer and bear sightings are so common place, that local newspapers and TV stations refuse to do stories on them anymore. I don't mind an occasional deer wondering onto the grounds, but a bear—that's another story. I unbuckle my belt in case I need an inadequate weapon in a hurry.

As suspected, the paper box is full of soaked newspapers. A partially open door on the mailbox is responsible for the wet correspondence. I cram the envelopes in my coat pocket and, like a tobacco cropper from days gone by, stuff the bundles of junk mail and newspapers under my arm. With my flashlight app, I give the mailbox a good look-see. No nooses, no coffins, and no night nurse—not a bad way to end the evening.

When I straighten, I see a swaying oval shape hanging from the yard lamp near the noise of the snapping branch. Even from this distance the familiar-looking shape gives me the heebie-jeebies. I jog to it, keeping my head on a swivel. It *is* a noose, and I'm certain it wasn't here when I passed by. I cram the noose into my other jacket pocket and look all around me.

Beaming exterior lights from the mansion do little in this rain to illuminate the darkened gaps between the sparse outdoor lighting. Beyond the gate, out on the public road, and an even blacker darkness faces me. My return route, a welcoming nature scene a few minutes earlier, is full of foreboding. And I have no idea if I can run, since we haven't gotten that far in my physical therapy. Even in my peak shape days it would've taken me a few minutes to make it back to safety.

I scan the mansion facade hoping someone is keeping check on me. No such luck, and to make matters worse, the library is dark now. I do a 360 turn, but at about the 180 point, the heavens open. Fat raindrops limit my recon. Nothing suspicious, but my gut says otherwise. Yelling won't get anyone's attention, and even if I had a gun to fire no one could hear it over the heavy rain.

I ease to the center of the driveway, away from the shrubbery, frothy with hiding places. An owl screeches from a nearby tree, then dive-bombs an unsuspecting toad not five feet behind me. Toaddy let's out a scream straight out of a B-grade horror flick and adrenaline shoots down to Pat and Charlie. My shoes slip and slide on the wet leaves and I do a burnout. Before I gain traction, muffled biped footfalls pound on the driveway behind me. As bad as I want to, I don't waste time looking back. I'm solely onto winning a race for my life.

Rain and wind blowing in my face silent the footsteps, so for a moment I'm safe…But out of nowhere, fingers rake down my back and slide off my raincoat. With less than a hundred yards to go, I will myself faster and yell bloody murder. Nearing the mansion, I trip the motion detector lights and jerk around, to locate my pursuer.

All that lies before me is a manicured lawn, a picture of deep green serenity. I put my key onto the lock and the door swings open. Did I lock it when I left the house? Have I let the attacker inside? Is a mass murderer holding my family hostage, or worse?

Slipping off my shoes, I tiptoe to the hidden gun safe in the foyer. I grab two Glocks and ease down the hallway. RH and Mr. Fisher are in his office going over paperwork. Jana and Jake are in the theater watching a movie. I turn to leave, but Jana's mommy-radar is in full scan mode.

"Dad, what are you doing?"

She hits a button on the remote and the house lights up like opening night on Broadway.

"Why are you armed?"

Before I can answer, RH says, "Put 'em down, chief. Slow and easy." I turn and face him—he's in a shooting stance with his service revolver aimed at my head.

"I thought I heard something…and I wanted to make sure y'all were safe."

"We're fine, Daddy."

My licensed drug-pusher, Jake, gives me another sedative and sends me off to bed. I lock my bedroom door and head to my window to survey the grounds. Someone was out there. A light but steady rain is falling, though, obscuring the entire field of vision. Fishing the noose out of my pocket, I pull the practically bone dry cotton cord though my fingers. A fact and clue I decide to share with no one.

CHAPTER FOUR

Cape does some investigating

Dawn, as Jana predicted, breaks dry and glorious. I hurry down-stairs to grab a quick coffee and check for clues along the driveway. Staring at an automated coffee bar with a plethora of choices, I realize quick coffee is out of the question. No one is up, not even staff, and I'm faced with options much easier to order than make; Mocha, Expresso, Chai Latte, Tall, Skinny, Neat and a host of other buttons, that describe fashion models better than coffee.

I find a jar of instant coffee, dump freeze-dried-crystals into a mug of water and nuke it. Taste is crappy, caffeine is kicking—good to go!

Cool air hits me when I open the door. Early morning sunlight filtering through the Lombardi poplars lining the drive, melts away last night's apprehensions. I head for the yard lamp that held the noose and note a length of cord lying near a poplar a few feet away. I wrap the soaking wet cord around my hand and whirl it like a watch fob. Mist slinging from the cord, cools my face like a splash of aftershave.

Figuring out why my stalker chose to hang the noose here is easy. Twin magnolias surrounded by flowerbeds conceal the light fixture from the mansion. Preparation this detailed leads to another question. Was our encounter happenstance or planned? I missed days of checking the mail, yet last night's walk to the box fit my routine. I decide to vary my exercise times, in case I'm being watched.

Footprints, about size 12, run parallel to the leaf-covered driveway. One footprint path crossing a broken limb ends any speculation about what or who made the snapping noise last night. Definitely a *who*, and likely a male, unless big-footed Amazons are roaming these parts.

The prints continue behind a second row of poplars for a short distance and back onto the driveway, explaining the footfalls behind me as I raced up the driveway. Approximately 100 yards from the poplars, stands a six-foot-high brick fence separating the mansion grounds from open fields Mr. Fisher also owns. Scaling the fence is no great feat, but it would take determination and purpose. As well as a total disregard of private property rights and a willingness to go to jail, since the grounds are patrolled by armed guards.

Anyone standing up to such obstacles and hazards, isn't hanging nooses all over the place as a prank! Of course, weird behavior doesn't necessarily make them a murderer, either.

Farther up the driveway, footprints spaced closer together indicate my guy was only toying with me. My footprints are those of a man running full bore, but the stalkers' prints suggest a walking gait, perhaps a stomping to intensify the sound. The casual nature of the prints remains uniform until they make a sharp right toward the brick fence. Once on an escape course, the spacing of the prints increases dramatically—he was running flat out. Maybe starting when I tripped the security floodlights on the portico.

One deep print indicates a launching point for a high jump. No way, an average person is high-jumping a six-foot brick fence? I pull myself atop the wall and look over, but sure enough there are two solid footprints where the stalker landed. Whoever made these tracks is well over six feet tall and versed in old-school western-roll high jumping. This person was certainly capable of walking me down, so why was I allowed to escape?

I unwind the cord in my hand and stretch it out in front of me. This maniac easily could have choked me to death with this very cord. Or armed with real weapons like guns, knives, or even a hatchet, taken off my head. Hairs on my neck, thankfully still attached to my head, bristle against my collar. No one is around but me, but I've got a distinct feeling of being watched. I survey long sections of the fence, because if an attacker is near, he is behind the brick wall.

"Hey! What you got there?"

My feet move like crazy but the muddy ground keeps me sliding in place. I get a little traction on centipede grass not covered with leaves, and leap for the pavement hoping to get a head start on my attacker. My leap falls short, though, and I face-plant in a puddle bordering the driveway.

"Whoa, Cape! Are you OK?" The voice does not belong to an assassin, a long-shot prankster, or a psychopath. At this moment, any of those would be preferable to that of Jake Draughon, grinning and breaking out a full-blown belly-laugh.

"Sorry, Cape—I didn't mean to startle you...Woo Hoo! You should have seen your face! Total fear! What happened to the cool, calm, ice-water-in-the-veins, airline pilot? Damn, that was funny!"

"Glad you think so," I say, sitting up to face my sweat-suit-clad son in law, out on his morning run. "Want me to do another face-plant on the driveway? Probably do a lot more damage over there." Jake pushes me down on the ground and wipes the mud from my eyes with his sleeve. Before I can protest he shines his penlight app into my eyes to make sure my pupils are dilating.

"Quit squirming Cape."

"My ass is in a puddle. Help me up!"

"Oh, sorry," he says, and pulls me up. During the lift, the cord winds up in Jake's hand. "What's this?"

If I tell him about the cord, I'll have to explain the noose. "I use it to stretch before I exercise…you know, like you suggested I do."

"Hmm, Cape Thomas following doctor's orders." Jake smiles. "Sounds a little fishy to me."

"Give it here and I'll show you."

"No, I believe you. It's just that I've never seen you stretching before."

"Well, Doc that's easy to explain. I do my stretching in the privacy of my room. You know, just in case I fall and crack my skull. I don't want to be responsible for you laughing your fool-self to death and leaving my daughter a widow."

Is his Hippocratic Oath coming to mind? "Cape, I'm sorry—I shouldn't have laughed at you. You're not mad, are you?"

"You call *that* laughing?" I said. "If you'd face-planted like that, I'd still be laughing. Matter of fact, I'd have snapped a picture and posted it on Facebook."

Jake dangles his iPhone at me. "Glad to know that."

"You got a picture of me on there?"

"Yep, sitting in the water, crying like a baby."

"You're not going to post that, are you?"

"Naw."

"Liar!"

Jake slaps me hard on the back, "C'mon let's go get some breakfast, *my* treat."

I stuff the cord in my pocket as we walk back up the hill. Part of me wants to tell Jake about the noose, but all that will do is upset Jana. Besides, after last night, there's no doubt I'm being targeted. Even if I don't help them by doing stupid things like turning the alarm off and leaving the door unlocked, Johnston and Kress will kill every member of my family to get to me.

Thank God my stupidity wasn't taken advantage of last night. We may not be as lucky next time. What if one of the kids had been kidnapped for ransom, or worse? I run more morbid scenarios through my mind, until one thing becomes clear. As long as I'm close to my family, danger is close to them.

Only one solution. I have to leave and go to a place where I have the advantage. With a little help from Jake, I'll get there.

"Dad, you're soaked." Jana grabs a dish towel and tosses it to me. "Sit on this. Jake, go get him a towel. What happened?"

I wait until Jake starts up the stairs before I answer. "Jake challenged me to a mud wrestling contest and, as much as I hate to admit it, he won."

"You're kidding me? He's a doctor, he knows how fragile you are. I'll kill him."

"I know," I grouse playing the pitiful invalid. "But that's not the worst part. Can you believe he took a picture of me after he muddied me up?" I make my bottom lip quiver. "And he's going to post it on, Facebook."

"Oh no he isn't!" She grabs Jake's phone and scans his pictures. "This is just not like, Jake."

"I know—and to gloat about it on social media."

Jana swipes the screen like a jilted lover keying a car. "There, problem solved! He didn't hurt you, did he?"

"Just my pride...and my back a little." I rub the small of my back like I'm auditioning for an Absorbine Jr. commercial. "I'm sure I'll be fine—in time."

Jake, walks back into the room with a smirk on his face. I give him a one-upsmanship, jack-ass-eating-briars grin.

"That wasn't funny." Jana says. "What were you thinking? Challenging him to a mud-wrestling match. *Really*?"

"Mud-wrestling match?" Jake said.

"You rolled him around in the mud. I saw the picture!" Jana said, "It's not funny Jake!"

While Jana glares at Jake, I cut him a dignified AeroMax Captain's public relationship smile.

"And you deleted the picture?" Jake said.

"Of course. I don't want people to think I married a bully!" Jana wraps the towel around my waist. "Give me your pants, Dad, and I'll put them in the washer."

"Thank you, darling." I call out as she stomps off to the laundry room.

"Smooth move." Jake says, "But how 'bout you tell her the truth now that your picture is deleted?"

"I suppose I could...But what are you prepared to give me for my act of compassion?"

"Compassion? Isn't, *Con*-passion, the right word?"

"Let's not quibble about words. I need a favor."

"You didn't concoct this elaborate ruse for a *favor*." Jake says. "What's up?"

"I want a clean bill of health. I want you to clear me to live by myself."

Jake shakes his head. "You're not a hundred percent, maybe not even eighty. You lost two whole days…and you're lucky you didn't crack your head on the driveway. I'm not releasing you. No matter how dirty you play."

"You know damn well drugs have something to do with that." I sweep my arms around, "And so does this place. It makes me jumpy. You saw me in the yard. I need peace and quiet in more familiar surroundings."

"Are you kidding? You love this place and we love you. The kids—"

"Come on. Don't do this to me. I love the kids, but Jana's right. I'm a bad influence on them." I put my hands together like I'm praying. "I'll work on my role-modeling while I'm healing."

"You're serious, aren't you?"

"Yeah, but don't tell, Jana. It'll hurt her feelings."

"You don't have to tell me not to hurt, Jana. My family is my only priority."

"I know that, but what I'm suggesting is a win for everybody."

"What do you have in mind?" Jake says. "A place of your own—here in Slick Rock?"

"Clear me to live in my own house. The familiar surroundings will help me recover quicker. You'll see. Besides, you said I need less stress. I don't have that here, Jake."

"I can't ride to Goldsboro to check on you every day."

"You can do it over the phone."

"What about, Jana? She'll never go for this."

"She will if you tell her I'll be OK. I'm not going to get any better until I'm back doing for myself. I can't do that here. Jana coddles me like one of the kids and the staff around won't let me lift a finger." I put my hand on Jake's shoulder. "Convince her, will ya? I need this."

Jake rolls his eyes. "Nothing would make me happier, because you're the rocks good marriages crash upon." Jake looks around for Jana. "It's bad enough you get me in trouble, but this stunt you pulled will make her even more protective of you."

"I rest my case! I'll tell her I was lying about the mud wrestling."

"How she bought your load of crap, I'll never know. You're some salesman is all I can figure." Jake looks to be in an epic battle between doing right by his patient or doing right by his marriage. "No driving at night?"

"You have my word."

"If you feel the least bit funny, you'll call me?"

"So fast it'll make your head swim."

"OK, I'll run it by her."

"You won't regret it, Jake. Thanks a million."

Confident Jake can pull this off, I head upstairs to pack, but Jana calls me into the kids' room to hear their prayers. Before they say Amen, Jana kneels and prays a new prayer. "Father, thank you for sparing my Dad and leading him to me. Please God, keep us all safe."

Talk about divine intervention, as a reason to leave! I reach for my handkerchief and instead find the noose, another sign.

"Off to bed so early?" Jana said.

"No, got something I need to do." I kiss them all. "I'll be upstairs if you need me."

My walk upstairs is interrupted by a flash of a woman who looks a lot like Louise. I top the landing in time to see the woman turn down another hallway and disappear. I haven't seen Louise since my first day at the mansion. If this is Louise, she's suffered an extended illness or avoided me for weeks.

I intend to find out before leaving. After turning down two hallways I come to stairs leading to the third floor, a place I haven't been. On the third floor are eight doors staggered on either side of the corridor. Farther down the corridor is, another. This mansion is much larger than I imagined. I go from door to door, checking each room.

Though the exterior doors are identical, the same can't be said for the rooms' interiors. Every room is furnished in a themed decor: Victorian, English Country, Colonial, Contemporary, Art Deco, Mediterranean, Moderne. Though the rooms differ they share one commonality, all are freshly cleaned. Unless Louise is cleaning on roller skates, I'm hot on her trail. But the eighth door I check is locked. I tap on it and whisper, "Louise?"

Not a peep. Michelle told me about Laura's room being locked after her death. My hunt for Louise will have to wait. From the moment I arrived here I knew I would eventually see this room.

Having a one-way conversation with a portrait of my soulmate hanging over a fireplace is no longer cutting it. I have to know everything about Laura Fisher. Even though a request of Mr. Fisher will get me inside, I don't want to share this moment with anyone, not even with

Jana.

Heart pounding, palms sweating like those of a teenager heading out on his first date, I face the door. A simple bedroom lock is no match for a pilot who's broken into half the FBO's in airports around the world. Trembling fingers remind me that lock-picking skills atrophy without constant use. Despite my rustiness, after a few well-placed swipes of a laminated pilot's license, the lock clicks open. I close my eyes and recall every aspect of my one date with Laura Fisher. Her smile, her wit, and beauty—I will never forget her or ever see her again. But her scent may still be in this room. Loaded with anticipation, I push the door open and inhale deeply.

Instead of my soulmate's lingering essence, a stale odor assails my nostrils. I acclimate to the dimness, but I have to cover my mouth to suppress gagging. Pinprick shafts of light shine through moth-bitten drapes covering three dirty windows.

This room can only be described as a boudoir. Yellowed linens strewn across the bed in a wild tangle capped by two pillows snugged together suggest a sexual romp of some sort. On the dusty floor are panties and a bra. At the foot of the bed is a pair of boxers. Definitely a sexual romp. Considering all the other bedrooms had themes, I name this decor, *passion room.*

On the night stand is an ashtray with two cigarette butts burned to the cotton filters. On either side of the ashtray are two highball glasses also coated in thick dust. A card, or stationery sheet of some sort leans against one of the highball glasses. I bend down to get a closer look. Through the dust I make out the first word: *Darling—*

"What you doing in this room? Get out of there!"

Louise has scared the living hell out of me. "Jeez! Don't sneak up on me like that!" I straighten up and head for the door.

Louise holds up both hands. "No! Mr. Cape, turn and *back* out. Use your same footprints!"

Intimidated by her menacing scowl, I obey. But with one foot lifted, I lose my balance and become a lopsided weeble-wobble. Too bad my rehab regiment hasn't yet addressed this daily task.

"Don't drag your feet. Lift 'em up high!"

I try hard to follow Louise's commands but before I reach the door I go into another high-speed-wobble. Louise jerks me out of the room. "How'd you get in here anyway...and why?"

"I thought it was Laura's room. I had to see it."

"This ain't Miss Laura's room. Her room is on the second floor, like all family members."

"How was I supposed to know?"

"You stand right here while I fix this." Like a technician Louise extends her dust mop and shakes it over my footprints. After several shakes she covers my tracks. Satisfied the room is like I found it, Louise slams and locks the door.

"What made you think this was Miss Laura's room?"

"It was locked?"

"Hah," Louise snorts, "They's plenty more locked doors around here." Louise lowers her voice. "In there's where he caught 'em."

"Caught who?"

"Louise, what's going on?" Mr. Fisher yells from the far-end of the hallway.

"Nothing, Mr. Fisher. I was just showing Mr. Thomas around the mansion. He wanted to see the observation room." Louise turns to me, "Ain't, that right Mr. Thomas?"

I have no idea where, or what, the observation room is, but I'm pretty sure Louise bailed me out of a bad situation. "Absolutely. Not a problem is it, Mr. Fisher?"

"No, but how do you know about the observation room, Cape?"

I don't know about the observation room. I'm not stupid either. A glaring anomaly of the Fisher Mansion is an oversized cupola atop the roof, something I noticed on my first visit here.

"How could I not?" I yell back to Mr. Fisher and smile big.

"Yes, yes…I guess that thing would intrigue anyone, but do hurry, Cape. RH has a suggestion that may be beneficial to your health and the family's safety. Perhaps we can discuss it at dinner."

Dinner, in the house of my grandfather was what high-brows call "lunch". Dinner, in the Fisher Mansion is what we low-brow Southerners call "supper." The difference in usage of "supper" or "dinner" for the evening meal is more than mere word-choice or a charming colloquialism; in reality the choice demonstrates a wide chasm that separating the "haves" from the "have-nots."

As a rule, I don't lie. If we don't visit the observation room, I'll be a bonafide member of Liars, Inc. "Louise, I guess I need to see that observation room."

"I ain't got time for that. Even if I stay hard at it, I won't get the third floor done today!"

"Mr. Fisher, may ask me about it at sup— ah, dinner."

Louise rolls her eyes. "We'll have to take the stairs, elevator don't go that far."

Neither Louise nor I speak as we make our way up the narrow winding stairs. We step onto a small landing at the top of the stairs and face an elaborately hand-carved oak door. "This door is never locked, in case you get the urge to snoop around some more." Louise says.

The room is an octagon-shaped with floor-to-ceiling windows set into each of the eight angles. The vista before us is nothing short of breathtaking. Only at altitude have I seen such an expanse of pastoral scenery.

"My God." I exclaim, at my bird's eye view of the thousands of cultivated acres that stretching out before us, "Does Mr. Fisher own all this?"

"As far as the eye can see." Louise says.

I treat myself to a panoramic view of what may be one of the last plantations in Eastern North Carolina other than the Orton Plantation in Wilmington. Acres of soybeans, corn, cotton, and bare-stalked-tobacco fields framed by loblolly pine and hardwood bottomlands seem to go on forever. But…there's nothing bucolic about the final leg of my turn. High-density residential subdivisions and apartment complexes bump right up to property lines of the, Plantation. "Urban sprawl? Why, Louise?" I whisper.

"Un-huh, but that urban sprawl you talking 'bout is what paid for all this," Louise mimics my earlier 360° turn, unwinding to in reverse.

"So all the development is on land he owned?"

"Still owns. Mr. Fisher only does commercial leases. He *never* sells land."

"How do you know that?"

Louise glares at me. "What you think because I'm a maid, I couldn't know that?"

"No, but isn't that esoteric information solely for family or business partners?"

"And you exactly right." Louise says. "My son and Mr. Fisher created most of that urban sprawl you looking at!"

I want to know more, but more questions may alienate Louise. Something I definitely don't want to chance until I know the answer to a one burning question: "My first morning here you told me, 'It's a good idea not to believe everything you hear and only half of what you see around this place.' What did you mean exactly?"

"You from the South, you heard it before."

That much is true. I've heard the adage hundreds of times, but I'm certain, Louise's usage is tinged with *gravitas*. "How about the locked room—should I see it and only half-believe?"

Louise shrugs her shoulders and continues to stare out the window.

"And you said, 'That's where he caught them.' Who are they?"

"First off, Mr. Cape, I know good and well you didn't *stumble* into that room. It's locked. How'd you get in there?"

I grin. "No lock is safe around me."

"You proud of that?" Louise says. "Think maybe you oughta respect people's privacy?"

"I'm not a thief—"

"Whole *lot* of safecrackers think that, but they in prison!"

"Sometimes I needed to be in places after hours. I…" Even I can't see where I'm headed with this. "I'm no thief."

"You family, an in-law," Louise says. "More likely, an outlaw! But they's lines you don't cross, rules you don't break in this house."

I understand why Louise is angry. My trespasses won't get me kicked out of the mansion, but they may get her fired.

"I was wrong." I hold out my hand to Louise. "Won't happen again… Friends?"

Louise doesn't shake my hand, but a tiny smile curls across her lips. "At least you got some manners. Something can't be said about other guests who stayed here."

There is no way to be sure, but I'm betting those *guests* weren't invited by Laura. "Bianca's friends, you mean?"

"*Friends?* Bianca didn't have friends."

"Acquaintances, then?"

"Victims."

"You mean like Jim Rodgers—"

"Don't ask me no more questions 'bout her."

"Sorry didn't mean to pry." I said.

"Yes, you did." Louise says. "I ain't putting family business on the street."

It's easy to see I need to change subjects or Louise is gone. "Why is the passion-room locked and kept in that sorry condition?"

Louise ignores my question and points to a large apartment complex across the way. "My son just finished those apartments."

"Wow, he must be rich…So why are you still working?" The words slip out and hang in the air like an axe about to fall. On me. "I didn't mean—"

"You said exactly what you meant." Louse says. "I take back what I said about you having manners. Well-mannered folks don't ask rude questions, Mr. Thomas." Louise freezes me with her cold black eyes and cuts me with her sharp tongue "Well, Mr. Nosy. My son *is* wealthy. He's also a state legislator. As for why I still work, I owe a debt to this place. I won't leave until it is paid in full, with interest."

"You mean you owe, Mr. Fisher?"

"I don't owe Mr. Fisher a dime. I owe this place for the successes and failures my son and family have enjoyed and suffered. I owe you, too. That's why I'm trying to be polite to you, but it's getting harder and harder."

"I don't understand?"

"The Good Lord does, and that's all that matters." Louise stands and grabs the doorknob. "When you first showed up snooping 'round here, rumor was you were after the Fisher Family Fortune. That turned out not to be true. Thank you for bringing our child home."

"So, bringing Jana home is the debt you owe me?"

"It is, and for that reason. I'm trying to be nice to you, but don't push your luck, Mr. Thomas."

"Laura, and Jana are they—"

"Laura could have spit Jana out of her mouth. Sometimes I get 'em mixed up."

"So you and Laura, were close?"

Louise nods. "Like a daughter to me… and even though some of the people here resented it. I was like a mother to Laura. She was older than my son—and white, but she doted on him like a big sister. Same as she did, Bianca. Difference is, Rafael *appreciated* Laura. Rafael is smart in his own ways, a natural builder, loves doing things with his hands. He hated school, but Laura made sure he finished college." Louise says, shaking her head.

"How about Bianca and Laura?"

"Laura spent many hours tanning to look more like Bianca and Rafael. Some cracker on the farm called them half-breeds, didn't know who Laura was." Louise smiles wide. "He found out real quick. Laura was ten, but she fired him on the spot. That sweet child!"

"I wouldn't know. I only met Laura once."

"Depends on what you mean by, *met*, I reckon." Louise leaves the observation room and I follow.

"Jana, told you about me seeing Laura when I was so bad-off?"

"She did, but she didn't have to. We have a mutual connection, Mr. Thomas."

"And that would be?"

"I'd rather not say."

"Other than Laura, you mean?"

Louise smiles.

"Did Laura, ever mention me?"

"Not by name, but said she was going be with you forever."

"Wish things had worked out that way."

"Huh," she snorts

Louise walks down the stairs, and when she gets to the bottom she looks back up at me. "Don't go into to places 'round here you got no business in. You understand, Mr. Thomas?"

CHAPTER FIVE

Time to move on

Cape T and Laura, bed escapees, are at my door watching me pack. They're wearing Super Hero pajamas that make them invisible so I'm pretending not to see them, but when I bring down my AeroMax Captain's hat, Cape T breaks radio silence.

"I want!"

I brush my fingers across the gold wings of the 737 cap I wore as a newly minted AeroMax Captain. Sarge sure was proud of me. Well, he never said as much, but in an unguarded moment at my pinning ceremony a tear ran down his face. He caught me looking and growled, "Damn cigar smoke, like to put my eye out."

Seeing Sarge choke up got me misty-eyed, too. "Well, put it out, Sarge, smoke's getting in my eyes, too." I told him. "What you trying to do, kill both of us?" We looked at his unlit cigar and laughed.

"I want. I want!"

I shoot Cape T toward the ceiling like Sarge did me when I was a kid. Before he comes out of orbit, Laura's climbing my leg. "Up, me up!"

I hang my hat on Cape T and send Laura on a moon-shot. As soon as her feet hit the floor she's snatching the hat from Cape T. "I want. I want, too!"

There's nothing left to do. I take my new 747 hat from its plastic cover and put it on Laura. "Now, listen up!" These kids aren't used to tough talk. I have their undivided attention and take advantage of the moment. Squatting down beside them, I give them, *The Speech*: "Now you, little birds may have fooled this airline into thinking you can fly, but I know better. So if you even think about screwing up, I'll be there to knock the sh—"

"Dad!"

"Stuffing, out of you!"

Jana's eyes are fire and ice, mostly fire. "Your language, remember?"

47

"I said 'stuffing'—"

"Only because I showed up." Jana is not playing the invisible game. "Kids, go to bed."

Stripped of their invisible super powers, the kids cry, then really let loose when their mom confiscates the hats. I expect a full-blown insurrection from our little angels and settle down in a chair to watch the show.

My daughter says, "Zip it!" and starts slowly counting, "1, 2, 3, 4..." Like a shot the kids are gone.

"What happens after, 10?" I ask Jana.

"I don't know. I've never gotten past, 5."

You can't argue with success, and besides I don't want to find out what happens after 5, either.

Jana rubs the smudges off the brims of each hat. "AeroMax said once you pass your flight physical, you're to report—"

"Come on, who are we kidding. I'll never—"

"Don't say it. I swear I'll never talk to you again if you do." The ice in her eyes melts and she sits on the bed. "Why are you leaving? Don't you love us?"

"Guess, you talked to, Jake?"

"Yes."

"He didn't give you any medical reasons?"

"None that made sense. Why don't you want to be here, Dad?"

Sometimes, the truth just will not work. This is one of those times. "First off, I want you to know if it wasn't for you, I would have negligible reasons to live. You've made life better for all of us. Look at Mr. Fisher, and Jake. My God, how lucky is that nerd to find a woman like—"

"Come on, Dad. He's smart, handsome, and could have had any woman."

"Matter of opinion...But you've seen him dance...the robot?" I do a little mock un-smooth and un-cool, Jake dance-move. "Even with my banged-up head, I got better moves than him. Good thing he's got a little Native American in him, or he'd be a total loser."

"Dad, Jake's not, Native American."

"Sure he is. His Indian name is; Two-Left-Feet-a-Dancing."

Jana loses it. I love her laugh and I'll miss it lots. Heck, I'll miss everything about my family. They are all I have in the world and I'll do anything to keep them safe.

She snuggles up and puts her head on my shoulder. "Don't go, Dad. We're making memories here and I want you to be part of them."

Boy, so do, I. "It'll only be for a little while."

"Promise?"

"I'll be as good as new before you know it."

"When are you leaving?"

"Early, I have some shopping to do and should be in Goldsboro by late afternoon."

"So I won't see you tomorrow?"

I shake my head. "You take care of Two-Left-Feet...and the kids... and Mr. Fisher—watch out for him, too." I give her a tight squeeze. "And most of all, you take care of my favorite girl."

"Dad, why are you *really* leaving?"

"Jana, until I learn to do for myself..." I grab the 747 cap and hold it over my head. "I'll never get well enough to wear this again."

"But you can recuperate here!"

"No, I can't. If I stumble on the steps, Mr. Fisher will have a crew out here the next day fixing steps that weren't broken in the first place. If I slip and fall, Jake has that damn—dang, penlight in my eyes and a syringe full of feel-good in my butt before I can stand."

"That's not it, either," Jana says. "You're leaving because I stay on you about trying to change the kids."

"You mean screw-them-up, don't you?" I put my hand up to quiet her before we end this moment in a bad way. "I never got to be a father, Jana, but after I survive the coma, I learn I'm a father and a grandfather, slam-dunk!"

"And you love it, don't you?"

"Yes, but I'm loving and learning as I *go*. In my day, guns and war toys, were OK, and were what we had, but now they're politically-correct footballs passed around at your snooty cocktail parties."

"Well! I don't see how my parties are, *snooty!*" Jana says, storming off before I can answer.

Damn! Of all the stupid things to say. Before I can go after Jana, RH fills my door-space. "Mind if I come in?"

"You can *move* into this room if you like, I won't be needing it anymore."

"Yeah, couldn't help but overhear you guys." RH pulls me to the side, "She's a little on edge about you leaving... She'll be fine." He puts both his hands in his back pockets and pokes out his barrel chest. "Before you go, I want to clear the air between us. I think you're making the right decision. Getting away from all this ruckus will do you good."

"I agree." I don't know what's come over me but I extend my hand to, RH. "No hard feelings?"

RH's grip is somewhere between being in a vise and getting my hand caught on an anvil as the hammer falls. I squeeze back like crazy but barely avoid getting my best hand crushed. "You make sure nothing happens to my family, now."

"Don't worry about that,"RH says. "And just so you know, we're really focusing resources on this case. I don't think anyone is trying to kill you—maybe scare you, but not kill you."

"I tend to agree."

"You do?"

"Yeah, because they keep letting me get away."

"*Keep letting you?* Have you been attacked again?"

No need to rock the boat. "No, I meant, 'they let.'" I point at my head. "Sometimes words don't come out right."

"You're sure there's nothing I should know?"

"Positive."

"Glad to hear that, because I've done a little investigating at the hospital," RH says. "I think the person in the selfie came from another floor and was tricked into doing that little show as a practical joke."

"What about me being paralyzed from that shot? *That* was real."

"Cape, I don't want you to take this the wrong way, but other than one unexplained marker, your toxicology test didn't turn up any drugs in you that weren't prescribed."

"So the night nurse didn't poison me?"

"Like I say, there's no evidence."

"So, I'm crazy?"

"I'm not saying that. You've been through a lot. Stress does funny things. Maybe you dreamed you were paralyzed?"

Despite the hard feelings I have had for RH, I'm starting to realize why my daughter and the Fisher family like him so much. "How about the coffin and nooses, RH? I didn't dream those up."

He laughs. "I know you have first-hand knowledge of that. We're pretty sure that coffin and noose thing is another scam on the Fisher Family Fortune."

"Yeah, but the missing heir has been found," I say.

"It never stops. Things like this have been going on since I was a kid," RH recalls. "Now that the heir has been found and DNA is proof-positive —folks are resorting to blackmail or extortion...the Fisher Family Fortune scam may never end, Cape."

I'll never be a rich man and for that I'm thankful. I can't imagine having people coming after you from all directions to steal what you earned. "Not my concern, anymore, RH. I just want some peace and quiet so I can heal."

He smacks me on the back, aggravating the heal big-time. "And I want that for you, too, Chief—sorry, *Cape*."

I wave off his words, "'Chief' is fine—the drugs make me ornery at times."

"You get well, Cape. I'll take care of things here."

My departure is later than planned so I get caught in late afternoon traffic. Somewhere between Greenville and Kinston, on NC Hwy 11 I catch a break. I want and need a slower pace than this bumper-to-bumper world I'm in. Soon a familiar tree-lined road catches my eye and I brake hard to make my turn.

A spirited blonde behind me isn't happy with my spur-of-the-moment decision, laying on her horn and flipping me off. Normally, I respond in kind to rude people. Today, I kindly purse my lips and blow her a kiss. Rather than another one-finger-salute, her thumbs-up rises from her BMW's sunroof and she waves goodbye.

A pickup behind her brakes hard and rides my bumper through the turnoff. I'm traveling way below the speed limit and the road ahead is clear. In spite of this, the pickup moves closer to my bumper.

There's a threat of rain, but I drop my windows to enjoy the still-warm temperatures of early fall. A quick glance in my rearview shows me I may be in for a road-rage incident, though. I did break pretty hard, and the guy probably thinks I cut him off. Aw, c'mon—it's too nice a day to deal with a jackass. I find a wide spot on the shoulder and pull over in a hardwood bottom intersected by a creek. The silver Ford pickup truck with dark-tinted windows slows, guns the engine, and races up the knoll on the far side of the creek.

My bladder is a little full, and since I'm parked and in no hurry, I opt for a nature break. A footpath beside the bridge, no doubt used by fishermen, provides ingress to the creek bank. About a hundred yards downstream, standing water brims over a beaver dam. I wind my way down a narrowing path, leading away from the creek into deeper woods. Without much sun or a compass it's really easy to get turned around in a forest. Throw in a noggin that's gone through trauma and there's a good chance I'll get as lost a golf ball in high weeds. I make my way back toward the creek until I see the beaver pond again and use it for orientation.

Recent rains have saturated Bibb soils along the creek bank. Without a fresh layer of fallen leaves, I'd be up to my ankles in mud. I consider turning around until I see an opening ahead covered in cinnamon ferns. A thin layer of convection fog hovers just above the fronds, giving this place a mystical air like another peaceful forest scene only I know of.

Then two car doors slam in rapid succession. Sound is easily distorted in the forest, but I'm certain the noise is near the bridge. A few pats on my pockets show me I didn't lock up or bring my phone. In fact, my phone, iPad, iPod and cash are sitting on the front seat. Jogging back to stop this robbery is out of the question—another fall could be bad news for my head. Nothing I can do but answer nature's call. Besides there's a decent chance the cops can find my stolen possessions in a local pawnshop.

A loud slapping noise nearby startles me. I jerk around in time to see a beaver smack the water with his tail. His warning echoes off the beaver lodge midway across the creek. Two females, pups in tow, slide down a mud chute and disappear. I don't get to see beavers every day, so I move closer to their lodge for a better look. My attack of curiosity allows the mud to suck my shoe off. I manage to contort myself into a position that leaves my dry sock resting on a cypress knee, but when water bubbles up around my shoe I stretch to save it from a soaking...almost there— only an inch away! But my socked foot slips off the knee, and I do a slow roll into a marshy, rotting mess.

Sitting in a deep mud puddle—second time in as many days—I halfway expect Jake to jump from behind a tree and snap pics for his Facebook page. A blaze-orange flash in a copse of tupelo trees stops my laughter—a hunter! Covered in brown mud, I can easily be mistaken for a deer.

"Hey, don't shoot! Had to whiz. Forgot it's deer season."

Not a peep from the thicket. I slip my shoe back on and stand up.

"Yo! Anyone there?"

A hunter in an orange vest zips between two gums. Probably has a deer in his sights, so the last thing I want to do is spook his quarry. Lots of people Down East feed their families on venison.

I wait a respectable amount of time and ease back toward my truck. An arrow whizzes by, only inches from my head, and thuds into a water-oak a foot from me.

"Hey, watch out! You damn-near hit me."

Another arrow zings past and buries its point in the water-oak next to the first arrow. Ducking down, I yell, "You idiot!" Still no answer, but I see another flash of orange gear about 30 yards away. Unless I'm crazy, this guy is maneuvering for a better shot—at me! I hug the tree and move to the opposite side from where the arrows were launched. Another whiz and thud. Vibrations from the quivering arrow hum against the bole of the tree. I'm being hunted without means of fighting back. Defense is my only option and hiding behind this tree isn't a plan.

I slide down the tree and sink back into the mud. Inch by inch, I low-crawl until the beaver lodge is in sight. Two options exist. I can run like crazy for the creek and risk getting shot, or stay in the relative safety of the mud. Snake-like, I slither along until the cool waters of Contentnea Creek consume me.

My bobbing head is all the shooter can target now. I'm no archery expert, but only a skilled marksman or lucky shot can get me now. Even though odds are in my favor, it's time to improve them. I dead-man-float under a low-hanging live oak and break off a small branch. The dark foliage blends in with the tea-colored creek-water for excellent camouflage.

A gentle current pushes me back to the bridge. Safely under the bridge, I paddle like mad for the bank. If an ambush is set, it's between the bridge and my truck. There's no cover from the bottom of the steep bank to the roadbed, factors the shooter has likely anticipated. Once I break out of the water I can't slow down until I reach my truck. Chilled by the cold water, though, my legs and arms are stiff. I push back and tread water until I'm looser.

I hit the incline in a sprinter's stance, grabbing at and pulling bahai grass clumps to reach the top. With a death grip, I grab the concrete bridge railing and fling myself over—landing in the path of two oncoming cars. Horns blare and I've never heard expletives sound so good.

Once in my truck, I lock the door, strip off my wet clothes, and crank up the heat. Cold air blows from the vents, so I reach for a stack of towels Jana placed on my backseat and come face to face with a noose.

My first thought is to head back and tell RH what happened. Then it hits me. Leaving the mansion did exactly what I'd hoped. Danger came with *me*, and even though they think I'm nuts, my family is safer. Still, someone's trying to kill me and I should file a report.

Locating the Slick Rock Sheriff's Department is a lot easier than finding a parking spot. Skies have opened up now. I'm in no mood to get wetter. A parking spot near a covered walkway offers a way to avoid another soaking. Or at least it does until rain begins blowing under the metal canopy. Again I go against my physician's advice and break into a sprint.

I don't slow down up until I reach a dry patch of concrete at the main entrance. Mud and water squish from my shoes, sounding like a bad case of diarrhea. Inside, is a glass door stenciled *Sheriff,* I'm inclined to scream bloody murder, demanding the immediate arrest of the crazed archer.

My second inclination is that my first inclination will likely get me another extended stay in the Slick Rock Trauma Ward. Not an option!

On the wall inside the door is a collage of newspaper and magazine articles behind a glass-enclosed bulletin board. I can't miss a headline front and center: **Kress and Johnston Get 25 years!** I linger at the display until I've read most of the snippets from the **Trial of the Century.** An event I missed, due to being comatose.

"Hi. May, I help you?" The soft, sexy voice belongs to a woman dressed in freshly laundered khakis with creases so sharp they could cut a path in the underbrush I crawled through. Her blouse is as crisp and bright as her smile. But in stark contrast to her clothing, she's wearing a muddy pair of waterproof Browning Featherweights.

"I need to speak with the sheriff, or a deputy."

She turns and starts down a corridor. I assume she's going to find an officer, but instead she stops at a coat rack and plucks a small leather case from a shearling-trimmed trench coat, that I'm pretty sure doesn't come from a department store. She flips the bifold case open: SHERIFF stamped across a gold star gets my attention.

"I'm sorry. You—you don't look like a—"

"Sheriff?" She says with an easy smile.

"I'm not sexist, though." I rush the words, raising my arms at the elbow stepping back, hoping she sees my remark for what it is, a dumb mistake.

"I get that a lot. Maybe I should wear a uniform to look the part?" Her accent is Southern, but not a local one, more Charleston-Beaufort, definitely, Low-Country.

"Naw," I grin, too wide. "You look just fine."

"Why, thank you sir." She extends her hand. "I'm Scarlett DuBois, Slick Rock County Sheriff. How may I help you?"

We shake. Though her hand is dainty, her grip is strong and firm, surprisingly strong.

"Sheriff, I think someone is trying to kill me."

"Hmm, didn't anticipate *that* being your problem—Mr—?"

"Thomas, Cape Thomas."

Scarlett beckons me into her office, sits at her desk and pulls out a yellow legal pad. "Do you know the person, or persons, trying to kill you?"

"Yes, I do."

"Care to name, or describe them?"

"Sure." I nod toward the bulletin board. "They're on your wall out there."

"Really?" Scarlett throws her pen on the pad and leans back in her chair. "Last I heard, Walter Cronus Kress and William Johnston are federal prisoners." She stands, walks me back to the bulletin board's press clippings and motions for me to join her. "The reason I know is that I worked for the Beaufort County Sheriff's Department when they were arrested." She points at a newspaper picture. "That's me escorting Walter Cronus Kress to the U.S. Marshals before the trial. Kress and Johnston asked for, and received, a change of venue. The trial was held at the Federal Courthouse, here in Slick Rock County where I worked first as a deputy."

"Well, I don't remember much about—"

"Mr. Thomas, we've never met. But I'm very familiar with who you are. And I'm also very knowledgeable about the Fisher family." Scarlett searches my eyes. "Should you be driving?"

"My physician cleared me to go back to Goldsboro. Call Dr. Jake Draughon, he'll verify my story."

"Not, necessary." Scarlett moves back behind her desk. I remain at the door. "You want to tell me what happened?"

"I guess I had a touch of paranoia. Sometimes I see things that I perceive as odd when others don't. I'll be on my way now." Without waiting for her to answer I turn to leave. Scarlett zooms around me, herds me back into her office and closes the door.

"Mr. Thomas, I didn't mean to insinuate that—"

"That I'm crazy? Hell, lady there's no shame in that. Jump on the bandwagon! There's plenty of company up there for you!" I snatch her door open. "Now, if you'll excuse me. I have an appointment with some mind-altering drugs." And so I won't be arrested, quickly add. "Prescription…mind-altering drugs."

"I really wish you'd tell me what happened." Scarlett pats my arm. I want to be insulted but I can't put my heart into it. Her warm eyes and smiling face are soothing.

"Why bother with a report? You already pegged me as crazy." I put my index finger in the air. "Oh, I get it. You have to patronize me because I'm connected to the Fishers, right?"

"Well, forgive me for being skeptical that two federal prisoners— incarcerated prisoners, mind you—tried to kill you!" Scarlett pulls her drawer open, tosses the pad inside and slams it. "You play it straight with me, I'll play straight with you. And for the record, I don't give a *damn* who your family is!"

"But what if the story I tell you doesn't make sense, are you going to yell at me again?"

Scarlett grabs a coffee pot from a credenza behind her desk and pours two steaming cups of black coffee.

"Tell you what. You tell me what happened and let's see where it leads. Fair enough?"

I recount the attack, and when I finish Scarlett motions for me to follow her. She grabs her wet raincoat and nods outside at a police cruiser in the parking lot. "Can you can show me the general area where the attack took place?"

"Yeah. I can show you exactly."

She stops in front of a storage room and hands me a hooded yellow rain slicker. While I put it on she runs her hands across a row of rubber boots. "Size 11. Right?"

"How'd you know?"

"No matter…"

"Well, you know an awful lot about me and my family. Seems only fair I know a little about you."

"I owned a shoe store in Winston-Salem and I have nothing else to say on that subject."

As promised, Sheriff Scarlett DuBois, doesn't divulge any more personal information—orally anyway. Other than general directions to the crime scene, we talk very little. While Scarlett looks out beyond headlights losing the battle against a black night made dimmer by rain, I focus on my driver. Her oval-shaped face, plays peek-a-boo with a flowing mane of jet-black hair. Appearing tired of the distraction, she flips her hair behind her shoulders revealing high cheekbones, aquiline nose, and full lips.

Her cruiser plies through a stretch of standing water covering the road and Scarlett's blue eyes dart from me back to the road ahead. When she tightens her grip on the steering wheel, sinewy forearms explain the firm handshake we shared earlier. If Scarlett isn't a gym-rat, I can't fly a Piper-Cub.

Something about the cut and fit of her outfit exudes a commanding presence, *haute couture*, if I had to bet. Uniforms project authority, yet Scarlett's manner of dress doesn't speak to the criminal world. Her style is designed for acceptance by her contemporaries, not a threat to her adversaries.

Baby crow's feet and fine worry lines over her brow suggest an age north of forty, possibly landing square on the big 5-0. Light from a billboard illuminates her flawless olive skin. I immediately shave ten years off my earlier assessment. Flashes of white teeth contrast nicely with her full red lips.

"Fifty." Scarlett says

"Excuse me?"

"You were trying to guess my age?"

"No—well, yes, I was. Old habit, sorry."

She nods, turns back to the road.

"Was a time when I was smoother at that and you wouldn't have noticed. I guessed younger, much."

She smiles, nice and warm. "I know it's been a struggle recently for you. How you doing?"

No more pitying and coddling—please. No conciliatory gesture to show you understand. Unless a bullet shattered *your* skull and put your life on hold for three years, you can't empathize, trust me.

"It *was* a struggle." I say through clenched teeth. "I'm *fine*, now."

"What ever happened to Ally Kress? She was at the trial every day."

Thank God, Scarlett gets it and changes the subject, but I don't want to talk about Ally Kress, either. "Last I heard she was marrying some billionaire entrepreneur—or doctor, maybe. Not surprising. Not too many rich-bitches care for damaged goods."

"Being a little hard on her, aren't you?"

"I guess so." I wipe moisture from my side window and look into dark rain. "Ally deserves a great life, one without me and my problems, anyway."

"What problems are those?"

I circled my temple with my finger. "You know—my head and thoughts…"

Scarlett smiles, "Word on the street is you'll make a full recovery."

"Yeah? Unless someone kills me first."

Scarlett turns and stares a hole in me. "Why do you say that? Has something like this happened before?"

Every part of me wants a conversation with Scarlett DuBois, but RH has enough to deal with, no need for me to put more, *words on the street*. "Nah, just this one time."

"If there's more to this than you're telling, I need to know, Mr. Thomas."

"Like I said. Just this one time."

Rain, pouring down at a good clip waits for us when we roll to a stop near the bridge. Scarlett dials down her wiper setting so the thumping becomes tolerable.

"Does this look like the place?"

"Yep."

The path is far more slippery than on my first trip down. We grab handfuls of cyrilla bushes to keep our footing. Just as I did earlier, we skirt the beaver pond and make our way to the ferns. Scarlett stops and points her flashlight at my earlier footprints, now filled with water. "Can you pick out the tree you hid behind?"

I point to the water oak and head out for it. "I'll do you one better than that—"

"Wait! This is as far as you go, Mr. Thomas. It's easier to preserve evidence when only one person is tromping around in the crime scene." Scarlett hands me her car keys. "I'll meet you back in the patrol car."

Normally, I'd protest, but Scarlett's wearing Jana's look when she's counting to 10. After many slips and slides I make it back to the cruiser. Once hot air is blasting from the vents I lean back in the seat. Headlights in the distance catch my eye but are obscured by fogged windows. I switch to defrost and zero in on the oncoming vehicle sporting a vaguely familiar light set up. A flash of gray zooms by and I'm almost certain it's the same Ford pickup that followed me earlier. I hop out to get a better look, but the driver speeds up and over the small rise.

"Friends of yours?" Scarlett said and steps onto the roadbed.

"Don't think so."

Empty handed, she slips into the driver's seat, executes a perfect "Y" turn and points us toward Slick Rock.

It's obvious she didn't find any arrows, but if she found my tracks, she may have found others. "Find anything?"

She unsnaps her rain slicker and kills the heater fan. "Ground's covered in ferns and leaves, plus heavy rain washed any tracks away, if there were any."

"So you don't believe me?"

"I didn't say that." Scarlett said. "But it is hard to see how an archer, intent on killing you, missed from such a close distance. The woods are pretty open and you did say you were sitting on the ground when the first arrows was shot?"

"Yeah, so?"

"Does the term, 'sitting duck' ring a bell?"

"Yeah, but—"

"We have a lot of skilled bow hunters around here, but not many who would miss that shot."

"Maybe so, but the third arrow was no accident."

"Three, are you sure? You said yourself, you were quiet so as not to scare the deer off—"

"I yelled."

"When, though?"

I strain to remember the sequence of arrows fired and my yelling. What was clear earlier is as muddled as the weather, now. I play out the scenario over and over. By the time we turn into the parking lot, I'm thoroughly confused. I fumble the door handle a couple of times until it finally opens. "Stop, let me out here."

"What's your hurry?"

"Thanks for investigating my delusion." I said. "Pleasure meeting you, Sheriff."

"Hold on, Mr. Thomas." Scarlett reaches into her rain slicker and holds up a plastic bag containing a steel arrow tip. "I dug this out of the tree you hid behind. I want you to fill out a report for me." Scarlett stares straight ahead. "I also want you to understand. I'm leaning toward this being a hunting accident. Not an attempt on your life—"

"Accident? One arrow would have been an accident. I may not remember all the details, but there were *three* arrows!"

"I have to go with the facts." Scarlett said. "I found one arrow, not three. Visibility was lousy and you weren't wearing orange. Hunters get anxious early in the season. Maybe they mistook you for a deer, and took off rather than face up to their mistake?" Scarlett puts the bag in her pocket. "And I hate to bring this up, but what are the odds of you being involved in *another* murder plot?"

"So you think I'm making this up?"

"I found an arrow and I'm willing to investigate. But I have to be objective—or what's the point?" She pulls out a silver Cross pen and hovers it over a small pad attached to the dash by a metal clip. "And just to be on the safe side, why don't you give me Dr. Draughon's number. Looks like you took a nasty spill out there. Besides, I'm sure your family would like to know about this incident."

One call to Jake from this sheriff and he'll pull my butt back home before my socks dry. "Sheriff, you're right, this is more likely an accident, not attempted murder. I'm going to Goldsboro and get a good night's sleep. I'll call Jake in the morning."

The rain turns into a light drizzle, and we head back to her office. "You can leave the coat and boots by the door." Scarlett walks over to a coffee pot and pours two cups and sets them on her desk. "Mr. Thomas, you strike me as a logical person. I think there is more going on than what you're telling me." She takes a sip of coffee, but holds eye contact with me. "It would take more than a few errant arrows to make a logical person jump to the conclusion that someone is trying to kill them. What's up?"

Part of me wants to level with her, but if I do I'll be pulled back to the mansion when my presence there endangers my family. I'm being targeted, but at least away from my family. I can live with that. "Odd things happen every now and then. Nothing earth-shattering. You've helped me see I tend to blow things out of proportion. I appreciate that." I say, and walk to the entrance door.

Scarlett looks out at the rain that is pouring again. "Take that raincoat. I'll walk you to your car."

"Naw, I'm good."

"Mr. Thomas, right now, you're *not* looking very logical." She smiles, "Do I need to make that call to Dr. Draughon?"

I drape the coat over my head and shoulders. "Do I look more logical, now?"

"Not a bit." Scarlett puts her hand on my back and guides me towards my truck. While handing her the raincoat, she points at the noose hanging on my back window. "Is that one of those odd things, you mentioned?"

"Nope. According to popular consensus, it's an errant length of cord."

She places her business card in my shirt pocket. "If that consensus changes, give me a call."

As I back out of the parking spot, my headlights illuminate a gray Ford pickup parked in the county impound lot. I'm certain it wasn't there when I first arrived. Or later when I left with the sheriff.

CHAPTER SIX

Miss Minnie and Jimmy

Miles roll by, happily distracting me by pouring rain, soft jazz, and thoughts of Sheriff Scarlett DuBois. Since I've awakened, no one's mentioned Ally—until now, that is. I guess they thought it best to wait until I asked about her. Not necessary, Ally's absence said it all. I Googled her and saw something about an upcoming wedding, whereupon Pride closed down my search.

Hearing her name makes me miss an emotion I haven't felt in a long time, love. Not love like I have for Jana and the kids, family love. Nor the love I have for old friends, brotherly love. No, the love I'm missing tonight, is a primordial one. That of two souls created from a rib, and then ordained as one: Soulmates.

I had it with Laura. Grace, and I flirted with it. Ally and I were destined for it, or so I thought. Maybe it's also nostalgia, or the human need to be part of a whole, but something about Scarlett DuBois evokes that primordial principle. And the *self-help* principle, too: To forget an old love, find a new love.

As my mind drifts again to the tall brunette, my truck drifts. Sounds of mud and gravel pounding my wheel wells, brings me back on point. I fight my urge to jerk the steering wheel and manage to keep the Yukon straight. When I stop, my headlights illuminate a white mailbox with familiar lettering: *Minnie Reynaud.*

Every time I'm lost in life, all roads lead back here. Like a magnet to metal I'm drawn down this muddy path. Tall bushes on either side of the path slap against my mirrors. The path is narrower and longer than I remember. Before I lose my nerve and shift to reverse, I'm in Miss Minnie's yard.

House and yard have succumbed to Mother Nature. A large limb from a gigantic oak once shading the old homestead, has flattened the front porch and a good portion of the living room. The yard is now overgrown

61

with dog-fennel and peppered with taller loblolly saplings. Empty Four Rose snuff tins scattered across the living room floor reflect my high beams like shiny broken promises. Rotting firewood connects portions of the caved-in porch to the house.

My God, is this how Miss Minnie died? Blind, alone, scared, cowering in a corner waiting for a howling storm to bring death crashing down from above? I should have taken care of her, like she did for me when I was a kid. How could I fail a woman who taught me to hunt, fish and swim like an otter? Under my breath I curse Gustavo Jobim for being such a lousy shot!

A freshly mowed path cuts across the overgrown yard. It's a surprise to me—I'm pretty sure Ms. Minnie doesn't have any living kinfolks. I know where the path leads because I made her final arrangements. I switch on my flashlight app and follow the path to her tombstone. REYNAUD engraved across the stone gives me pause: why is it the marker is aligned north to south? A glance at a moss-covered oak shows otherwise. She is buried in accordance with her Christian faith, east to west. I lay my hand on the tombstone and kneel to pay my respects.

Even with eyes closed and in deep thought, I can't shake the feeling I'm being watched. A light touch on my shoulder opens my eyes. Looking down—Holy Moly Peggy Coley! I see a hand on my shoulder.

Launching myself across the tombstone, I roll into the weeds beside the path. No protection here—must find cover before the archer draws a bead on me. No time for that, but I grab up a fistful of mud, slinging it at my attacker. It works! Even in the dark, I see him turn to protect himself.

"Stop, Cape, are you nuts?"

"What the hell?" I light up the man with my phone. "Jimmy?"

An old trademark grin spreads across his familiar face. Jimmy extends his hand and pulls me up. "Looked like you were praying, didn't mean to scare you."

"Well, you failed miserably!" I report, wiping new mud off old mud. "Whaddaya mean sneaking up on me like that?"

"I called your name. I guess with the rain beating down on the umbrella, you didn't hear me."

Instead of the bloodshot eyes I expect to see, Jimmy's eyes are clear and focused. He's wearing a nice tailored raincoat, a bit soiled, but nice. "Dang Jimmy, you look spiffy."

Jimmy wipes at his own mud. "Hard to stay spiffy 'round you."

"Why you all dressed up?"

"I'm not. These are my normal work clothes."

"You dress up to do lawn work?"

Jimmy grins, again. "Naw, I don't do yard work anymore. Went back to my old profession, CPA."

CPA? I toss my umbrella down, look up at the pouring rain, and laugh like a hyena. "Good God, I *am* crazy. I'm standing at a grave talking to my imaginary friend, Jimmy the Yardman, who thinks he's a CPA!"

When I finally finish laughing Jimmy picks up my umbrella and holds it over his head. "Now a case can be made, that a man who throws away a perfectly good umbrella, is crazy. But I don't *think* I'm a CPA, I have papers to prove it."

I reach across the tombstone and grab Jimmy's arm before he disappears.

"I'm real, Cape." Jimmy said. "What's wrong with you?"

"It's been a weird day—and night."

"Tell me."

"I stopped to walk in the woods and take a little nature break earlier. Someone tried to kill me. That's my version anyway, Slick Rock County Sheriff, a real looker, thinks it was a *hunting* accident." I sit on the tombstone. "I thought I was recovering, Jimmy, but maybe I need to check myself into the hospital again."

"Come on, Cape. Let's get you out of this rain."

We hit the yard, and I notice an SUV, obviously Jimmy's. A figure inside stirs and I look at Jimmy. "Don't tell me. You have a wife?"

"Nope, an old friend of yours."

"Who?"

"Get in the backseat, see for yourself."

I slide into the back seat and immediately see "Miss Minnie!" I grab her from behind and hug her like she just returned from the dead, and in a way she has, to me.

"Boy, your hands are filthy! Quit pawin' at me. You acting like a heathen," Miss Minnie said. "And you smell like a rotten fish!"

"Sorry, Miss Minnie, it's been one heck of a day."

"Put you cheek up here beside my face." I do as she tells me and she kisses me on my cheek. "And you need a shave."

"Now, Miss Minnie," Jimmy says, "You're being mighty rude to your favorite patient."

"Patient?" I said.

"That's right," Miss Minnie said. "Without my medicine we'd a lost you."

I peek around the head rest to scope her out. Maybe, like me, she's having trouble with reality because tears are streaming down her face. "Miss Minnie, are you crying?"

"Crying! What I be crying for?" She tugs at her coat collar and points to Jimmy. "These ain' tears. I'm sweatin'. I told this jackass to turn the heater down!"

It is awfully hot in the car.

Jimmy lowers the climate control. "Well, you said you were cold, earlier?"

"Don't you get hot when someone's trying to roast you?" Miss Minnie says.

"You could have turned the heat down…"

"How I gonna see the numbers?"

"My mistake" Jimmy says.

"Miss Minnie, when did you give me medicine?"

"Heck, Cape, she was at the hospital almost every night for two years."

"I thought I was dreaming?"

Miss Minnie points at Jimmy. "He came, too."

"Why didn't you come back to visit when I woke up?"

"Why, you well then! I got other people needing me. Ain't got time to socialize."

"Well, nobody mentioned you were there." I say.

"Didn't nobody know, but a young doctor," Miss Minnie says. "Not ever'body *believes* in my medicine. Other doctors and nurses run us out first time Jimmy got us there."

It's incredible that she's alive. But it's more incredible that a blind woman found me. "How did you know, Miss Minnie?"

"It was on the news. But I had this vision of you dying," She says pointing at Jimmy. "I told him to get me into that hospital or you gonna die."

"I called a few doctor clients, and sure enough, they're getting ready to pull the *plug* on you!" Jimmy says.

"He say, 'If I get you in there, can you save him?'" Miss Minnie says. "I tole him, 'I'll do all I can do.'"

"You did that for me, Jimmy?"

Jimmy nods. "When you used to get drunk, you always told the story about Ms. Minnie giving you the sky, and how she saved your life, more than once. I figured she could do it again."

The whole time I was recuperating no one mentioned pulling the plug on me, not even, Jana or Jake. "Miss Minnie. The doctor, do you remember his name?"

"He be—Jake. Handsome man."

"Miss Minnie, you're blind—"

"Nice people is nice-*looking* people."

"Like me." I chip in.

"*You* ain't nice," Minnie says.

"Or handsome," Jimmy says under his breath.

I ignore their potshots and get the facts. "Jake Draughon. You're certain?"

"Jimmy, tole him 'bout my remedies. Doctor Jake, say he inter-rested in such things. He snuck us in around midnight and stayed there so we didn't get throw'ed out." Miss Minnie said. "First night I see you, Dr. Jake say things ain't looking too good, and you might be brain-dead."

"What did you say, Miss Minnie?"

"I tole Dr. Jake, don't be too worried 'cause this fool been acting brain-dead most of his life."

"I bet that got a laugh out of him?"

"Naw, he pretty serious, 'cause when I whispered in your ear, he say, 'Damn, he's responding to *you*.' After that, Dr. Jake showed up every night to let us in and studied my doctoring. He didn't mention nothin' 'bout unplugging you after that."

"Miss Minnie, what did you whisper to me?"

Cackling, Miss Minnie says, "I say 'Boy! Git up from there, or I'll whup the tar out of you!"

"Seriously?"

"Naw, I'm funnin', you, boy. I sang you a little song."

"What song?"

"Hush, little baby don't you cry—"

"You're kidding!"

"You heard it before, when you little. Don't you 'member?"

"Yes, but I thought that was my mama."

"Taught ya' mama that song when she was little."

Is it possible that I only heard Miss Minnie singing? If that's the case, there is no Mansion, no Mama, and no Jesus!

"Did you tell Jake about the song?"

"Naw, that song wouldn't mean nothing to nobody but you. I showed him my remedies I used on you each time before I treated you."

It's hard to believe. Straight-shooter, Jake let a shaman practice on me in his hospital! It's even harder to believe my mother wasn't singing. But that's not right, I heard my mother, not Miss Minnie. I know what I saw —what I felt.

"Did Jake take you seriously...I mean, take notes?"

"Took notes, compared notes. Dr. Jake, say my medicine might be psychological as well as physiological. Said he heard of stranger things, and what could it hurt anyway. Then one night, just before you woke up, he say not only is this the strangest thing he ever seen, but the strangest thing he ever heard."

"Exactly what kind of remedies did you use, Miss Minnie?"

"Well, at first Dr. Jake wouldn't let me put a poultice on your head wound. He asked me what was in it. I don't share my medicines with average folks, but I figure since we both doctors, it be all right. He wrote down the ingredients, then he say, 'My goodness, that the base of some name longer than that nose on your face.' Ask me where I got that knowledge and how I got that weed, plant or seashell 'cause it not be endemic to this area. I finally had to tell him how when I was younger my grandmother showed me how to find the cures from the ocean, shores, and marshes that fed and protected us." Miss Minnie smiles, talking about the days of her youth. "God, Almighty provides a cure for every ailment the Devil can conjure up—if you know where to look for them. My mama taught me the medicine."

Funny, but for some reason I thought most homeopathic medicines came mainly from the mountains and rain forests, but not for Miss Minnie's. I'm no scientist, but I'm pretty sure I do remember hearing that the ocean contains, most, if not all of the major elements. Iodine, a rudimentary antiseptic, comes from the ocean. Maybe Miss Minnie is on to something, but her medicine apparently interests Jake much more than it does most doctors. And her medicine story is the first clue she's ever given as to where she was born and raised.

"Miss Minnie, were you born on the coast?"

"None a' you business. Ever since you little you always asking foolish questions. Don't make no difference where I come from. I'm here now, that's all that matters."

"Miss Minnie, remember the raft I made? You said it wouldn't work, too flimsy."

"And it was, too. You like to drowned your fool-self when she broke up."

"That's when you taught me to swim. You made me float, too. I asked what if I float away? You said trust the water, that it would take me to safety. What'd you mean?"

"Life come from the water and all waters lead to the ocean."

"Why, that's science, but I thought you were a Godly woman."

"Who a better scientist than, God? *Genesis* 1:2 say, 'And the earth was without form, and void; and darkness was upon the face of the deep. And the Spirit of God moved upon the face of the waters.'"

"So the Bible says life came from water?"

Miss Minnie sighs. "Ain't changed a bit. Always asking fool questions.

Let me answer one question 'fore you asked another question OK?"

"Yes, ma'am!" It's never a good idea to press Miss Minnie. Back in her younger days she would have accused me of *sassing* her and switched my hide.

"Big part of life is water." Minnie says. "Without it nothing lives. First thing God created—water. "

"What other cures did you use on me?"

"I used gris-gris and don't ask me where to find *that* in the Bible. You asleep, couldn't drink no remedy—I had to do something!"

Gris-gris or mojo bag, is a combination good luck charm and small satchel that holds roots, herbs, even small stones and sometimes scripture. The purpose can be to ward off evil spirits or attract good ones. I'm starting to understand Jake's reason for letting Miss Minnie and Jimmy into my room. "Did you burn candles and use magic powder?"

"Don't be foolish—my powers don't need magic. You in bad shape and you here now. I must'a done something right."

Undoubtedly, Jake has a video collection of Miss Minnie's, witch-doctoring. When I'm fully recovered and at a time when I least expect it, the footage will show up on his Facebook page. I'd never say this to Miss Minnie, it would hurt her feelings. She doesn't understand that only modern medicine saved me, but Jimmy? Now, that's another story. "What were you doing, Jimmy? Let me guess, helping Jake film Miss Minnie?"

Jimmy snaps around in his seat. "Wasn't like that, Cape! Jake, didn't see it that way either."

"So y'all believe in voodoo?"

"No, but I believe in Miss Minnie after I saw what was in her gris-gris bag." Jimmy nods at Miss Minnie. "She prayed, too."

"You think prayers cured me, Miss Minnie?" I ask.

"Course I do. Why you think my medicine so powerful? And before you ask another fool question, that power is *the* Power—the power of the Holy Spirit!"

"And Jake went along with the praying and voodoo-ing—didn't make fun?"

Jimmy says, "At first I asked Jake, if we could come pray for you. He was reluctant, but when he met Miss Minnie, he was starstruck. Jake said it didn't look good for you, as I said, but said it definitely couldn't hurt."

Miss Minnie jumps in, "When he saw my cures and prayers workin' he stay right in there with us writin' things down, askin' me all kind a questions. Not foolish ones like you ask, neither."

Of course Jake would be interested in any medicine that worked, even spiritual ones. Doctors do that, but I got a feeling that video footage of this fiasco is going to show up at a most embarrassing time for me. "Did he video you, Miss Minnie?"

"I don't know nothing about video?"

"He did." Jimmy chimes in.

"Well, it doesn't matter now." I hug Miss Minnie and Jimmy, "Thanks for coming and saving my life!"

"Only the good Lord knows why I bothered. Where people gonna spend *thanks* anyhow?" Miss Minnie removes my arm from her neck. "And I tole you one time, keep them nasty paws off of me. You need to wash."

"Yes, ma'am." I un-hug Jimmy, too. "So do I owe you anything?"

"Owe me for what?" Miss Minnie said.

"Saving my life—you said you can't spend my *thanks.*"

"Didn't say no such thing—"

"You insinuated—"

"Hush up! I said where people gonna spend, thanks. You don't owe me nothing for saving your sorry butt. You owe other people. Maybe people you ain't met, yet. You understand?"

Ah, *Paying it forward*, and everyone thinks that's such a new concept. "I do, Miss Minnie."

Miss Minnie tilts her head to one side and puts her hand behind her ear. "Barn owl coming in from a night of hunting, be daylight soon." I have 20/20 vision yet barely see the owl flying by the windshield—and Miss Minnie heard it? A flash of lighting in the distant gloom precedes a faint roar of thunder. "Storm be gone by morning." Miss Minnie turns to Jimmy. "C'mon, boy, let's get home."

"Miss Minnie, did Jake let anyone *else* in the room, for secret visits, besides you and Jimmy?"

"Dr. Jake, didn't want nobody to know about us being there. We met you daughter one time, but she didn't stay long."

"How about a lady named, Allison Kress, Ally?"

"Don't recall that name, do you, boy?"

"Nope." Jimmy says. "We got to go, Cape."

We make arrangements to meet for lunch, real soon.

CHAPTER SEVEN

Not so Home Sweet Home

Unlike Miss Minnie's place, my home looks better than when I left it. My yard is clearly a contender for yard of the year. Jimmy, now a suit-wearing CPA, can't be responsible for the transformation. There's only one answer: Jana has expanded Fisher-family beneficence to extended family members…not a bad gig!

I hit the garage remote and dig around for my phone, expecting that my house has had an extreme makeover to match my fabulous yard re-do. Couldn't have happened to a dump that needed it more! Before I get inside, my phone rings. "Dad, where are you?"

"Just finished riding through my awarding-winning yard and now pulling into my immaculate garage—"

"What took you so long to get home? I've been checking your security-system log all night. You had me worried sick, why didn't answer your phone."

"You can check *my* security system?"

"Yes, and please don't answer my question with a question, it's very annoying. Especially when I'm worried about you. What took you so long to get home?"

"I stopped off to see Miss Minnie, and I guess I left my phone in the truck. She told me she met you in the hospital. Why didn't you mention that?"

"Jake, insisted I come and meet her. She's a little strange…"

"She's not strange, she's special. Without her I probably wouldn't be here."

"Dad, Jake said she's a witch doctor or something. He's taken with her, too, but she's not someone I want the kids around."

"Jana, Miss Minnie—"

"Dad's, She's nice, OK? I just don't see us becoming friends."

I love my daughter, but she's moving so fast right now, she doesn't have

69

the patience to sit and listen to people, letting them reveal their character to her over time. And plain enjoying that!

"Well, Jana, the kids couldn't have a better friend, and neither could you. Miss Minnie—"

"OK, OK. According to you and Jake, she walks on water, I get it." Jana said. "Have you been inside, yet?"

"No, I've been admiring my beautiful landscaping, can't wait to see it in daylight. Man, this garage has a place for everything and everything in its place. I didn't think it was possible. Hey, you didn't throw away my stuff, did you?"

"By stuff, you mean junk?"

"How in the world do you confuse, collectibles with junk?"

"*Collectibles?*"

"Fine, have it your way. You didn't throw away my junk, did you?"

"No, your *collectibles* were inventoried, boxed and moved to storage. Come on, Dad. Forget the garage and go inside."

"Just opening the door now, and—oh boy!"

A noose dangling over the kitchen island, over rides everything Jana has done to the room. My breath goes short and shallow.

"Do you like it?"

I walk over to the island to get a better look. Same as the rest of 'em.

"You don't like it, do you?" Jana said.

"No, I don't like it." I pause for effect. "I *love* it! You're so talented, Honey. Thanks, so much!"

Jana gushes on about all the changes she's made, step by step, and how hard it was to get things that I would love.

Keeping my eyes on the noose, I ease back to the garage. I don't want to see any other surprises in the room right now.

"I know you'll freak when you see the bathroom!" Jana promises. "Where are you right now, Dad."

I grab my 357 magnum from the console, check the cylinders, and cock the hammer.

"I hear your truck alarm. You're back in the garage, aren't you?" Jana says. "Your junk is safe, Geez!"

"It's not that. I forgot my, ah—sunglasses."

"It's *dark* outside."

"I meant, *reading* glasses."

"You had me worried for a second there."

"You know, Honey, rather than have a play-by-play, how 'bout I soak in each glorious room and call you in the morning? It's late, to be honest,

I'm beat."

What's burning? I walk around my truck to make sure the smell isn't coming from the garage.

"You're like the Grinch Who Stole Christmas."

She's right, but I got pressing business. "I know, but Jake told me not to over do it." Something *is* burning.

"I know. You should rest. Oh, I wish I could be there to see your face." Jana says. "Promise you'll call me first thing. I'll be up by 6:00."

"I promise."

I step back inside and realize this smell wasn't present when I first entered the house. Light shines through a crack in the mudroom door. I'm certain that door was closed and the light off when I passed it to get into the kitchen—and found the noose. There are two logical answers: my brain is whacking out again, or I'm not alone in my house.

"I love, you Jana." I whisper.

"Something's wrong, isn't there?"

I tiptoe to the mudroom door and push it open slowly with my foot. It sticks a little. A highball glass with a two-finger-pour sits beside a burning cigarette in an ashtray on the vanity. I don't smoke and I haven't had a drink in years. My brain may short out occasionally, but I know I did not put these here.

"I'm just tired. Call you soon, g'night, Honey."

I sniff the glass—Scotch Whiskey. I roll the smoldering cigarette over and read the label, Nat Sherman. The smoke is stinking up my house. I wet my fingers, snuff out the cigarette, and return it to the ashtray.

I slip my phone into my pocket to use a two-hand grip on my pistol. Like a cop clearing an area on TV, I go room to room sweeping my gun side to side. On the way to my bedroom, a stinging burning sensation unlike anything I've ever felt before, blooms out from the dead center of my back. It can't be a wasp, or bee; has to be a ground hornet to inflict this kind of pain. I brace against the wall. In spite of exerting all my strength to stand, in no time I face-plant on the floor. I'm not allergic to bees but sense I'm going into anaphylactic shock.

A ringing and buzzing phone wakes me with a jolt. After three tries, I fish it out of my pocket.

"Dad, I've been waiting for your call. I've been up for an hour."

What the hell? I make it to my knees and crawl straight ahead. Light from the low-hanging sun fills my bedroom. My watch shows 7:15 AM.

"Jana, the strangest thing, a ground hornet stung me. I've never been allergic to stings before, but I passed out."

"Dad, you need to come home, right now. I'll call Jake and—"

"No, Jana. I appreciate your concern, but stop coddling me!"

"OK, OK—so how do you like the re-do."

"It's gorgeous, Honey." I try to stand but my legs are weak, like paper lanterns. "I—I'm groggy."

"Dad, please let me send Jake."

"NO!"

"You don't have to yell."

"What time did we hang up last night?"

"Why?"

"What time!"

"Security History says you opened the garage door at 1:48 AM." Jana said. "Please, don't yell at me. I'm just worried about you."

"Sorry, honey." Aw, what a jerk. "Tell you what, if I don't feel better after a nap... I'll give Jake a call. Deal?"

"Sure, Dad."

"I didn't mean to yell. I love you, Jana."

I'm missing almost five hours. Something doesn't make sense. I go to the bathroom to look at the sting. A small ring of blood and a tiny hole in my t-shirt mark the spot where I felt the initial sting. I've been stung plenty, but I've never had a sting that left a hole in my clothes.

I fish Scarlett's business card from my pocket and dial her number. "The consensus has changed. Can you send a deputy by my house?"

"I'm on my way, Cape."

I grab a quick shower and wait for Scarlett. Warm water soothes my burning wound and clears my head. I toss on some old jeans and a clean t-shirt, then slap on a little cologne. Something I wouldn't do for just any law enforcement officer. A uniformed Scarlett DuBois arrives at my door.

"What's going on?"

"Well, good morning, Sheriff."

Scarlett, repeats her question in the same focused tone, and I figure I read more into our first meeting than was there.

"Had a few surprises when I arrived home."

"Such as?"

"See for yourself." I step aside and point her toward the mudroom. I'll show her the noose last. Maybe even discuss her findings over a cup of coffee in the kitchen.

"Closed off both rooms. I know you don't like people contaminating crime scenes."

"Where're we going?" Scarlett says.

"Straight ahead, door in front of you."

Again, the mudroom door sticks—no re-do there. I give it a quick kick, and move aside so Scarlett can enter.

"If those CSI shows are realistic, you should find some DNA on that cigarette butt." I said, "I picked the glass up, but I didn't touch the cigarette filter."

Scarlett walks over to the basin and surveys the room.

"Obviously I'm missing something?"

I join Scarlett in the room. Ashtray and booze are gone.

"There was a shot of whiskey and a cigarette in an ashtray." I tap the vanity. "Right here."

"Are you sure?"

"I'm not crazy, dammit! I know what I saw—and smelled!"

"Calm down." She says. "You said you picked the glass up. Maybe you moved it, and forgot?"

"There was a smoldering cigarette in an ashtray and a glass of Scotch." I slap the vanity. "Right here!"

Scarlett, sniffs the air. "Smells like Lysol to me, not a cigarette."

"I know what I saw."

"What time did you arrive home?" Scarlett looks at knob on the back door. "Door's still locked. Do you have an alarm?"

"According to Jana, I do. She said, my security history, what ever that is, shows I opened the garage door at 1:48 AM."

"You said a 'few' surprises. What else do you have?"

"A noose, hanging above the island." I open the kitchen door, we file in, the island in our sights, and the noose is gone.

"You did say—noose?"

"It was here last night."

"Was it like the noose I saw in your car?"

"Yes."

"Is it still there?"

"Yes…Hell, I guess—maybe?"

We look in the truck and the noose is hanging right where it was. Scarlett snares the noose with her Cross Pen. "Mind if I keep this?"

"Be my guest, I have no use for it."

"You didn't get home until almost 2:00 AM." Scarlett notes. "That makes for a long day. Did you have a drink to relax?"

"I don't drink. "

"Why didn't you call me when you first noticed something was wrong?"

"When I was checking things out, a hornet or bee stung me. But—there's a hole in my t-shirt and blood."

"What were you doing from the time you left my office until you arrived home, some five hours later?"

How is it, cops automatically assume innocent people are guilty? I consider tossing Scarlett out, but decide to answer.

"Visiting friends?"

"Where?"

"Miss Minnie's place."

"Minnie Reynaud?" Scarlett asked.

"Yes."

"That place has been abandoned for years."

"It wasn't last night."

"You're sure?"

I slow-breathe to calm down. Losing it will only make things worse.

"Positive, Sheriff."

Scarlett looks at her watch, presses the little microphone on her epaulet; "16, you anywhere close to Minnie Reynaud's place?"

"Just passed by it, why?"

"Look like anyone's been there recently."

"Standby, I'll check."

"You don't believe me?" I say.

"How many people do you know who visit people at abandoned homes?"

"16 to Sheriff."

"Go ahead."

"Storm blew a tree down across the path last night, maybe longer ago."

"Roger, 16."

"I was there last night. You can ask Miss Minnie or Jimmy the yardman...Well, Jimmy's a—"

"I took this call because the department is stretched thin. If just one deputy misses work, we don't have enough manpower to staff nightshift. I don't have time for games."

"What do you mean? I'm reporting a *crime* here!"

"You always *bathe* in cologne when you meet officers, or was that just for me?"

"What's that got to do with anything?"

"I think you know." Scarlett said.

Scarlett pulls out the same note pad and silver pen I observed last night. "Are you reporting a crime, or is this a social call?"

The bloody t-shirt in my bedroom. Probably not a good idea to suggest Scarlett check out my bedroom for evidence. "I wasn't hitting on you. I wear cologne. Is that a crime?"

Scarlett's foot tapping the tile floor scatters my thoughts.

"Rhetorical question, Mr. Thomas?"

To order my scattered thoughts I press both sides of my head—an exercise in futility. "I guess I don't have anything to report."

Scarlett slides her pen into her shirt pocket.

"Good day, Mr. Thomas."

I slam my front door, head back to my bedroom and shower again. Even though Scarlett didn't answer, my question deserves an answer. When did it become a crime to wear cologne? Granted, it hasn't been my routine lately, but I shaved and wore cologne everyday at AeroMax. And no matter what Scarlett DuBois thinks, I wasn't making a play for her. She's too tall, flawless, and shapely for my taste!

While I'm thinking about it, I scroll to my new contact information for Jimmy—bingo. At least I have proof I met with Miss Minnie and Jimmy. Crazy sheriff may lock me up for lying.

From the edge of my bed I stare at the deck where Laura visited me almost six years ago. I could sure use her help again, but Laura's return from the dead had one purpose—to bestow her birthright on Jana. Mission accomplished! I may have my problems now, but I took care of business back then—and I'll solve this problem, too.

Think! There's a message or clue from last night's break in, but what? Inanimate objects can't move by themselves. To make sure Scarlett didn't overlook something, I head back to the mudroom. No, whisky, ashtray or cigarette, not one thing out of place, except a lingering lysol smell.

From the mudroom I meander to my bar, a place I spent a lot of time in the past. Sitting on the counter is a bottle of Glenfiddich 25-year-old Rare Oak. Obvious source of the liquor, but the highball glass and ashtray are still a mystery. I don't smoke, yet bringing in cigarettes would take no great effort. Why Nat Shermans? Certainly not a common brand.

My highball-glass inventory, turns up nothing like the glass from last night. An undisturbed coating of dust, indicates none were never considered as props. I make a mental note to tell Jana her cleaning service sucks. I'm sure she's paying them a bundle, too. For that kind of money, my house should be spotless! Since I don't smoke, the ashtray, like the highball glass was brought here. Why the elaborate ruse if the props were to be seen only by me? Whoever perpetrated this ruse has no way of knowing, but their efforts were wasted. I don't have a clue what they symbolize, if anything?

I uncork the whiskey and hold it over the drain—wait! Who in their right mind pours out booze this expensive? I pour a double shot and swirl the amber around. A rich oaky aroma fills the room, ahhh, so I let the whiskey roll across my lips and down my gullet. Warmth spreads nicely, melting away Scarlett's icy behavior.

Booze won't fix what ails me, but neither will anything modern medicine offers. At least this illusory elixir is agreeable to my palate. I pour another double and down it in a gulp.

"Time to crack this case." I Google expensive highball glasses. Diamond Glencairn Scotch Tasting Glass is my fourth hit and a dead ringer for the prop. I don't bother looking for ashtrays—I didn't pay any attention to detail.

I pour another drink and walk through the house admiring Jana's do-overs. In my bar, framed photographs cover an entire wall. Smiling faces, of coworkers in AeroMax uniforms center the collage. Group shots of, captains, first officers, and flight attendants who served on planes I captained look out at me. Many are labeled; *Get Well soon, Captain Cape Thomas!* for example.

I can't believe I have a daughter who loves me this much. I pause at a picture of Jana with Jake and the kids. What would they think if they could see me now, throwing back shots like I did in my heyday? The upside of drinking: I feel like I did back then. Young, bulletproof and not worried in the least about anyone killing me.

On another wall, a gaggle of beautiful women, all connected to me at one time or another. I haven't seen or heard from most of them in years, except for the last four. Linda, Grace, Joy Higgenbottom and, Allison—Ally Moore Kress finishes the lineup. At one time, I could have made a life with any of them. Now, I can't get a gangly, knobby-kneed-cop to give me the time of day.

I can't remember the names of some of the women, just their nicknames; Bodacious, Double D, ShortStack, Little Debbie SnackCake, Holly Dolly, Sexy-Mexi…and on and on. Then I try to place the contenders. Linda, happily married to a doctor, and the kids she always wanted. Grace, after falling from the high-life turned to missionary work as an ordained minister, last I heard. Her good works extended to a project she never gave up on, CPA Jimmy Swain. Joy, as far as I know, is still in Charlotte doing part time acting gigs. My gaze finally comes to, Ally, ah sweet Ally.

I sip my drink. Now are you marrying a Doctor or rich entrepreneur? I gulp down my drink and fill it. "Ladies, I'd like to propose a roast—well, that, too. But I meant *toast*. Here's looking at y'all for looking good—

Salut!"

CHAPTER EIGHT

Off to Charlotte

A ringing noise splits my head like an axe blade striking a gong. I scramble to find my phone and somehow manage to kick the empty Scotch bottle on the floor into a metal barstool. Shards of glass fly across the floor but most stay gathered around my bare feet.

"HELLO!"

"Dad, why are you yelling?"

"You woke me. What do you want?" I can't see the shock on Jana's face but I don't have to. I know I've hurt her feelings. "I'm sorry, Honey. I broke a bottle while I was searching for my phone."

"What kind of bottle?"

"Um, a Coke bottle."

"A *glass* Coke bottle?"

Dumb! What comes in glass bottles anymore? Wine, liquor, beer—and not one of them'll work for me right now. "Maybe? Hell, I don't know! All I know is I have glass all over this damn place. I'll call you back."

"Dad, are you OK? And please watch your potty mouth!"

"Dams hold water, you know that right?"

"The ones with n's don't."

"Point taken. Now, if you'll excuse me I need to wash my mouth out with soap, lye soap." I tell her. "I'll call you."

"Well, I hope you're in a better mood."

"Odds are tipping in your favor."

One step, and I frost my sole with broken glass. Hopping around on one foot while still drunk is stupid, plain stupid. Trying to levitate to safety, and failing miserably, cannot be described in any way, shape, fashion or form without potty-mouthing. Even with all the lye soap ever manufactured, I can't clean up my tirade of the next few minutes. After an hour of picking glass splinters from my soles and my carcass, I hunt for broom and mop. I find neither.

In all the months I've been gone, Jana's cleaning service helped themselves to my cleaning stuff. To hell—heck with it. For what she's paying them, *they* can deal with this mess!

I settle down on a couch and look at my memory walls. All the people in the pictures seem to be staring at me, shaming me. I glare back at them. I'm grown, and if I want to drink, by God, I'll drink! I move closer to the pictures and close one eye so I can see to glare better.

Though, I know most of the owners of these disapproving eyes, one person in particular stands out. I'm certain I don't know the woman, yet in a strange way, she's familiar. Stepping back to focus on this gorgeous mystery woman, I lose my balance, grab the picture to steady myself and pull it off the wall. Sitting on floor with the picture on my lap, I realize why this beautiful creature looks so familiar.

She's Ally's daughter, Celine Seabolt, now a famous movie star. Taped to the corner of the 8 x 10 is a smaller picture in stark contrast to the stylishly framed picture in my hands. It is an add-on and not part of Jana's original display. I don't remember seeing it last night, but how did I overlook it?

No one could have overlooked such a glaring anomaly, something so obviously out of place. The smaller picture must've been put here *after* I passed out. I scrutinize the shot and realize it is a panoramic-selfie. The selfie taker is wearing a harem-girl costume, only her eyes are visible, and I've seen those eyes before. She is holding a noose that frames Ally and Celine. The noose looks larger than the nooses I've found, but it's not, it has been photo-shopped.

My hands start shaking like crazy. I don't have time for this. I need to get my act together. If I'm right about who took this selfie, there's a good chance Ally is in danger.

I fill a shot glass with vodka and knock it back. My hand steadies. Dozens of people are in the background behind Ally and Celine, all of them are in period-costumes. Littered throughout the shot are light sets and mike-booms of various sorts and sizes. This picture was taken on a movie set! I know nothing about movies, but if this isn't a wrap party, I can't fly a kite, much less a 747.

I pour another shot and knock it back. I need to know where and when this photo was taken. I race to my computer and type in: Celine Seabolt Movies Latest to Oldest. "Oh, Hell-o-Pete. Bingo!" Celine's latest picture is *Nymph of the Nile* a parody of the old 40's and 50's Cleopatra movies. According to this article the movie wrapped last month. So this selfie is only weeks old, at the most. Only cast members go to wrap parties, I think. If that's the case, my *night nurse* may be named in the credits.

Gotta warn Ally! I grab my phone, but this isn't something to discuss over a phone. I can't call, but I can't rush down to Charlotte with some wild tale about someone trying to kill her, either. She'll think I'm there to beg her back into my life. What's wrong with me? My pride isn't important—the night nurse is real, and dangerous. I have the proof right here in my hands.

Wait a minute, wait a minute! Warning Ally isn't the most pressing problem I have. I unlock the gun drawer in my desk and grab my Glock 43. Whoever taped this picture onto the frame may still be in my house. I peep down the hallway and a shadow that looks an awful lot like a man holding a gun gets my attention. Inch by inch, I low-crawl to the doorway showing the shadow, roll in front of the door and shoot a raincoat hanging on a clothes tree. "Dammit!"

Time to sober up. I sit in a cold shower, for what seems like hours. Still drunk, I nap until the booze wears off then head out for the Queen City.

Two hours from Charlotte my call to Ally is answered by, Donna Sue Hobart. A woman who claims to be, *The* personal assistant to Celine Seabolt. I tell her my name and why I'm on my way to Charlotte. Donna covers the phone with her hand and whispers, "Some guy named, Cape Thomas, is on his way here with an urgent message for Mrs. Kress? Kook, or do we know him?" A voice, I'm guessing, Ally's says, "Definitely a friend. When can we expect him?"

"How long before you arrive, Mr. Thomas?"

"A little after lunch."

"I'll leave your name at the gatehouse."

Charlotte traffic is flowing well and I'm making much better time than I imagined. Ally's exit is only a few miles west of the Concord airport exit. I have a little time to kill and there's no better place to kill time than an airport. Besides, it's Monday and a rain-delayed race means the NASCAR Air Force will be landing in Concord right about now. A few of the guys I flew with at AeroMax, pilot for some of the race teams now. With any luck, I may bump into one of them and get a job co-piloting— as soon as I pass my physical. Got to knock some rust off before I report back to AeroMax.

I pull into the parking lot and watch the owners' and drivers' private jets land and taxi to the terminal. Even after all these years, seeing planes land still excites me. Most of the star-struck fans in the terminal are gawking at the drivers, but I'm hoping to find a familiar face among the pilots finishing up paperwork. After ten minutes I don't recognize any pilots in the terminal. I turn to leave and a woman points at me and shouts, "It *is* you!"

Like an Olympic long jumper, Joy Higgenbottom Meredith, leaps across the room and straddles my waist. Not a move I'm expecting. I grab on to her to keep us from falling. Unfortunately, the only place to grab is her very shapely derriere. In the process of maintaining our balance, I shuck her tight black skirt all the way up to the small of her back. The entire terminal populace—well, men anyway, stop idolizing celebrities and turn their attention to Joy. "Cape, it's feeling a little breezy in here. Is my skirt up around my waist?"

I trace the hem of the skirt with my fingers. "I'm pretty sure it is." I tug at the tight fitting skirt but realize it's not coming down. "Hope you're not wearing granny-panties."

She laughs, then whispers in my ear, "Not even a thong."

"Oh, boy!" I get us behind a potted plant and put her down.

"Think anyone saw anything?"

I do a peekaboo through the greenery. The masses, including most of the drivers, are still staring at us. "Definitely *something*."

"Tell you what," Joy whispers, "Why don't you get my bag, pretend like you're a cabbie, and I'll wait for you in the parking lot?"

"Sounds like a plan!"

When I walk outside with Joy's bag, I don't see her, but a shrill whistle and frantic waving at the far end of the parking lot reveals her location.

"Damn, that's one for the grandkids." Joy says.

"You have grandkids?"

"No, do I look like a grandmother? I'm only forty!"

"Well, I'm only fifty and I have two. Beautiful twins."

Joy smiles. "That's nice you feel that way."

"Feel what way?"

"About the kids."

"What about them?"

"Well, I guess they're step-grandkids." Joy brushes my hair back. "Hope that little incidence in the terminal doesn't get back to your wife. I'm sorry, I had no idea you were married."

Joy's statement is like a cold-hard-smack of reality. Women I thought couldn't live without me, or me them, don't know and apparently don't care, about my close brush with death.

"Wow. We've got some catching up to do."

"So, you're *not* married?"

"Nope. I just can't seem to find the right—"

"Oh, come on, Cape! Not the one-who-got-away story!"

It seems like a hundred years since anyone has mentioned that story.

"No way!" I put up both hands to stop any further accusations. "And I promise that pity-the-poor-orphan is also gone from my repertoire."

Joy smiles and hugs me. "Good."

"You hated those stories that much?"

"Cape, those stories, to a woman, anyway, are like being told to go straight to hell. Women want men to be honest and open."

I disagree with Joy's premise but stay silent. Those stories saved me from commitment and that in turn saved me from heartbreak, not a bad tradeoff. On the flip side, the stories probably also stopped me from finding, *the one*. Grace, would think that for sure, and, to be honest, Linda would be justified for feeling that way, too. But Ally? I laid my soul bare to that woman and what did my honesty get me—heartbreak to the ErosMax!

"Can I see you for lunch?"

"I have some free time now. Coffee?" Joy says.

Coffee with Joy, in spite of her lack of concern for our past friendship, would be a good time. But I have to warn Ally even though I suspect our meeting won't end well—the more I think about how Ally dumped me, the madder I get. Despite my fury, Ally's life is in danger and I need to warn her.

"I have some important business to take care of this morning."

Joy straightens her skirt. "Let me guess, a woman?"

"Yes, but it's not what you think."

A cab turns into the parking lot. Joy steps forward and signals to it. "How about drinks, later?" she says. "That's my final offer."

"Works for me. Where and when?"

We update our contact information while the driver loads her bag. I think about my promise to Jake not to drive at night, but what the hay, if I play my cards right I may not have to drive later. *Drinks?* Another example of Joy's being out of my loop, or she would know I quit drinking years ago. Well, except for my little relapse last night…but it's true I haven't felt the urge to camp out on skid row drinking my life away. I handle my liquor fine now.

"Give me your phone."

I hand it over and she whispers our meeting place into my navigation app. "After drinks you're coming to my place for dinner, I have someone special I want you to meet. What would you like?"

"I'm not exactly sure about the entree." I give Joy a going-over from head to toe, "But I know exactly what I want for dessert."

"As long as it isn't *me* I guess we'll do just fine." Joy blows me a kiss from the backseat as the cab takes off. I strut back to my truck feeling pretty good. "Still got it!"

From the gatehouse a guard motions me to pull into the visitor lane and stop. "Who you visiting, sir?"

"Allison Moore Kress."

The guard gives me a funny look. "Do you have that number?"

I look at my phone and repeat the last number I called.

He dials the number and turns away for privacy first. "Your name, sir?"

"Cape Thomas."

"Right. I must be getting old. They called your name in earlier, sorry." And I'm motioned through the gate.

Mystic Trail is full of grand houses, and the farther down the road I go the grander the houses become. At the very end of the road, I see my destination. Pulling down the visor mirror, I give myself a quick going-over. My heart is racing like a teenager's on a first date. Satisfied I'm halfway presentable, I pop in a mint and begin my long walk up the drive.

A doorbell serenades me for what seems like minutes. I consider knocking, but just before I do, the door slowly opens. Standing in front of me is the most beautiful human being I've ever seen. Everything about her is familiar, but I know we've never met.

"Hi, Mr. Thomas." She says stepping aside. "Please come in."

I flew quite a few celebrities back in my AeroMax days, and met a lot of them, too. Truth is, most of them don't look so hot in person. I used to think that was because they dressed down to go incognito. After a while you figure it out, though. Many celebrities are just plain ugly, inside and out.

Not so this woman, and besides being beautiful, she sounds just like Ally. "Ms. Seabolt, you're even prettier in person than you are in the movies." Before the words hit her ears, I regret saying them. No telling how many times she's endured this backhanded compliment.

She nods and exhales. "That's kind of you, but I'm jet-lagged and hardly presentable—please forgive."

Before Celine Seabolt tries to convince me further that she's not gorgeous, the house phone rings. She answers it and points to a sofa at the far end of the living room. I sit and take a gander at all the flower arrangements crammed into the room. Must be nice to have so many adoring fans.

"Please, make a donation to a favorite charity, if you wish to pay respects. And thank you so much," Celine says to the caller as she paces across the room and looks out the window. I follow her gaze. What I see as a welcome sight, a florist with flowers coming up the drive, seems to upset Celine. She marches to the door and turns to me before she opens it. "I'm sorry Mr. Thomas. I'll be with you in a moment."

Celine points at the deliveryman. "I said no flowers!" The man stops, and shrugs. While he tries to figure out his next move, another florist's van stops behind his. A woman and another man jump out, hustling four giant arrangements to the front door. The bewildered first deliveryman sets his flowers down in the drive and takes off.

The new arrivals look to Miss Seabolt. She points to a spot near where I'm sitting. "Just put them over there." The young man lingers in the foyer shuffling from foot to foot. I expect he needs the bathroom, but that isn't the first desire he wants fulfilled.

"Ma'am, I'm your biggest fan. May I have your auto—"

"*Silencio*, Leonardo!"

The woman who admonishes, Leonardo sets an arrangement down in front of me and rushes back to the foyer. "*Perdona me*, Miss Seabolt. My grandson helps only part time." Celine nods and offers a weak smile. Without a word she fishes stationery and a pen from the credenza in the foyer and turns to him.

"Leonardo, was it?"

"Yes...but my friends call me, Lenny."

"I'll make it out to, Lenny." Celine says. "After all, we're friends now, aren't we, Lenny?"

"Yes, Ms. Seabolt!"

If I wasn't a fan of Celine's, I am now. I've got half a mind to ask for her autograph, too. Who doesn't want to be friends with Celine Seabolt?

While Celine signs Lenny's autograph, the older woman sets Leonardo's arrangement beside me and whispers, "Sorry for your loss, sir."

Loss? I look around the room taking in everything. These flowers aren't from Celine's adoring fans. These flowers are memorials for the woman in the pictures lining the walls, Ally Kress. No. It can't be!

I push past the old woman to study Ally's photographic life trail: Young Ally Kress in equestrian grab stands in front of a magnificent steed bedecked with a wreath of roses around his neck. Ally Kress wears a tiara and a blue sash emblazoned with the words *Miss North Carolina*. Local and national dignitaries are pictured with the vivacious woman, no doubt touting her good deeds too numerous to list.

No wall is long enough to display all of Ally's accomplishments. If I were allowed to include one photograph missing here, it would be of

Ally's heroic actions in Edenton. Without her there that night I would have died. And without Ally's help, Jana may never have been found. In this moment I realize I will never have a chance to repay the debts I owe Allison Moore Kress.

I stumble to Celine and Lenny still in the foyer. So many things have gotten scrambled in my brain—please let this nightmare be just another one of those delusional moments—not reality.

The young guy is still gushing about some movie Celine starred in. I don't care about that, and I push him aside. "Ally's dead?"

All of them look at me, none more incredulous than Celine Seabolt. "Isn't that why you're here?" She whispers. The foyer begins to tilt and the walls rotate. I grab the delivery woman to steady myself.

"Here." Celine Seabolt points toward a chair and guides me over to it before I fall. The door bell rings again, and now Celine growls, "That better not be more flowers." She swings the door open and screams. "Take them away!"

The older woman moves beside Celine and whispers, "I know you are angry that they send flowers, but the flowers are their words. They cannot find enough soft words to comfort you." She regards her grandson, "It is the only way your fans can show their love. With your permission my grandson and I will stay here and handle any other deliveries—"

"You're *so* right. I'm sorry." Celine says. "It's just that...I really haven't had time even to grieve myself—then all *this* comes."

"Not a problem. You rest and Leonardo and I will handle the flowers."

"But, your boss—"

"I own the shop, Maria's Flowers. It is no problem." She points to new delivery people gathering at the door. "I will line the walk with the rest. We can move them to the service tomorrow, *sí?*"

Celine nods and guides the couple onto the porch. "Thank you. Please don't think badly of me."

"No *señora*."

Celine pushes against the door, and locks the dead bolt. "I know I don't need a dead bolt in Charlotte, it's a habit." She moves away from the door and slumps down in the chair across from me.

"I'm sorry you had to see that. I'm not a Hollywood bitch, but losing Mom has drained me." Celine grabs her clutch from the desk, snaps it open and pops two pills into her mouth. "I know what you're thinking, but I don't do drugs, and seldom even drink for that matter. I have a heart condition."

I nod. "What happened to, Ally?"

"Suicide." The word seems to drain the life from, Celine.

"Are you sure?"

"She left a note."

"So why, then?" My question must seem rhetorical, or that's the way Celine treats it. A long silence cloaks us.

"I have asked myself that a thousand times." Celine plucks a tissue from a box on the credenza and wipes her eyes. "Last time we talked, she seemed so happy. She had decided not to deny herself the pleasure of being with the man she loved."

"Her husband, you mean?"

"No." Celine returns to her chair and smiles wistfully. "My mother was a remarkable woman, Mr. Thomas. On one hand, she made me the center of her universe, but on the other she completely hid that from the world, and especially from Walter Cronus Kress. An amazing feat, don't you think?"

I smile and nod. No need to interrupt, I've heard this beautiful story before.

"Do you know why she did that?" she asks me.

"Actually, I do. She was worried for your safety."

Celine exhales a long, low, breath and sinks back into her chair.

"The very first day Walter went to prison Mom flew out to see me. She saw that he could no longer harm us and she could go about being with the man she loved. But something happened."

I want to tell Celine, why I'm here, but more than that, I want to hear why Ally turned from me.

"She wouldn't tell me what, but she felt threatened, I know that. That's why she wasn't there for you when you came out of your coma. That's why she lied about her plans to marry someone else."

"Ally never married?"

"No. She publicized those plans as a ruse to keep Walter from destroying those she loved. She used those same tactics for years to keep me safe." Celine stands and walks to the collage of pictures and regards them longingly. "You, whether you were aware of it or not, were part of that universe Ally Kress was determined to protect."

"The man she loved—that was me?"

"Yes, and she loved you very much. She felt Walter and William Johnston were after not only her, but anyone she loved. That why she spread her false wedding plans. She created a common but fictitious name, for her *fiancé*. No, James Jones that I know of was ever engaged to my mother, but she hoped a search for him would lead Walter and William Johnston away from *you*."

God, I called her a rich bitch and I said I hated her! Hated a woman who was willing to give up everything for me? I never deserved Ally. And I don't deserve this generous explanation from Celine Seabolt. I don't deserve to be alive.

"She kept in touch with, Jana. When she heard you were considering moving back home, she was determined to be there with you—"

"Jana knew about the sham wedding?"

"Yes, and so did her husband. They agreed it would keep you safe, too."

The coddling wasn't imagined, then. Jake let me go home because he knew Ally would be there to look after me. "Then why didn't my family tell me, Ally was dead?"

"They don't know. I should have called, but it's been only a week since she died, and I'm simply devastated and exhausted. I can barely keep myself in tissues!"

"The flowers and pictures, aren't they for her funeral?"

"I had her cremated shortly after the autopsy. We had a service for her in L. A."

"What the hell? I could see you being so busy you couldn't call, Jana. But you knew how she felt about me!"

"Mr. Thomas, I know you're upset. But this is something my people handled for me."

"Your *people*—!"

"Mr. Thomas. I wish I'd handled it differently. But what's done is done. The service is tomorrow at three. Come by in the morning and I'll try to answer your questions." Celine pressed her temples. "But right now, I need some rest."

Celine Seabolt, a woman who dominates screen and stage, now seems small and frail. Honoring her wish is the least I can do, but I have to know. As much as I hate to, I pose my question. "How did she die?"

Celine Seabolt points to the balcony over the living room. "They found her up there, hanging from the bannister." Tears stream down her face and she is racked by sobs.

"Hanged"?

"Please, no more…"

"I know, but I do have something to tell you. I think once you hear this, you will agree with me that Ally's death was no suicide."

I explain the nooses, miniature coffin, coins, pictures and even the unaccountable appearances of the whiskey and burning cigarette in my own house last night. When I finish, I expect lots of questions but I'm not prepared for the only one she asks.

"Mr. Thomas, have you ever considered a career as a screen writer?"

"Excuse me?"

"What a fascinating tale."

"It's not a tale. I can prove it!"

She simply nods and gives me a wry smile. I get it. She's been told that I don't have a grasp on reality. At times.

"Ah yes, I'm sure you can, Mr. Thomas."

"No, I know what you're thinking—"

"Then I'm sure you'll understand why I must rest." She opens the door. "Mr. Thomas, we can talk tomorrow." Celine shuts the door behind me and clicks the dead bolt.

I nod to the floral grandmother and Leonardo on the walkway. As I pass, she whispers, "*Dios mio!*" and stares down to the street.

A woman, standing beside a delivery van and wearing a Scream Mask sets a wreath down at the end of the driveway. The wreath is adorned with a ribbon embossed with words I can't read from this distance. I race down the walkway, the van driver burns rubber back toward the gatehouse. I stop long enough to read the banner: Mother & Daughter Reunion and attached to the wreath is a noose, just like those in my own, growing collection.

I snatch the noose from the flowers and run back up toward the locked door. But what's the use?

Even if I show it to Celine, she'll never believe me. I jump in my truck and slam the accelerator to the floor. This has to end right here, right now. I fly by the gatehouse only to be held up by a school bus unloading a passel of kids. For what seems like an hour, the kids meander across the street. The delivery van is long gone.

I leave my truck idling by the roadside and race back to the guardhouse. The guard puts up his hand for me to stay outside, but I throw the door open and scream. "I need your identification information for the van that just passed through here. Better yet, call it in to Charlotte P.D. Tell them Ally's Kress' killer is in the van!"

"Whoa, pardner! Normally, we do log delivery vehicles in. Today's been crazy. So we just let the florist vans roll through."

"You're kidding me! What about your security cameras?"

"Yeah, there's one up there… but its been on the blink."

"Dammit man! Call the cops! Give them a description of the van."

"Which one?"

"You are an *idiot!*"

CHAPTER NINE

Things go from bad to worse in Charlotte

I tear down the street from the gatehouse, hop into my truck, and nudge into the bumper to bumper traffic. If I get a break I still may catch the delivery van. But after going no where for ten minutes, I understand why Charlotte is called Car-Lot.

I check out the noose on the seat beside me. Though identical to the others, a chilling reality appertains to *this* noose. The horror Ally, must have felt as she was flung over the railing so high above the floor below. No one deserves to die by having their neck snapped like that, especially one as kind and gentle as Ally.

It's time to let my family know that whoever is targeting us has raised the stakes. Now, the penalty for letting our guard down, is death. RH Carter, in his usual prompt and efficient manner, picks up on the first ring.

"RH Carter, go."

I see a van across the road in a parking lot that looks a lot like the one at Ally's and click on my blinker to check it out. A Good Samaritan driver beside me, thinks I want the left lane and let's me in. When he realizes I'm turning across two lanes of oncoming traffic, he loses it. I can hear him cussing over the traffic.

"Hello, hello. This is RH Carter, is that you, Cape?"

"Yeah, had to make a turn, sorry."

"What's up?"

"What's going on with the noose and coffins definitely isn't a game." I guess the driver behind me gets madder when he sees I'm on the phone. He lays on his horn like it's broken.

"Where are you? New York?"

"No, why?"

"I haven't heard horns blaring like that since I left the city."

"I did something stupid and I'm paying for it." Thankfully oncoming traffic clears for a second and I make my turn into the parking lot. A large heavy-set man, tosses a box into the van loaded with mattresses, hops in, and drives off. Not the van I saw at Ally's.

"What happened in your house, man? There's broken glass from a liquor bottle all over the floor!" RH says. "Did you get in a fight with someone? Is that why you say this isn't a game?"

The shame of falling off the wagon overwhelms me. "How do you know about that?"

"I guess when you left you forgot to set the alarm. Jana got a call from the alarm company and asked me to check it out. Did you report the attack?"

Boy, of all the people in the world, why do I have to confess to big-mouth RH Carter?

"There wasn't an attack, RH—unless fighting with yourself during a drunk counts. I fell off the wagon, but I'm back on it now. Did Jana see the mess?"

"No, I kind of thought that's what happened. I cleaned up the place myself."

"I took stupid—"

"Don't be so hard on yourself. You've been under a lot of pressure." RH replies. "Blowing off a little steam probably did you good. You didn't hurt yourself, did you?"

RH's sympathy catches me by surprise. Again he suddenly acts and sounds human.

"Naw, just soiled my dignity a bit."

"Never heard of that killing anyone."

"I got bad news, RH."

What's going on, chief? You sure you're OK?"

I want to answer, but thinking of Ally and knowing I'll never see her again hits me hard. My mouth moves, but no words come out.

"Cape, talk to me. Tell me where you are and I'll get help to you."

"It's too late. You can't help—it's Ally."

"Where is she? Tell her to hold tight. I'll have agents there in 10 minutes!"

"Ally's dead...and the killer's hiding behind a Scream Mask. I tried to catch him, but traffic is bumper to bumper."

"Tried to catch him? Call the cops. That's what we do and we're pretty good at it!"

"I told the guard to call the cops. I was trying to catch up to the van— but the killer will never be caught because the security firm are slack asses! Their security cameras don't work. Can you believe that!"

"What security camera? Tell me exactly what happened."

I shake my head to clear it. This isn't how pilots handle emergencies. RH, is right—I have to get it together. "So much happened so fast, it's hard to put together. I wasn't prepared to walk into a funeral. I wanted to warn Ally that someone might be after her, too, and, to be honest, give her a piece of my mind. Dammit, RH, I was too late. I said mean things about Ally, but Ally loved me! What's wrong with me? I'm like a lit Roman Candle. I never know when, or who I'll go off on next."

"When and where did you see the killer?"

"At Ally's place north of Charlotte, just now."

"I thought you were at a funeral! Dammit, Cape, this is a murder! Don't give me this story piecemeal. Tell me the facts and put it in some chronological order!"

I explain exactly what happened in chronological order just as if I'm reading it from my logbook.

"No one else saw this person in the mask?"

"The woman helping with the flowers did, but Celine locked the deadbolt and I couldn't get back into the house to tell her. I don't know if Celine knows about the driver in the mask."

"If Miss Seabolt has no idea about the perp, you better head back to Ally's. Sounds like you're the only one with details. The police will need to talk to you, and when you finish with them come back home. This place is like Fort Knox now. Security is all over the place."

"I'm not ready to go back and there's not much I can tell the cops. I saw a van and rather than try to get the plate number, I ran back to my truck and tried to chase them down. So stupid!"

"Cape, you gotta quit tryin' to be a cop."

"Go to hell—I was trying to help!"

RH makes repeated calls back to my number, but I ignore him. I lay on my horn, and forcing my way back into traffic. On the way back to Ally's my anger at RH metastasizes into a full-blown case of road rage.

The guard comes to my car smiling and holding a placard of some sort. "Here you go. Put this on your dash and the next time you come use the residence lane, no need to stop."

"How about the cops?" I said.

"Cops?"

"I told you to call the cops!"

"I called Ms. Seabolt and she said it wouldn't be necessary to call the cops. The person you saw was promoting her latest movie. What you got excited about was part of a movie trailer."

"She told you that?"

"Well, her assistant, and she asked me to stop all deliveries and made it very clear that you're the only visitor allowed during the rest of her stay."

Unless Celine Seabolt's latest movie spoof of ancient Egypt includes nooses and Scream Masks for props, this story is bull crap. I grab the guard by the collar and pull his face to mine. "What I saw wasn't a movie trailer prop but who I saw is likely the killer of Ally Kress. Call the cops, something doesn't add up. I'm going to talk to Ms Seabolt *and* her assistant."

I park in the same space in front of the house and make my way up the walk. It doesn't appear that more arrangements have been added to the walkway since I left, but I notice two glaring omission. The *Mother and Daughter Reunion* wreath is missing and so are Maria and Lenny. Oddly enough, the Maria's Flowers van is still here. What the crap is going on here?

I reach for the doorbell, but the door's slightly ajar. Strange, considering Celine Seabolt closed and dead-bolted the door twice in my presence. I knock on the door and step inside, but just as I am about to close the door, I notice an arrangement in the foyer that wasn't there earlier. I read the ribbon across the wreath (*Exitus Acta Probat*) and fling the door open. Hanging from the very bannister where Ally's life ended is Celine Seabolt, hanged by the neck.

I rush up the staircase and reach down for her shoulders—no way. Downstairs again, I grab a chair to slide under her so I can support her legs. Of all things that make no sense, I slip in a soapy puddle of water directly under, Celine's body and bang my head on the floor. Though addled, I manage to get back on my feet and place the chair in the center of the puddle. Her legs are cold to the touch, and there's no saving this woman. The beautiful Celine Seabolt is now another footnote in history —another of those movie stars who died way too young.

Celebrities, as much as they are maligned, at times are just like us except for their very familiar faces. Or at least Celine Seabolt struck me that way. Somehow she seemed older than twenty-nine, maybe because she was a public figure for so long, making her first movie when she was nine. Twenty years in any business makes you a pro, and there is little doubt that Celine was tops in her profession.

I call 9-1-1, but before I get an answer a cop slinks into the foyer and yells, "FREEZE"!"

I do as he says and he *still* throws me to the floor. "Stay there, or I'll blow your head off!" is his second greeting.

Of course he rushes up the stairs to try and save a person who can't be saved. "She's dead." I say.

"Push on her legs!" He yells to me. "I can't reach her!"

I stand up, but stay in place. "I'm the one who asked the guard to call you. Let me show you something."

"What?"

I reach for the noose, but the cop already has his drawn weapon aimed at my head.

"It's not a gun." I say, entirely fed up—exhausted, in fact…

"Bring it out nice and easy, then."

I dangle the noose in front of me.

"What's that? A noose?" He barks.

"I found it on a wreath—"

"This is a crime scene. DON'T TOUCH ANYTHING, YOU GOT THAT!"

"Go to hell! I've been through this before. And, for your information, I found the noose before this became a crime scene! I've been getting nooses like this for weeks now."

"YEAH, well I want to hear more about that," a detective rushing into the foyer yells. "Get the paramedics in here, now!" he tells the hapless cop.

Within seconds the house is abuzz with EMTs, more cops, photographers, and a group of people with CORONER written across their jumpsuits. Once everyone is performing their duties to the detective's satisfaction, he saunters over to me. "Who are you?"

"Cape Thomas."

"You related to the victim?"

Easy question, tough answer. I've *known* Celine Seabolt for an hour, but had things worked out between Ally and me. I would have been her step-father. Once I fill him in on my connection to the Kress family and tell him about my burgeoning noose collection, he closes his notebook.

"Stay put."

I stay put.

The detective joins the coroner next to the body, but after a few minutes he returns.

"I think the killer was a delivery person." I advise him.

The detective ignores my speculation and instead initiates a line of questioning that will establish a time line. In any case, he asks me for the third time if I'm sure of my departure time. "I didn't write the time down, but it was a little after 12:30. Ask the gate guard—I spoke to him before I chased the van."

"I'll do that." The man makes another entry on his notepad, then questions the forensic team, "Anyone know what the writing means?"

I follow his finger pointing at the wreath with the words: *Exitus Acta Probat.*

"The end justifies the means." I counsel him.

The detective snaps closed his notepad and makes a beeline for me.

"Did you send the flowers? Or, more specifically, did you send this wreath?"

"No. I didn't know Ally was dead until I arrived."

"And how is it you know Latin?"

"My grandfather was a lawyer."

"Hey, Detective—need you in the kitchen, now!"

"What it is?"

"More bodies."

I stand to follow the detective. He whirls around and points at a chair. "Sit, and don't touch a thing until I get back."

Another covey of EMTs floods into the house and heads for the kitchen. After five minutes or so the detective comes back to me.

"Do you know anyone named, Donna Sue Hobart?"

"I believe she is the lady I spoke with earlier. She identified herself as the personal assistant to Ms. Seabolt."

"How about, Leonardo Silva?"

"His friends call him, Lenny?"

"Not anymore, they don't. How about Maria Clara Silva?"

"She is Lenny's grandmother and she owns Maria's Flowers here in town."

"So you know them?"

"I met them here, Detective, Very briefly. About an hour ago. Seemed like very nice people."

"I'm sure they were."

"Are they dead?"

"Yes, they are." The detective puts his notepad in his jacket pocket. "You know anything about how they died, or did you have anything to do with their deaths?"

"No."

"Mind submitting a sample of your DNA?"

"Be glad to, as soon as you tell me your name, rank and serial number."

"Sorry" The detective takes out his badge and dangles it in my face. "I'm Detective Darius Martin, Charlotte P.D."

"Thank you. How can I help you?"

Detective Darius Martin leans back, rests his elbow on the arm crossing his midsection, and puts his chin in the palm of his hand. "Let me get this straight, you came here to visit Mrs. Kress, but you didn't know about her funeral?"

If there's one thing cops do well, that is ask questions. Lots and lots of questions, often the same ones over and over. After another, apparently satisfactory explanation, Detective Martin, requests that I stick around, then rejoins the coroner's group. This time their conversation turns intense.

I'm fairly certain, Detective Martin will ask me about the delivery van driver when things calm down. In the meantime I decide to look at Ally's pictures. Just as I am about to stand, I notice a familiar-looking cord protruding from a drawer of the antique French desk in front of me. Curious, I pull the drawer open.

"What the hell are you doing!" Detective Martin asks charging me like a bull in the ring. "This is a crime scene, you idiot! How many times do I have to tell you that? I told you to stay put, and I mean *stay put!*"

I lock my eyes on the noose laid neatly across an opened pack of Nat Sherman cigarettes in the bottom of the drawer. The detective picks up on my gaze and shoves me aside. Like a surgeon he uses his pen to lay the nooses on top of the desk. "Thirteen," He says loud enough for the forensic team in the kitchen to hear.

"Thirteen?" I ask.

Detective Martin blows out like a whale. "Yeah, does that number mean something to you?"

"Uh—bad luck."

"You bein' a smart ass?"

"You asked a question, and that's my answer."

Detective Darius Martin: hands me his business card. "You're not the only one who has been receiving these nooses. Mrs. Kress made a complaint months ago about the same thing. Counting the one you found earlier, this is the thirteenth noose that I've collected so far." He scribbles another note and looks back at me. "Are you the same Cape Thomas connected to the noose case in Greenville?"

"I am, but how do you know that?"

"We're working with SBI, and they are working with an FBI guy with personal connections to the family."

"Yeah, I just spoke with him, RH Carter, I told him about Ally."

"Did you tell him about Ms. Seabolt?"

"No."

"Why not?"

"She wasn't dead when I spoke with him."

"Well, don't mention what you've seen or heard here today. We'll control what information we release, understand?"

"Loud and clear. But just so you know. Word on the street in Greenville is all of this may be a prank."

"Maybe that's the word on the street, but you haven't heard that from the police. This is, and always has been, a serious investigation…and it just got a lot more serious."

"Are you guys working with Sheriff Scarlett DuBois?"

"This is a local, state and federal investigation. We meet regularly to exchange information. As far as I know, no Sheriff named DuBois, is part of this investigation. That doesn't mean she won't be. Have you told her something relevant to this case?"

"You'd have to check with her on that."

"Why's that?"

"I'm not sure she takes much of what I say seriously." I said.

"Sounds like you got on her bad side…"

"Exactly."

"I'll give her a call."

"Thanks for being honest with me, Detective Martin."

"If you think of something when you get back down there and report it to her, how about you call me, too?"

I make up my mind to visit with Sheriff Scarlett DuBois as soon as I get back to town. And if I have a choice of who I report to, it will be Scarlett, not Darius Martin. Besides, this will give me a chance to prove that I'm not some creep who hits on every woman he sees…and I'm pretty sure she thinks I'm one of those.

"Celine, told me Ally's death was a suicide?"

"You understand," Detective Martin says. "I can't talk about this case because it is ongoing, right?"

"Yes, I do. But just in case what happened to Ally and Celine happens to me, I want you to know it wasn't a suicide."

For the first time since I've met Darius Martin, he cracks a half-assed smile. "I'll make a note of that, Mr. Thomas."

I check my watch. "May I leave now? I have a date in a few hours."

Detective Martin thumps the card I'm holding with his thick index finger. "Sure, but if you think of anything, or if something suspicious happens, while you're in Charlotte, I want to know about it, understand?"

I think about telling him about the bow and arrow incident in the woods. And the strange time lapse and evidence missing from my house.

But he'll get that from Scarlett when he calls her.

I look at the body bag the coroner is zipping up and start for the door. Detective Martin steps in front of me and lowers his voice. "If what you've told me, checks out, I won't arrest you, right now. But you're a person of interest. If I call, make sure you get back with me, asap, understand?"

I stop at the gatehouse on the way out. Something is bugging me and this guy has the answer. Again, the guard motions for me to go to the window rather than come inside, as he did earlier. I guess if someone horse-collared me, I'd do the same thing.

"Sorry, I grabbed you."

"How may I help you?"

"Have you ever spoken in person with, Donna Sue Hobart, Ms Seabolt's assistant, before today?"

"Yes, I met her with Ms. Seabolt. People who live here are very nice— seems like only the visitors are buttholes."

"Yeah, like I said, I'm sorry about that. Did the woman who put me on the visitor list sound like, Donna Sue Hobart to you?"

"A police detective just called, and asked me not to talk to anyone about the Kress Family."

"Well, yes or no is hardly talking about them, right?" I said.

"You'll have to excuse me. Another potential, butthole just rolled up." The guard grabs his clipboard and steps out to the visitor's lane. No need to hang around.

CHAPTER TEN

Gettin' ugly in the Queen City

My late lunch is at Meat-n-3 on College Street near the bar where I'm meeting Joy. I eat slowly, hoping time passes quickly—it doesn't. With more than an hour to kill, I decide to walk to the bar Joy whispered into my phone. The direct route to the watering hole is all uphill, so by the time I get there, I'm thirsty.

"What'll it be?"

"Cold beer."

The Lock, Stock & Gun Barrel, like most bars in Charlotte, is preparing for Happy Hour. Several dozen patrons, like me, though, can't wait for the normal 5:00 PM kickoff. Before I'm served, three more join our ranks of Early-Timers.

I sip my beer and try to wrap my brain around how so many murders took place in such a short period. The cops didn't say, but more than one person had to be involved. Detective Martin, unless he's lying, said there was an ongoing investigation and the nooses were part of it. Why wouldn't the cops tell Celine that Ally's death was, at the very least, suspicious? Or does the existence of a suicide note determine the cause of death until proven otherwise? The blaring TV behind the bar distracts me.

"Breaking News! Oscar-winning actress, Celine Seabolt and others have been found dead in a Charlotte home!"

Conversations about Celine's death gin up at tables all over.

"Overdose, I guaran-damn-tee you!" A petite blond with thick Appalachian accent, surmises to her two girlfriends. "No doubt!" one agrees.

"Such a pity. How old was she? What was she doing in Charlotte?" another patron wonders.

A guy across the room adds his two cents, "Crazy bitch probably killed herself! Hollywood stars can't *stand* success."

I pluck my server from the chaos. "Bring me a Scotch. Make it a double."

The madness continues. "Yeah, definitely overdose!"

"Suicide!" yells another.

"Well, it's the same thing. You take drugs and die, that's suicide."

"Well, I just hate it. She was my favorite actress."

"Why in Charlotte? Was she from here?"

Speculation and hostile comments buzz around me like angry bees. I knock back my drink and order another.

A young guy at a filled-five topper holds his IPhone and turns the screen toward the crowd. "My bud at Channel 8 says it's a suicide."

What the hell does it matter how Celine died? Truth is, it doesn't, but for some reason I want the world to know that Celine Seabolt wasn't some drugged-out actress who killed herself. She was a child, grieving the loss of her mother, and she was jet-lagged; no overdose, no suicide. I think of the last autograph she signed for Lenny—and she was a class-act.

"She was murdered! Dammit!" I yell.

"Did he say she was murdered?" the blonde asks her friends.

I make my way to the register and settled up my tab. I'll wait for Joy outside.

"Damn! Drugs ruined another perfect piece of ass! That's my headline," a guy hunched over his barstool snickers.

The scene is hauntingly familiar. In Raleigh Ally Kress rushed by a register exactly like the one I'm staring at now. I wonder how Ally would react to these comments being made about her daughter. My parent side answers. *Exactly the way I'd react if someone was ragging on Jana.*

Anger boils from my gut like vinegar poured on baking soda. I turn and face the crowd. "CELINE SEABOLT DIDN'T DO DRUGS!" Suddenly everyone in the bar is silent, looking at me. Hell, even I'm looking at me in the mirror behind the bar. An eerie quiet spreads through the bar, sucking up the good cheer. I look at the guy with the IPhone. "SHE DIDN'T TAKE HER LIFE. I DON'T GIVE A CRAP WHAT YOUR BUDDY AT CHANNEL 8 SAYS!" As my words reverberate in the room, it dawns on me:I don't have to yell to be heard. "Celine came home to hold a private memorial for her deceased mother. I'm sure she was tired and probably depressed, but she wasn't suicidal."

"How the hell do you know that?" IPhone man challenges me. "You a reporter, or just a damn know-it-all?"

The bartender raises an eyebrow and nods in agreement to the question. "Yeah, how *do* you know that?" he echoes, chin up and gauging me.

"Settle me up." I grunt and hand the bartender two twenties.

"Well, tell us, Mr. Know-it-all," a woman from the crowd yells. "Are you her *Dad* or somethin'?"

"Nah, he ain't black enough for that," a guy at the bar says, and then adds, "Her mammy was white."

It is the prettiest 1-2 punch I've ever thrown and the end result is perfect. The mouthy guy lands on his backside and slides to a stop against a wall.

In the movies, a punch like that, pretty much ends the fight—not so in real life. This guy leaps up like some Kung Foo fighter and blitzes me with a passel of kicks and punches. I break out running, hoping to out-distance his fury. He's having none of it and keeps pounding away. I grab a beer mug off a table and break it over his nose. He bends over and grabs his face, then he stands and continues his charge. Unbelievable! I look for something else to bean him with.

Two full mugs sitting on the table with the blonde catch my eye, and I slam them on either side of his head. Remnants of one of the mugs crashes into the bar mirror, shattering it. I heave the handle of the other mug at a guy who stands to help his buddy. That guy's fall in slow motion, like a giant oak going down. The momentum of my wild toss launches me toward the door, and I go with the flow. As luck would have it, there's Joy, so I spin her around.

"Let's go, Honey, it's too hot in here!"

"Cape, are you drunk?"

"Just getting started." I grab Joy's hand and we run down the sidewalk. "Where's your car?"

"I took a cab so I could ride back with you."

"Come on!" We jog down the street until I realize we're running away from my truck. "We have to double back—"

"Why?"

"Cops!" I yell and drag her in the other direction.

"Why are we running from the police?"

A squad car rolls to a stop in front of the bar. I grab Joy's hand and pull her across the street. "A guy called Ally 'Mammy'. It hit me wrong!"

"Alley Kress?"

"Yes. She's dead, Joy—"

"I know. I wasn't sure you knew when I saw you at the airport. That's one reason I wanted to see you tonight."

Two cops run into the bar and scramble back out, apparently in hot pursuit of us. The cops look across the street at us. I push Joy against the wall and kiss her passionately. The cops jump in their cruiser and take off. Joy knees me in my cojones and pushes me away. "Stop! I'm engaged, dammit!"

I suck wind and kneel on one knee. "You're engaged?"

Before she can answer, the bartender yells at me from across the street. "Stay there! The cops want to talk to you."

The return trip to my truck is all downhill. We run full-bore and don't talk until we get to my truck.

I pop the lock on my Yukon and toss the keys to Joy. "Get us out of here."

"I can't drive something this big."

"Well, give it a try Honey, 'cuz I sure can't drive." We make it onto the one-way street that runs back past the bar. Joy is driving so slow the bartender has no trouble getting my plate number. It's just a matter of time before the cops arrest us, but for the moment, I feel alive! Which is a dang sight better than dead, though invitations to death seem to follow me everywhere I go.

"Cape Thomas, what's wrong with you?"

"You mean the kissing thing?"

"Well, there's that, but you're so different from the Cape I know."

Joy is right. I am different. Jake promised that one day things would return to normal, but after today I realize there is no normal. There's just life and death. You belong to one, or the other, and the commonality that connects the two is a state of mind. I fling Jake's prescription pills out the window.

"Was that your medication?" Joy ask.

"Yep."

"What's it for?"

"To calm me down, help me see things clearer."

"And you don't want to see things clearer?"

"Joy, for the first time since I've awakened, I see things crystal clear."

"That's a good thing, right?"

"Hell yeah!"

"Explain."

"Ally tried to insulate her family from the world, yet it got her daughter killed. My family won't pay that price."

"What are you talking about? You're scaring me."

I look at Joy's wild eyes and decide my morning activities aren't a good topic for us. "So, you're really engaged?"

"Yes, I am." She flashes a big smile and a small diamond ring.

"This morning at the airport...I thought you wanted—"

"To hop in the sack with you?"

"Yeah. You know, like old times?"

"I take back what I said about you." Joy giggles. "You haven't changed a bit!"

"That's good, right?"

"Cape, you've always been bad in that way."

"What way?"

"Has it ever occurred to you that a woman can't do you a favor, or even talk politely to you without you thinking she wants to sleep with you?"

"What it is with you women nowadays?" I said. "Are all of you men-haters?"

"No, but we'd like to think we're more than sex objects."

"We spent a lot of time in the sack. How am I supposed to know you're not like that anymore?"

"This morning I made it very clear that I had someone special, someone I wanted you to meet?"

"I wasn't thinking about a fiancé."

"Well, who did you think that *someone special* might be?"

"Maybe a *special someone* for a threesome—"

She slaps me hard across the face. "I'm not like that and you know it!"

I rub my jaw. To be so small, Joy packs a punch.

"Well, what do you have to say for yourself?"

"We were talking about people changing…I thought."

Joy slaps me again. "Have you lost your mind or are you just brain-dead?"

I see a Sonic sign and motion for Joy to pull in so I can get something to drink and dilute my alcohol buzz.

"Jake, wonders about that, too. He never says the brain-dead part, though."

"Who's Jake?"

"Jake Draughon, Jana's husband, and the doctor who saved me. He's also a friend of the doctor who saved Jana."

"Who's Jana? And what did they save y'all from?"

I notice blood dripping from my nose and right hand. The skin across my knuckles is split all the way across. I press the speaker button and order lots of napkins and two Cokes. "It's a long story." I see a police cruiser turn into the far side of the parking lot. It won't take them long to find us. "A story for another time." I reach over and give Joy a peck on the cheek. "I'm sorry for being a jerk, but can you to do me a favor for old times sake?"

"If it has anything to do with sex, forget—"

"Nothing like that. I don't think I'm going to get to meet your special someone. I want you to tell him that he's a lucky man. Women like you are a real treasure, Joy."

"If you don't have dinner with us, I'll never speak to you again, Cape Thomas!"

Suddenly, blue lights, flash around the interior of the truck like a Kmart special discount.

"I think I have other plans, Honey."

The fear on Joy's face is heartbreaking.

"Let me do all the talking—OK?"

Joy nods her head. "What's going on, Cape—this is more than bar fight isn't it?"

"Yes, someone's trying to kill me. Can I count on you if I need a friend?"

Joy looks me dead in the eyes and becomes cool, calm and collected. " You can always count on me, Cape Thomas."

"Good, follow my lead."

The cops in the cruiser draw their weapons and point them at us. "Hands up! And keep 'em where we can see'em!"

When one cop snatches my door open I look at Joy and yell, "You called the cops, you sorry bitch! Get outta my sight! I ought'a kill you!"

As an actress, Joy, I hope, picks up on my cue. If the cops think she's with me, she's going to jail, too. The shock on Joy's face and her sudden tears look real enough—I hope they fool the cops. I feel terrible, and start to apologize, but before I can say anything else, the cops slams me on the ground. The cop on Joy's side of the truck says, "Don't worry, ma'am. You're safe now!"

Not the best impromptu plan ever devised, but seems like it worked.

CHAPTER ELEVEN

Law breaker

The officers in the cruiser are professional, prompt, and efficient. Within thirty minutes I'm charged, booked and jailed for assault, public drunkenness, communicating threats, and disturbing the peace. Apparently yelling at the top of your lungs to a TV crew filming a protest in front of the Charlotte Police Department that the department is owned by Walter Cronus Kress merits the trumped up charge of disturbing the peace. I have no problem with the other charges.

My previous encounter with law enforcement took place in an interrogation room after MarKay's murder. This is my first time in a holding cell, or a lockup of any sort for that matter. The bleak and austere surroundings aren't exactly dirty, but a tad uninviting. Much like the greetings I receive from the current occupants of Charlotte P. D.'s Holding Cell-D.

"What the hell are you looking at?" the guy sprawled on the lower steel bunk asks as I survey the seating arrangements, or lack thereof.

"Yeah, you got a problem?" the guy from the top bunk adds and sits up to get a better look at me. "How 'bout I knock your ass out 'cuz I don't like your looks—whaddya think 'bout that?"

I glance down the corridor, hoping to see a guard, trustee, or at least a friendly custodian with a spare set of brass knuckles. Not a soul in sight.

"I asked you a question!" Top-bunk guy yells, "You gonna answer me, dickhead?"

Bottom-bunk guy is intent upon adding some blood to the water. "Looks like he ain't got no respect for you, Bobby Ray."

I smile my best *Thank-you-for-flying-with-us-today* smile, hoping it'll diffuse some of the hostility festering up in Bobby Ray.

"Look, fellas, I don't want any trouble."

Bobby Ray, twists his face into the nastiest sneer I've ever seen. "We ain't no *fellas*, punk bitch. I'm Mister Bobby Ray Holland, and this here's my 'sociate, Mr. Tyrell Hardison. And we 'bout to open up a can of whup-ass on you, *Fella*."

"Guys...I apologize—"

"Guys? We look like *guys* to you?" Tyrell asks.

"Gentlemen? How's that work for you?"

"*Gentlemen?*" he smirks. "We got us a real smart-ass here, Bobby Ray."

For the most part, except for today, apparently, I try to avoid trouble. These lowlifes aren't on the same program. As Bobby Ray Holland, prepares to launch himself from his roost, I grip one of the iron bars at the front of the cell with my left hand and swing all my weight into a wild haymaker. My right lands square on his chin and sounds like a golf ball connecting with the sweet spot of a well-swung driver, solid. Bobby Ray, goes from vertical to horizontal in less than a second.

Tyrell, eager to help his associate, lunges at me from the bottom bunk. I grab the frame of the top bunk and pull with all my might. My handhold move works perfectly as I slam my knee into his face and reverse his forward motion. His head jerks back so violently I worry for a second that I've broken his neck. When Tyrell shakes his head, though, I know I'm in for a beating unless I take charge. I jerk Tyrell off the bunk, straddle him and whale away. Tyrell scrambles to get under the bunk, but I keep pounding and stomping him.

Cops, too busy to monitor the closed-circuit TV when I was about to get my butt kicked, evidently can't turn away from the screen. A team of four rushes down the corridor in riot gear. The lead officer has a shield of some sort and the guy behind him has a stun-gun. Before the team reaches the cell, Tyrell bucks like a bull and almost flips me under him. By a stroke of luck, my foot braces against the cell's stainless-steel toilet. With that leverage I'm able to hold Tyrell under me and whale away on his head some more.

Suddenly, everything I think I know about electricity goes out to lunch. Fifty-thousand volts of electricity won't kill you, but dang near it, as it turns out. I stiffen up like a board, and Tyrell seizes the moment for payback. His punches bouncing off my head and torso are barely felt as long as the high voltage is coursing through my body. But as soon as the voltage dies, I note that Tyrell has a punch like a mule's kick—a mule immune to the blows of billy clubs raining down on him. I can only assume the team has but one stun gun since Tyrell's beating goes on forever. The last thing I remember, before the cops light me up again, is getting one full-force kick into Tyrell's groin. 'Tis but a Pyrrhic victory.

CHAPTER TWELVE

More Hospital time...

The effects of the sedative dissipates in stages. My left eye is fully opened but I have only a narrow field of vision in my right eye. Yet through this eye I observe Detective Darius Martin scanning what appears to be an X-ray image.

"What you got there?" I say.

Detective Martin clips the film on a lighted board attached to a stainless steel cart. "Doctor said you were stuck in the back with a needle, not stung by an insect." Martin turns off the chart board and looks at me. "You got any idea how a person with a needle can get close enough to inject an armed man, without being seen?"

I'm not sure whether the question is rhetorical, or even meant for me. Questions about a small puncture wound seem irrelevant considering the pop-knots, contusions, and abrasions adorning my body, thanks to my jailhouse beating. I roll my head around to see who else may be there. Seeing no one else, I figure he's talking to me.

"Don't have a clue."

"You told Sheriff DuBois you felt like something stung you when you were searching your house?"

"Right, right. Yeah, it burned but the pain went away quickly—that was a needle?"

Detective Martin clicks the backlight on again and points to a perfect circle in the middle of CAT scan image. "Yep, 10 gauge needle according to the doctor."

"I must have overlooked it, 'cause I sure don't remember seeing a syringe after I woke up. It has to be in my house... Maybe they'll find it and some fingerprints, or—"

"Didn't turn up when Sheriff DuBois searched your house."

I try to sit up but a giant rubber band is strapped across my chest.

"What the hell?"

"You got a little restless last night. They strapped you down rather than sedate you again," Detective Martin said. "Want me to undo you?"

"That'd be nice." When he unlatches the rubber strap I try to raise my arm, but handcuffs attached to my wrist clang against the bedrail.

"Want to undo this while you're at it?"

Detective Martin looks into both my now wide open eyes. His look is one I've seen before on another cop's face. "We just got the autopsy report on Ms. Seabolt. She has a puncture wound exactly like yours, and we think the injection incapacitated her. In fact, all the victims have a wound like yours. What about that, Mr. Thomas?"

They say when cops start asking questions you should start asking for a lawyer. But, following sage advice has never been my strong suit. Besides, I've always felt like that advice is for guilty people. One thing I am certain of, brain-damaged and all, I'm innocent.

"Well, Detective Martin, I think the same person who killed Ms. Seabolt, and probably Ally Kress, Donna Hobart, Lenny and his grandmother, tried to kill me. That's what I think, but I'm no top-notch homicide detective stocked with trick questions contrived to trap an innocent person, either."

The policeman pushes his face closer and closer to mine until there is a total visual eclipse of the room caused by Detective Darius Martin's face. "Or—you perhaps practiced on yourself with this, as yet, unknown drug. We do have a witness who says you were very upset with, Alley Kress. So let's call that motive.

We also know that you were the last person to see, Celine Seabolt alive and, you're also the person who discovered her body." Martin eases back in much the same manner he moved forward. "Some people believe in coincidence, Mr. Thomas. I don't happen to be one of them. I seek the truth. And I don't have time for any of these unexplained time lapses you seem to suffer at the most convenient times. Now let's start over again until we can account for every moment of your activities, OK?"

"You're the boss."

"Do you drink, Mr. Thomas?" It's an honest question, but not one I'm prepared to face. I prefer to think my falling off the wagon was a lapse in judgement, not a life style change.

"It's a simple question, Mr. Thomas. Do you drink?"

"I quit for a long time, Detective. I had a relapse—recently."

"Did you have a drink at Mrs. Kress' home?"

"No."

"You're sure?"

"Positive."

"Do you smoke, Mr. Thomas?"

Finally, an easy question and one I can answer categorically.

"Not in years."

"You're sure?"

"What is this, *you're sure* bit?" I do my best stare-down on Darius Martin—but he doesn't blink. "I have an occasional short-term memory lapse, that's it. Asking me the same question in fifty different ways is wasting your time and mine, understand Detective?"

Darius Martin opens a carry-on bag that holds the highball glass, ashtray, and cigarette I discovered in my mudroom.

"Where did you get those?"

"Why, do you recognize them?"

"They were on my mudroom vanity."

"You're sure?"

"Stop trying to trap me, damn you! I didn't murder, Ally, Celine, or anybody else, for that matter. I'm *innocent*, you idiot!"

I figure Darius Martin is going to pick me up and snap me over his knee.

"Mr. Thomas, I ask these questions to convince myself that you *didn't* kill anyone. You flying off the handle, lends credence to the possibility that you did. Now, if you answer my questions in a calm, rational manner, I may look at you differently. How you choose to proceed from here, will determine whether I let you go or book you for the murders of Ally Kress, Celine Seabolt, Donna Hobart, Leonardo Silva and Maria Clara Silva."

Darius Martin squeezes the handcuff on the bed railing until there are no clicks remaining. "Do we understand one another?"

Hearing the names of all the people who died, is a sobering moment. God, have mercy on their souls. "Fine." I lie back in the bed and close my eyes. "Ask your questions."

"How do you explain your fingerprints on a glass found in a place that you didn't have a drink?"

"I—"

"And your DNA on a cigarette, that you never smoked?"

"I picked the glass up to smell the liquid, then I wet my fingers to put out the cigarette so it didn't set my house on fire."

"Do you have other glassware in your house that matches this glass?"

"No, I checked."

"Do you know that this glass matches other glasses at the Kress home?" Martin said.

"I'm not surprised."

"Why is that?"

"They're expensive, Ally, would have things like that in her house. I wouldn't."

"And how do you know the glass is expensive if you don't own it?"

"I did an online search." I said.

"Can you explain how a glass from the Kress home made its way in to your home, 120 miles away, where you touched it, then back to Charlotte without you knowing it?"

"No, I can't, Detective. All I can do is tell you the truth, and I have. You can believe me or not."

"I want to believe you, Mr Thomas. But do you hear how far-fetched your answers sounds? Objects don't move on their own. Do you agree?"

"I have no idea how the glass got to or left my house. I did a search for that type of glass on my computer because it wasn't mine. Check my search history!"

"Don't think I'll have to. Your story corroborates what the lab found. There was none of your DNA inside the filter of the cigarette."

"So I can go?" Dumb question.

"At one time, you and Mrs. Kress, were in an intimate relationship, right?"

I've never been big on kiss and tell. Unfortunately, when we made love Ally was a married woman. "We were headed that way, but it's been years since I've seen Ally. Check with Slick Rock General Hospital. They can easily verify my story and besides, that's none of your business!"

"I'll take that as a, yes. Did it make you mad that she dumped you?"

"I was hurt that she didn't visit me in the hospital."

"Hurt enough to seek revenge on her and her family?"

"Go to hell! It wasn't like that. Celine said Ally had plans to marry—"

"Yeah, going to be hard for, Mrs. Seabolt to back that story up, huh, Mr. Thomas?"

"Ally Kress was one of the finest women I've ever known. Unfortunately, we never had a real honest-to-goodness date. We were two people with nothing in common who were thrown together by circumstances that should have killed us. Surviving that extreme hazard drew us together and what happened, happened. My daughter knows the truth about Ally's plans to marry me. I know you won't believe her, but I'm telling you the truth. I didn't want to kill Ally Kress, I wanted to marry her." The thought of how close Ally and I came to having a life together is more than I can bear. The loss wracks me, and I don't care if Detective Martin locks me up and throws away the key.

Darius Martin places his hand gently on my shoulder, a move I figure to be another interrogative tactic.

"I knew Mrs. Kress though various charity events, here in Charlotte. She was, indeed, a fine and caring person. She did a lot of good for a lot of people. I knew a little about Mr. Kress and his rigid temperament, too. I'm sorry things didn't work out for you two, Mr. Thomas. Thank you for being honest…and a gentleman. Now let's go over the events from when you arrived in Charlotte."

I go over and over the timeline with Darius Martin. He checks my phone calls against a printout of Celine Seabolt's cell phone and home phone calls. After what seems like hours, he reaches across my bed and unlocks the cuffs.

"Does this mean I'm free to go, now?"

"Your bond for the bar fight was posted by RH Carter. We decided not to charge you for the damage you inflicted upon Mr. Holland and Mr. Hardison."

"Mighty nice of you, but why did you arrest me, then?"

"You were never under arrest, Mr. Thomas."

"Hell, if I wasn't—I was handcuffed!"

"You looked a little hostile to me. I cuffed you for my sake."

"You cuffed me to make me *think* I was under arrest!"

Detective Martin does the total-eclipse move again until I am staring into his shark-black eyes. "I want you to understand something. Five innocent people were murdered in my city. I will do whatever it takes to solve those crimes. The only reason I don't lock your ass up right now is because I don't have enough evidence. Plus, I do believe you've been honest, but that doesn't mean I think you're innocent. Like I said, I don't believe in coincidence…and until I have proof of your innocence, you won't even have a dream that I can't show up in. You got that?"

I close my eyes and mumble, "Loud and clear."

Seconds later when I opened my eyes, the room is empty. Planning is another trait I've never perfected, but my next move doesn't require a lot. The killer hit pay dirt twice, and showing total disregard for human life by killing three people who happened to be in the way. Why I wasn't killed is a mystery to me. Whatever the reason, it isn't coincidence—he has a plan. I can't change his plans, but I can change where and how we play the game.

My safest bet is to get to the Fisher Mansion that's being guarded by a small private army. That's my smart move—but not the safest move for my family. I snatch the IV from my arm and head to the nurse's desk to gather up my clothes and personal belongings. The sooner I put a scent on my trail, the sooner Ally and Celine's killer will find me.

"You can't check out! This is a hospital—you must be, *discharged*". The nurse plays the word like it's a get-out-of-jail card only doctor's can deal. Nuts to them.

I do some dealing of my own, and play the Nathan Hale Fisher *money card* and Jake Draughon *I-know-a-doctor-too-card*.

Apparently someone around here has been checking the newspapers or streaming news on their phones. The Kress-Seabolt murders, despite best efforts of the police, have been connected to the Fisher's DownEast.

Back in my hospital room, I dial Joy's number. She's got the key to my freedom..

Joy, unlike RH, doesn't answer on the first ring, or even the tenth for that matter, so I leave a message. Ten minutes later she finally returns my call.

"My arrest papers say you signed for my truck?"

"Why should I even talk to you? You threatened to kill me!"

"Misguided chivalry, if you missed what I was trying to do."

"Well, I thought that—but you were scary."

"Trust me, witnessing scary is a whole lot better than experiencing jail."

"Are you, OK?"

"I'll be fine, once I get home. Where's my truck?"

"Police impound lot." Sounds of papers shuffling like someone's digging in a trashcan fill my ear. "Got it! Want me to text you the address or take you there?"

"Text it. I've caused you enough trouble for one day—a lifetime, actually. You're not still mad, are you?"

"A little, but I still want you to come to my wedding."

"How come I never get the girl?"

"Maybe because you never *want* the girl?"

She's right. Funny how when you're on top of the world, you don't need anyone in your life. But when the world's crashing down on you, you want someone to stand with you. And as much as I hate to admit it, for my love of flying free, I've never wound up with the girl—that selfishness means I've never deserved one.

"Joy, you've always been a good friend to me. I appreciate that."

"You're not coming to my wedding, are you."

"Nope."

"I won't ever see you again, will I?"

"Only if your man mistreats you."

"He won't. He's a great guy. I wish you could've met him."

"So do I." A scroll coming across the bottom of my room TV lists the name of the others killed with Celine Seabolt. "One last favor?"

"I'm not having sex with you, Cape."

"That wasn't the favor."

"What then?"

"The kid who was murdered with Celine Seabolt, his name was Leonardo, and his friends called him, Lenny. Somewhere in his possessions is the last autograph Celine Seabolt ever signed. Can you make sure his family knows that?"

"Why?"

"Could mean some money for his family. Funerals are expensive."

"Ah, that's nice of you."

"Just following the lead of great leading lady, Celine Seabolt. She was a class act."

"I'll make sure they know." Joy's voice drops off to a whisper. "You're a pretty classy too, Captain Cape Thomas—I'll miss you."

I wish that were true, but in a few years, when Joy has kids and builds a life with her wonderful guy, I'll become little more than a fleeting thought during her rare moments of melancholy.

I change into my clothes and cram the brown vanilla envelope stuffed with my arrest paperwork inside my backside waist band. Same as I did when I worked for AeroMax. According to my phone GPS the police impound lot is a mere 5.3 miles from my the hospital. With any luck I'll make it to the lot before their 6:00 PM closing time.

Walking among tall buildings makes the distance seem shorter for some reason. As I approach the outskirts of town, the wide-open spaces ahead dispel that illusion. It's a little after five and most small businesses and shops along the street are closing as the setting sun ducks behind Charlotte's skyline.

I consider calling a cab, something I should have done from the start, but my GPS indicates only a mile left to my destination. Even at this butt-dragging pace, I'll make it with time to spare. To be on the safe side, I opt for a direct route since I'm on foot.

An alleyway leading downhill toward an abandoned factory is my straight shot to the impound-lot. The alley, once paved, is now strewn with gravel, debris, and full of potholes. Gravel crunching under my feet drowns out street noises from up the hill, but a revving engine somewhere close by shuts off before I can pinpoint it.

The silence puts me on edge. I ease past a rusting loading ramp, and the engine roars to life, much closer, almost as if the vehicle had coasted downhill to avoid detection. I turn to locate the vehicle, and a broad beam of light floods the narrow passage. I move to the side of the alley. However, rather than continue toward me, the driver stops about a hundred feet from me and revs up again.

The truck rocks from side to side like a prancing iron-steed. I motion for the driver to pass, but he stays put, revs the engine again, then shuts off the lights. In the twilight I see the outline of a light-bar across the cab of the truck. I'm not sure, but the light setup seems to be the type used for safaris or night hunting. In addition to the light-bar, a bank of fog lights are under the bumper and two additional spotlights are mounted in the grill.

Idiots kids out having fun, I figure, and resume my journey to the impoundment yard. The truck begins to back away and I pick up my pace to increase the distance between us. Shoulders along the alleyway narrow to nearly nothing as I approach two low-slung buildings on either side. I take a quick peek behind to see if I can spot the truck, then ease into a jog. The last thing I want is to get hemmed up in an alley with some juiced-up kids.

The length of this alley is much longer than I estimated. Even running at full speed, it will take me time to clear this chokepoint. I turn and see the truck coasting down the hill with its engine off so I break into a full-fledged sprint.

A thundering noise behind me reverberates off the brick walls, and again light floods the alley. No turning around now. I charge through the chokepoint. Leg muscles I haven't use in while burn down to my aching feet. Noise from the engine is deafening, so close I can feel the sound waves bouncing off the building. I turn to check the distance and the truck grill slams into my hip, sending me sprawling down the alley on my stomach. I scrabble to my feet and stumble but maintain my balance, only inches ahead of the bumper. The driver races the engine and jams into me again. I tumble headlong in the gravel and roll toward the building, hoping to find a crawlspace, but the facade is solid all the way to the ground. The truck goes to idle and reverses away from me. I stand, shade my eyes against the blinding light, and yell, "You've had your fun, now leave me alone!"

The driver eases back another fifty yards and guns it. I take off running again, but the grill clips me hard enough to send me flying ten or fifteen feet down the alley. Sand-gravel burns into my palms and knees. But even on all fours, I can see the end of the building less that a hundred feet ahead. I don't bother trying to stand—from a sprinter's stance, I break out running, like I've never run before. Rocks and gravel slinging off the spinning tires and hitting the metal body sound like machine gun fire.

No need to look back, either—by sound alone I know if the truck hits me I'm dead. Just as I reach the end of the building I execute a perfect 90-degree turn and continue running down the other side of the building. The truck roars by at full-bore. I only catch a glimpse, but I'm pretty sure it's the same gray Ford pick-up truck I saw on the bridge near Slick Rock.

The truck slides to a stop and kicks up a rooster-tail as it spins back toward me. I dive down a steep brush-covered embankment and tumble onto the street right in front of the Charlotte Police Impoundment Lot.

A mechanic's work-light hanging from a long cord is the sole source of light in the building. Because it looks more like a garage than a police annex, if not for the sign out front, I'd swear I'm in the wrong place. This lot, is little more than a junkyard of wrecked and evidence cars—clearly a dumping grounds for local towing services. The rumbling noise of the truck up the hill slows, no doubt to find a route leading downhill to me. I rush the building like a war hero going after a machine-gunner's nest. All I want is to get inside the building and away from these crazy idiots. The door is locked, so I bang on it to like a mad drummer when it doesn't open.

"Pull!" a stocky guy at his desk yells. "What the hell! Are you crazy?"

Panting like a dog, I snatch the door open and spit out my answer before he calls the cops. "Need, to pick up, my truck!"

"What's your hurry? We don't close until six. Geez, what happened to you? Look like you run through a meat grinder!"

I look down at my knees and see how accurate the cigar-smoking mechanic's analogy is. "If you think the front's bad, checkout my back side. I got road rash on both cheeks."

The mechanic walks over to me and pulls something off the back of my shirt, "Yeah and that ain't all. You got this, too." He hands me a feathered dart sticking into the manilla envelope covering the small of my back.

"So that's why they weren't in a hurry to chase me down?" I gasp.

"They who?" the guy asks.

"Some crazy kids—or a psychopath."

"You want me to call the cops, or an ambulance?"

"No!" I rush my response. I have no desire to spend anymore time with Detective Darius Martin. "Just some kids out having a little fun, I'm pretty sure. I don't want to go overboard and get 'em in trouble. Serves me right for some of the crazy things I used to do."

The mechanic hacks up a loogie, and spits it in a trashcan beside his desk. "Yeah, I should'a went to jail for some a' stuff I did when I was a kid, too." The mechanic gives me another good going-over. "Looks like *they* went a little overboard with *you*. They need their asses kicked. You sure you don't want me to call the cops?"

"Naw, I did most of the damage to myself. Over-reacting—like a wuss!"

The mechanic nods, "Guess you'd know. Whatcha here to get?"

"Black Yukon."

"Got it right here in front. Some lady called, said somebody was on the way to get it."

Joy, how thoughtful of her, I think. Then again, maybe not.

"That would be my friend, Joy?" I said.

"Naw, won't no American name, she didn't sound like no, Joy, neither."

"What'd she sound like?"

The mechanic closes one eye and looks up, as if the answer is scrawled on the ceiling. "Sounded sort of foreign—real sexy. Had a funny-sounding name, but it won't, Joy, I know that. Wanted to know if she had your ID if she could get the vehicle. I said sure, long as you got cash. We don't take checks."

"Is that legal?"

"Your paperwork said, *arrested*. Most time *they* don't come by in a few hours like the parking violators do—so we let their families or friends pay. Whatta they lock you up for, anyhow?"

"A misunderstanding?"

"I hear you." The mechanic does a laughing-cough mixture. "You got yer driver's license?"

"Got it right here." I rummage through my personal items from the hospital and realize, two things are missing: the selfie of Ally and Celine and my driver's license. "You're not going to believe this—"

"If you ain't got an ID, you ain't getting this truck."

"Pilot's license, work?"

"Never seen one before, but after what you been through. I guess it'll work."

We finished up the paperwork and I promise him a free ride on AeroMax when I get back to work. He slaps me on the back and we do a little male-bonding. I cram the receipt into the manila folder, that may have saved my life and slide it beside my seat. I stick the dart in an old bill envelope and put it in the dash pocket. At some point and time, I'll turn it over to law enforcement, but not to Detective Darius Martin.

CHAPTER THIRTEEN

Down to Faison

Out on the Interstate, every car behind, in front, and beside me raises my suspicions. Other than Joy, I told no one about my plans to pick up my truck, and yet someone with my license almost beat me to it. Why go to so much trouble to steal my truck when others could be stolen easier? Then it hits me, maybe they don't want my truck for itself—maybe they want to track it. What better way for killers to plan a surprise attack than to know my every move?

At the last possible second, I whip the Yukon onto the rest area exit ramp and make sure no one's following me. I park at the far end of the lot away from other travelers and check my truck. When no obvious tracking devices turn up on the exterior, I check under the hood and chassis. Everything looks fine. Only one option left. I open my phone and remove the battery. Without power the internal GPS can't send or receive signals.

I need to make a call but I don't know the last time I've seen a payphone. If there's one around it has to be in the facilities and refreshment area. I drive toward the halogen-lighted area. Nothing, dumb idea. Under the bright lights, I snap the battery back into my phone and call Jimmy.

"Cape?"

"Yep, I need your help."

"Where and when?"

"Miss Minnie's place in about two hours. I want you to help me set up house keeping there."

"House keeping?"

"I'll be staying there, for an extended period."

"Something doesn't—"

"And don't try to call me, Jimmy. I'm running silent and deep as soon as I hang up."

"Silent and deep? Isn't that what submarines do?" Jimmy said.

"Yep, but people can do it too. Don't you ever watch old war movies?"

"Yeah, I think the term you're looking for is radio silence…" Jimmy said.

"Whatever, but don't keep talking about it, somebody may be listening. I don't want people to know I'm staying out there."

"Cape, you feeling, OK?"

"Don't start with me! I'm not crazy. I'll explain when I see you."

As soon as I hang up, I remove the battery and run silent and deep—dammit! If someone is trying to track me, the game just got more difficult.

The ride from the Cleveland School exit to the Newton Grove exit is a time of reflection. Why am I still alive and others dead? It's not like the killer hasn't had ample opportunities to finish me off, yet I'm still here. Ally got nooses, same as me; Darius Martin even confirmed that she took them to the police, but did she get coffins with coins and photographs? I'd ask Detective Darius Martin, but why would a cop who regards me as a *person of interest* discuss his case with me? Obviously he isn't.

A gray Ford pickup, I haven't noticed passes the car behind me and snugs up close to my bumper, just like the move the pickup made on me the day I was attacked at the creek. I turn on my blinker to exit for Newton Grove. The pickup follows my lead. From the car lights behind the pickup it's easy to see the truck doesn't have extra lights on it. But other than that, the truck is identical in every way to the attacker's truck in Charlotte. How difficult would it be to remove an add-on light package? Probably just a matter of undoing a few bolts. If this is the attacker, he has to think I called the cops. That being so, he'd definitely remove any objects that made him easily identifiable.

Instinctively, I grab my phone to dial 911 and remember the battery's in my jacket pocket. Traffic is heavy on Hwy 50, even at 9:00 PM. While I wait for traffic to pass, a plan pops into my head. I'm tired of running and if I don't move, this guy is going nowhere. His only escape is back down the exit ramp. Before the thought gets out of my head a semi rolls up behind the pickup and he's trapped like a rat.

This is my chance! I may die, but at least there'll be eyewitnesses. Two more cars fill the ramp now, completing a solid blockade on the exit ramp. My heart is pounding in my chest like a jackhammer dancing on granite.

Traffic clears on Hwy 50 and the pickup honks its horn for me to go. Instead, I jump out, rush the truck, scream, "The hunted becomes the hunter! Get out!" and jerk the door open.

The young mother inside leans across the seat to protect her baby in its car seat. At that, the semi driver sees my act of heroism as a road-rage incident and scrambles down from his rig. "What in the hell's wrong with you? Leave that woman alone or I'll break your damn neck!"

One of the two cars parked behind the semi whips onto the grassy shoulder and stops beside my truck. A young man jumps out with a phone in one hand and a gun in the other. "I dialed 911. We can wait for the cops or I'll drop you where you stand. Choice is yours, Bub!"

"Please, Mister, don't hurt my baby."

One look at the terrified mother inside the gray Ford pickup and I wish the guy *would* shoot me—I'm an idiot!

"I'm so sorry," I mouth to the mother and turn back to face the trucker and gunman. "A guy in a truck like hers tried to run me over—"

"Save it for the cops," the gunman says. In less than five minutes a deputy's car pulls in front of my truck with blue lights flashing.

For ten minutes, in front of the cruiser's spotlight and in plain view of the motoring public, I play a game of Simon Says with the deputy. "Walk this line—Put you feet together...Tilt your head back...Touch your nose...Well," the deputy finally says, "You ain't drunk, but somethin's sure as hell wrong with you."

After passing a battery of questions designed to reveal my proclivity for road-rage-itis, I become somewhat human. Once the deputy hears the story of my attack in Charlotte he even becomes a little sympathetic.

Since I hadn't assaulted anyone, or been armed, the deputy deems the incident and my threat to the young mother a case of mistaken identity. I start toward the pickup to apologize to the young mom, but the deputy has other ideas. "Sir, if you get close to her again. I will arrest you."

"I want to—"

"She wants you to leave. You're scaring her baby, understand?"

After the excitement of the last few minutes, I need something to calm me down. The traffic circle in Newton Grove is just the ticket! I ride around the circle five times, because I love the idea that a grove of trees surrounded by white crepe myrtles is the epicenter of a municipality. Untold numbers of commercial opportunities have, undoubtedly, presented themselves to build on the land, but the wise citizens of Newton Grove stand united against developing this bucolic ground. The town, state and country are enriched by their resolve to keep their "grove."

The mind-cleansing of driving the circle has me looking forward to the serene drive from Newton Grove to Faison. By the time I reach the intersection of Highways 50 and 403 I'm good with my decision to hide out here. No way my nemesis can know this area better than me. I'm no odds maker, or much of a tennis player, but I'd score this: Advantage Cape.

Fresh tire tracks on the dirt path to Miss Minnie's means Jimmy is early. The sight of Miss Minnie standing next to the his car warms my heart. "Thanks for coming!" I tell them, then shake Jimmy's hand and hug Miss Minnie. To my surprise she hugs me back.

"This place gets mighty cold in the winter, and the power company folks say they can't turn the 'lectricity back on 'til it gets inspected." Miss Minnie, says.

"Not a problem, anything else?"

"Well, since you asked..." Miss Minnie spits out a long stream of tobacco juice. "This ain't the best idea, you've ever had, boy—then again, ain't nothing unusual 'bout that."

I go over what happened in Charlotte and so they can provide feedback.

"Cape, I'm not one to get in your business, but if five people died in such a short period of time, sounds to me like you're poking a hornet's nest," Jimmy says.

"That's the whole purpose of me coming here. I'm not going to confront them, I'm hiding out—big difference."

"You got your escape covered?" Miss Minnie asks.

"Can't imagine anything happened to it." I reassure her. "But, I'll make sure tomorrow."

"How about Jana and the kids?" Jimmy said.

"That base is covered. RH, hired a security company, and he's a member of the task force."

"Why not go back there?" Jimmy says. "That's the smart play, if you want my opinion."

"I know, I know, and everyone else agrees with you." I tell him. "I just don't see it that way."

"You ever think that they might not be after you, but somethin' you got?" Miss Minnie asks.

"What do you mean?"

"Seems like they could've killed you anytime they wanted too. But you still alive. What if they need you? If they want to cut you away from the herd—you playin' right into their hands," she says, making a slicing motion with her hand.

Miss Minnie, and Jimmy have valid points, but they haven't thought this through.

"That mansion is not a fortress—I know they can get to me there."

"Do you know that for sure?" Jimmy asks.

No need to tell Jimmy about being chased from the mailbox to the mansion. I trust Jimmy, but if I tell him about that night, he'll tell Jake and I'll be back under lock and key. Besides, that story will upset Miss Minnie.

"I don't, but what does it hurt for me to stay out here a few days? I need solitude, and cleaning this place up will be great therapy for me."

Miss Minnie shakes her head. "You welcome to it, but you better off laying up in that big mansion than being out here in the country livin' like a fool-ass-hermit."

Jimmy nods agreement, but he knows this conversation is over. I scribble a note to Jana, and Jimmy promises to deliver it, since I'll be silent and deep. I stare at the hovel before me and smile. Except for the part of looking like a 'fool-ass-hermit,' I'm feeling pretty good about my plan.

"Chainsaw and gas are under the corner of the house along with some kerosene and a lamp." Jimmy pats a Yeti cooler on the ground in front of him. "Got canned goods and little fresh meat right here. Your suitcase is inside the door, and I didn't pack any fancy clothes." Jimmy grabs a 410 shotgun and two boxes of cartridges off his backseat. "It's the only weapon I own, but it's perfect for all the small game 'round here. I'll be by tomorrow to check on you and drop off some more tools."

My eyes stay locked on Jimmy's car until it disappears into the woods-line. As the dust settles so does my anxiety. One trip around the house and it becomes clear just how much work lies ahead.

The oak tree across the front porch is more than 20" in diameter. Just to clear the front entrance will take hours and midnight is fast approaching. Even though the temperature is in the mid-fifties after an hour of wrestling with the chainsaw I break out in a light sweat. But then just before the moon is directly overhead, a path to the front door is open for business.

I lay splinters of fat-lighter under firewood in the wood heater and light it and a kerosene lantern off the same kitchen match. In the back room I find a small fold-up table, a cot and a sleeping bag. Things I didn't think to request, but something a former homeless person like Jimmy, knows are needed. Then it hits me, how did Jimmy get this stuff in here? Though it's a shotgun design, the back door is wedged into place by a sagging wall. The front door blocked by the oak would have allowed *him* to enter but not the bulky items.

I set the lantern on the floor behind the heater where I find a perfectly round hole bored into a floorboard. When I pull up, a small trap door rises! And I thought I knew this place like the back of my hand. Jimmy must have spent a lot of time here with Miss Minnie, so it makes perfect sense. Miss Minnie took this homeless boy in when the rest of the town shunned him, explaining why the two are so close, though I've never bothered to question their history before.

While flames dance an exotic number around the firewood in the stove, I chainsaw the back door open. A hand pump stands over a wash basin resting precariously on a rough-hewn wooden drain tacked to the porch railing, and a partially filled bucket of water sits on cinderblock steps leading to the overgrown backyard. I wonder who to thank for the priming water, Jimmy or Mother Nature. But hands down, I give Jimmy credit for my good fortune—especially for the cot and sleeping bag.

Lifting the handle, I fill the throat of the cast-iron pump. Braying jackass sounds come with the first few pumps, but then comes the payoff —fresh cold water. I cup my hand over the spout and drink my fill of mineral-water.

Smoke is filling the house, so I rush to adjust the damper, and like magic, the layer of smoke makes its way up the metal stovepipe and out the chimney. I tweak the damper adjustment, heighten the lantern flame, and lay my sleeping bag on the cot. Despite my rudimentary surroundings, I'm feeling quite decadent.

Deciding what to have for dinner is a matter of rummaging through canned goods in two paper sacks sitting atop Jimmy's Yeti cooler. My selection is based on the first-out first-eat rule. Seems canned pork-n-beans and a tin of sardines are tonight's bill of fare. I pull the lid off the beans and sit them on the stove. While the beans warm, I add some apple cider vinegar to the sardines packed in olive oil. Almost ready to dine...

What's this? Spotty flashes of light move around the walls and slowly merge into a giant ball of light filling the room. From the front door, I see two sets of headlights bouncing down the path. I pull my culinary adventure off the stove, grab the shotgun, and drop down through the trapdoor. From under the house I see a well-worn path leading to the outhouse at the edge of the woods. As one car stops behind the outhouse, I fade into the woods beside it.

A deputy exits his car, approaches the other car, and calls, "That's the truck the nut-job was driving."

"Cape Thomas, you mean?"

"Yeah, Sheriff."

The deputy who investigated my putative road-rage incident must've followed me to Miss Minnie's and I missed him doing that. Damn! I have two choices. I can high-tail it farther into the woods and hide, or come out and face the music. Something I'm pretty sure will happen even if I decide to go with option one.

"Hello!— Is there a problem?"

The deputy spins around, grabs and aims his pistol in one motion. "Is that a shotgun?"

"It is." I slowly raise the gun into the air with the barrel pointed skyward, "Mighty late for visitors—wasn't taking any chances."

Sheriff Scarlett DuBois gets out of her car. Though she isn't dressed in a uniform she looks much more official than she did last time I saw her. "It's called investigating, not visiting."

I nod. "Evenin', Sheriff. I beg to differ. Nothing to investigate here."

"Smoke coming out of an abandoned home is worthy of a look-see for a rural sheriff's department," the deputy says.

"Fair enough. But as you can see, there's no emergency here and I haven't broken any law." I clarify.

"Well, that may be true now. But if the young lady who you terrified earlier tonight had followed my advice and pressed charges, that wouldn't be the case. Since she chose to cut you some slack because you reminded her of the father she lost last week—you're a free man."

God, not only was the poor mom worried about her child, she has just lost her father, too. Guilt settles in my gut, and I promise to make things right with that young mother no matter what the cost.

"Sheriff." I look at the deputy, "I explained to your deputy what happened. I feel terrible about that, it was—"

"You know, Mr. Thomas, if you'll quit taking the law into your own hands and let us do what we are trained to do—things like that wouldn't happen."

She's right of course, but sometimes extenuating circumstances get in the way of logic. I think of the statement Darius Martin made in Charlotte: 'Some people believe in coincidence, Mr. Thomas. I don't happen to be one of them.'

As questionable a character as Detective Darius Martin is, I do have something in common with him. No way in hell is coincidence behind all that's been happening to me. "I agree. That's why I came out here to get away from all that—out of sight, out of mind, if you will?"

"That brings up my next question. According to county tax records you don't own this place—and I know it's not rentable. What gives?"

I explain my relationship with Miss Minnie and assure her my stay here isn't illegal, and won't be long-term. Sheriff DuBois, turns to her deputy, "I've got this. Get back to your rounds. I've got a few more questions for Mr. Thomas, and I'll call you when I'm back on patrol."

The deputy nods and heads back to his cruiser. Sheriff DuBois doesn't speak until the deputy is well down the road. "Want to tell me what happened in Charlotte?"

I wonder if the deputy has told her about Charlotte or if she already has the lowdown from Charlotte PD. Not that it matters. If she wants to know what went down in Charlotte, all she has to do is request the report from Detective Darius Martin.

"They say a good cop never asks a question unless they have the answer. I'm sure you know exactly what happened in Charlotte."

Scarlett DuBois, smiles, "I confess. I did get a briefing from my deputy."

"Case closed. I really appreciate you dropping by," I say turning to walk back into the house.

"Mr. Thomas."

"Yeah."

"You didn't mention that a gray Ford pick-up truck like the one that attacked you in Charlotte, was also like the one on the bridge the night I found the arrows. Just wondering how you managed to leave that out when you were talking to my deputy?"

I do the twirling thing around my temple with a finger. "It's no secret. I forget things."

"Yes, and it's no secret that your memory lapses come at the most... convenient times."

"Look, Sheriff I have nothing to hide, if that's what you're getting at..."

"Actually, you *are* trying to hide something."

"Like what?"

"A body."

"Whose body!"

"Your body, Mr. Thomas. Who are you hiding from?"

"I've done nothing wrong. I'm here legally and I think you need to move along."

"If you don't want to talk to me that's fine, Mr. Thomas. But as soon as I leave here I'm going to contact Detective Martin and see if you had another memory lapse. Good night."

Well, well, imagine that. Due to their woefully inadequate investigation skills, these two cops will still figure out a way to frame the only *person of interest* they have in the murder of Ally Kress *et als*. One way or another I'm going to have more discussions with Scarlett DuBois or Detective

Darius Martin. But if those are my choices, I'm going with Scarlett DuBois rather than Darius Martin.

"Actually, I was just fixing myself a midnight snack—care to join me? We can talk then, if you have the time."

"Just so happens, I do have a few minutes to spare, Mr. Thomas."

CHAPTER FOURTEEN

Country Livin'

My guest stays close behind me as I pick my way across the recently cleared, but still busted-up porch. Empty snuff cans get kicked out of our dining area and I set a broken board on top of two empty five-gallon plastic lard buckets. "I haven't had time to shop for furniture. Think that board will hold both of us?"

Scarlett casts a wary eye on my creation, grabs a section of newspaper from the firebox and spreads it across the dusty board. "You know, they say a house isn't a home until it's given a woman's touch."

I stand back and give her *touch* a little look-see. "Well, don't that just make all the difference in the world!"

Scarlett's smile comes in easy, refined. I don't know her background, but money says she's from money. I turn back to the wood stove and get on with preparing supper.

Carmel streams of bean juice boil over the sides of the can and sizzle atop the wood stove. I wad up the two remaining sections of the *Calypso Gazette*, Scarlett's decorating source, and use them for potholders. "Dinner is served!" I announce and set the beans down beside the tin of sardines on a galvanized washboard, our buffet.

"I haven't eaten anything since lunch." Scarlett eyes the bounty laid out before her and mockingly licks her lips, "Umm, the beans actually smell pretty good, and are those sardines?"

I dig around in the paper sacks Jimmy brought and find a pack of plastic forks—and an unexpected treasure. "Not just sardines, imported sardines in olive oil, and an extra bonus, voila—dessert!"

Scarlett looks at the Moon Pie and breaks out laughing. "God, I can't remember the last time I had *these* foods, but I can tell you this, I've never had them in a combo!"

Our dining experience is going much smoother than I thought possible. Until, I realize Jimmy forgot paper plates. More than likely, he figured I wouldn't be entertaining. Or he just knew I'd man-up and eat from the cans like a proper hobo. A quick glance at my dinner guest, shows me this gal knows nothing about being a hobo.

"I guess this is a long way from what you're used to at the Fisher mansion?" Scarlett says.

"Why, yes it is, Sheriff, and I do apologize, but it seems my manservant packed the cutlery," I twirled the plastic forks around my fingers, "yet completely overlooked the fine china." I point to the beans and tin of sardines. "We'll have to share, taking turns, if you don't mind?"

Scarlett DuBois, has an infectious gut-deep laugh. We double over and guffaw like two old friends from way back. A line from Charles Dickens comes to mind: *There is nothing in the world so irresistibly contagious as laughter and good humor.*

Scarlett lifts her plastic Dixie cup in a mock toast, and sips the fresh-pumped water.

"Oh dear...I'm not one to complain with my mouth full, but this wine is fresh as rain..." She takes another sip. "But with the bite of mineral-laced well water."

"*Impossible!*" I say in French, and rummage through the sacks feigning surprise at not finding wine. "By Jove...he'll *pay* for this!"

Maybe it's the long day we've both endured, or more than likely some law-enforcement tactic Scarlett is employing to get me to soften up and talk? But it doesn't matter, I'm completely at ease with Scarlett DuBois.

Before we chow down, Scarlett reaches over and grabs my hand. Her eyes are closed. Good gravy, what's going on here?

"Father, thank you for this food. Let it nourish our bodies, our hearts, our souls, and minds so that we may become better Christians. Amen"

I don't know what to say, so I echo her "Amen." Seems to fit.

We alternate sampling the beans and sardines. In this lull of frivolity, I tell her about my attack in Charlotte.

"Well, you certainly jumped right from playful to serious. Why is that?" Scarlett said.

"I didn't want to forget and not tell you the whole story—that's why you stayed, right?"

"Yes."

Scarlett's direct, honest answer inspires me to be the same. "I have nothing to hide, Sheriff."

"I appreciate that." Scarlett says. "So why do you think they didn't flat-out run your over?"

It's a simple question, but doesn't strike me as genuine. Cops ask lots of questions in various ways to make sure you give the same answers. It's like they want to trip you up. I don't have a problem with Scarlett doing her job, but I want to be more than a *person of interest* in some file folder, a classification I've already earned with Detective Darius Martin.

Flames from the open stove door reflect off Scarlett's blue eyes and highlight her olive complexion. High cheek bones and raven hair suggest a mixture of Cherokee and, considering her surname, French linage. Her visage holds my gaze until she cuts her eyes at me. The earlier cologne incident pops into my head and I turn away. Embarrassed, I focus on the glowing coals in front of me. My thoughts drift to Ally—she too was warm and beautiful.

"I saw you looking at me." Scarlett says. "Being a cop doesn't mean I'm not a woman."

"I don't want to get off on the wrong foot again." I lean over next to her and pull out my collar. "No cologne— smell?"

Scarlett bows her head and interlocks her fingers. For a second I think we might be in for another prayer, but instead she stares into my eyes. I avert my gaze again, so she cups my chin in her hands and searches my face. "It's important to me that people, especially men, see me as a police officer, first." She drops her hands from my face. "Maybe I went a little overboard with the cologne complaint?"

"Naw, I got what I had coming." I rake the glowing coals in the stove to one side and add another piece of firewood. "Before my injury, I knew how to act. Women liked me back then. I'm not a sleaze bag. Even though I came across as one."

"Your reputation preceded you. I'll admit I was on alert." Scarlett says with a gentle laugh. "I think you're a nice guy. But—and I don't want you to take this the wrong way—with sleaze bag potential."

"Wrong way is about the only way a fellow *could* take that! People change, Sheriff. Now, while we're on the subject of potential…" I let the word hang out there.

"What's *that* supposed to mean?"

"Means, you got the potential to be a really nice person—if you flip that enormous chip off your shoulder."

"Easy for you to say, you don't have to prove yourself everyday."

"How about this, if—or when, I ever blur the line between you being a cop and a lady—"

"I'll delineate them so fast." Scarlett snaps her fingers, "it'll make your neck snap, Mr. Thomas!"

"Uh—how about you wait until I cross that line, before you break my neck?"

"I'm sorry." Scarlett bows her head and mumbles, "That was uncalled for."

It is at this moment that I decide to trust Scarlett DuBois. "Come with me." I said.

"Where're we going?"

"You asked why the attacker didn't run me over. I think I have the answer." Back outside the night air is cool and crisp. Ambient light from the house and moon overhead light our way. Side by side we stroll to my Yukon. I hand Scarlett the envelope with the dart. "Be careful, Sheriff. It's sharp. There's some kind of funk on it, too. Probably give you a nasty infection if it sticks you."

Scarlett removes the dart and holds it under the dome light. "Where did you find this?"

"When I was running away from the truck, he must have fired this dart at me. It missed me and stuck in a file folder tucked into my pants."

"Do you mind if I have this tested?" Scarlett asks.

"Tested for what?"

"Drugs—poison?"

"That's not it. You want to see if you can trace it back to me somehow."

"I know it's hard for you to trust others, Cape. Especially since you're having trouble believing your own eyes and ears, sometimes." She hands me the envelope and dart. "I want you to know that you can trust me. If you don't want it tested—"

"Got nothing to do with testing. Darius Martin said all the murder victims were stuck with a 10-gauge needle. Same wound I have, that I thought was an insect sting, by the way. He wanted me to explain how someone could get close enough to stick me with a needle and I not see them. And like you, he thinks my 'memory lapses' are a ploy to hide the facts." I hand her the envelope. "Run your test. Like I said, I have nothing to hide."

"I believe you."

"What?"

"Everything about you says you were trying to protect your family, Ally Kress, and Celine Seabolt. Call it woman's intuition, or a cop's radar, but I don't see you as a suspect in the Charlotte murders."

Well, hallelujah—finally a cop who believes me.

"Detective Martin, said you didn't find a syringe in my house, but did you find a dart?"

"No, but if one was used in the attack on you, maybe they took it with them," she says.

"What if the attack on me in Charlotte was a teen prank, gone bad?

And this dart is just a dart? That's puts us back to square one on these puncture wounds."

"I guess anything is possible, but when's the last time you heard of kids shooting darts at someone? Nowadays they shoot bullets, real bullets. And I'm not so sure this is a gaming dart. It's too small—I'm pretty certain the tip is a 10-gauge needle."

"Why darts?" I said. "If the goal is to kill me they *had* a shot, pun intended."

"Exactly, there's a reason someone chose darts over bullets. The test results may lead us to a reasonable conclusion."

"Yeah, maybe, but how does a glass and ashtray wind up in Ally's house with my prints and DNA on them?"

"I don't know."

"Darius Martin thinks I'm lying to him, but I know I didn't put those items in Ally's house, why would I? Unless I *am* crazy."

Scarlett pats my hand. "I'm going to be candid with you. I had a long conversation with Dr. Jake Draughon. He said nothing about your recovery is out of the norm for someone who suffered an injury like yours. I think your memory lapses will soon be a thing of the past and your testimony can be taken at face value."

"And it can't now?"

"That didn't come out right. I thought you might find what Dr. Draughon said uplifting—I don't want to argue with you." Scarlett said.

"What did he say?"

"Dr. Draughon, said you should make a full recovery… If you stick with your therapy program at the hospital—very hard to do from here."

"Sheriff," I say with my best welcome-aboard-I'm-your-captain smile, "I know what you're up to. This is no follow-up on the road-rage deal. You're teaming up with my family to get me back to the mansion where they want me to sip warm milk and idle my days away in some blissful, drugged state. Well let me tell—"

"Stop right there!" Scarlett holds up her hand like a traffic cop. "I did promise your family that I would check on you. I'm the sheriff, that's what families expect us to do. But I'm not part of any conspiracy to get you back to the mansion. Frankly, I can see why you want to trade that life for this one."

I wait for the punchline, or at least her laughter, but neither comes.

"You don't think I'm crazy for hiding out here?"

She looks up toward the sky. I follow her gaze. The number of stars looks to be in the millions.

"Funny how a simple thing like eliminating light pollution intensifies the beauty of God's creations." Scarlett says. "This place reminds me of my home in South Carolina." She points to the shack behind us.

I may not be a mind reader, but I'm right about her South Carolina accent.

"That's hard to believe," I say. "I picture you coming from much grander circumstances."

"And you would be right. I was reared on a six-thousand-acre plantation—and here's another bit of information you may not know. My family was acquainted with the Fishers. I knew Lara and Bianca from debutante balls."

"So how do you know," I nod toward the shack behind us, "that life?"

"Nearby on our property was an abandoned shantytown with houses very similar to this one. My father restored the little town for me. My friends and I used it as a play place for years...until we went off to college, actually." A faint smile lights her face, but she also has a hint of sadness in her eyes.

"So you used that place to run away from your real life. Is that why my hiding out here makes sense to you?"

"In a way, I guess that little town was my refuge," Scarlett says, "Sometimes rich and powerful men forget that their children are human beings, not possessions. You can buy many things with money, but love isn't one of them. Not to say my Dad didn't love me, but he wasn't the easiest at showing his feelings."

I thought of how Bianca and Laura were treated by Mr. Fisher. I can't be sure, but I'm almost certain Scarlett shared more than a debutante season with Bianca and Laura.

"Seems like girls in your situation have two choices. They either conform to please, or rebel and flee. Which path did you choose?" I ask.

"Very, intuitive, Mr. Thomas. Those were exactly my choices."

"So which path did you take?"

Scarlett lets my question hang, then responds with a question of her own. "Which do you think?"

Again I thought of Bianca. "You rebelled. How else would a daddy's girl, debutante, wind up in law enforcement?"

"An analytical, man. I'm impressed."

Like most men, I'm a little cocky, especially when I'm dead on about something. I poke out my chest and preen a little like Cocky, the USC Gamecock.

"Well, I don't like to brag...but I'm pretty good at reading people, heh, heh."

Scarlett ignores my bravado and I can see she's about to deflate and agitate. "Oh my, I feel like I've led you into a bit of a box canyon."

"Whadd'ya mean?"

"I didn't rebel, Mr. Thomas. I was a model daughter and I married my high school sweetheart."

"Come on! Daddy's little girl toting a gun and tracking down bad guys? No way *that* flew if your Dad is anything like Nathan Hale Fisher."

"I loved every minute of being a Daddy's girl. I make no apologies for that. And you're right—my father wouldn't approve of my career." Scarlett tightens her jaw and grinds her molars. "Ironically, through, he is the reason I chose this career."

"So I'm not as good as I thought at reading people. But I get the sense I'm stepping onto sacred ground here—"

"You didn't find my office bulletin board decorated with Walter Cronus Kress trial tidbits a little unusual?"

I remember seeing the bulletin board, but it didn't set off any alarms at the time. "The only recollection I have of the trial is what the hospital staff call, 'getting me up to speed'. I'd really like to read all those press clippings of yours one of these days, if you don't mind?"

"Oh, you were quite the hero. Ally Kress, saw to that. She gave you all the credit for taking down Johnston and Kress"

"Well, it isn't true. Without the evidence that Ally gathered those snakes would never have been convicted."

"So you don't think of her as a rich-B-itch, anymore?"

I thought back to that snide remark about Ally that I made to Scarlett. She's the one, then, who told Darius Martin that I was mad at Ally.

"I thought Ally walked away from me without even a good-bye. That hurt and I lashed out at her. As it turns out, for no reason. You see, Ally loved me. More than I imagined. Celine, told me Ally had made up her mind to be with me, but then she was murdered."

My voice trails off as I recall Darius Martin warned me not to talk about the case, yet here I'm blabbing about puncture wounds and whatever... He didn't specifically say, but I'm assuming that means blabbing to other law enforcement agencies, as well.

"You want to elaborate on that statement? I thought Ally's death was ruled a suicide."

"Under warning by law enforcement, I'd rather not. Besides, I really want to hear your story about Kress and Johnston."

"And I'd like to know everything about this attack on you and your family. However, it seems like you're holding things back, not only from Detective Martin, but from me as well."

"Like what?" I say.

"Why does Detective Martin consider you a person of interest?"

"He didn't tell you?"

"Yes, of course he did, but I want to hear it from you."

"What is it with you cops? You're always trying to trick people. What are you, the good cop to his bad cop? I've been down that road before! Read Detective Martin's report. That's all I have to say on the subject!" If I forget one little detail, my dinner guest will ship me off to the Charlotte jail.

"Well, you don't have to yell."

Scarlett looks hurt and I'm feeling a little like a sleaze bag.

"Sorry, I didn't mean to yell—and besides, I did give you the dart, not Detective Martin—which means I trust you. I made Detective Martin a promise I'd keep quiet, and I always try to live up to my word. My grandfather used to say that a man not worth his word, is not worth much."

"Fair enough." Scarlett said in a tone that leads me to believe we're done for the night—but I'm not.

"I'd like to hear more about why you keep a bulletin board of the Johnston and Kress trial?"

Scarlett tightens her jaw again and stares straight ahead.

"My family thinks I'm obsessed with Walter Kress and William Johnston, too. With them that topic is also taboo. So what's the deal with your bulletin board?" I redirect.

Scarlett refuses to look at me, but does begin to talk. "I keep it because, like you, I have a connection to Walter Cronus Kress." Anger rises in her face. The way she lets her raw emotions show surprises me. Not a trait I associate with cops.

"Walter Cronus Kress is the main reason I made law enforcement my career." She pauses and I sense, no, almost *see* her mind, flipping through pages from her past.

"My father, as do most business men, had a line of credit with various banks. He dealt primarily with The Farmers and Maritime Bank. For years they had a wonderful working relationship, right up until Walter Cronus Kress added the bank to his portfolio. My father knew of Kress and decided to switch banks as soon as he found out about the sale. Unfortunately for him, credit dried up and the prime rate shot up to over 15%. That was in the late 90's and early 2000's. He was forced to cross-collateralize to keep the bank happy and the cash flowing. Eventually, the bank forced him to use all his holdings as collateral.

Kress replaced the local board with his own team. They cherry-picked assets that were undervalued with huge future-earnings potential. My father's plantation was prime pickings, considering the looming real estate boom. Long story short, Kress and his cronies got the land and reaped millions. My father faced bankruptcy."

I nod my head as she finishes. "Sounds just like the Walter Cronus Kress I know. You said 'faced.' I assume your dad got things back on track?"

"Not exactly." Scarlett says through clenched teeth. "It took years, but he decided to sue the bank and Kress for unfair trade practices. Kress hadn't counted on that. As it turns out my father had a helluva case."

"So he beat Kress at his own game. Great!" I said.

"Again, not exactly," Scarlett said, "My brother, an attorney, and Dad disappeared on their way to federal court in Charleston. They haven't been heard from in five years."

Sometimes when a story is finished, we are obligated to comment. This isn't one of those times. As her story sinks in I'm reminded of how Ally and I were marked for death on the Chowan River. There is no doubt in my mind that Walter Cronus Kress is capable of murder—of planning it, anyway. The surprising part, is hearing how long Kress and Johnston have practiced their craft.

"After my brother and father went missing, I knew Kress had plans to finish me off. That's why I entered law enforcement." Scarlett smooths out her stylish pantsuit. "Until you brought Kress and Johnston down I wore a uniform everyday. I wanted to remind Kress that I was after him. It wasn't until he was in prison that I started wearing civilian clothes."

"Well, I'll happily take credit for your dressing stylishly. But I think we both know the credit for taking down Kress and Johnston goes to Ally and Jim Rogers. I was a bit player, despite what Ally told the court."

"And I was at the trial. Without you showing up at the Chowan Quail Plantation, Ally Kress would have died, according to her own testimony," Scarlett said.

"I wish I could have been as timely in Charlotte—I fell for a diversion that cost Celine Seabolt her life."

"Four people were murdered that day. It's hard to believe one person could have stopped them by himself."

"I don't know how many people were involved in the murders, all I know is I wasn't. No matter what Detective Darius Martin thinks!"

Scarlett gives me the look that says I'm yelling again, but doesn't give me the cold shoulder. "I'm going to share the information you've given me with Detective Martin. It may help him get a clearer picture. But try to remember, Detective Martin is only doing his job."

"Bullcrap! I'm his prime suspect, so he's not looking for the real killers.

That's not doing your job!" I pound my truck hood. "You told him I was angry at Ally—and that's the reason he's wasting his time investigating me!"

"He's investigating multiple murders—but yes, I told him you called her a bitch." Scarlett says.

My head feels like it's going to explode, my peripheral vision dims, and I feel myself spinning out of control. Scarlett braces me against my truck. Even so, I do a slow slide until my butt is flat on the ground.

"Sit tight, Cape. I'll get paramedics out—"

"No." I grab Scarlett's hand. "If you call them, I'll end up in that damn hospital." As I tilt my head toward her, the circle of darkness retreats.

"You're pale as a watermelon's bottom."

"I'm fine." I slide back up the truck and hang on. "I have something that may interest, Detective Martin, but I'd rather you have it."

I reach in my coat pocket and hand her the noose I found on the wreath.

"Is this the noose from your truck?"

"What noose from my truck?"

"The one I saw the first night you stopped by my office."

I'd forgotten about that. But a good law enforcement officer wouldn't forget.

"I found this one at Ally's"

"You tampered with evidence at a crime scene?"

I shake my head slowly trying to think of a way to tell my side of the story so it doesn't sound like I really tampered with evidence.

"It's not as bad as you make it sound." Judging by the look on Scarlett's face, my statement sounds idiotic rather than reasoned. "I stuck it in my pocket and forgot about it. Wasn't like I was trying to conceal evidence."

Scarlett jiggles the noose in front of me. "'Fraid he's probably going to have more questions for you."

Great! Bring 'em on.

CHAPTER FIFTEEN

Who Needs a Lawyer

With her evidence secured, Scarlett and I go back into the house to finish our supper. While I'm busy chasing down the last forkful of beans at the bottom of the can. Scarlett stands akimbo and slowly tilts her body side to side like a feline stretching. "Aaaah, sure feels good to stretch after being cramped up in that car all day," she moans.

I can't tell if this is a come-on, or if that's just me getting my sleaze-bag on again. Whatever, I can't take my eyes off her curves. Whoa. This day may turn out to be my best one in a long time.

Scarlett bends from the waist and places her palms on the floor, a move I couldn't make if my feet were nailed to the floor and the entire Carolina Panther's football team sat on my neck. I'm guessing this is some type of yoga position—downward-facing dog, maybe? From my rear-facing advantage, nothing I see reminds me of a dog. She stands, letting her hand gently drop onto her phone. "As a professional courtesy, I should call, Detective Martin and leave him a message." She explains. "I think he may be interested in how I came into possession of the dart and I'm sure he'll want to know about the noose—you mind?"

Before I can answer, she's hits his number and starts pacing in front of the stove. Rather than intrude, I step out onto the porch.

"I understand that, but he could have just as easily not mentioned it," Scarlett tells him.

Though I'm only getting half the conversation, it's not hard to figure out that Darius Martin isn't happy with me. I walk out into the yard rather than eavesdrop further. In a few minutes, Scarlett walks onto the porch and gives me a wave.

"Up late, huh?"

"Yes, he is actually working on this case."

"I guess he's ticked that I didn't report the attack when it happened?"

"Just a little," Scarlett surveys the overgrown yard. "You should have filed a report while they were better able to catch them."

"Maybe I would have if he didn't have a nasty habit of handcuffing potentials suspects and pretend they aren't under arrest. I don't like him and I don't trust him. When I see him again, I'll be lawyered-up."

"He didn't request an interview, just a report."

"Can I email it to him?"

"If it will make it easier on you. I can help you fill out your report and send it to him over a secured server. We can send RH Carter a copy, too, if you like."

I peel a hunk of rotting wood from a porch post and make a mental note of my next project, "That's fine. It's time for me to let the experts handle this. I'm obviously hindering their investigation. The sooner I get out of the way, the sooner they can solve the case."

"About that." Scarlett said. "There's another reason I wanted to stay and talk with you tonight."

"Yeah, I figured you'd finally get around to the truth. What do you want?"

Choosing her words carefully, she says, "My deputy noticed something in your truck today, during your traffic stop. It could be damning evidence."

"Sounds serious. Should I hire an attorney?"

Scarlett looks me dead in the eye. What I think is a rhetorical question is anything *but*.

"Probably."

"So I guess after your little talk with Detective Martin, you think I'm guilty?"

"No, I think you are innocent." Scarlett says. "But you asked, if I think you should hire an attorney."

"Only guilty people need attorneys!"

Scarlett holds up her right hand and extends her index finger. "Number 1: You are in possession of a noose, identical to other nooses found in Ally's home. Who's to say you didn't plant the others and keep one? Number 2: According to Detective Martin, you and all the victims have an identical wound likely caused by a dart, similar to one you have in your possession."

"I told you how I got the dart!"

"So you say, but there are no witnesses—"

"The mechanic at the impound lot. Geez!"

"And what if he has a terrible memory in a year or two? You didn't file a police report. Any prosecutor worth their salt could tear your story to pieces." Scarlett continues her list. "Number 3: You made disparaging remarks about Ally Kress that could be—"

"I apologized for—"

"Again, a prosecutor would love to go after that statement in a court of law to establish, motive. Number 4: You were the last person to see Celine Seabolt alive and you discovered her body—"

"No, the grandmother and the kid were the last ones to see her alive." I say.

"They're dead, murdered by the same person who killed, Celine."

"The gate guard saw the killer leaving in the florist's van. I can give you a time for that. From the time I left to chase the van until I returned. Couldn't have been more than a 15-minute window."

"You mean the gate guard who has mysteriously disappeared?"

"Explain, that."

"My guess is he will turn up sooner or later," Scarlett says.

"Dead, you mean?"

"Yes."

"The video tapes in the guard house—there were multiple cameras, and I saw at least three. Surely the guard was wrong, and at least one camera was working?"

"The security company confirms what the guard told you. The cameras, all of them, were malfunctioning. So there are no tapes to corroborate your story. They do have a log of you signing in and out. As a matter of fact, you were the sole visitor of Celine Seabolt."

"What's the fifth reason? Wait, no don't tell me. Let me guess: They have a video of me slashing away, murdering everyone, including, Ally. Cops are so dirty!—well, not you."

Scarlett rolls her eyes. "Do you own a crossbow?"

"No, not even a bow and arrow, for that matter."

"Would you mind opening the back door of your Yukon for me?"

"Not a problem." As we walk back to my truck, I think again about questions police don't ask, unless they have the answer.

I pop the door and Scarlett pulls out a crossbow wedged between the rear seat and storage compartment. "Number 5: My deputy spotted it earlier when he stopped you today. I think it may belong to a hunter we found who has been missing for a couple of days."

"When you say missing, you mean—"

"Dead, *very* dead."

"Am I a person of interest in his death, too?"

"No. According to the time-line the coroner established, it couldn't have been you."

"How's that?"

"You were present and accounted for in a Charlotte jail. Besides, why would you lead me to evidence I wouldn't have found?"

"You mean the arrows you found near the bridge?"

"Yes."

"I know the evidence is stacked against me, but do you really think I killed anyone?"

"I think the person who attacked you in Charlotte planted the crossbow in your truck."

I think back to the mechanic at the impoundment lot. How easy would it have been to get by him? Damn easy!

"Just to be clear, Sheriff. You don't think I'm guilty, but you think I need an attorney?"

"Yes."

"OK, I have a question for you."

"Shoot."

"When did my family request that you check up on me?"

"The afternoon that you left the mansion. Why?"

"This may sound weird to you, but as soon as I left the mansion, a pickup started following me. Was it you?"

"No, why would I follow you? Your family provided me your address and license number."

"The night I was attacked. I never told you where I was attacked. Yet, you stopped almost in the place I originally parked. I find that a little strange."

"You mentioned a creek. There are only two between my office and Hwy. 13. I guess I got lucky."

Luck, or coincidence? Like Darius Martin, I'm beginning not to believe in either.

"Just curious—when my family asked you to check on me, did they mention anything about a miniature coffin with pictures inside?"

"No, they didn't mention anything about coffins, miniature or otherwise. Care to enlighten me?"

"Maybe another time. But for the moment, let's say their actions give a little credence as to why I'm in this place."

"How so?"

"Sheriff, seems like everyone, including my family and RH are operating off of hunches. Some officials, like you and Darius Martin, seem to be diving down rabbit holes to pin the murders on an innocent man."

"I am not in that camp, and I don't think Darius Martin is either."

Scarlett says.

"Yeah well, you may not be, but Darius Martin sure is."

"He's not, Cape!"

"How can you be so sure?"

"Because if he thought that, you'd be in jail—dumbass!" Scarlett grabs both my arms and pulls me close to her face. "I shouldn't have said that. I'm sorry. It's just that when you disparage law-enforcement officers, I want to smack you. Most cops are good people."

"Not a problem. Lately I seem to have that effect on lots of people."

"Does it have anything to do with your accident?" Scarlett asks.

"No—I'm just a dumbass." I pull away from Scarlett and maintain eye contact. "You know, it's the weirdest thing. When people try to kill me, I expect law enforcement to treat me like a victim. When that doesn't happen and cops question me instead like a suspect, I tend to get cynical, real cynical—and lots of people can't handle my cynicism."

"I assume I fall into that category?"

"Teetering on the edge, Sheriff—teetering on the edge."

"Then tell me about photos and coffins, tell me everything so I can understand."

"Can't help you. I'm out of the loop, for health reasons, or so they say. I did find out from Detective Martin that there is some type of joint, local, state, and federal task force focused on what they call Kress-Fisher. I think RH is the federal agent on the case, but I could be wrong. As I said, I'm not in the loop."

"I understand why my department isn't included—nothing has happened in our jurisdiction. But I think the crossbow attack on you in Slick Rock County changes all that."

"I recall, you were pretty sure the attack at the creek was an anxious hunter?"

"That was before we found the crossbow hunter, who may have been the person who shot at you."

"Why?"

"We didn't get a chance to question him."

"How did he die, by the way?"

"It's is an on-going investigation, so I can't talk about it."

"Fine, then I'll consider everything that happens to me from this point forward to be part of my own on-going investigation. Nice seeing you for dinner, Sheriff, but I have nothing else to say."

Scarlett tries to stare me into submission. Nothing doing. I stare right back—I mean what I say and she knows it. I may be out of the investigative loop, but the agency I decide to share my information with is the agency that cracks this case. Sheriff Scarlett DuBois is no dummy. She knows, for the moment anyway, I hold the key to this investigation.

"Technically," Scarlett says, "and this goes no further, agreed?"

I nod.

"He drowned, but in a bizarre way he was also hanged."

"Come again?"

"The victim was put in a tidal pool in Hyde County with cement blocks tied around his feet and a noose around his neck. He was given an inner tube to hold on to with a noose tied to it. For a little while, anyway, he could lift the blocks enough to keep from drowning by holding onto the float. At some point fatigue caused him to let go of the inner tube. At that point he was going to choke to death or drown. Looks like he took a big gulp and ended it quickly."

"Was he connected to Kress or Johnston?"

"Not as far as we can tell. Just a case of being in the wrong place at the wrong time."

"But he shot at me with that crossbow and knew what he was doing —"

"According to what we do know. Mr. Sauls was an expert marksman. He could have killed you ten times over."

"Then why didn't he?"

"As I said, unfortunately, we didn't get a chance to talk with him. But, we think someone may have put him up to it as a joke or a gag. That's sheer speculation."

"So the person, or persons, who put Mr. Sauls up to shooting at me, probably killed him?" I ask.

"Exactly, but rather than provide us with clues by buying a crossbow and arrows from a local retailer, they decided to murder him, an innocent person who happened to possess weapons they knew how to use, quite effectively as it turns out."

"And the gray Ford pickup?"

"I'm almost certain it belonged to the crossbow hunter."

"But the truck in Charlotte—it looked just like one that passed me on the bridge near Slick Rock."

"The crossbow hunter was a blowgun hobbyist. As I said, it looks like the killer used the tools his victim provided."

"Have you ever heard of someone this ruthless or cold-blooded?"

A vacant look comes across, Scarlett's face, as if she's checking out of the present and moving into the past. "Yes, I have. In the case of my brother and father. To tell you the truth, what they did to them was even more gruesome."

This is the second time Scarlett has referenced the dark story of her father and brother. If there is a Walter Cronus Kress connection between what happened to her family and mine, she's taking her sweet time explaining. I think about pressing her for details, but the resolute look on face says she'll tell that story in her own time, not mine.

"What you've told me makes me even more determined to keep this danger away from—"

"Go home, Cape. Your family is worried about you. Trust me, Nathan Hale Fisher has enough protection around the mansion to make the Secret Service envious. No one is getting into the Fisher mansion, unless they have an invitation. You'll be safer there..." and Scarlett does a slow pirouette with arms outstretched and palms turned upward, "than staying in this place. It's barely better than a...a lean-to!"

My accommodations are arguably lacking, I'll give her that. But comfort isn't the reason I made this choice.

"Maybe you're right," I say. "And maybe my family is right. But until I feel that way...I'll be staying in this damn lean-to. Got it?"

Scarlett's face flushes and she looks like a pressure cooker stuffed to near-explosion by my cynicism. "Fine. It's a free country, but know this. That freedom also includes my right to drop by and check on you—anytime."

"Aren't you forgetting property rights? You can't just waltz out here—"

"You don't own or lease this property. Technically, I can lock you up for trespassing."

"Why don't you, then?"

"Now, now—we both know Minnie Reynaud would give you written permission like *that*." Scarlett snaps her fingers in my face.

"Does help to know people in high places." I smile evenly just to piss her off.

"Why is it so important that you stay here? I'm just not getting it."

"Despite what you, and apparently everyone else thinks, there is some logic to my plan."

"Well, do tell, Mr. Thomas. Do tell!"

"I figure if I hide out here, alone, it's less likely that my family gets caught up in the hunt. The bonus to that is I can draw the killer out into the open. I know this place. There is one way in and one way out. Perfect trap, wouldn't you say, sheriff?"

Scarlett arches her brow, "No, it's not. You're displaying that same chivalrous-macho attitude that got my father and brother..."

Her voice trails off so I fill in the blank for her. "Killed?"

"It's too late for them. I just can't in good conscience let you stay out here like a sitting duck!"

"You got two little problems, sheriff."

"What's that?"

"I'm a grown-ass man, and this is a free country!"

I hate awkward pauses in conversations. I especially hate awkward pauses in well-meaning conversations. And in spite of my wish to remain independent, I appreciate Scarlett's concern. After what seems like an hour, Scarlett breaks the silence.

"I did promise your family I would check on you."

"However, acting on your promise violates my privacy."

Despite her efforts not to show emotions, deep lines of consternation span Scarlett's forehead.

"Just hear me out." Scarlett says. "I don't really think this will intrude on your privacy too much, anyway. I can set up some surveillance that will act as an early warning system. That alone won't keep you safe, but if someone comes snooping around here, I'll know about it in real time. And it will allow me to keep my promise to your family yet not tie up a lot of my time."

"What makes you so sure someone will find me? Call me crazy, and many have, but I'm not as stupid as I look." I take my cell phone and battery and place them on the drainboard trough near the hand-pump. "I'm off the grid and have been since I left Charlotte."

"That will buy you only a little time. People are nosy. Even out here in the country. Sooner or later, if the right people want to find you, they will."

"And when, or if *they* do, I'll take appropriate action."

"How?"

"Like I said, there is one way into this place and one way out. I have an escape route that only I know about. I found it when I was a kid. I'm also armed, and if I'm cornered, I will shoot to kill."

Scarlett steps off the porch, kicks at a small clod of dirt, and focuses on it rather than me. "Aren't you in a scheduled physical therapy program at the hospital? All that coming and going is sure to draw attention to this place. "

I rub my aching shoulders and arms, "I know I'm not at 100% yet, and maybe I need a little more therapy, but just the cleaning up I've done around here today has worked wonders for me. That dang chainsaw is whipping me into shape—not as good as physical therapy, but I'm stopping that program. Jake will be proud of me, he's a big holistic guy, you know."

Scarlett smiles. I'm making a little sense to her and me, and that feeling allows me to open up a little more. "And there's another reason I want to be here. This place, Miss Minnie's place, needs a lot of repairs. I saw the look on her face when she left tonight. She didn't want to leave—this is her home. She wants to live here. This is where she wants to launch from when it's her time to *March with the Saints*, as she calls it."

"I don't know where she comes from, but I know she wants her mortal remains to rest here for eternity. Go look at her tombstone. It's laid out east to west, according to Christian culture, not north to south 'like heathens' as Miss Minnie tells me." It's hard to think of Miss Minnie dying, but at a hundred years old, dying is a distinct probability, not a remote possibility.

Scarlett's face softens and she whispers. "You love her, don't you?"

"It's hard to explain. In some strange way she's always been my connection to my mother, grandmother and even to my daughter, Jana. For that matter, she made sure I connected with Sarge because she knew he was crucial to me getting into aviation."

I laugh, "As for loving, Miss Minnie. I'll tell you and anyone else who cares to listen. I love her with all my heart, and though she pretends not to know me half the time, Miss Minnie loves me, too."

Scarlett looks back inside the house and notices the broken windows and missing doors. "Looks like a lot of work even for a skilled laborer."

"I'm a handyman of sorts and this old place isn't in as bad a shape as I thought. Jimmy's bringing me a few hand tools. With his help, I know we can make this place livable again."

Scarlett pops the lock on her cruiser. "Want to come with me while I scout out some places to put those security devices? It is OK if I install them, right?"

"You can't put an alarm system in here. There's no power. That's why I'm getting hand tools—"

"Well, duh," Scarlett says, "I didn't think you were using the wood stove as a mood-setter. I'm talking about setting up some solar-powered infra-red game cameras."

"How does that help? You still have to come out here to check them, right?"

"They're wired for satellites. Any movement that trips them will send images directly to my computer."

"That's in real time?" I ask.

"As soon as they're tripped, I'll get a live feed."

"Get out of here! I had no idea hunting is so high-tech now."

"And that's what worries me, Mr. Thomas. You're not a perfect candidate for the *hunted becoming the hunter*, you know."

Scarlett walks to her cruiser. The interior light pops on as she opens the door. She grabs a folder off the dash and pulls a long flashlight from its holder on the driver's side door. She tests it by lighting me up like a Christmas tree. "You ready?" Her fingers brush down my forearm as she turns to go. I'm trying to discern if her move is accidental or on purpose.

Meanwhile, she's in full stride, yards ahead of me. I jog to come abreast of her on the path leading to the woods-line. Scarlett switches off the light and we walk in silence.

Light from the full moon casts our shadows far ahead of us. It's been a while since I've been in the country—so long that I've forgotten how truly peaceful silence can be. From the contented look on Scarlett's face, she's enjoying this moment, too.

"You're an urbane individual. Flying all around the world and being very social, as I understand. Do you think you can really abide such a slow-paced life?"

"Very *social?* What's that supposed to mean?"

"Wine, women, and song." Scarlett says. "People talk, Mr. Thomas, especially to law enforcement."

Part of what Scarlett says is correct. Oh, I had plenty of wine, and more than my share of women, good women, but song? I can't carry a tune in a bucket. I understand why locals think of me as being a little different. For the most part, people from here date locally. Most marry young after knowing each other since childhood. They have kids who have kids who stay on here, too. Of course, like the rest of the country, the divorce rate is higher than it should be, but all in all this place is good for family life. Even Jana, a person raised with no family, agrees.

"Sheriff, I've been around the world, visited many places and done things a little different than most folks around here, I suppose. But one thing holds true…home is never the same once you leave it. Even if you only move a mile or two down the road."

"That's true, the home you leave for college is never home again. Why is that?" Scarlett said.

"I think changing family relationships over time has a lot to do with that. I can tell you that what people consider normal in one part of the world can be seen as strange in another."

"Meaning you don't see yourself as *very* social on the world stage, but understand why people here think you might be?"

"Exactly, Scarlett. Don't mind if I call you, Scarlett, do you?"

"No, I kind of like it, actually. And I agree with what you said."

"Good, now that I've de-socialized myself and we're back here again, tell me about this high school sweetheart you married."

"Let's just say it didn't work out, OK?"

"Sorry to hear that."

"Why?"

"Who doesn't like a happy ending?"

"I love happy endings. Tell me a story about you that has a happy ending, Cape Thomas."

"There is only one story about me, but it doesn't have a happy ending."

"Tell it anyway," She laughs.

"I don't want to bore you with it. I call it: 'My-One-Who-Got-Away-Story.'"

Scarlett laughs deep and genuine. "I've actually heard that story before!"

"You're kidding me?"

"Nope, Ally Kress told me about it at the Kress and Johnston trial."

Just hearing Ally's name makes me sad. I guess Scarlett picks up on that.

"Why don't we just stick to my original question? Not the wine, women and song one, but how do you plan to adapt to such a slow-paced life? You won't even have TV."

Thank God for someone who won't let me slip into a funk. "Well, I'm glad we're back on topic. Because it just so happens that a long time ago this place was like a second home to me. I spent all my spare time out here when I was a kid."

"Is that how you know, Miss Minnie so well?"

"Sort of…but no one really knows Miss Minnie—she's always been an enigma."

"I know. That rumor that she's a 100 years old? I asked her if that was true," Scarlett snickers, "and she told me her age was none of my damn business!" We both laugh.

"Sounds 'bout right. When my grandfather deeded her this farm, he tried to find a birth certificate or marriage license to make sure her name was correct on the deed. But turns out she has no documentation in this or any other county in North Carolina that he could find."

"So, she wasn't born here?"

I grin. "Heck, if I know. I asked her that once. Got the same 'None a your damn business' answer you got. I never asked, but I'm pretty sure, my mother and grandmother knew everything about Miss Minnie…and I'm just as certain she knew everything about them. Miss Minnie always called them, *special*."

"Special?" Scarlett repeats.

I don't really want to go into the nutty-side of my family. Scarlett is from South Carolina, so there's a pretty good chance she knows nothing of my family history, even though she knows the Fishers.

"What a lovely way to describe mental illness," Scarlett says.

So much for thinking my family history isn't part of community lore.

"They weren't mentally ill...they...saw things. Things others couldn't —"

"Like you saw Laura Fisher?"

"Where'd you get that?"

"Sorry, I know you don't remember, but that came up in the trial."

Great! One more reason for AeroMax never to rehire me. "Laura and I never had conversations—"

"I know, but she led you to your daughter. The way Jana explained it in court was so beautiful. My favorite part of the trial, even if it was deemed irrelevant by the defense."

Before I can comment, Scarlett stops and shines her flashlight on an aerial photograph in the folder she's carrying. "I'm going to put dual cameras here, one on either side of the path." She traces a finger around the small creek that surrounds the property. "As far as I know there's no other crossing, right?"

"Nope. Like I said, one way in and one way out. Except for my secret passageway."

"You really do know this property, don't you?" Scarlett asks.

"My grandfather bought it at an auction, years ago. The farm was in pretty bad shape, but my grandmother sort of forced him to buy it. As soon as he closed on the farm, he deeded everything, including the old house, to Miss Minnie."

"What a lovely story," Scarlett says. "It reminds me of something my father would have done." In the bright moonlight I see tears on her cheeks. That won't do.

"Hey, now that you finished your survey—you want to see something?" I ask.

"You sound like a kid about to divulge a great secret. How can I resist?"

"Follow me." We half-walk half-run along the edge of the woods to the corner of the field. A narrow, small sandy path cuts through the hardwood bottom facing us. Shafts of moonlight filter through the limbs overhead and illuminate the white-sand path. "Sugar-sand," Scarlett bends over and scoops up a double handful, as the grains sifts between her fingers she squeals, "This is like being in Candy Land, I love it."

"Farmers around here call it 'dead-sand.' That's one reason this place sold so cheap. Poor crop land. Nothing much grows on dead-sand but long-leaf pines and a few scrub oaks. Once you hit the Bibb soils along the creek, it's another story. You'll see."

"I like sugar-sand better. Dead-sand, sounds morbid."

As we near the creek, the path becomes a sandy beach framing the black-water creek. Lush green cinnamon ferns layered row on top of row outline the sugar-sand beach. Water oaks, strung with Spanish moss stand like bearded sentinels on either side of the creek. A gigantic poplar rules a spit of land in the middle of the creek, and its tree-roots form a natural waterfall across the breadth of the stream. Moonlight reflecting off the bubbling waters below resembles strands of diamonds flowing on to the sea.

"My God! It's an enchanted forest," Scarlett gasps. Her voice, cushioned by the surrounding flora, comes out whispery.

"I call it the Huck Finn place." For a moment the sights and sounds of the forest isolate us from the world—and each other. I think of Jana and the twins. I hope I live long enough to share this place with them. A sadness comes over me, knowing I'll never be able to do so with Laura or Ally.

"Why, Huck Finn?" Scarlett asked.

"Well, it was a rare time in my life when I discovered this place. Back then I mostly read books about airplanes and flying. But the day I wound up here, I'd just finished, *The Adventures of Huckleberry Finn*, by Mr. Mark Twain.

"I took one look at this little creek, and though it was nowhere near as majestic as the Mississippi River, I knew it was my ticket to the world beyond. I ran back to Miss Minnie's for her ax. That was early on a Saturday, and by noon I had enough saplings chopped down and cut to size to make a raft to take me to the Atlantic Ocean, and the world beyond!"

"No way you made it to the ocean—did you?"

"Well, I would have…except for how I lashed the poles together."

"Do tell."

"My grandfather was a miser of sorts, keeping me on a tight budget. I couldn't afford to buy the rope I needed…and then it hit me. Shoelaces! He had at least twenty pairs of wingtips shoes, and I robbed every one of them of their laces.

"You can't see it from here even in daylight." I say, pointing down the creek. "But I made it to the first bend. Then I got tangled up in the shoestrings and logs. The current was swift, the waters were black. I tried to paddle, but I was like a fly in a fast-moving spider's web. The more I struggled, the more hazardous my situation. Panicked, I thrashed, kicked and cursed. As pieces of the raft dug into the creek bed, I face-planted with them on the bottom.

"I held my breath as long as I could. But after exhaling, the water coming into my lungs felt like fire. All of a sudden these arms grabbed around me and we shot off the creek bed to the surface. I tell you, that day I thought of Miss Minnie as a super hero. She still had her eyesight back then. Once back on the bank, she started CPR—and she was like a machine! After I started breathing, she said, 'Boy, you mean to tell me you got on that water and didn't know how to swim?'"

"Aw, I was swimming pretty good!"

"'Well, pretty good, ain't good *enough*!' Then Miss Minnie tanned my hide, and rightfully so. I think she spanked me because she was scared that I came so close to drowning."

"Why would you think that," Scarlett says.

"When I think back to that day, I remember how Miss Minnie rocked me in her arms and cried out "Praise Jesus! Over and over…That's the only time I'd seen her cry and really show emotions, but, of course, she later denied it."

"What happened then?"

"Well, she got down to the business of teaching me to swim. She said, 'Boy, you ain't leaving here today 'til you can swim to my satisfaction'. Here I'd almost drowned dead-away, and she forced me out into the creek again! She taught me how to dog-paddle, do the breaststroke, crawl, sidestroke, backstroke, and any other kind of stroke you can imagine. Last thing we did, she taught me to fetch."

"*Fetch*, like a dog?"

"Yep, she threw a hammer in the water and said, 'Go git it, boy'. Turns out swimming underwater is my forte. I stayed under the water so long Miss Minnie said I was like an otter at heart."

"Did you salvage the raft after that?" Scarlett says.

"No, but had I known the consequences of not replacing those shoelaces, I would have. I worked the rest of that summer cleaning my grandfather's law office to pay for all those laces…And —like all good lawyers—he inflated his damages."

"So at an early age you learned that crime doesn't pay?" Scarlett said.

"Well, that—and never skimp on materials needed to get the job done right."

"Is this your secret passageway?"

"The beginning of it."

"How do you cross the creek, swim?"

"Nope, swimming to the other side will just get you to that little island you see there. On the other side is a pocosin, thick and impassable."

"So how do you get to your secret passageway?"

"Now if I told you that it wouldn't be a secret, would it, Sheriff?"

"You aren't going to tell me? Kind of defeats the purpose of showing me this place, no?"

"Nope, just means the time for telling isn't right."

"I look forward to that day." Scarlett shivers, "It's nippy out here."

"Yeah, guess we better head back."

Just before we're back at Scarlett's cruiser she turns to me. "Would you mind if I visit you again? Not an official visit, a social visit. I'd really like to see the Huck Finn place in the daylight—and I can't wait to see the secret passageway."

"As long as it isn't an official visit, you're welcome to stop by anytime, Scarlett."

CHAPTER SIXTEEN

Johnston & Kress 5 years earlier

Bright and early, before Cape Thomas was up, Scarlett DuBois had one camera set along the entrance and two more strategically placed along the Huck Finn path. Before she made it back to the blacktop, her cruiser's radio crackled to life.

"You 10-42, Sheriff?"

"Nope, 10-41, heading over to Taylor Town, then down to Faison."

"10-4."

All things considered, the meeting went well. Not exactly as planned, but her cameras were in place and she could now monitor him in real time. Pretty slick move, she thought. Then again handling men had always come easy to her. Cape, as expected, was more than receptive to her coy advances. She thought of how his eyes nearly popped out of his head when she stretched in front of the stove—changed man, indeed! Thank God he hadn't bathed in cologne this time, nor had he broached the subject of dating.

Old Cape had boxed himself in with his assertion of being a Southern Gentleman rather than a sleazebag. What a crock—the guy was clearly a womanizer who'd gotten knocked off his game after a brain injury. As soon as he healed he'd be back to his hound-dog ways in no time. Men—all real men anyway—like leopards, never changed their spots. That's what made them so predictable.

But the next man-sized-task, on her agenda would not be easy. William Johnston was no pushover, and unlike, Cape Thomas, he was a worthy adversary. Nothing in her arsenal of female wiles would play well with Johnston. Hard to deceive a true master of deception—and a misogynist too boot.

The worst part of meeting Johnston was having to be regaled with his tales of being the prison-bitch. She imagined him as a naked, pasty-white pervert earning his title of Oreo-Double-Stuff, with two paid Mandingo cellmates. Never a fan of aberrant behavior, Scarlett DuBois, was more than thankful Johnston's proclivity for depravity didn't draw him to prey on women and children. Not having to hear any fantasies like that made her necessary visits with him disgusting but not intolerable.

A much as she despised Johnston, he was responsible for her being Slick Rock County Sheriff. That position, ironically, made it possible for her to extract very soon her ultimate revenge on Johnston and Walter Cronus Kress.

Five years earlier, driven by indignation, anger, and press clippings heralding the **Trial of The Century** of her father's nemeses, Johnston and Kress. Scarlett had managed to land, the right job, in the right place, at the right time. Law enforcement veterans from across the country, looking for exposure that would lead to certain advancements, wanted to be involved in the highly publicized trial.

Most applied to Pitt County where the crimes took place, but she guessed the defense would ask for and rightly receive a change of venue. One look at the map of eastern North Carolina and she knew an impoverished county like Slick Rock would be the likely place for the trial.

Suddenly, the sleepy little county had been inundated with stacks of over-qualified applications for positions of Deputy Sheriff. The trial had everything—attempted murder, international drug cartel connections, money laundering, human trafficking, and counterfeiting. The cast of characters was a scriptwriter's dream if or when the trial was made into a movie.

Johnston and Kress, avatars of evil with their high-powered defense team, were on one side of the courtroom. Pitted against them were what the press described as, a newly appointed, country-boy, federal prosecutor and his star witness, the beautiful Allison Moore Kress, wife of defendant W. Cronus Kress. Eastern Carolina had never seen and likely would never see again a trial like this.

Every type of media descended on the quaint but way too small Slick Rock County Courthouse. Well-known national and international journalist became regulars at meat-n-3 diners and local bars. That potential clash of cultures morphed, oddly, into an harmonious gathering that mystified sociologists and participants alike. Long-term friendships between sophisticates and country-folk had endured to this day, showing that more unites this country than divides it.

Scarlett entered the job hunt with an application on top of the pile, but three strikes against her, too. First woman applying to the all-male Slick

Rock County Sheriff's Department, a non-resident, and a card-carrying SEC fan in the heart of Pirate Nation.

While other applicants were over-qualified and mostly male. Scarlett possessed natural assets her competitors lacked—brains; political connections; and at 45, looks that still could stop a clock.

In spite of her lackluster law-enforcement background, Sheriff Calvin Oliver had taken a liking to her. Even so, things weren't looking good for her. That is until she batted her eyes and promised the sheriff she would do anything, *absolutely anything*, to get the deputy position. As expected, male-chauvinist, good-old-boy, Calvin Oliver took her at her word. The sound of a zipper coming down shocked her at first. When she looked over and saw Sheriff Calvin Oliver's fly open she knew the position was hers. When she finished, all he said was, "Swallow the evidence and you're hired."

Though it was degrading to womanhood, and to the women who follow in her footprints, to land a job by granting sexual favors, Scarlett was certain the ends justified the means. Besides, she also knew that the only score that counted was the final score, and the game she was playing was just getting started. As long as her goal of serving vengeance on the men who had destroyed her family, was facilitated, she didn't give a damn what feminists—or the world, for that matter—thought of her means.

Her attitude carried over at the sheriff's department. The other deputies, all male, thought she was stupid for taking the lowly prison transport job. Justifiable reasoning—after all, she was the *private stock* of Sheriff Calvin Oliver and might've had any job in the department save his.

Other deputies hated the verbal, and in Scarlett's case sexual, abuse screamed by criminals from the backseat when carted off to prison. But Scarlett used the long, hard rides to toughen her mental resolve. The best part of the trip was flashing a warm smile at the prisoner when she reached the prison gate and giving her standard send-off. "Have a nice day, Fresh-meat."

Despite the degrading work she did it without complaint. One day soon, when she was alone with William Johnston and Walter Cronus Kress, it would all be worth it. Even with the best representation money could buy those slimeballs would not walk out of said Trial of the Century as free men. Once they were convicted, she would transport them to Raleigh for processing—not that they could trust living that long.

That had been her original plan, but when opportunity knocked, she snatched the door wide open. After sentencing, Johnston and Kress, shackled and in handcuffs, were brought to the sally port—at that vulnerable second becoming sitting ducks. It had taken all her self-discipline not to gun them down when they smirked at her, Johnston speaking first.

"Good morning, Deputy, DuBois!"

"Good morning, Mr. Creepy," Scarlett sang out as she slammed her knee into Johnston's groin. Kress, avoiding his own greeting, raced to the other side of the cruiser and hopped into the back seat.

"What the hell was that?" Johnston whined.

"An attention-getter—now get in there and shut up!"

"All I said was 'Good morning'…"

Scarlett grabbed Johnston by the collar, shoved him into the back seat, and slammed the door. Even socially acceptable pleasantries sounded vile coming from this hypocritical scumbag. She buckled her seat belt and adjusted her rearview mirror. Of all the lowlifes she'd transported, this was by far her most unsavory cargo. Once they were both looking at her, she pulled a small bottle of sanitizer from her utility belt and slathered her hands with the cleansing gel. Slowly she worked the gel in and around her fingers, making sure the men knew she was cleansing away their slime.

"We know your Daddy," Johnston said. "Former client of Mr. Kress, isn't that right, Walter?"

Kress pretended not to hear and stomped the floorboard of the cruiser in rapid succession. Same-lame-game he used during the trial—killing little floor-bugs that only he could see. And a ploy to justify his insanity plea—that no one was buying, including the Superior Court Judge.

"Did you hear me, Deputy?" Johnston said through the wire mesh cage.

Scarlett ignored Johnston, again. His admission that he knew her father was throwing her off her game. Not once during the Trial of the Century had he even acknowledged her presence in the courtroom. Now he was admitting something she had been prepared to beat out of him.

"Yeah, I know. That's why I took this job." Scarlett said.

"Hero envy?" Johnston sneered.

Again she ignored the question, instead making eye contact with him via the rear-view mirror. Hard to believe this once-pudgy man now weighted less than a buck-fifty. The new look only made him bare-boned, butt-uglier, and more obnoxious.

Johnston leaned up to the cage just behind her head and whispered. "I.Q. Test, Deputy—you willing to take a million in exchange for our freedom?"

"Screw you and your money!" Scarlett yelled and immediately

regretted it. Never show a lawyer emotion—how many times had her brother pounded that into her? Emotion stirred a lawyer's killer instinct like blood in the water set off a feeding frenzy among Great White Sharks. If Johnston was in a court of law just then he would've used her mistake to his advantage. Too bad for Johnston he was in the back of a police cruiser, and at her mercy.

"Your father is a brilliant man. I doubt he would turn down a proposition before he heard it. Then again, your father doesn't have your morals." Johnston shook his head. "I don't mean that as a compliment, by the way. Had his morals not gotten in the way, your brother would still be alive."

Is a brilliant man? This slime bag knew damn well her father and brother were dead. Hell, he killed them! Maybe not with his own hands but, by all accounts, Johnston and Walter Kress ordered the hits. Why pretend her father was alive? Ah yes, to cloud her thinking with emotions. Well, what Johnston didn't know is how deep she could bury her emotions thanks to all those screaming prisoners she had delivered to prison.

Scarlett stared at Johnston in the rearview mirror, enjoying how her cold reserve pissed him off. Rather than validate her victory, Johnston settled back into the bench seat and pretended to enjoy the bucolic scenery they were passing by at a state-regulated 55 mph. A good five miles rolled up on the car's odometer before Johnston tried another angle. "Wonder why I referred to your father in the present tense"?

"Nope." Scarlett barely glanced at her rear-view mirror when answering.

"I know where they are."

"Liar."

Johnson broke into a grin. Just as he'd done at his trial when his defense team was about to score points—a rare occurrence. Rather than go away, Johnston centered a knowing smirk dead center of her rearview mirror, making it impossible for Scarlett to ignore him.

"You mean you know where their bodies are located, right?"

Johnston slid up close to the cage. "You really think we killed them and got away with murder, don't you?"

"Shut up, Johnston. You killed them because they agreed to testify against you!"

"Let get the facts straight; we were never charged." Johnston snarled. "And they weren't going to testify! They were turning state's evidence to save their miserable hides."

"Sit back and shut up. I don't want to hear another word out of you!"

But while Deputy DuBois made a conscious effort to ignore her backseat passengers, Johnston was busy slipping his newly gained svelte frame into a contortionist position. He slipped his arms under his feet and fed a looped wire coat-hanger through the cage and around Scarlett's throat. The thin-gauged wire bit into her neck like a cookie-cutter into dough. Air and blood flow stopped at the same time. The pressure in her skull built until her eyes bulged. Just before she lost control of the car, Johnston released the pressure and she gasped for air. "What is that!"

"An attention-getter, to use your word!" Johnston waited until her eyes were focused on him. "You do realize that your life is in my hands, right?"

"Yes,"she croaked.

"Pull into the rest area coming up—and no funny business, or you die."

Johnston scanned the area like a hunter looking for prey. "Go further down. Not that one…the space on the end. Right here, stop!"

In one last moment of resistance, she tried to key the radio mike with her knee but Johnston immediately threaded the hanger back into the soft skin around her throat. "I said no funny business!"

"You'll never get away with this!" Scarlett moaned.

"I don't intend to." Johnston looked around the immediate area of the cruiser and then looked for signs of movements in the distance—nothing was amiss. He had as much time as he needed to make his case. "I'm going to tell you exactly what went down with your brother and father. You do know they were turning state's evidence, right?" Johnston waited for an answer that wasn't coming. "If you don't admit that, I won't tell you what happened."

Though her father and brother were accused of belonging to the largest counterfeiting ring in the South, Scarlett never believed it. Doing some money-laundering for Kress and Johnston? Sure, that evidence was plain and simple. Her father had gotten in over his head with the bank, a Walter Cronus Kress owned bank, and turned to crime to get out of debt. In the process he involved many of his friends, including politicians, judges, and other prominent business people. When her father and brother were kidnapped on their way to testify against their former associates, and were later rumored to have been murdered, lots of crooked big-shots sighed with relief.

"I understand they planned to turn state's evidence to right some of the wrongs they had committed."

"Who the hell told you that?" Johnston howled.

"Both were honorable men!"

"They were rats! Rats! Who planned to double-cross everyone, including friends and family, to save their miserable hides. Wake up and try living in the real world!"

Scarlett nodded her head. Johnson was right about that—immunity had been their goal. Some family members still wouldn't talk to her. But if she ever wrote a book on her justifiable homicide of Johnston and Kress, her own "righting-the-wrong" card was going to be played. Her father and brother would come across as heroes on her silver screen.

"Fine, I'll start living in the real world if you stop pretending my father and brother are alive."

"Your brother's dead. Your father is alive."

"Impossible! He would have contacted me by—"

"The F.A.R.C. and E.L.N...mean anything to you?"

FARC, Revolutionary Armed Forces of Columbia and ELN, National Liberation Army. Who hadn't heard of them? But why was Johnston invoking these far-flung entities? Her brother and father had gone missing in South Carolina.

"What the hell do they have to do with *my* family?"

"Ransoms paid for returning individuals they've kidnapped is their primary source of income. A similar group has developed a constant income stream from kidnappings rather than the sporadic payments the FARC and ELN receive. Perhaps you've heard of—ISIS?"

"I don't understand—Dad and Jon have been missing for over three years. Besides, you cannot be believed."

Johnston again squirmed in the seat to survey the area around the cruiser. Was he expecting someone? "Your father is alive because he has the goods on some very powerful people. Walter here included. Id'nt that right, Walter?" Walter Cronus Kress nodded and stared back outside as if he were a patron donor at a boring comedy of manners.

"Everyone wanted to kill them. But your old man was smart enough to hide some *insurance* or easily transferrable information, that could bring down a lot of powerful folks. It's called, a Dead Man's Dump, in legal lingo. Even I admit it was a brilliant move."

To Scarlett, Johnston was a helluva good actor, a facile liar, or he was telling the truth. To reveal which one, Scarlett decided to try a lawyer-trick her brother had passed along to her. "Why did you say my brother was dead—to make your lie more believable?"

Her taunting started paying huge short-term dividends when Johnston's face twisted into a nasty sneer.

"I'm a seasoned lawyer, Bitch! I have no reason to lie. We're headed to prison, not a round of golf at the country club. You want the truth or not?"

"You wouldn't know the truth if it slept with you."

"Ms. Deputy, I thought you were smart enough to make a deal and save your old man. I guess not…"

"Tell your story. If it makes sense, I'll do anything to save my father."

"I was going to spare you some gory details. But since you doubt me, I'll share my first-hand account just as I saw it. When I finish, I'll have a couple of life-or-death options for you." Johnston pulled with all his weight against the wire, and once again Scarlett's eyes bulged in pain from their sockets. "Or I could just kill you now?"

"No, please…I *have* to know what happened."

Johnston slacked off the wire. "Fine, but keep your trap shut until I finish, understand?"

Scarlett nodded and sucked in lungfuls of sweet, cool air.

"N.A.R.C.O., was holding them at the time. They brought your father, Jon, and two Guatemalan captives into this courtyard. They demanded your father tell them where he had stashed the damning evidence. The group stood to make millions if they broke him.

"As a matter of full disclosure, Walter and I had brought the money that would procure the evidence. Your old man, of course, opted not to tell them. Smart move as I saw it, but turns out it's not a good idea to piss the NARCO folks off. Anyway, the damage is done. NARCO brings in a portable limb-chipper like tree trimming companies use. They fired the machine up and ran a couple of small logs through it. At first I didn't get why they wanted a pile of mulch that had built up behind the machine. Then WHAP! These two goons grabbed one of the Guatemalans, and tossed him head first into the mouth of the chipper. The pile of mulch instantly turned blood-red! Oh Man! The cruelest and coolest thing I've ever seen! The guy didn't even have a chance to scream.

Now the second Guatemalan started jumping, twisting, and fighting with everything he had." Johnston looked at Scarlett in the mirror—and was gratified to find her hanging on every word. "So, in broken English he started begging your father to spill the beans. But your old man just shakes his head.

"The goons have a plan B for this second Guatemalan. Rather than throw him in head-first, they tied a rope to the guy's hands and slowly fed him into the wood chipper, feet first. Talk about blood-curdling screams…it was nasty! Guy screamed for mercy right up until the machine gnawed into his intestines. Shit flew everywhere…and the smell would've gagged a maggot." Johnston observed the horror in Scarlett DuBois expression and continued. "Your brother, Jon, must have figured out his fate. Before anyone could stop him, he kicked off his shoes—I still haven't figured that one out—and dives head-first into that damn wood chipper. Talk about *Balls*."

Scarlett DuBois slid down in her seat until the makeshift garrote tightened against her throat. The pain was nothing compared to what her brother must have suffered. She tried to apply more pressure, only dying could make her feel better. There was only one love greater than the one she shared with Jon, and that was her love for her father. The two men were everything in her life—protectors, confidants, and best friends. How had the man she loved more than Jon let this happen? And how horribly he must have suffered, too. Oh, God, what a terrible story... what a terrible world!

"Why didn't my father save him?"

"There was no saving him. Your brother saw that if he spilled the beans, they both died. What your brother did worked, too. His death only toughened your old man's resolve. He didn't give a damn what they did to him after that. He wasn't telling. He must've figured, too, that if he told he'd be wasting Jon's life and now his self-sacrifice. And make no mistake, they tortured the hell out of your dad. But he wouldn't talk. They even nailed one of his nuts to a board...and after that, they had to come up with another plan. Only way your old man was giving up the goods was if someone cuts him a deal that included your safety and his."

"How do you fit in?"

"Let's just say we're...trading partners with N.A.R.C.O. They're animals, but astute business people, too. I've convinced them there is a way that we can all win if they give me a little time with you."

"How so?"

"The people who will be spared public humiliation as well as prison time certainly have no problem looking the other way. We conduct business as usual, politicians keep promising to put us out of business, but then they don't lift a finger against us because they keep getting re-elected with the money we *donate*. It's The American Way."

"So what stops this group from coming directly after me? Surely they can reap greater rewards without paying you a cut."

"Oh they've thought about it, I'm sure. But things get real shitty real quick when something happens to a cop. The last thing any of us needs is more heat! Jeez! So, everyone agreed to go along with my plan. All I have to do is get a moment alone with you, like we have now. But before that can happen, along comes this idiot, Cape Thomas trying to be the knight in shining armor for his jungle-bunny-lover—but you know the rest of that story. Long story short, Cape Thomas's stumbling into our little money-laundering scheme and getting us put in prison is a set back, that's all. The fact that you had the good sense to get into law enforcement has kept you alive.

"But for you to be beneficial to your father, you'll need to be in a position of influence—and we've arranged for you to have that position. Your old man knows this and has adjusted his demands accordingly. Now he has this hair-trigger threat out there to take his own life if his terms aren't met. We call that a Poison Pill in the corporate world."

"What does *that* mean?"

"Once the shit starts rolling downhill, it will snowball until everyone is smothered in stench and destroyed. Your old man is a diabolical S.O.B."

The worry-lines etching across Johnston's face made her a proud of her Dad for the first time in years. "So why are you telling me all this? If I live, I'm going to report this. Surely you know that?" Scarlett said.

"Yeah. Goodie two-shoes, and we figured that. There's no doubt you're a good cop."

The backhanded compliment made Scarlett smile. Even the vilest most corrupt man in the world knew she was incorruptible, except for the execution she was planning for these two.

"But," Johnston continued. "You don't want your old man to die. So we have this deal for you that will save both you and him."

The smile faded from Scarlett's face. They have her number. Nothing is more important than her father's life—not her honor, not her loyalty to law enforcement, not anything else under the sun. Surely there was a way to save both her father and her career?

"I know you're thinking there must be a way to save your father and still make sure Walter and I get our just rewards. You're wrong, I assure you. Only one way can possibly save your father...and that's my way. Understand?"

"No! You're lying! How can you save anyone? You can't even save yourself from prison?"

"Listen to me, Sweetie. If the story of how your brother died bothers you, the death they have planned for your father is far worse. Far!"

"You won't kill him. Or you already would have killed him—"

"Our group made a bad call when we sent your old man and brother off for safekeeping. If N.A.R.C.O. had lived up to the original agreement, things would be different. They figured out they could make a lot more money by bargaining for your father's deadman's dump. We pay these animals a yearly fee...that they keep increasing, and the ransom we agreed to pay to get him back has gone through the roof. If we don't get him back soon—"

"You're lying. You're still calling the shots. This is just some bullshit to make me—"

"Oh, you're wrong about that. I'm scared as hell of these animals, we all are. Only time we get around them at all is to pay them. And even then we devise a method of payment that insures our team's safe return. These double-crossing sons-of-bitches would hold *us* for ransom and kill us in a minute if we didn't have firewalls to keep us safe."

Suddenly the obvious hit Scarlett like a low-blow in the gut. "I don't believe a word you're saying. My father would have tied Jon's life into this deadman's dump, he wouldn't have ever let Jonnie Boy die!"

"They kept them separated so they couldn't discuss strategy. I'm sure you were included in the insurance, too. Jon must have concluded your old man would talk if his or your life was threatened. Guess he knew his death would toughen your old man's resolve and save you, too. 'Crazy, magnificent bastard' is all I can say, and I didn't even like the guy!"

Jon gave his life to save Dad and me, Scarlett thought. Jon, *Jonnie Boy*, always the exemplary, Eagle Scout, valedictorian—number-one brother and number-one son. And Johnston could have no way of knowing, Jon loved shoes, even had his initials, JD engraved on the heels after his first nice pair were stolen at gym class. She couldn't be sure how much of Johnston's story was true, kicking off his shoes is something Jon would have done.

"Those bastards!"

"I agree, but that doesn't change the situation." Johnston said. "You and your dad can still walk away from this. Don't let your brother's death be in vain."

"You don't care about us. You just want to save—"

"Myself! Guilty as charged, but if we all get what we want, what's the downside? You live to come after me another day. Don't be stupid!"

"Who are the people who will be destroyed if my Dad's information is released?"

"You don't want to know."

"Yes, I do. My brother died because of them!"

"I won't tell you names, but some are very powerful people, some of them live in Washington. Their positions of power are the only thing Walter and I have to bank on right now, even though we're headed to prison. So you may ask why we care what happens to our former colleagues. They have assured us that they will issue us end-of-term pardons if we keep our mouths shut and make sure your old man does the same."

"Only the Executive branch can do that."

"And they will have done nothing more than every elected leader in modern times has done—Democratic and Republican."

"Guess the Bible nailed it: money is truly the root of all evil."

"You're right. The Bible is what politician swear on, not what they believe in. All they can think about is the money they make after taking the oath on that Bible. Until they can't be bought and sold, career politicians are a commodity just like oil and gas...and considering how beneficial that is to so many, is it really such a bad thing?"

"So what am I supposed to do, just let you go?" Scarlett said.

"Nope, we have no plans to escape. We need you to keep your job, in a slightly elevated position from Deputy. We have a deal worked out that will set you and your father up in Samoa, which doesn't have an extradition treaty with the US. With the money you and your old man get, you can hire an army to protect you. But that won't be necessary."

"Why so? And how can we trust you?"

"Our colleagues are like the rat in the trap. They don't want any more cheese, they just want out of the trap. It's cheaper for the group to set you and your dad up in Samoa than it is to keep paying the ransom fee. Our trial and conviction has really gotten our associates on edge. They figure if we can be tried and convicted, so can they—and they're right."

"How long before I can see my father?"

"Unfortunately, it may take five years. About as long as it will take us to get pardons."

"Five years!"

"Hey, it's not like we want to be in prison that long either. If we had more cash to spread around we could get things done a little quicker."

Scarlett jerked her head toward Walter, "Oh, come on. He's Walter Cronus Kress!"

"Yes, he is, but his assets have been frozen by the Feds, and that crazy wife of his has given away any joint assets she controlled! Plus, this mess Cape Thomas has gotten us into has really put a dent in our on-hand cash reserves. We have a little cash-flow problem. But, we've got a plan to replenish those funds even while we're in prison. Your old man will be safe, don't worry about that." Johnston salivated like a starving man eyeing a thick, juicy steak. "All we have to do, when the time is at hand, is make sure some people who may oppose our pardons disappear."

"You mean Allison Moore Kress?"

"Yes, and Cape Thomas and family, if he recovers."

"And by disappear, you mean *kill*?" Scarlett said, "They are innocent people—"

"They are not people, they are impediments!"

"I won't kill innocent people!"

"You won't have to. We have those bases covered, as a matter of fact the cleansing won't start until you and your dad are out of the country."

"I can't stand by and let innocent people die."

Johnston pulled the coat hanger back through the cage.

"That's fine, Deputy DuBois. If you prefer to save strangers over family then you obviously have the constitution to deal with the consequences.

"In exactly two weeks you will receive a video of your father being killed 'inch by inch.' If you are not familiar with that process, allow me to explain. Your father's limbs will be severed with machetes one inch at a time, starting with his toes and fingers. It will be an excruciatingly painful death." Johnson smiled again at her image in the rearview mirror. "You may now take us to Raleigh for our processing to Federal Prison in Atlanta."

Scarlett closed her eyes, trying to erase the terrifying vision Johnston had stealth-planted in her brain. Focusing on her father still being alive, however, helped her focus on her wake up to the job at hand. She had to buy time, contact the FBI, or at least notify her superiors.

"Wait. I have to have some proof that my father is still alive. You can't expect me to take what you say at face value." Scarlett said. "Surely you can understand that?"

"All I understand for certain is this." Johnston sneered. "At precisely 9:45 AM EST, five minutes from now, a van will pull up beside your car. Two armed men will exit, their guns drawn, and demand our release." Johnston pointed to a security camera mounted on a light pole between the service area building and the cruiser. "A live feed from the camera you see there will record your decision to work with us and save your father, or you will sign his death warrant."

"What if I agree to this madness?"

"The van will flee with their accomplices and never be heard of again. Your heroic deed will be captured on camera and televised around the world. You will be hailed a hero in Slick Rock County. So proud of you will the citizens be that they will elect you sheriff in the next election."

"That's impossible! Sheriff Oliver loves his job and he has the people snowed. They will never vote him out—"

"Not only will Sheriff Oliver not run for re-election, he will endorse you as his candidate of choice."

"He won't. I promise you he will not resign and he will not be intimidated by you."

"That may be, Ms DuBois. But we know for a fact that Sheriff Calvin

Oliver will resign, or he will suffer a scandal beyond his imagination. We have video of the little favor you bestowed upon him to gain employment with the Slick Rock County Sheriff's department."

"I don't know what you're talking about!"

"I'm not into porn," Johnston said. "But I'd pay to see your performance on the ole sheriff again—if I were offered the chance."

"Go to hell! I only did that so I could get a chance to kill you two!"

"That should be the last thing you want to do now. If we die, so does your father...and are you really willing to sign your old man's death warrant, Deputy?"

"But, I'm not a native of Slick Rock. I have no political expertise. I don't see how I can possibly be elected."

"Oh, it can happen. Politics is nothing but a power game fueled by money. Cape Thomas, in his own bumbling way, did us a favor. Not only are we going to teach his new family a lesson. We are also going to reclaim the Fisher family fortune—it's ours anyway, you know. Thomas should not have stuck his nose where it didn't belong. Old man Fisher is vulnerable. You do know that a member of the Fisher family dealt with us before, right?"

"If Mr. Fisher dealt with you before, why would you have to extort him?"

"I didn't say Fisher dealt with us, I said a family member. Trust me, if you exploit your relationship with the Fisher family we'll have all the money we will ever need. But in order to do that, we need the full cooperation of the Slick Rock County Sheriff." Johnston looked at the digital clock on the dash. "What's it's going to be, Ms. DuBois? We have less than a minute. If you don't play-act with these gunmen you can expect your own copy of the video of your father's death in two weeks."

"I'll do it. I'll do it!"

Johnston rushed his words. "Don't aim for them. Shoot just over their heads but make it look real."

Relief flooded through her. It would be a game, play-acting—no one would die.

A black van with dark-tinted windows eased by the service area building and headed straight for the cruiser. Scarlett unsnapped the strap holding her service revolver and yelled, "10-33" into her radio.

"Bitch!" Johnston screamed. "You just signed your old man's death warrant."

"You wanted it real—right?"

"Ah, good thinking, deputy!"

When the first gunman bailed from the van, Scarlett took aim just over his head and fired. Her target returned fire, striking her dead-center in her bullet-proof vest. The impact of the bullet knocked her to the ground as Johnston yelled "Kill her!" from the back seat.

This was no game. The gunman were here to grab Johnston and Kress. From a prone position Scarlett DuBois leveled her gun, but the perp who fired at her jumped back inside the van. She re-targeted and connected with a head shot to perp # 2. Occupants from the van snatched up the dead man and disappeared as quickly as they'd arrived.

"You lying son-of-a-bitch! They were going to kill me," Scarlett said, rubbing the bruise that is forming behind her vest. "If I hadn't been wearing—"

"You never report to duty without a bullet-proof vest," Johnston said.

That was true, but how did they know that...? Hell, they knew everything, so why wouldn't they know that? "All that talk about my father and brother was bullshit, wasn't it! I foiled your damn escape attempt, didn't I?"

Sirens were fast approaching the rest area from the interstate. Johnston rushed his words. "You will get a video of your father soon to prove he is alive. The plan worked to perfection. We had to make it look real."

"But your guy is dead!"

"Just as we planned it. Your training kicked in and you did what you had to do. You were shot to trigger your training. You did notice the man you killed never fired?"

"Yes, he had the drop on me, too. I figured he froze, scared. I could see it in his eyes."

"Exactly," Johnston said.

"Why didn't he fire? Don't lie to me!"

"Without you, Deputy, our plan doesn't work."

"Why didn't he fire?"

Again, Johnston seemed to read her mind.

"Don't worry. The man you killed was a felon and a fugitive from the law." Johnston sat back in the seat and snapped on a pair of handcuffs, something Scarlett had not noticed he was missing. Her emotions had gotten in the way and she had indeed forgotten some of the basics. Just as she was being distracted now. "That doesn't mean he was stupid enough to take a bullet. Why didn't he fire?"

"Unfortunately for him, he also happened to be a father." Johnston said. "His kid was in the van. Had he fired on you, his son would have—"

"You scumbag! Is there no line you won't cross? A kid has to watch his father die?"

"On the bright side, at least he didn't have to see a force for good die."

The first of many patrol cars came speeding down the exit ramp into the rest area, lights on and siren wailing.

"Tell your story any different than what that camera will show and you will watch your father die, too."

Johnston stuck a handcuff key through the cage, "You may want this."

"Who gave you the key and the coat hanger?"

Johnston shrugged his shoulders. "I really couldn't say. That was arranged by someone else."

"Was it someone in the sheriff's department?" Scarlett tried to hide the urgency in her voice. If the department had been infiltrated, there was no way for her to play both sides against the middle. And no doubt about it, for her perfidy, Johnston would make sure she saw her father die.

"Money is a powerful motivator, Deputy. Could have been anyone— from a mechanic who services your cruisers to a friendly judge…You just never know about such things."

Johnston was right about that. You never do know about such things, but you can figure them out. Just like she figured out things on the night she was elected Sheriff of Slick Rock County. Nathan Hale Fisher, even though he lived in another county, turned out to be her biggest financial backer in the Slick Rock County race for sheriff. And she won in a landslide.

CHAPTER SEVENTEEN

Sheriff and the Puppet Master

Sheriff Scarlett DuBois, checked her remote live-feed surveillance at Minnie Reynaud's place. No way any comings or goings could escape her knowing about them. Having Cape Thomas under virtual lock and key made for a relaxing ride back to her Slick Rock office. That feeling faded as soon as a text chimed on her phone. The number was not familiar, and the sender's coded message was:

We have a problem contact me asap WJ.

REPLY: *On my way to Atlanta tonight. As planned SD.*

No, now reside Macedonia Prison Farm. Come today.

Macedonia Prison Farm? How could William Johnston be in a state prison only an hours ride or so from Slick Rock? Today William Johnston and Walter Cronus Kress were federal prisoners with 15 years of their 20-year sentences still ahead of them. Federal sentences could be shortened only one way—by pardon, just as Johnston had promised five years earlier.

But they couldn't be pardoned. No politician was stupid enough to grant pardons to these lowlifes unless he or she was out of office or not up for re-election—and that couldn't happen until January, when political terms expired.

Even with their connections, Johnston and Kress had to pull the ultimate insider's hat trick to get transferred from Federal prison to a state prison system. Was it possible her Dad's Dead Man's Dump had reached to the very pinnacle of the federal government? Or, could the text be a hoax? Had Johnston's method of reaching out to her on prepaid phones, as they had done over the past five years, been discovered by the penitentiary in Atlanta? Were the feds trying to set her up?

These thoughts put Scarlett DuBois in an analytical mode. A good mode to be in preceding any visit with William Johnston. When Johnston first proposed, hell, shoved the offer down her throat of an idyllic life in

Samoa without any extradition treaty with the U.S. she had had to take the deal, even if she hadn't been under work pressure and time constraints.

What daughter wouldn't have done the same to save her Dad? Her only regret was the kid in the van who had to watch his own Dad be executed by a law enforcement officer. SBI had analyzed the video evidence and found her actions justifiable, just as Johnston knew they would—but it still *was* an execution. That fact had kept her from having a peaceful night's rest for almost five years. Something about taking a human life changed you, she could see—even under justifiable circumstances.

Scarlett shook her head to clear her mind. But the clarity gained from that only brought up more questions. Why the strange text from Johnston? Had something happened to her father? Had Samoa signed an extradition treaty with the U.S.? Was Johnston trying to weasel out of their deal or change the terms?

Scarlett, rather than grab a few hours' sleep on the cot in her office, began her trip to Macedonia Prison Farm at first light. Though she had put many criminals in the sprawling complex, she had never visited the place before.

When she rolled to a stop at the guardhouse the guard inside snapped to attention and fired off a brisk salute. Scarlett returned the salute and waited until the guard pushed his clipboard through her window before she said, "Good Morning."

"Good morning, Sheriff."

"Just curious, do all incoming officers receive a salute?"

"I'm originally from Slick Rock County, Sheriff. I know what you did to clean up that place. I'm a big fan, and so is my family."

"Well, thank you." Scarlett sat up taller in her seat and took the clipboard from the guard. "I'm here to see some prisoners, just want to make sure they're here before I sign in."

"What's their names?"

"William Johnston and—"

"Yes, ma'am. Johnston and Kress came in bright and early yesterday morning."

"OK, that's what I heard, but aren't they Federal prisoners? Just wanted to make sure someone hadn't gotten their wires crossed?"

"I don't know about wires crossed, but they're both here. I processed the transport detail in myself. Anything else, Sheriff?"

"No, thank you."

"Don't forget to print and sign by your name, ma'am."

Macedonia Prison Farm is a 5,000-acre prison in eastern N.C. that started out as housing for prisoners with life sentences who worked on chain gangs. In the early 1900's, the state, intent on making sure the prisoners paid their debt to society, put the inmates to work farming and building their own housing. Eventually, the prison switched over to being a medium-custody facility and introduced vocational and adult educational classes to prepare the inmates for jobs when they returned to society. Though Johnston and Kress had absolutely no right ever to belong in society again.

On her walk from the superintendent's office, Scarlett noticed a buff man holding a feeding bucket and waving for her to join him on a bench near a catfish pond. Until she could see his face, she had no idea who he was. "You must be living well?" Scarlett said, and sat down beside Johnston. "I didn't recognize you."

William Johnston, put his bucket down stood and slid his hands over his sculpted buttocks. "Loving well, actually, but unfortunately I'm in between, uh *gigs*."

"Johnston, you perverted, bastard! Why would I want to hear that?"

"Now, Sheriff." Johnston, said pouting a little. "Oh, never mind, but I *am* 'living well,' so to speak. Hope your father is in good health?"

"He's existing, but he knows that good health awaits him in Samoa."

Johnston reached out to shake Scarlett's hand.

"Get that nasty grabber out of my face, Johnston, no telling where it's been."

"Now, Sheriff, how are we ever going to become real friends if you keep hurting my feelings?"

"Our deal doesn't call for that, Johnston, and when does Dad move to Samoa?"

Johnston pulled his hand back and wiped it on his pants leg. "There's a little glitch, so we need to talk."

"First, let's talk about your little killing spree. That wasn't supposed to start until my Dad and—"

"You mean Walter's ex?"

"And others!"

Johnston kicked his feed bucket across the path.

"That's the reason for my message! We saw that idiot, Cape Thomas, yelling at the top of his lungs on live TV while he's being arrested that Walter Kress controls the Charlotte PD. The heat his little tirade put on us doesn't help our pardon situation," Johnston said. "Not that we aren't pleased that the slut and her half-breed kid are gone, but we didn't order those killings."

"Come on. I know your plans, so don't lie to me!"

Johnston eyed the prison yard like a bird of prey out for a juicy morsel to calm the sheriff. "Until you've lived years in a 6' x 8' cell, you can't appreciate the simple wonders outside even on a prison farm. The sun on your face, a sudden breeze, crickets chirping, birds singing, and thunderstorms. People on the outside take them for granted every day. As long as you are on the outside you never think about them, but once you're locked in behind prison walls, you yearn for them like crazy! You think about them all the time, just hoping you don't forget your memories of them—the simplest things!"

He turned and swept his arms around the farm. "Yet, even though this is paradise compared to a concrete cell, it's still prison. A place where eyes and ears are always watching and listening. This is not living, Sheriff. It's barely existing. Walter and I have never aspired to merely exist. We're movers and shakers—people who make a difference in the world. We can't spend any more time being irrelevant and cooped up. We want back in the game of life." Johnston leaned in close and Scarlett stepped back. "I'm telling you the truth, Sheriff. So listen carefully—find out who is doing these killings and stop them before they do more damage to our chances for pardons."

"We want the same things as you, but I don't have jurisdiction where the murders occurred." Scarlett said.

"That may be, but the next likely target lives in your jurisdiction."

"You mean Cape Thomas?"

"Exactly."

"Never thought you'd want Cape Thomas protected?"

"You know why we have to do that. Cape Thomas thinks we're behind the killings. He blabs about it all the time. If anything happens to him, people are going to think we killed him too, and for good reason, I might add.

"Whoever is doing these killings is after Cape Thomas—he's the next logical victim. That puts you in a position to solve this case. After you do, you and your father will live a life like you were accustomed to in South Carolina. Perhaps even better. But I promise you this, if Thomas screws up our pardons, you'll live with the nightmares of the inch-by-inch execution your father suffers."

Scarlett thought of her options. She had only two. Option one: If she didn't work with Johnston and Kress to help them with pardons, her dad was as good as dead. If she helped them get pardons, there was a high likelihood Johnston and Kress would double cross her and the people who feared her dad's dead man's dump.

"How did you manage to get out of the Federal system, anyway?"

"Less call it a flaw in the legal system, but that's not important. What is important is that we avoid publicity. Our return to the state prison system caused nary a murmur from the general public because we were on the back-burner, forgotten. With our new status as medium-security prisoners, we can easily win our pardons. Unless publicity from these murders spotlights us, again."

"You have no involvement whatsoever in the Charlotte murders?"

"Well, I must admit, that poor Walter was so looking forward to adding some excruciatingly painful touches to Allison Moore Kress's demise. But you can eliminate us as suspects, Sheriff. That puts you way ahead of this Taskforce chasing dead-end leads that they hope connect us to the case. "

Not even a hint of remorse that five people were murdered. Just some regret that Ally and Celine's deaths weren't more painful because he and Walter were denied the pleasure of torturing them. "I'm only one person, Johnston, it's hardly fair to expect me to do alone what a task force can't do."

"You're a Sheriff! Use all your departments resources! Find out who is doing this and stop them before the public heat becomes too great on our politician friends. If that happens, the money-grubbing cowards will *never* pardon us. If we don't get those pardons we can't generate cash. If we can't generate cash—and I hate to keep belaboring the point—you know what happens to your father."

"I thought my father was good to go. Solving this case wasn't part of our deal. Besides, if you get pardons before my dad gets to Samoa, what guarantee do we have that you'll follow through?"

"Even though the pardons will free us, we still have to depend on our friends' influence to get us back in the game. Trust me, we don't want to start life over at the bottom."

"Why is my father in more danger now, then?"

"Things change, Sheriff. Just like the blood suckers that raised the ransom for your father. We paid half and the other half is to be kept in escrow until you and your father are safe in Samoa."

"So what's the problem?"

"We don't have the cash to pay into escrow. They won't notice the shortage until the due date a few months away."

"How can I help with that? Sheriff's don't make that kind of money. And just so you know: Slick Rock is a poor county. My department has very few resources!"

Johnston watched a cardinal hopping along the edge of the catfish pond. In a quick flutter the bird speared a rhino beetle and secure its breakfast. "Jackpot!" Johnston whispered.

"Excuse me?"

"Jackpot, Sheriff"

"You lost me." Scarlett said.

"You heard of the Fisher family fortune?"

"Who hasn't? Some people think it's code for Mr. Fisher's wealth, others think it's some hidden treasure worth millions just waiting to be discovered."

"It's the latter, Sheriff, and not millions, *hundreds* of millions."

"And we know this, how?"

"Walter and I put the money there."

"Well, tell me more."

"I'd rather not say any more—like I said there are too many eyes and ears watching us in prison. The clock is ticking, Sheriff. We have to be out of here to gain access to the Fisher family fortune, but political terms end in January—so pardons must be announced before then."

"You know where the fortune is?"

"No, but we have an idea, and we know for sure it still exists. I can't talk about it. I want to know what your plans are to solve this murder case and clear us."

"It's almost impossible to solve a case like this in that length of time."

"Then do the impossible, Sheriff. There's a lot riding on it! How much do you know about the case?"

Scarlett briefed Johnston on Cape Thomas and her call to the lead detective, Darius Martin.

"What about the coffin and nooses, you didn't mention those?" Johnston asked.

"How do you know about the coffins, or the nooses?"

"The better question, Sheriff, is why didn't you tell me everything you knew about them?"

"I've seen only one noose and all I know about the coffin is what Cape Thomas told me yesterday."

Johnston looked around the yard and motioned for Scarlett to lean closer. "The cops don't know this yet, but the coffin was hand made by a source who built many custom pieces for Walter's banks. Walter recognized the craftsmanship as soon as he saw pictures of the coffin. The coins are very rare, but after checking, I saw they are coins from a collection Walter started years ago. That ties Walter to this case. I haven't been able to verify this yet, but I'm almost certain the cord the nooses are made from is manufactured by a company I foreclosed on when they couldn't pay my firm's legal fees. We're being framed, and once someone connects all those dots, Walter and I will be headlines in every news outlets across the country."

"How do you know all this?"

"Our little smuggled prepaid phones are good for getting messages out, but information also flows in, even behind prison walls, my dear."

"Maybe so, but only one explanation matches the information you have," Scarlett said.

"Impress me, Sheriff."

"You have an inside source who is on the task force, don't you?"

Johnston thought back to all the high-profile inside information sources his firms had paid in various non-traceable compensation. During political season all anyone talked about was the 'broken system' and how to fix it. The system, whether the public cared to know it or not, was in perfect working order and yes, it *was* rigged. Influence, was, is, and always will be for sale. Just as every person had a price, and no one was better at exploiting that fact than he was.

"Answer my question, Johnston." Scarlett said. "Who do you have on the task force? I don't have all day!"

"I'm sorry. My mind was wandering to one of my favorite topics, politics."

"Only because you *own* most of the politicians."

Johnston smiled with a half-lidded glance. "Just as we own you, Sheriff. And to answer your question, we do have someone on the Taskforce, but I won't compromise them. Not just yet, anyway, though they have proven to be a little disappointing lately." Johnston shuffled his feet in the gravel —reminding her of Kress's courtroom footwork.

"I will, however, pass along to you what little information they have been able to ferret out. Although, I was hoping the dire situation your father is in would be enough incentive for you to bring this investigation to a speedy, successful conclusion."

"I don't need more incentive. I need clues, facts, and the latest leads from the Taskforce."

Johnston handed Scarlett an envelope. "And those, you now have."

"What if they search me when I leave?"

"They won't."

"What happens when I solve the case?"

"I like your confidence, Sheriff. Are you sure you don't have information that you need to share with us?"

"I have an inside source to the Fisher fortune."

"Cape Thomas?"

"Exactly. And I have the capability to monitor him 24-7."

"I really do wish you would reconsider becoming friends. We could use someone with your skills, making you a very rich woman."

"I want my father and a life in Samoa—and to never hear from you again."

"Feeling's mutual, bitch!"

Scarlett's scenic ride back to Slick Rock was interrupted by a call from, Detective Darius Martin. "We found a gray Ford pickup, registered to Jimmy Sauls of Slick Rock. The hunter killed down there?"

"Murdered. But yeah, he's the guy," Scarlett said. "Does the vehicle still have custom exterior lighting?"

"Yeah, looks like some safari hunting setup, plus a bunch of fog lights under the front bumper. Sound familiar?"

"Sounds exactly like the truck, Cape Thomas, described to my deputy when he was trying to explain why he attacked a woman in a gray Ford pickup on ramp off of I-40." Scarlett said.

"So you've interrogated, Cape Thomas?"

"I've talked to him—we generally do that before we read someone their rights, and only after that do we *interrogate* them, Detective Martin"

Darius Martin ignored the dig. Sheriffs were elected—they were politicians, not real cops. They could operate like Andy and Barney, real cops are on the clock.

"Mechanic here said, Thomas was skinned up—something about a bunch of kids chasing him. You notice anything like that?"

"Some minor abrasions on his hands and face, nothing serious."

"His story sounds bogus as hell to me. He mention anything about a dart?"

"You know, Detective, I appreciate what you're trying to do, but rather than interrogate me, why don't I get Cape Thomas to file a report on the incident? I'll even help him fill it out."

"Suits me. I guess if I have any follow-up questions I'll ride down there and talk to Mr. Thomas."

"Long ride, why not call?"

"Well, I've tried that, but my calls go straight to voice mail. I think he's avoiding me."

"Guess he doesn't like your interrogation techniques…" Scarlett said.

"He's a little high-strung. Looked like the type who could fly off the handle. When he was in jail he got into it with up a couple of punks in the drunk tank."

"I didn't get that vibe, but maybe you're right. When can I get that pickup down here? We need to go over it for possible evidence."

"When we saw it, it was registered to a murder victim so we turned it over to SBI. But it was wiped clean, very professional job, according to them. You can contact them if you want to know what they found. Only thing I noticed was some arrows that looked like lawn darts. I'm not a hunter." Darius Martin paused. "But my guys who hunt said they were crossbow arrows. That mean anything to you?"

"It's a long shot, but it may tie in to a report a man filed a while back. I'll keep you posted if it checks out. How about the your Kress-Seabolt case—is it connected to the Fishers in Greenville?"

"We've had some developments, but we want to play things close to the vest for a while—I'm sure you understand?"

I sure do, Scarlett thought, and I hope you'll understand why I need to play things close to *my* vest. "No problem I thought since Cape Thomas had set up camp here in Slick Rock County you might want to pass along any information that may pose a threat to him?"

"Set up camp? Doesn't he live in a mansion?"

"He does, but Mr. Thomas is a little eccentric. He thinks living in a shack with no power or running water will keep him and his family safe."

"That's why I never go down East. Too many unpredictable, hair-triggered backwoods trappers and moonshiners down there for me! Why make life hard? Rather head on over to Publix's to shop, then to a local watering hole for drinks. Now I love the beaches, but I don't stop once I leave Raleigh."

"Too bad, Detective. A lot of natural beauty and friendly people between Raleigh and the beach." Scarlett said.

"Well, in that case, next time I head to the beach, maybe I'll swing by Dead Rock and we'll have a cup of coffee or something—maybe compare notes?"

"You're welcome any time—and it's Slick Rock, Mr. Martin."

"Slick Rock, yeah. Like I said, I don't get down that way much. And Sheriff, just to clear the air, we'll get you a full briefing as soon as it's feasible—I'd appreciate the same courtesy if you come across anything."

"No problem, Detective Martin, I'll get back with you as soon as I do a little more investigating." Scarlett called dispatch and veered south toward Taylor Town.

"Yes, Sheriff?"

"I'm going to be 10-20 out at Minnie Reynaud place. Make a note that Cape Thomas is now living at that address. I put surveillance up on the place, but I don't want anyone else checking those cameras, understand?"

"Yes, Sheriff."

CHAPTER EIGHTEEN

Fixin' the old place up

Morning and thudding boots hit my porch at the same time. I grab my shotgun and roll behind the wood-burning stove. The cast-iron stove gives me plenty of cover and a line of sight through the open doorway. "Better make tracks, friend, or your shadow going to have a gap in coverage!"

"It's me, Cape." Jimmy said. "Don't shoot!"

"I won't, but I should. What time is it?"

"I told you I'd be here at first light."

A small nimbus of morning sun behind Jimmy seems to balance atop his head.

"First light? Who the hell keeps time like that?"

Jimmy ignores me, steps back off the porch, grabs an armful of lumber from the bed of his pickup, and dumps it on the porch, or what's left of it. The noise is deafening.

I sight down the barrel of my shotgun and consider the consequences of murdering Jimmy to get another thirty minutes of shut-eye.

"I went by the building supply place in Clinton yesterday," Jimmy says. "Probably didn't get near enough lumber, but it's a start." Before I say a word, Jimmy splays three boards across the porch joists and starts hammering away. I stumble out onto the back porch, and gather up a double handful of water from the cistern, and splash my face, prime the pump and put on a pot of coffee.

For three hours Jimmy and I hand-saw and nail boards until the porch is finally covered. In the process we work up a thirst that stale coffee won't quench.

"Want some water, Cape? I got some in the cooler."

"Water?" I rub my back and clench and unclench my cramping hands. "Any other choices?"

"Couple of sports drinks and a Coke?"

176

"That's it?"

Jimmy pushes the ice around in the cooler and slings the frigid water from his hands. "That's it. What you want? Store is just down the road, they probably got anything you want. What'll it be?"

"Oh, I don't know. See if that have a backbone with a few less miles on it, or a couple of hands that don't cramp so much. If they don't have that, I'll take a hot-stone massage from a dainty-footed geisha."

Jimmy shakes his head. "How about I just bring you back a whole case of, man-up? You're an embarrassment to the rugged individuals who built this country."

"Well, let me make a suggestion to you and your rugged-country-building friends. Next time you build a country, don't leave out the dainty-footed geisha girls, savvy?"

"Geisha girls?"

"Yes, they're a national treasure we, as a country, have failed to embrace."

"Boy, you airline pilots. Talk about a spoiled bunch! Coke, water, or sports drink?"

"Toss me a water before you get off on another topic you know nothing about," I said.

"What's that supposed to mean?"

"As if you know anything about rugged individuals."

"I slept on the ground a many a night in your old greenhouse. You never heard me complain about needing a massage."

I think back on some hurtful things I said to Jimmy when he stayed with me and I wonder why he's here. I wouldn't hang around someone who treated me like I treated him. "Yeah, about that... I'm sorry about calling you a grungy drug addict."

Jimmy gives me that old familiar smart-ass grin of his. "Guess that means you're just fine with calling me a good-for-nothin', sorry-ass-drunk, then?"

He's baiting me and spoiling for some trash-talking. I'm more than happy to oblige.

"I apologize. I thought, 'Sorry-Ass-Drunk' was your last name, Jimmy —"

"Well, that was my surname, but I've added a few letters behind it."

"Oh yeah? Like what?"

"C-P-A. You got any letters behind your name, Mr. Thomas? All professional people do, you know."

"No, but I have more than just three letters in *front* of my name."

"I'll bite."

"C-A-P-T-A-I-N, as in Airline Captain. What all little girls and boys want to be when they grow up."

"Okay, you win—never met a kid who wanted to grow up to be a CPA."

As we sip our water I remember back to the first time I met Jimmy Swain, A.K.A. Jimmy the Yardman. "You know when you first showed up with Grace, I was against you staying with us."

"I know that, Cape." Jimmy brushed off the toe of his new boots behind his pants leg. "Remember when I didn't wear shoes?"

"Yeah, only time I ever saw you with shoes on was when it snowed. How the heck did you stand that?"

"When liquor and drugs get hold of you, your only necessity is your next high."

"Yeah, but Grace was always buying you shoes or giving you pairs of mine. Wasn't like you had to pay for them."

"I had to make them last. That's why I waited till it snowed before I wore them."

Jimmy looks far across the field out front. The tears in his eyes soften his face. "You ever hear from Grace?"

"No, I never do."

"Do you know what happen to her?"

"Can't really say, all that time in the hospital kind of knocked me out of the social loop. Probably married again, kind of a hobby with her, you know."

"Grace wasn't like that!" Jimmy pulls his shirt sleeve across his face and wipes off beads of sweat over his brow. "She ever tell you the story about how we met?"

"If she did, Jimmy, I don't remember."

"Don't reckon you would."

"What's *that* supposed to mean?"

Jimmy cracks open another water and takes a long swig. "Grace saw me lying on a railroad track. She got me up and took me to your place— I never really thanked her for that."

"Yeah, Grace always loved a stray—dogs, cats, CPA's."

"It's called compassion—"

"Railroad tracks, that's a heck of a place to pass out, you big dummy. You're lucky she came by."

Jimmy moves a stepladder to the corner of the porch and climbs on. "Wasn't passed out, Cape. That was the first day I'd been sober in years."

I look at the man before me, and his confession starts to sink in. If not for the kindness of a woman I disliked for a long time, Jimmy Swain

CPA, wouldn't be here helping me today.

"While you were snoozing through first light, I put some tar on the roof. Should stop the leaks, but we need to replace some of these beadboard panels that water damaged." Jimmy positions his claw hammer in the perfect spot and pries off one of the rotten beadboard panels from the porch ceiling. The panel hits the porch with a 'whoosh' and clears the air between us as we stand regarding it a moment.

"I'll get Grace's number for you, Jimmy. While we're on the topic, I never thanked you for bringing Miss Minnie to the hospital and saving me."

"That was Miss Minnie's idea to save you," Jimmy deadpans, "I told 'em to pull the plug."

"Come on, Jimmy, I'm serious. If you hadn't have done that. I'd have died." I'm becoming way too emotional, now, like Jake warns me about since I left the hospital.

"I was just joking, Cape. You all right?"

"Yeah, yeah. I just get a little choked up thinking about how I treated you, yet you show up to help me in spite of that. Hell, Jimmy, to tell you the truth, you and Miss Minnie are about the only friends I have left. I appreciate you playing down how crappy I treated you."

"I was a freeloader—I deserved it."

"No, you didn't. It's just that for some reason, you were invisible to me." I said. "I mean I remember looking at you but never really seeing you. Not the obvious potential you had. I mean, my God, you're a CPA!"

"I was homeless for all those years before Grace brought me home. What hurt the most about being homeless was people looking at me but never seeing me. See, Cape, when you're homeless other people don't look you in the eyes. If you scrape together a little money and go shopping, well, you feel proud of yourself. Especially if you earned the money, which I always tried to do. And when you spend it, you want people to acknowledge that you're a viable part of society. But people don't ever see the homeless as trying to become better. They give you a handout or food, but they never see you as a person because they never look you in the eyes."

"Why do you suppose that is?" I ask him.

"Eyes are reflective, like mirrors. I guess people are afraid to look because they may not like what they see. Or maybe compassion is a burden they can't bear?"

"I never knew till today you were on the verge of taking your life, Jimmy. I wish I'd tried harder to be your friend. Guess I'm one of those people who looked at *themselves* and didn't like what they saw?"

179

"Let me stop you there, Cape, before you get back on that depression train. If you have a minute, I got a little story to tell you."

"About me?"

"Yep, you may remember it, but I doubt you will. What you did wasn't a big thing to you, but at that time in my life in made all the difference in the world to me. That day is the day I set myself on a path to be successful. You got time for me to tell it?"

"Only if it's a good story about me, I don't want to be reminded again of how bad I was."

"It's a *good* story, man!"

"Well...OK, then."

"It was during that time when things got rough for you. The bank called in your notes and you were scrambling to get money any way you could. You remember?"

"As much as I'd like to forget, I can't. Hard times."

"Exactly, and they were for me, too. I'd *borrowed* so much money from you back then. I said it was for food but it was for drugs. You pretended it was for food, too. I got high and I felt rotten for lying to you. I never paid you back, though I meant to. Then one night, you left your door open. I heard you calling around begging everyone you knew for a loan. That's when it hit me, that not only were you broke, but you also owed money you couldn't pay back.

The next morning I got up early and worked in the neighbor's yard— she paid me $100.00. I knocked on your door to give you that $100. I must have looked a little hollow-eyed to you because you said right off, 'Come on Jimmy. You look like you could use a good meal and I know I can.'"

"I remember that—and you paid for the meal! That was mighty nice of you."

"Cape, I'm not stupid. When the waitress took the money, you pretended to go to the bathroom, but instead you ran the waitress down and got my money back and gave her a credit card. But she came back to you and asked for another card because they rejected the first card, didn't they?"

"Walter Kress and William Johnston were putting terrible pressure on me and even went after my credit cards. Yeah, the place turned the first card down."

"Next day when I was working in the yard, I found the fifty dollars mixed in with the change the waitress brought back to the table."

"Why did you do that, Cape?"

"Well, I had a little cash on me and the waitress agreed to play along, so she brought the change——"

"That money wasn't in the change she brought back, I counted it. You slipped that money in my pocket when I wasn't looking. Why'd you do that when you were broke, too?"

"I guess that's the first time I looked at you as an equal. You looked so proud when you told that waitress, 'I got this.' Then I realized that was probably every

cent you had to your name, and I just didn't feel right taking your money."

"A man like that, makes a mighty good friend, Cape. That's why I showed up at the hospital with Miss Minnie."

"Jimmy, I was wrong earlier."

"About what?"

"About all the little girls and boys wanting to grow up to be airline pilots—the real smart ones want to be like you."

"I got a lunch meeting. I'll see you tomorrow, Cape."

I watch Jimmy's pickup until it disappears in a cloud of dust, finish hand-sawing the last board for the porch ceiling. No sooner is it nailed in place, than I see another cloud of dust kicking up on the path. When the car turns into the wind, Sheriff Scarlett DuBois' cruiser emerges from the dust. I jog over to my Yukon, pop a breath mint, and stand by my truck looking cool when Scarlett rolls up. "Afternoon, Sheriff, you out checking building permits?"

"You got one?"

"Nailed to that service pole that's soon to be energized."

Scarlett smiles, walks up on the porch, and I follow behind. "Boy, hard to believe you did this much work in two days?"

"Well, Jimmy helped with his battery-powered tools. Soon as I get juice, I'll be able to use my old plug-in ones."

"What color you going to paint it?"

"The porch ceiling, you mean?"

"Yes."

"Haint-blue, of course."

Scarlett busts out laughing. "Now, how did I know the answer before I even asked the question?"

"Miss Minnie would kill me if I didn't color it up to keep the haints away. She's funny like that."

"What self-respecting Southerner isn't?" Scarlett said. "All this work on the old place makes me think you're not going to take my advice and head back to Greenville?"

"Ah, Sheriff, can't we talk a little more about Southern customs before you ruin the moment? Questions like that make me think you're here on official business…"

I move in front of Scarlett to let her know she's not welcome to come any farther. "You know my invitation to drop by anytime doesn't cover official business. I'd appreciate a call beforehand if that's the case."

"It's a *semi*-official visit, OK?" Scarlett flashes a movie-star smile, "I need to check the trail cams…and I enjoy our little banter sessions. Is that such a bad thing?"

My watch-out-Cape radar is going off like crazy. On one hand I think Scarlett may enjoy my company, but I also know law enforcement can, and will, use your emotions against you. "Only been a couple of days since you put your cameras up, so what's the big rush to check 'em this soon? Besides, I thought they went through a satellite."

"Probably a glitch or maybe the solar panels aren't getting enough sunlight, but for some reason they quit on us."

Not that I know anything about trail cams, but Scarlett's explanations seems plausible…But it could be another sneaky police tactic. I don't care. Being alone is not how I want to end my day.

"You want to look inside? Jimmy and I tossed around a few ideas on how to fix the place up, you want to hear them?"

"Let me guess—you're either sticking with the traditional shotgun-house decor." Scarlett said, "or thinking about shaking things up with some worldly-airline-pilot-pizazz?"

"You're good! Definitely pizazz, but I'm in a real dilemma."

"Pray tell."

"I can't decide if I should go for a high-end swanky-Fifth-Avenue apartment look, or really blow the budget with a decadent Parisian Panache?"

"Why not mix the two?" Scarlett offers, rolling her hands like she's shaping cat-head biscuit dough.

"Stick to sheriffing, I thought you had potential, but you'll never make it as a designer, honey-child." I give her the old one-eyebrow-raised look Americans get when they venture overseas. "Where were you born—the backwaters of South Carolina?"

"Indeed, I was fortunate enough to be born and reared in that great Palmetto State, but not in the backwaters or backwoods." Scarlett said. "During my debutante days, unfortunately, there were times that I did venture at times to the lesser of the Carolinas—but I don't recall you being one of the gentlemen at those functions?"

Boy, Scarlett knows how to put a fine point on our obvious class differences. Her reference to the possibility of my attending a cotillion, brings up images from *Beauty and the Beast*.

"OK, I got nothing for you there. I couldn't get into an affair like that even as a server. Hate I didn't get to see you all gussied-up in a ballgown, though. I bet you were a sight to behold, and indubitably the prettiest girl at the ball."

Scarlett fights it, but a blush darkens her olive complexion. "You sir, are deceptively charming. Or are you just being nice so I'll stop bugging you?"

Of all the dumb things to do at this critical moment when I'm making headway, in what may morph into a beautiful relationship, I choke on the stupid breath mint. My eyes bug out of my head and my face takes on the baby-blue color that haints's fear. Scarlett bear-hugs me in a Heimlich maneuver. A couple of jerks later and the mint launches from my larynx like it's riding atop a Saturn V Rocket, ricochets off the wall in front of us, and bounces back in Scarlett's hair. I think about trying to brush it out before she finds it, but my need to breathe exceeds any chivalrous intent.

"You, OK?" Scarlett asks.

Cough, gag, another eye-watering-cough, a little snot-dribble down my chin, and I am OK. "Whoo-Boy, thought I was a goner!"

Scarlett plucks the mint from her hair and displays it on the palm of her hand. "Is this a breath mint?"

I barely glance at it. "Peppermint candy—I think?"

Scarlett throws the mint into the yard. "Wasn't striped like peppermint candy…"

"Well, it *could* have been a breath mint."

"Did you pop that breath mint, just for li'l ole me?"

"No, my mouth was dry. Don't remember when I put it in."

Scarlett gives me the squinty-eyed look of a prospector standing before a motherlode of fools' gold.

If you're a male reading this, you'll identify with what I'm feeling at this moment. You know when in spite of your best efforts you try not to sneak a peek at a woman's cleavage, but you do anyway, and she nails you? That's exactly how I feel right now.

"But why did you pop a mint?"

My cologne faux pas is fresh on my mind, and I don't want to get busted a second time.

"I didn't want to talk to you with stinky breath?"

Scarlett rests her palm on her nightstick and drums her fingers on the shaft. She breaks out laughing, doubling over, then I laugh, too, and it hits me. I haven't shared a moment like this with a woman in a long time.

"I'm a sucker for honesty. If you'd have given me a BS answer, I'd have teed off on you again. You know that, right?" Scarlett says.

"Yep, one blip on the BS-meter, and I knew you'd run me in."

Just by the look on her face I can tell the next thing out of Scarlett's mouth won't be good.

"How about rather than run you in, I escort you back to the Fisher mansion?"

"Sheriff, you're a real killjoy. How about you leave—"

"Hear me out." Scarlett looks hurt, but I'm not so sure I'm buying it. "Detective Martin found the gray pickup truck in Charlotte. Very likely the one that chased you down. I don't think they want this information out in the general public, but I don't care. Detective Martin also said he found a highball glass and cigarette with your DNA on it at Ally's?"

"The glass and cigarette came from my house. I told him that, but the jerk didn't believe me. So why are you telling me this if Charlotte PD doesn't want it to get out?"

"Because they found something in the truck that may tie into the attack on you here in Slick Rock."

"Where did they find the truck?"

"Near the police impound lot. They found some crossbow arrows inside...and I bet you donuts to dollars they're connected to the crossbow we found in your truck. I'll also bet those arrows match the ones I found at the creek."

"What! That's impossible!"

Scarlett's jaw drops, "You don't believe the crossbow and arrows are linked to your attack at the creek? You're the one who was screaming bloody murder!"

"Well, that may be true, but I don't believe any self-respecting cop, is going to bet *donuts* for dollars! *Donuts*, get it?"

Scarlett's eyes burn a hole thorough me, "This is not funny! Someone is trying to kill you. What happened at the creek the day we met was no accident. These people are serious, Cape. They killed Ally Kress and Celine Seabolt, and I believe you're next!"

"I get it. I get it. But maybe a little levity in the midst of people trying to kill me and cops treating me like a person of interest isn't such a bad thing."

"Well, it was kind of funny." Scarlett starts laughing again and tries to talk as well. "Donuts—cops! God, I needed that!" Scarlett wipes tears from her eyes and turns serious again.

"I have to tell you this, even though I shouldn't."

"Well, don't," I say. "Let's just forget about killers and cops. Let's talk about decorating this place—though you have zero taste."

"I have to—it's important and the real reason I'm here."

"Fine, go ahead and ruin my day."

"The people you're so sure are responsible for the killings, probably aren't."

"You mean Johnston and Kress?"

Scarlett, diverts her eyes like she's lying. I'm no cop trained to pick up on deception, but I know something isn't right.

"You obviously know more than you're telling me. If it's not Kress and Johnston, who's trying to kill me?"

"I don't know."

"Then why label *them* innocent?" I said.

"I shouldn't. Forget it."

"Does RH or the task force think so, too?"

"I don't know—I'm not included in their briefings."

"It has to be them. I—we put them in prison for Christ's sake!"

"There's really no proof that it is Johnston and Kress. Stop jumping to conclusions, Cape."

"You're jumping to conclusions. I'm standing on solid ground!"

"They may be suspects, but there's not one shred of evidence tying them to these crimes. I think they're being framed!"

"Why do you think that?"

"Because Johnston and Kress are prisoners up at Macedonia Prison Farm." Scarlett looks me dead in the eyes. "I talked to Johnston there today. He swears it's not them—"

"You talked to Walter Johnston…Today?"

"Yes." Scarlett admits.

"And you *believe* him? That is a lot more ludicrous than cops betting with donuts."

"Don't say another word until you hear me out!" Scarlett yells. She tells me about the deal Johnston and Kress have worked out to get into the state prison system and why these yahoo's are in Macedonia.

"Fine! Someone screwed up and they do their time in a state prison. So what, but I do care *where* they do their time. Macedonia is what, an hour from the Fisher mansion?"

"Yes."

"You don't find it a little funny that they show up in North Carolina just as Ally and Celine get—"

"They were still in Atlanta when Ally and Celine died."

"Why can't they send them to a prison in the western part of the state? Why stick them so close to Slick Rock?!"

"I don't know. I don't work for the Bureau of Prisons!"

"Well, I didn't mean to tick you off. Again!"

"It's not that. I'm letting my feelings get in the way of my job. I shouldn't have told you about Johnston and Kress. I could get in trouble for that."

"I'm not going to tell anybody…When you say feelings—"

"I like you, Cape," Scarlett says, "I guess during the trial when Ally spoke so glowingly about you, I wondered—nothing."

"Wondered what?"

"I wondered what it would be like to find a man like the one Ally described. I fantasized about my dad coming to find me, like you did Jana. But, my dad is not a hero like you—"

"I got lucky. I'm sure your Dad—"

"He's done bad things, very bad things." Scarlett's bottom lip quivers and I feel terrible for yelling at her.

"I don't want to talk about Dad anymore. I need to go check my game cameras," and she brushes right past me.

"If you don't mind a little company, I'm going to the Huck Finn place. Maybe you could join me there after you check the cameras?"

Scarlett puts her hand on my forearm. "I'd like that."

CHAPTER NINETEEN

Love is in the air...

As we arrive at the fork in the path, a sound like thunder or heavy artillery rolls across us. I glance up at the starry sky. "Seneca Guns!"

Scarlett looks at her phone. "Won't be long till I get calls to investigate."

"From who?"

"Non-natives who know nothing about Seneca Guns. I never knew about them until I moved here, either. First report I got, a woman called in and said some rednecks were shooting cannons at her house," She recalls laughing. "I believed her and went out to investigate. That story still gets mileage around the Sheriff's department. What do you know about them?"

"The phenomenon is one of the great mysteries of Coastal Carolinas —and the world, for that matter. Not even scientists know what makes the booms. Some theorize they're caused by earthquakes, others think a mysterious gas rises from the ocean and explodes. But they're all just theories. The only thing known for certain is that the sound that rolls across the ocean and slams into the land is real. We know that because sometimes the booms are so powerful they break windows in beach houses."

"Why couldn't that be earthquakes?"

"I'm no scientist, but only the windows rattle, houses don't shake. Pretty solid case for percussion, not so much for shifting tectonic plates."

"How do you know?"

"When I was a kid, I spent a lot of time on Topsail Island. Seen and heard it firsthand."

"Wow, so what do you think it is?" Scarlett said.

"I can tell you what my Grandfather told me. Naw, I better not tell you. That old story may prove once and for all that both sides of my family are crazy, not, uh 'special'."

"Cape Thomas—" Scarlett grabs me by the arms and spins me around to face her. "You tell me this very second!"

She's playing with me, but I like the attention and hatch a plan to get more. "It's based on my grandfather's original theory and I've expanded on it. Not a story an elected official, like you, would put much stock in—its based on conjecture and hearsay."

"Are you kidding me? A potential explanation of one of the world's true mysteries, and you wonder if I want to hear it?"

"I…better not. I've never shared the idea with anyone outside my wacky family." I walk off but Scarlett grabs me by my collar, stopping me in mid-step.

"If you don't tell me…I'll lock you up!"

"You know, since my stint in the big house with hardened criminals up in Charlotte, a threat of jail-time doesn't scare me…"

Scarlett crosses her arms and taps her foot—she's clearly tamping down a hissy-fit.

"A holding cell is hardly the *big house,* and I understand the, *hardened criminals* were two local punks sleeping off a drunk!"

"Career criminals—rotten to the core, I assure you, and we were in the belly of the Beast. Make no mistake about that," I do my best Barney Fife impression. "Yeah, time in the Beast hardens a man. Your threat of an overnight stay in your li'l Mayberry jail doesn't scare me. What else you got, Copper?"

"This." Scarlett pulls my mouth to hers, we kiss deep and passionately. Not a move I am expecting, but I can certainly learn to live with it.

"Now, Cape Thomas, tell me!"

"I don't know if my story is good enough to deserve all that, but I'll do my best."

"See that you do." Scarlett pouts, flicking her tongue across her full lips, then eyes me from head to toe. "And keep this in mind, mistah. I'm a Southerner, good stories turn me on."

"That being the case, let me give you a little family history. My grandfather was a lawyer and a religious man. He also was good at laying out his case, but he always let people draw their own conclusion…sort of like a jury does."

"I'm very familiar with the concept. Lay out your case, Mr. Thomas."

I grab the lapels of my make-believe suit and continue. "As I was saying before I was so rudely threatened, Nature is full of examples of total opposites. Thrust, Drag; Lift, Gravity; Positive Charges, Negative Charges; and opposing magnetic fields, just to name a few. These forces of nature are always battling, just as nature and mankind are constantly at war. We see examples of it every day, so we can agree it exists.

"Then we have God and Satan, and the never-ending argument of whether they exist. Conversely, there's little argument about the existence of Good and Evil. Most people believe both exist in some form or another. Yin and Yang, Karma and Fate, being examples. Now these are invisible forces, thus can't be measured or proven. Let us group all of the aforementioned invisible forces into two categories, Good and Evil.

"Good and Evil are manifestly a part of our everyday lives. Certain groups of people see them operating in daily life more than others do, but particularly folks in law enforcement, like yourself, see them. It's not so hard to imagine that every now and then, these diametric extremes get fed up with each other. Sort of like two drunks in a bar who have to take their differences outside. You with me?"

"Yes—and the scary part is, your logic is starting to make sense to me."

I give Scarlett the old evil eye and dress her down a little bit. "A simple yes would have sufficed, Sheriff." I tug on my lapels again and dive back into my story. "These battles are so devastating that they can't be fought in our everyday world. Good and Evil *know* they can operate on an apocalyptic scale and they also know that if they destroy the world, they destroy themselves. So the Two agree to throw down in a place on earth that's like a big padded cell to contain the damage. That place is right off our coastline, on the horizon where the ocean meets the puffy clouds— that explains the muffled sounds. Like our aforementioned drunks, they start off pushing each other a little, but eventually pull guns the size of cannons, and blaze away causing that ruckus we just heard. And that…is my family's theory of the phenomenon called, Seneca Guns. "

"How do we know who wins?" Scarlett said.

"Ahh—I asked that, too, when I was a kid. My Grandfather answered me with an old Indian adage, probably related to why the Seneca Guns have an Indian name."

"Well, who wins each time they have a fight, Good or Evil?"

"The one we feed."

Scarlett presses against me and whispers, "Your family's theory is much more compelling—even romantic—than the scientific ones." Scarlett kisses me again and holds my face in her hands. I can't turn my head, nor do I want to. "Did you mean it when you said you've never told that story to anyone outside your family?"

"Not that I recall. Why does that matter?"

"It just does." Scarlett twirls a tendril of hair and looks more like a budding debutante than a full-grown police officer. "Are you sure you haven't?"

"Yes."

"Don't ever share it with anyone else," she says softly.

"Why?"

"I'm old fashioned, and I've had poems, mostly bad, written for me. Once a successful author from Atlanta named a character after me. I've never had anyone present a theory to me that may explain one of the world's great secrets—only to little old me."

"OK, other than my family, I'll never share that theory with anyone else."

"Promise?"

"Scarlett, my word is my bond." I search her eyes and catch a glimpse of her soul. "You'll never need a promise, or an oath from me."

"I believe that about you."

Scarlett gives me a quick peck on my lips and heads off to check her cameras. "I won't be long. Maybe you can make us a fire?"

I take out my trusty Zippo and give it a flick. "That I can do."

I break off on the path lined with cinnamon ferns that leads to the Huck Finn place. My boots sink into sugar-sand and I struggle for traction. Now that the guns have quieted, only the whisking of my jeans against the dried fronds breaks the silence of the deep woods.

This path is, and I hope always will be, a portal to my childhood. In the solitude of the moment, I think of Ally. I push her memory from my mind and fill it instead with images of Scarlett and the excitement of our kiss. A pang of guilt stabs my gut, but only for a second. Nothing would please Ally more than for me to find happiness.

When the creek comes into view, I grab up two sweet-gum-balls and press different colored leaves onto each of the spiked seed pods. Not exactly perfect sailing vessels, but adequate for the contest I devised as a kid. Before the makeshift vessels hit the water I pick the red-tinted maple leaf to beat the yellow poplar leaf over the hundred-foot run to the miniature waterfall downstream. Halfway into the race my leaf racers get hung on a low-hanging branch midstream. Undaunted, I go back to the starting point and rig two more sweet-gum balls with leaves. This time I toss them to the far side of the stream where the current runs faster. The poplar leaf gets a jump on the maple, but once my odds-on-favorite orients itself down stream, the race is on. I trot down to the waterfall anticipating a photo-finish as the gum balls jockey for position on the turbulent backstretch. Just a yard from the finish line I feel a light tap on my shoulder, and turn, expecting to see Scarlett.

A pair of flinty copper eyes, only feet from mine, light up the darkness between us. I step back, sinking into soft muck and slide toward the rushing water. Grabbing for a limb, I expose my torso and my ninja-garbed attacker lifts a blowgun to her lips, firing a dart into my chest. As I did in the hospital room, I reach out to grab this form or the night nurse, but instead of disappearing into thin air, she plucks the dart from my chest, whirls around, and lands a flying kick to my chin. The force of her powerful kick sends me flying backwards into the creek.

Again I feel the paralysis seeping into and infusing my entire body. I cannot move, but at least I'm floating. My body, like the maple leaf, begins to turn and heads down stream toward the water fall. I hear the rushing waters spill over the poplar-root dam. As I yell, air rushes out from my lungs, but I am unable to inhale. Chilled water fills my mouth and trickles into my lungs. I manage to gulp in deep breaths of air, mixed with water, somehow staying afloat.

I open my mouth to yell before I go over the spillway but succeed only in filling my mouth and lungs with water. The pressure from the falling waters flattens me on the bottom of the shallow creek. My eyes are open, but the water surrounding me grows darker and even colder. I forget my surroundings for the distance place I've visited before. "*Hush, little baby, don't say a word, Mama's gonna buy you a mockingbird.*"

The water above me splits and a human form dives for me. I have no defense, and if the night nurse does nothing else she can simply watch me die. I close my eyes and feel her lips on mine. She blows a cooling breath of air into my burning lungs. I feel her grabbing my collar, and her feet plant firmly on either side of my body. We rocket to the surface and in two strokes she has me lying on my side, water flowing out of me like an artesian well.

Once the water stops draining, Scarlett rolls me over and begins mouth-to-mouth. I cough but am unable to breathe on my own. Scarlett does mouth-to-mouth for another few minutes till I finally begin to sip air on my own. "Cape, what happened?"

I try to talk but the best I can do is grunt. There just isn't enough air in my lungs to project words.

"Oh, my God, you've had a stroke!"

Feelings start to ease back into my body and I roll my head from side to side, "No! Night nurse got me!"

"There's someone here?"

I nod.

Scarlett unsnaps her holster and draws her weapon. She surveys the area around us for any immediate threats, then drags me halfway over to an oak draped in Spanish moss.

"You doing, OK?"

My dead weight is too much for her to move any farther one-handed. She holsters her pistol, grabs me with both hands, and gets me to the tree. For a woman, or a man even, Scarlett is strong. I struggle to stand but realize I can barely move, "Weak, but feeling is coming back."

"What happened?"

I tell Scarlett phrases about the attack by the night nurse. She walks over to the scene of the crime and picks up the ball cap that must have flown off her head when she dove in for me. It's the only dry clothing either of us has at the moment. Rather than put her cap back on, Scarlett gingerly places it over a muddy depression near the creek. A catfish feeding breaks water near the bank, Scarlett draws her weapon and fans it in front of her as she backs up to the oak. "I found a great foot print over there. I want to get a cast made of it. Think you can walk?"

"Not yet, but if you give me some time I feel like my strength's coming back."

"Obviously it was a poison dart again."

"Not a poison meant to kill, this paralyzes. And it's non-analgesic. I felt and knew everything that was happening."

Scarlett looks around, "I'd go to my patrol car and get help, but I don't want to leave you alone."

"Why not call on your radio?"

Scarlett unclips the microphone attached to her epaulet and taps water from it. "I saw a mass of bubbles coming up from the creek and figured that was your last gasp. I didn't think just dove in."

I take a couple of deep breaths and enjoy the purity of the cold air, "I'm glad you did. At first I thought you were the night nurse coming back to finish me off."

"Why do you call her the night nurse?"

I explain everything that happened to me in the hospital and at the mansion. "You pretty much know what happened in Charlotte, but I'll go over it again if you want?"

"No, but why didn't you tell this to the police earlier?"

"I felt like the hospital attack was my imagination, and so did Jake. To be honest my imagination still gets the best of me. I hear a noise and imagine the night nurse is there, even though I know she's not. I'm spooked, I guess. The other stuff I didn't tell because I thought the family was blocking me out of the loop. I realize now, that they're trying to help me, even RH."

"Does that mean you're giving up the rugged life and going back to the mansion?"

I really want to face Scarlett, when I deliver this comeback, but the best I can do is breathe on my own and lie against the tree, "Sheriff, we already talked—"

"Before you answer. You need to know this. The trail cameras didn't stop working. As a matter of fact, other than the lenses being painted over in black, they work just fine."

So even at my best the night nurse is able to come onto the property without me having a clue. She's also able to avoid detection by some fairly sophisticated surveillance equipment. "You think she's still out there?"

"Maybe," Scarlett says as she moves into the darkness away from the creek and me. I hear leaves rustling and branches snapping. When the noise stops I call out, "Scarlett, you doing that?"

Scarlett eases down beside me and whispers, "Yes, I put up a perimeter around us. Unless she's a ghost, too, she's going to make some noise getting to us—or walk on water."

"I wouldn't be so sure of her making any noise. She got right up on me with that blowgun, and I never heard her." As soon as I say that I start shivering uncontrollably, "Chills." I said.

"Hold on, maybe I can help with that." I barely see Scarlett in my peripheral vision, but I'm pretty sure she has a couple of 9 mm cartridges in her hands. She presses them against a small river rock, works the bullet away from the cartridge, and pours the gunpowder on top of the rock. Scooping up some dried leaves and small twigs, she places them on the rock with the powder. A few strikes against another rock and an errant spark brings her project to life. She blows softly into the smoking heap and the glowing embers illuminate her profile.

I notice for the first time that the tendril of dark hair she twisted earlier is highlighted with steaks of gray. A flickering tongue of flame reflects off her blue eyes and almost flawless olive skin. Only the fine lines around her eyes and lips suggest she is a day over forty. Once again, Scarlett purses her full lips and blows into the half-lit tinder cupped in her hands. From the ambient light, I realize just how exquisite she is. The woman before me would fit nicely onto any TV or movie screen across America and I can't take my eyes off her.

She lifts her watering eyes from the smoking pile, coughs, sniffles, and gives me a demure smile. "Whooo, that smoke got to me."

"Probably should have mentioned, I still have my lighter in my pocket."

Scarlett sniffles again. "That leads me to believe you either have a thing for snotty-nosed women, or you have a sadistic streak. Which?"

"I'm ashamed to admit it, but I've had a snot-fetish forever. Some kids went for the pin-up models back in the day. I was always on the hunt for that elusive, watery-eyed, snotty-nosed woman."

Scarlett puckers up and tries to plant a runny-nose kiss on me. I turn away but in the process slip lower down the tree trunk.

"I should let you lie there, you know," She chuckles.

"Probably not a bad idea." I look beyond the rim of light cast around us. "Won't the fire make us better targets?"

"Strangely enough, I took a statistical weapons course once and blow guns were included. If memory serves, anything past 60 feet and the accuracy drops off sharply."

"That's pretty far if you think about it."

"That distance would also require a direct line of fire. With all the vegetation in this place, she would have to be much closer," Scarlett pats her 9 mm, "and then she would be at a distinct disadvantage."

"Jeez, I'm cold."

Scarlett gathers some small branches and tosses them onto the fire, "Won't be long and the heat should reach you. I'm going to help you get your shirt off so I can wring it out. It'll dry quicker."

As Scarlett struggles with my shirt I can't help but notice her firm, tight body pressing against her wet clothes. Her breasts are full and sway naturally as she gives my shirt another firm tug. "Ah, success," she says, and lifts my shirt above her head. She ties one end of the shirt to a small sapling, and wrings out more water. Like a *bona fide* survivalist, she breaks off a forked branch, jabs it in the ground, and hangs the shirt by the fire.

"I take it this is not the first time you've done this?"

"Nope, camped all the time with my dad and Jon—Jonnie Boy, my brother. I'm a hunter, too."

"Really? You certainly don't look the part."

Scarlett snaps off another forked branch and pokes it into the ground. With her back turned to me she starts to unbutton her blouse. She slowly peels off the wet garment and moisture on her skin glistens in the firelight. "My Dad always said he raised two sons—I was such a tomboy."

"You sure don't look like a tomboy, or any other boy, for that matter." A simple case of what comes up comes out. I try to get off this topic. "I mean, it's great that you and Jon are so close, and—"

"*Were* close." Scarlett says without looking at me.

"Your brother and dad are *missing*, right?"

Scarlett moves our steaming shirts back away from the fire, "You know how you said you wanted to be honest with me when you told me about what happened in Charlotte?"

"Yeah?"

"I want to be the same with you, so this is between us, OK?"

"Sure."

"I'm pretty sure my brother is dead. I know my father is safe for the time being, but he's in great danger."

"I hate to ask a crazy question, but why don't you go rescue him? I mean you are the law…"

Scarlett frowns. "It's complicated. Let's talk about it another time."

I strain with my arms to sit up. Surprise! I can move myself up the oak tree a few inches, "Hey, I'm getting some feelings back in my arms. Legs still feel like two logs, though."

"Great!" Scarlett turns away from the fire and scoots toward me on her knees. "Want me to try and help you stand?"

"It's no use. I'm not feeling anything below my waist."

"Can you feel the fire?"

Her question is innocent enough, but as I look at her dressed only in a bra and pants I feel another fire stirring. A fire I haven't felt in a long, long time. "Yes, I do." My eyes linger over her voluptuous shape for too long. I cut my eyes away, but my point of focus does not go unnoticed.

Scarlett stares into my eyes, moves her hands behind her back and unhooks her bra. The bra falls away and she pulls her arms through the straps. Now she sits completely naked from her waist up. "Is this what you want to see?"

Over the years sexual desire is said to diminish yet I have not found that to be true. What does change among consenting adults of a certain age is the unwillingness to play, *the game*, or *dick dance*, as a young copilot of mine used to say. Perhaps the knowledge that there is more life behind one than ahead vanquishes the inhibitions of youth, or maybe frankness, like wisdom, only comes only with age.

"Do you want me, Cape?"

Before I can answer, Scarlett comes near, brushing her lips along my neck. Her wet hair falls on my chest and cascades along my lats and abs. She moves lower kissing my chest, then stomach. I feel her fingers undoing my belt and unbuttoning my jeans. Her kisses follow the zipper as she pulls my jeans apart. The cold night air and heat from the fire dances across our bodies. I feel her tongue flickering, circling, teasing, until the warmth of her mouth and throat envelopes me. For a moment I sense the night nurse watching us. Then I close my eyes as Scarlett moves up and down. If I die at this very moment, I die a happy man.

Scarlett stands, unfastens her pants and steps out of them. I watch as she straddles me and slowly sinks to her knees. She leans forward and her hard nipples trace lightly across my chest. Our lips meet. I wrap my arms around her and let my hands slide along the flair of hips stopping just above her buttocks. We kiss deep and hard. I cup her buttocks in my hands and guide her down on me. She makes a soft moaning sound as we complete our union. Scarlett places her hands on my chest and pushes herself up. She grinds and gyrates to a frenzied beat only we can hear.

I push into her, matching my thrusts and parries to hers. She digs her fingers into my back forcing me to press deeper into her warmth. I grab her hips and slide her back and forth against my hardness again and again and again. Just before I explode, Scarlett lets out a wrenching moan and collapses on top of me.

She inhales deeply and plants her breasts firmly against my chest. I feel the pounding of her heart lessen as her breathing slows. She snuggles against me and faint hints of her perfume tease my nostrils. With no concerted effort our breathing syncs into an easy rhythm that makes us one. I kiss Scarlett on her forehead, she looks at me and smiles. "It's been a while. I needed that."

I move Scarlett's open hand over my heart and press it against my chest. "You made me feel—"

"Stop." Scarlett stands and begins pulling on her clothes. "Let's not ruin a good thing here. It was fun. Let's leave it at that." Scarlett said.

Boy, my brain damage again. Dumb, dumb, dumb! "Fun! Yeah, that's what I meant by feeling—"

"You feeling better?"

I nod, "I think I can walk now."

"Good, let's get to my cruiser. I need to call this in."

Within 10 minutes of her call for back-up, Miss Minnie's place looks like a scene out of a T.V. cop show. From my perch in the ambulance I get a clear view of Scarlett surrounded by cops in suits, peppering her with questions.

"You sure you're OK?" The EMT asks.

"A little tightness in my chest, but other than that I feel fine."

"We're going to transport you to the hosp—"

"No, hospital!" I snap and immediately regret it, "My son-in-law is a doctor. I'll have way more medical care than I'll need in a couple hours."

"Sorry, sir."

"I *do* appreciate the offer. It's just that I spent a lot of time in the hospital." I said. "Please open this door for me. I need to talk to the sheriff."

I step down the steps and wave to her. She excuses herself from the crowd of officers and pulls me by the arm behind a mobile police lab van. " You OK?"

"Yeah. They took some blood samples for the hospital," I nod at the mobile police lab beside us, "and I guess these guys get some, too?"

"Good, if we find out what drug she's using, it will go along way toward solving this case."

"You're enjoying being Queen-of-the-Court over there?"

"Making a difference is why I ran for sheriff." Scarlett gives me that little mischievous smile of hers that I'm really starting to like. "Thanks for almost getting killed, Cape—this way I can be relevant in the Task Force investigation."

"Nothing I won't do for our local law enforcement." I rub the gauze bandage taped to my chest. "And thanks for your perfect timing."

The group of cops look at Scarlett. "Guess your friends want to hear more?" I note.

"I'm sure they do. I have to go, Cape." Scarlett grabs my hand and squeezes it. "But before I do, you know I was kidding about you getting killed, right?"

"I wasn't. A few seconds more and I wouldn't be here, thanks."

Scarlett looks at the group of cops. "I told the task force everything, by the way. They're coming by my office to pick up the arrows and I told them you would give them your nooses, OK?"

"Sure, I'm *out* of the detective business. I just want people to stop trying to kill me so I can concentrate on getting back into the cockpit. I really miss flying, Scarlett."

"That's sounds *sooo* nice."

"Me, flying again?"

"No, the way you say my name. I like it when you call me, Scarlett—it sure beats Sheriff."

I shuffle from one foot to the other, trying to be honest before she gets away. "It took this attack to get me thinking about my safety. You're right, I should go back to the mansion."

Scarlett covers her face with her hands. "Oh my, God, I never thought I would live this long—you're amazing!"

"Really, what did I do?"

"All my life I've heard of these elusive men who listen to advice from women—but until now, I've never actually met one. My heart is aflutter."

"Keep that up and I may not be willing to get killed next time, either!"

Scarlett gives the impatient group a glance. "I really need to go—forgive me?"

"Of course." I take Scarlett's hand. "I'd like to see you once I get settled in at the mansion. Maybe you could have dinner with us? Meet my family."

"I'd really like that."

Family? This is the first time in my life that I've asked someone to meet my family.

"So are you headed back to the mansion now?"

"Yep, via Wilson."

"Long way around. Your best shot is up Hwy 13 to Slick Rock and then it's a straight shot home."

"I know, but when Jimmy was helping me with the house he told me about an old friend of mine who has retired and moved to Wilson. As a matter of fact, her husband was my mentor, Sarge. I should have stopped by long before now." I look at my watch, almost 10:00 PM. "Hope she'll see me this late…"

"Oh, I'm sure she'll make time for Cape Thomas."

"I don't know. Not too many people have been glad to see me lately."

"You know I need to get out of these wet clothes. Shouldn't take too much longer to wrap things up here. How about I meet you in Wilson after you finish your visit?"

"I'd like that, but it may be late when I leave." I said.

Scarlett pulls me around to the side of the lab truck, away from prying eyes. You have your kisses, and then you have your world-class kisses, and then you have your, storybook-one-for-the-ages-kiss. That's the one that Scarlett and I share. Our bodies seem to levitate into an invisible sphere that separates us from the world for a few rarified seconds.

"What was that for?" I ask.

"A little incentive to end your visit early."

I remember Scarlett's earlier warning about not getting serious.

"Hey, I'm always up for more fun."

"Yeah, about that—I want more, Cape."

CHAPTER TWENTY

Seeing Betty Again!

Scarlett's mentioning the nooses on my backseat brings me to a skidding stop at the fork of the Huck Finn Place and Scarlett's trail-cam path. I grab the nooses and jog over to Scarlett, still the center of attention in the gaggle of cops. "You need these, right?"

She smiles. "Thanks, I forgot all about them," Scarlett looks down the path at my truck, "You, may want to get your tail light checked, it flickered—maybe a faulty bulb?"

"Will do, Darlin'."

Scarlett steps away from her associates and pulls me behind the mobile lab. Are we headed for another kiss?

"In front of other officers, address me as Sheriff, understand?"

I match her coolness with a little chill of my own. "You can count on that, *Sheriff*."

I jog back to my truck and buckle in, but before I shift into drive, a deputy steps from the side of the path and lights me up with his flashlight.

"Step out, sir, I'll need to check your vehicle."

"Why's that?"

"Sheriff's says since the perp hasn't been caught, nobody leaves until their vehicle is checked."

Scarlett yells, "He's good, Bill. Let him go."

The deputy looks up the path at Scarlett and switches off his light. "You heard the lady, move out."

On the drive to Wilson, I give Betty a call. She assures me the late hour isn't a problem and she can't wait to see me. Funny how five years has changed nothing between us. Especially in our case, true friends do pick up where they left off, no matter how much time has passed between visits.

Sarge is gone now, but I'll never think of Betty without thinking of Sarge—and I'm sure Sarge appreciates my sentiment. My feelings for both are easy to discern—my evolving feelings for Scarlett are murkier.

On one hand she wants to have fun, yet—she also says she wants more. Understanding womankind is beyond mankind's abilities! All I know is what I want—to find a love like Sarge had.

From the corner of my eye I catch a glimpse of the Zebulon/Outer Banks exit sign and slam on my brakes. In spite of my best efforts, I miss my chance to join I-587. Rather than wreck a dozen cars behind me, I ignore the constant nagging from my GPS to make a U-turn and decide to return to my missed exit via downtown Wilson. Not a drive I mind making considering Wilson's sights, the Whirligig Park alone is worth the trip!

Wilson, once a city of old-monied families, now embraces development and growth. The place has transitioned into a beguiling scape that draws the *nouveau riche* from nearby Research Triangle Park (RTP). At the same time, grand trappings of the Old South are on display at every corner and in between. Mansions built and bought with fortunes made in tobacco, farming, forestry, industry, construction, and banking grace tree-lined avenues and even the side streets of *Wonderful Wilson, its brand-new brand*. Mixing amicably in this bastion of Southern Aristocracy are young entrepreneurs and high-paid executives from everywhere who snap up these grand homes at bargain prices compared to RTP comps. As a result, trendy bistros, cafes, and malls have sprung up to accommodate the varied tastes of new citizen-commuters. Streets and thoroughfares are clogged with exotic hybrids, luxury imports, and high-dollars SUV's.

On the outskirts of Wilson, in the bedroom community of Sims, North Carolina, newer upscale subdivisions continue the luxuriant theme, and my GPS guides me into one of these lavish oases. I check the address again just to make sure. The street and house number on the mansion are a perfect match, but not a place I expected to find Betty Bishop. I note my arrival time, 11:00 PM and promise myself to beat my one-hour drive time on my next visit from Miss Minnie's place to Betty's.

Six Doric columns support a wraparound veranda with steps that flow down to an immaculate manicured lawn. I make my way up the steps and head for matching double doors, at least 12 feet tall. The door bell chimes for seeming minutes. Finally a college-age kid opens the doors.

"May I help you, sir?"

"I'm here to see Betty Bishop?"

"You must be Cape Thomas?"

"I am."

"I'm Ethan Warren." Ethan extends his hand and we shake. "Betty's expecting you."

Betty is smaller, more fragile than I remember, but still the same old Betty, except for the oxygen tube at her nose. What *is* different are her opulent surroundings—nothing about this place is like Sarge and Betty's old place. As a matter of fact, this place is devoid of every single thing that made their old house a home. No oversized lumpy recliner, no errant airplane parts sitting on the kitchen table or counter, or model airplanes scattered on the sideboard. Not even her prized curio collection she and Sarge added to on their annual trips in the old, broke-down RV. And the thing I miss most of all is the lingering smell of stale cigars. Funny how you can miss things almost as much as you miss people.

"Cape Thomas!" Betty screams. "Get over here and give me some sugar."

Five years melt away just as I hoped they would. It seems like only yesterday that Betty and I last talked. I kiss Betty on the cheek and admire the stylish divan she's perched on. "You look fabulous—and this place. Man! Looks like something right out of a magazine."

"Still a silver-tongued devil, you are!" Betty smiles and struggles to sit up straight. "Just a damn liar. Who the hell looks good with a plastic hose hanging from their nose?

"Well…not a look everyone can pull off, I'll give you that." I lean back and use my fingers to frame her like the movie folks do. "But, it'll take more than a plastic hose to mar a classic beauty like Betty Bishop!"

Betty goes into a fit of prolonged coughing and laughter. For a moment I think about calling 911. Ethan, in the corner of the room, gives me a look that says everything is okay, so I don't.

Betty clears her throat and takes a sip from a sports drink bottle with a long plastic straw. Her eyes sweep the room and settle back on me. "Well, at least you didn't lie about the room. It does look like something out of a magazine." Betty scrunches up her face. "But to tell you the truth, Cape, I never feel comfortable in this damn place!" Betty looks at Ethan who is smiling and rolling his eyes.

Betty ignores him and studies me. "What'cha doing showering with your clothes on?"

Even with the truck's heater on full blast, my clothes are still noticeably wet. "Long story—besides, I didn't come here to talk about me. Let's talk about our favorite topic, Betty Bishop."

"Fascinating topic, to be sure." Betty says. "But aren't you cold?"

"Naw, I'm good."

"Ethan, get Cape a towel—and why don't you go do the grocery shopping while we visit?"

"You don't like me shopping at Wally World, but they're the only ones open this late."

"Well, make yourself scarce, I'm sure you can find something to do."

Ethan, brings me a warm towel and shakes my hand again, "Good to finally meet you, sir. I've heard many stories about you."

"All good I hope?"

Ethan looks at Betty and they break out laughing.

"Affectionately told, if not all 'good', sir." That said, Ethan is on his way to Wally World.

"Who's Ethan, Betty, your nephew?"

Betty puts her chin on her hand, like she's really in deep thought. "He's what you call a, uh, gigolo. Does that sound right, Cape?"

"No, you're thinking of something else, Betty, maybe valet or aide?"

"Well, I hear it on TV all the time—hell, I can't remember. I just use him for sex," Betty says.

Oh, *please* let her be suffering from dementia. "Sex, you're fantasizing about sex—right?"

"Naw, I have sex with *him*. He's an animal, a real artist. He spreads me out and uses me like a blank canvas."

"Well, you wouldn't think it to look at him, he looks a little young—but I guess you would know…"

"Wait!—'Boy Toy'! That's the new word, Cape. Yeah, and the younger the better, as far as I'm concerned." Betty wiggles on the divan. "I tried dating, but men today just pussyfoot around. Self-conscious? Whoo! I like to get it on quick—down and dirty without all the malarky."

OK, maybe Betty and I *haven't* picked up where we left off. I'm not sure I've known this Betty. "Well, ah, there's something to be said for the—ah, direct approach."

Betty falls back on the divan in a laughing fit. "I wish the hell you could see your face, Cape Thomas. Ha, ha! Boy, you are *old*!"

"What?"

"What's wrong with you? You know I don't have no damn boy toy! He's a college kid who sits with me. Runs errands"

I'd like to answer but I'm about to roll on the floor laughing. "I jumped on that one like a hobo on a ham sandwich, Betty!."

"Oh Lawd." Betty tries to sit back up and goes into another spell of cough-laugh. "Help me up before I choke myself to death. Boy, I sure wish Sarge could'a seen your face!"

"I do, too!" I wipe tears from my face and try to picture Sarge fitting into these posh surroundings. "Speaking of Sarge, this place doesn't even look like a place he would visit, much less live in. What's the deal?"

"My family built and decorated it, but there's not a comfortable seat in the place. Well, except for one." Betty points to a corner of the room. "Get my walker, Cape. We'll go back there and do our visiting. You gonna love it!"

Betty walks and I hold onto her arm. We stop in front of a plain door that looks nothing like the other doors we've passed. "Press that button."

I do as I'm told and the door opens revealing a small elevator. We cram into the tight quarters. "I fought them tooth and nail over this, but I got what I wanted even if it is in the garage."

The elevator goes up two floors and the door opens. I immediately recognize an almost exact replica of Sarge's airport office in Goldsboro. It's not perfect, but if I woke up drunk in the place, I'd think I was back in Sarge's office. Even the air has a lingering smell of cigars.

"If you're wondering about the smell, I come in here every day or so and smoke a cigar." Betty confesses.

"But you hated his cigars, huh?"

"I did, but it didn't take me long to realize if I lost that smell, I'd lose, Sarge." Betty wipes at the tears quick to her eyes. "I just couldn't bear that, Cape. For sixty years we stood hand in hand, us against the world, and I loved every minute of it."

I walk behind the desk, flop in Sarge's old chair, and throw my feet up on his desk—just like the old days. "This is great!"

Betty walks over to end of the desk and picks up a remote. I figure she's turning on a TV or something. The next thing I know, I feel like I'm being tasered with a bazooka. The jolt knocks me clean out of the chair. I pick myself up and check my backsides to make sure I'm not on fire. "It still works?"

"Like a charm."

"Why'd you do that?"

"You broke a rule."

"Sarge's rule—not yours. That thing hurts. I can't believe it works."

"You know, Sarge didn't build junk. I wish I had a dollar for every pilot he zapped with that thing. It was made especially for you, but he got a lot of others with it, too. He sure got a kick out of telling the story about the first time he got you."

"Ha! I even remember his name for it: Cocky-Pilot Shocky-Seat. He introduced me to it the day I soloed. He cut my shirttail off, like old pilots do, and he told me, 'Since you are now a pilot, that makes you a man. 'Have a seat,' Sarge said. 'You've earned it, my boy!'

"Like an idiot I flopped down and threw my feet up on his desk—and he zapped me! I looked like a cat clinging to the old florescent light hanging over his desk. 'Let that be a lesson to you, boy. Don't ever get so big for your britches that you think you can fill old Sarge's chair. You understand, boy?'"

Betty howls again, "That's just the way he told it." We break out laughing again. Though neither of us mentions it, no matter how good I get at telling this story it'll never be as funny as how Sarge told it.

"Sit back down, Cape."

"Betty, I haven't got so big for my britches that I think I can fill Sarge's chair. I don't need another reminder. That thing's got a kick like a thunderbolt!"

"Ah, sit down. I won't shock you again." Now, I trust Betty and love her, too. But, I'm not stupid.

"Naw, like I said, I'll pass."

"Oh, sit down. There's something in the desk drawer I want you to see."

Reluctantly, I sit down again, but keep a wary eye on Betty and the remote.

"Quit being so skittish and pull the drawer out. I'm not going to shock you again, I promise."

I see Betty's finger move as she presses another button on the remote. I jump out of the chair before it shocks me. Then, to my surprise the whole wall in front of us moves up like a hangar door. I see my truck parked on the street outside. "Well, I'll be! From outside it looks just like an exterior wall."

"I know. The entire east wall is a facade. It's the only way the HOA would agree for me to have my hangar door."

"Home Owner's Association?"

"Hitler's Old A-holes, if you ask me! I swear it's like living in a Communist country! Better drive you truck in here, or they'll tow it."

I pull my truck inside and drop my windows so Sarge's cigar scent can permeate it. I miss that smell, too. As soon as I join Betty on the balcony overlooking the garage, she points at the desk drawer, "There's something in there that I want you to have."

I'm a little wary of another one of Sarge's booby traps. Like I said, I trust Betty, but I still ease the desk drawer open. In front of me is a picture album. Written across the top of the book in Sarge's chicken scratch are the words: **Captain Cape Thomas.**

I open the album. The first picture I see is that rebellious day I showed up at the airport against my grandfather's wishes. The next picture is of me taking my first flying lesson and a picture from the day I soloed. Written across each of them are the same words as on the cover of the album **Captain Cape Thomas**. The last picture in the album is of me in my captain's uniform standing in front of my 747. Across this picture are the words: **Best stick-and-rudder pilot in the skies. Good job, boy!**

"You know I was with him the day he bought that album," Betty said. "It was the day after you took your first lesson."

"When did he add 'Captain Cape Thomas'?"

"The same day he brought it. He knew it was your destiny. He never told you, but I can't count the times he's shown that album to pilots and passengers passing through the airport. When he got to that last picture of you, he'd puff out his chest and say, 'That's him today, a 20,000-hour 747 captain with AeroMax Airlines. You find yourself flying with him, you're flying with the best, buddy. I trained him!'"

Funny how you know a man all of your life and never realize how special he is—until he dies. It just dawned on me that I never told Sarge I loved him. Then again, I don't think I ever told my Grandfather so, either. Doesn't matter, I'm sure they knew how I felt about them. "I'm glad I got to see this," I hold up the album, "I barely remember Sarge taking these pictures."

Betty points to a picture of me and Sarge boarding the first 737 I captained with AeroMax, "That one is my favorite. Sarge never was one for posing, I snapped it without him knowing. Do you remember what he was yelling about?"

"Like it was yesterday. He said, 'Cape Thomas, you might have fooled these people into thinking you can fly this damn airplane responsibly, but I know better. That's why I'm flying with you today. You try any funny business and I'm going into that cockpit and knock the crap out of you!'"

We laughed, we hugged, and we cried. "He's buried at Maple Forest," Betty said.

"Is that here in Wilson?"

"Yes, he was buried in our family plot. I'm from Wilson, you know."

"I didn't know that, and I didn't know you and Sarge were so set. This place is huge."

"My family is very wealthy Cape. But that didn't matter to Sarge. He wouldn't let me spend a dime of family money on him. We always lived off his salary. You *know* how he was."

"Sarge had his pride—a lot like my grandfather in that regard. I wish they could come back for just a visit so I could tell'em I loved them. Pretty sure I never did that."

"They knew," Betty pulls the picture of me and Sarge off the wall and puts it in a packing box on the floor. "Hand me that album. I want to put that in here, too. I got some more stuff packed for you over there. It's got your name on it. You can take it now, or come back after I'm out of this place."

"I can't take this, Betty. You keep it all and we can look at it when I visit you again. I'll come and see you more often. Why're you moving, anyway—the HOA devils?"

"I'm not moving." Betty's eyes sweep the room before she looks back and settles on me at me. "I'm dying, Cape. Sarge would want you to have all this—so do I. You were like a son to us."

I hear Betty's words just fine. It's processing her words that I'm having trouble with. "Betty, don't give up. Modern medicine is amazing. Look what they did for me. I'll call Jake, he— "

"Cape, I am *so* ready to go. Living without Sarge has been the hardest thing I've ever done. Soon we'll be together again." Betty smiles angelically, "I can't wait for that day. You'll see us again one day, too."

I guess the look on my face shows her my thinking.

"You *are* a Christian, aren't you?" Betty said.

Unlike my pat answer for why I never married, this subject is one I can never seem to come to terms with.

"Betty, I tried, but it just hasn't worked for me."

"Did Mr. Willard know? He was a fine Christian man. He raised you to be one, too. I know that for a fact."

"I never missed a chance to disappoint him, I guess. I've seen so many wondrous things from the cockpit, I know there's something bigger than mankind. I'm just not sure the Bible gets it right."

"You're a grown man and you're smart, but you can trust me when I tell you this: the Bible *got* it right."

"Sarge, never struck me as a Christian man?"

"Strongest Christian I ever knew!"

"He cussed, and drank, and Sarge had a temper when he got riled up..."

"All those things are true, but hear this: Noah was a drunk, Rahad was a whore, Moses was a murderer, and the Apostle Paul killed Christians. So Sarge was in pretty good company, and he helped lots of people, many of whom never knew—same as he did you. He fixed bikes and gave them to poor kids. He fixed people's cars and never charged them a dime."

"Is that why he kept all the old cars in his maintenance hanger?"

"Yes. He only worked on them at night when you pilots weren't around."

Funny how you see someone every day yet never pay attention to what they're doing. I even helped Sarge push those old clunkers into the hangar, but never realized how quickly they rolled out under their own power.

"He always said he didn't know if he could help them 'cause he was an aircraft mechanic, not a grease monkey'. He said things like that to keep people from thinking he was a big softie. That's why I loved him— that's why I can't wait to see him again."

"You make it sound like you have an appointment?"

"I'm going to hospice this coming Monday. Doctors don't think I'll last long—no fight left in me."

"But I'm not ready for you to leave. I love you, Betty. I'll come by and see you every day, it'll be like old times, you'll—"

"Now don't you get me to crying, Cape Thomas."

"Don't go—"

"My time here is finished, and that day comes for all of us, Cape—like I said, I'm ready to go."

"Can I visit you at the hospice?"

"I'd like that." Betty gives me a remote for the garage. "Use and keep this. I willed this house to you—"

"What about your family?"

"They'd haul all this stuff off to the trash pile. I know you'll make a place for it, even if you sell the house."

"I don't want to talk about you dying…"

Betty's eyes light up like the Vegas skyline. "Me, either! Let's talk about your love life!"

"On second thought, let's talk about you dying." I shrug my shoulders. "I got nothing on my love life."

"Aw, come on, it's only fair. I told you about my, boy toy, and I know you can't go long without a woman. Who is she?"

"Well—"

"I knew it!"

"She's different, Betty. I can't figure her out."

"That's nothing new, you've never been good at figuring women out, but they never seem to have a problem gettin' your number."

"This one doesn't seem to want that, or at least that's what she said. Then she said she did, so she's kind of hot and cold, if you know what I mean?"

"Psycho! Better leave that one alone, Cape. She's into mind games."

"I don't know about that. Scarlett's really nice. I like her—"

"Let me guess. Extremely attractive, smart, and sexy."

"Yep. How did you know?"

"It's what you always go after, but in a few months she won't measure up to your dream girl and some other gal will catch your eye—"

"I'm not like that anymore, Betty. Ally changed all that. But I guess you haven't heard about Ally?"

"Haven't heard about her, but I can tell you this. Go back to this Ally, and drop the psycho chick."

"Ally's dead—murdered and that's why I have on this drip-dry attire."

"Oh, my!"

Betty's phone rings and I wait for her to answer it. Instead she ignores it, like she doesn't hear it.

"Want me to get that for you?"

Betty shakes her head and groans. "I don't bother with that thing. That's why Ethan's here. When he gets back he'll check and see if it's important."

In spite of her efforts to be sociable, Betty is drained—I can tell by her body language that our visit is over. "Tell you what. I'm a little tired. It's been a long, stressful day. How about I come back this weekend. We can go out to dinner and I'll tell you all about Ally."

Betty uses her walker to stand and leans on it to keep her balance. "Afraid I won't be much of a date—but Lord knows you need some dating advice."

"No, no!" We'll paint the town and have fun—nothing heavy."

"Well, if that's the case, you won't do." Betty points at the box of memorabilia and gives me a note "Take that with you, and here are the directions to Sarge's grave. Cemetery is closed from dusk to dawn."

"Why you telling me that?"

"Because I know hell or high water won't keep you from seeing him tonight. I'm telling you about the hours so when they lock you up for trespassing, you won't be mad at me."

"I could never be mad at you, Betty."

"I know. Call me if you need bail money."

"Count on it...Hey, your towel?"

"Leave it in the mudroom—it's the door in front of your truck."

"Got a shower in it?"

"Yep."

"Mind if I may take a quick shower? I got a change of clothes in my truck."

"Be my guest. Use the remote to close the garage when you leave."

"Want me to walk you back to your couch?"

"Nope, that's my boy toy's job."

"He's not here…"

"You're getting Ethan and my *real* stud muffin mixed up—"

"Say wha—?"

"Good night, Cape."

After I close the garage door I realize I still have the towel in my hand. I toss it in the back and head out to Maple Forest.

I pull the picture of Sarge and me from the cardboard box and prop it up on my console. The ride to Maple Forest Cemetery is like the cemetery itself, dark and quiet. As expected at this late hour, parking isn't a problem. I swing into a spot under a street lamp across from the school and give Betty's map a quick peek.

One look across the grounds and I realize I won't need a flashlight to find the Westmoreland family plot. Far across the graveyard, a 30-foot tall monument, just as Betty's note described it, catches my eye. The Guardian Angel, who has watched over deceased Westmorelands for almost 200 years, probably isn't used to late-night visitors, but for some reason I don't think he'll mind.

I hit the lock button on my key fob and start out. After a few paces I remember the picture on my console. I want to share it with Sarge. I turn back just in time to see my interior light pop on and right back off. My first thought is that I'm being broken into. I break into a run but recall that key fobs, like phones, can be butt dialed.

Once I have the picture it seems silly to lock my truck. Let's face it, denizens of graveyards don't have larceny in their hearts; even so, carrying out a crime would be a tough task. But ever since those nooses started showing up in my unlocked truck, I've developed a habit of locking it. As soon as I hear the metal thud of the locks and the horn beep—I head out for the monument.

In the past, graveyards spooked me, yet lately I feel a strange calm in visiting them. Maple Forest feels different. Even though there is some ambient lighting, it isn't daylight-bright. Shadows from the eclectic monuments and tombstones scattered about seem to move with me as I walk along. My footsteps crunching on the gravel path have a stereoscopic sound to them, almost as if someone it matching my cadence, step by step. A quick glance behind verifies that my imagination is playing tricks on me, but I am alone in the dark—in a place where I have no legal right to be.

I can make out some of the names, dates, and epitaphs on the tombstones closer to the path, but I use my keychain light to illuminate those farther away. Some have scripture etched upon them, others are adorned with angels or lambs. Not one of them elicits any emotion in me. Until my light shines on a glossy black-marble plaque near the Westmoreland Guardian Angel:

Hiram 'Sarge' Bishop.

Of all the thoughts and emotions I expected to run through my mind at this moment, only one turns up. I never knew Sarge's first name was, Hiram...*Hiram?* I shine the light around to see the other Westmorelands and spouses and children who share this plot with Sarge. Jefferson Westmoreland III, Lawrence E. Westmoreland II, Senator Carlton A. Westmoreland, and wife Priscilla Prescott Westmoreland, and dozens more, row upon row. Blue-bloods every one—I'd bet anything on it.

"Sarge, it looks like you definitely out of your league, buddy." I kneel in front of the marker and place my hand over Sarge's name. "I hope these highfalutin' Westmorelands are doing right by you. I'd have come sooner, but except for a little luck and a good doctor—I'd be in the grave, too."

A light rustling noise behind me ends the conversation. I shine my light in that direction, but the beam doesn't travel very far.

"Anyone there?"

Ah, my crazy head—acting up again. I turn back to Sarge. "I know you're feeling pretty flush in this esteemed neighborhood, and you have every right, but I got my on little eternal, pad of my own little eternal pad. I've never been one to brag, Sarge, but mine's made out of marble, not just the stone, either. Got my name carved on it, too: 'Captain Cape Thomas Loving Father'...thanks to my daughter.

"Yep, that's right, I got a kid, Sarge, a beautiful daughter you'd like, Jana. She's the spitting image of her mother, Laura. She's the lady you called, the 'one-who-got-away gal.' I got grand-kids, too. If I hadn't been in a coma when they were born, I'd pushed for Cape T being named after you, rather than me."

I hit the light by mistake and ruin my night vision.

"No offense, but I'd probably pushed for him to be named, Sarge or maybe Bishop. Hiram probably wouldn't have made the cut! I'll bring pictures of them next time I come." I prop the picture up against the plaque and lay the album beside it. "Betty gave me this album. I'm glad she did. I never knew you were proud of me. I kind of thought you always wanted to kill me because I screwed up so often. Now, some of that was probably due to our lack of communication channels—and that was a two-way street, Sarge.

"I never thanked you for giving me all those flying lessons because I was young and stupid. I told myself that washing an airplane every now and then was an equal trade-off. So I'm a little late, but thanks, Sarge.

I flip though the album and shine my light on a picture of my shirt-tail cut after my solo flight and kneel in front of the marker. "Remember this? You said it wouldn't make a good snot rag, and it sure as hell would never be a treasured aviation memento. If that's the case, why'd you framed it...you old softy! I miss you, Sarge. It must get lonely out here, but you'll have company soon. Betty is on her way and she can't wait to see you again. Now that I know where you are, I'll be a regular visitor. Probably bring Miss Minnie with me, too. Hadn't been for you two, I'd never been a part of the sky."

I close the book and notice some grass clippings from a recent mowing on one corner of the grave marker. I kneel and brush the clippings away. "I know this is coming late, too, but...I love you, Sarge."

More clippings are farther up the stone and I stretch way out to get at them, too. Then just inches in front of my face, I find a pair of familiar-looking black canvas slippers. The same slippers that nailed me on the chin at the Huck Finn Place.

At this range, the night nurse can't miss me with her poison dart. A shiver as cold as the marble tombstone passes through me—without someone around to resuscitate me, I'm a dead man. My only hope is to pretend I don't see her, then quick get the drop on her.

I gently place the album on the grave marker, talking to Sarge the entire time, "You know, you once told me that you'd always be there for me...DON'T FAIL ME NOW, SARGE!"

I lunge for the shoes, but my attacker leaps vertically and I wind up flat on my belly in the grass. I feel her feet, then her weight as she lands on my back and, just as quickly, broad-jumps off. A glimpse of her, and roll for cover behind a low border wall. A shadowy 10 or 15 feet from me, she somersaults and rolls between two tombstones. Her black outfit matches perfectly with the surrounding darkness. Though I can't see her, I feel her watching me. Scarlett said 60 feet is pretty much the accuracy-range for a blow gunner. I have to put that distance and as many obstacles as I can between me and this crazy woman—or game over.

I begin a slow, backward low-crawl toward my truck. In the distance, I hear footsteps along one of the many gravel paths that crisscross Maple Forest. I can't be sure, but they seem to be headed away from my truck. In the race for my life, I get to my knees then into a sprinter's stance, jumping and running like crazy.

Maybe it's my imagination then, but I feel fingers raking my back! Lowering my head, I sprint straight for the well-lit street. A wrecking-ball dressed in black flies across my path, so close I can feel the breeze. I dive into the gravel and curl into a fetal position waiting for the mortal dart sure to come. After a full minute and no telltale sting, I sit up. Just beyond me is the bright halo cast by the street light near my truck. Other than a lone dog barking in the distance, silence falls around me.

I fumble in my pocket for the key fob. If I make it to my truck and have to unlock the door, I'll be a sitting duck. Instead of unlocking my truck, though, I hit the panic button. My blaring horn goes into a spasmodic fit, and lights in nearby houses pop on! I don't know how to shut the damn alarm off. The best I can do is press every button on the key fob at least a dozen times. The Maple Forest Cemetery community is clearly wide awake by the time I get my truck opened and the alarm stopped.

Inside the safety of my locked truck, I see flashing blue lights atop two Wilson City PD cruisers racing my way at high speed. I think about telling the cops I don't know the cemetery is closed from dusk to dawn, but realize I'm parked right in front of the sign with that notification printed there.

"Show me your hands!" The officer, under thirty, yells at me as she draws a bead on my forehead.

I give her the my AeroMax Airline Captain smile and stick both hands beside my head. "Hello, officer." For the first time I notice that I have scrapes and cuts all over my arms from the tumble I've taken in the gravel. "I got spooked. I started running and fell."

The officer moves closer with her weapon still trained on my forehead. She motions for the other unit to cover the back of my vehicle. Another officer in the cruiser lights up my truck with his spotlight.

"Get out of your vehicle, now!"

As harrowing as this is, all I can think about it the call Betty will soon get to bring me the bail money—that woman is clairvoyant!

"Officer, can't you just write me—" Before I finish my statement the officer opens my door and snatches me to the ground. Two more cops pop up the back hatch, guns at the ready.

"What the hell!" I said.

"Mr. Thomas, someone from Sims Proper HOA told us they wrote your tag number down because you were parked on the street." Boy, Betty was right about this HOA's Storm troopers.

"They also said they saw someone get into the back of your vehicle."

"They must be mistaken—nobody else was in my truck."

"Are you sure?"

"Yes, I drove my truck into Betty's garage because I wasn't supposed to be parked on the street. So nobody but me was in my truck. I would have seen them."

"You're certain no one was in your truck."

"I didn't search, if that's what you mean, but yeah, I'm certain no one was in my truck."

The cop opens my back compartment and feels the carpet. "Have you hauled anything back here recently that could have leaked?"

"No, why?"

"It's soaking wet back here."

"Well, I tossed a towel back there, but it wasn't soaking wet?"

The officer gets on her radio and soon more police cruisers surround the cemetery, scanning the grounds with their spotlights.

"We got a call from Mrs. Bishop's residence. The caller said you were in danger—that's why we're here."

"Well, that's nice, but I'm good."

"Why are you here?" The cop looks at the sign with the posted hours. "Can't you read?"

"Betty gave me an album from her husband, my mentor, Sarge Bishop. I don't pass through Wilson a lot and I wanted to see Sarge before I left."

"So you ignored the posted hours?"

"I did. Are you going to arrest me, officer?"

"No, looks like you've been through enough, but don't do it again. Where's the album you mentioned? It's not in your truck."

"It's by Sarge's grave."

"Take me to it."

As we walk the officer shines her light on the path. I look for tracks but see only one set, mine.

"What spooked you Mr. Thomas?"

"I had a head injury a while back, so sometimes I imagine things."

"What did you imagine tonight?"

"I thought someone was attacking me, but I guess I imagined it."

"Does that happen a lot?"

"Only when I'm alone in dark places, apparently."

"Maybe you should avoid dark places?"

"I think I'll do that...Just curious, why are so many cops here? I mean I know HOA's are powerful, but I parked on the street for a very short time."

"The call we got from the Bishop residence said someone riding in your vehicle was going to kill you. We came as fast as we could once the

HOA verified someone was in your vehicle."

"This caller you're talking about, was it Betty Bishop?"

"No, the caller wouldn't identify themself."

"Sound like a young college guy?" I said.

"No, the caller was a woman."

"A *woman?*"

Our conversation ends at Sarge's grave, the officer shines her light on the album. "Is that it?"

"Yes, thanks, Officer."

As we walk back to my truck, I look again for footprints in the gravel—nothing.

"You have good evening, Mr. Thomas. And no more late night visits to the graveyard, understand?"

"You have my word on it, Officer."

As the cops pull off, I check my phone and see several missed calls from Scarlett. I lay the album down on the passenger's seat, but snugged around the back cover is a noose that holds a note in large block letters:

SO SORRY ABOUT BETTY, IT WAS FOR THE BEST.

CHAPTER TWENTY-ONE
Back to Greenville

I make a beeline to Betty's, calling Scarlett on the way. "I think something happened to Betty. Can you meet me there?"

"Why didn't you answer your phone? I've been calling for an hour."

"Yeah, I just looked at my phone—I'll tell you more later. The important thing is that I found a note from the night nurse on the picture album I left in the graveyard."

"The graveyard? What does the note say?"

"Hold on." I turn on my interior light and grab the album. "It reads: SO SORRY ABOUT BETTY, IT WAS FOR THE BEST."

"She could be toying with you."

"She wasn't toying with Celine and Ally."

"I'm calling Wilson County Sheriff's Department. It may be a trap! Wait for them before you go in."

"Can't do that. Betty needs me."

I park on the street, then halfway to the house, I remember the garage remote. Before I get back to my truck, a runt with a big flashlight blinds me. "You can't park out here after 9:00."

"Don't worry. I'm parking in the garage."

"You parked on the street before—"

I start for the guy. "I don't have time for this!"

"I'm calling the cops!"

"Do that, pissant!"

The garage door opens like its greased with molasses. Inside, I find Betty hanging from the balcony...just like Celine. The nosy neighbor follows me in, then runs off to call the cops. I push a chair under Betty and try to lift her up. Her legs are cool to the touch, though, and I have no doubts that she's dead.

On the stairs leading to the balcony I find the body of Ethan. A picture of Sarge, Betty, and me from the album I brought to the graveyard is pinned to his chest with a dart, like the one that missed me in Charlotte. But clearly the dart is not the murder weapon—I know his neck is snapped. A sticky note on his forehead reads: *What's wrong with this picture?* Ethan's body is warm. I check for a pulse—nothing.

I crawl along the floor to Sarge's desk, ease the desk drawer open, and pull out his service-issue 45. With my left hand I dial Scarlett, "Did you call the cops?" I whisper.

"Yes, they're on the way."

"Betty's dead and there's some collateral damage— guy named Ethan. I can't remember his last name."

"Why are you whispering?"

"I'm not alone."

"You think the killer is still there?"

"Yes."

"Why?"

"I'm looking at her."

"I'll be there in 30 minutes!"

Standing before me is my attacker from the graveyard. I have the phone in one hand and manage to hide the gun—that may not be loaded!—in my waistband. She motions for me to stand, then to stop, and pulls a Samurai sword from a sheath at her side. She must have watched one too many ISIS videos, but an over-the-top beheading ain't happening as long as I'm armed.

Snatching the pistol from my belt, I shuck the slide to make sure a round is chambered. She jumps back, ducking behind the desk. I know a bullet didn't chamber—she doesn't. "Drop the sword!" A command I would have no problem following if I brought a knife to a gunfight. Far off in the distance sirens wail and I get bolder. "You make one wrong move and I'll—"

Night Nurse up and flies across the desk like she's wearing a jet pack, then kicks me in the chest with both feet. I reel backwards but manage to hold on to my empty weapon. She steps on my gun hand, smashes the hilt of the sword in my temple like she's driving a fence post into red-clay, and...

When I come to I'm looking at the shiny patent-leather shoes of the cop who helped me in the graveyard.

For the next half hour, I answer a myriad of questions, none that seeming relevant to solving the murders. 'Course, I'm zoning in and out all the while. The cops want to focus on my attacker, I want to focus on my attacker's employers, W.Cronus Kress and William Johnston. When I mention their names, I'm told for what seems like the hundredth time: "Without some type of proof, or evidence Johnston and Kress can't be charged." Just as I'm about to lose it, Scarlett walks in. She stops to talk to the cop, who I assume is the lead detective, then comes over to me.

"How you doing?"

"Not too good, but a lot better than Betty and Ethan."

"I'm so sorry. They said you refused medical help?"

"I did."

"Why?"

"Let's just say I'm developing an aversion to medical staff…How did you get here so fast?"

"What do you mean?"

"It took me an hour to get here, you said your eta was 30 minutes when I called you. If you left from Slick Rock—"

"I was just over the county line. When you didn't answer your phone. I got worried. I came as fast as I could and I wasn't going the speed limit."

I rub the growing knot on my head. "I better let Jake have a look at this. Can I go now?"

Scarlett reaches for my hand, "I'm sure I can work that out."

"Good, I want to see Jana and the kids."

"Mind if I ride with you?" Scarlett said. "My deputy can drive my cruiser back to Slick Rock."

"Sounds good."

As we leave, my headlights illuminate the inside of Scarlett's cruiser. The person sitting behind the steering wheel bows their head to avoid my bright lights. If that's a male deputy, he has the smallest hands I've ever seen or the driver is female. Must be a new hire… But I'm certain Scarlett is the lone female in the Slick Rock Sheriff's Department.

For the first five minutes or so we ride in silence. I keep trying to get my head around something one of the cops at the park pointed out. "The cop said the back of my truck was soaking wet, I threw a damp towel back there, but the carpet shouldn't have been *soaking* wet. Do you think the Night Nurse caught a ride with me from Miss Minnie's place?"

"It's very possible—I tried to call you."

"Before your deputy checked my truck, you ordered me through the checkpoint, why?"

"I was doing you a favor. You were already running late for visiting, remember? Besides, how is someone going to slip into your truck with dozens of law officers around?"

"Good point."

"Did you stop anywhere along the way?" Scarlett said.

217

"No, I drove straight through to Wilson, and if the killer was in my truck all the way to Wilson, why didn't she kill me? She had every opportunity in my truck, at the graveyard, and at Betty's, yet she chose to let me live. Why? "

"Obviously we're dealing with a psychopath. Betty was killed to inflict pain on you. That's probably true of your family, too, if she can get to them?"

"But why didn't she kill me? It would have been so easy."

"Hard to inflict pain on a dead man. For some reason I think this has as much to do with vengeance as anything." Scarlett said.

"What if I had driven straight to Greenville rather than stop off to see Betty? I would have delivered the killer to my family!"

"First of all, you're only speculating about someone being in your truck." Scarlett turns and looks at the back of my Yukon. "But to tell you the truth, there were clues."

"Guess I better remind the guards to check family as well as guest, from now on?"

"Never hurts to be safe," she agreed. "I haven't discussed this with the Taskforce, but I don't think what happened to you at the creek was an attempt on your life."

"Well, that may be, but I sure thought I was a goner! Why do you think that?"

"Let's say you're right about the night nurse in your truck, and she's soaking wet, right?"

"Yeah."

"So why is she soaking wet?"

"Good point. She didn't fall in the water—so it couldn't have been her in the back of my truck, right?"

"No, Cape. If she had been in the water, she had another purpose."

"That's right—she knew I was immobilized, not a threat. But you! She went in the water to kill you!"

Scarlett turns and looks over the back of my truck. "We don't know that's what happened. All the same, I'd like to have my guys go over your truck. Water is a great destroyer of DNA evidence, but we may get lucky. Do you mind?"

"You can have this truck, take it apart if you have to. I'll buy another one."

I realize that I-587 is going to get us to the mansion much quicker than I want. Scarlett and I are making headway on this attack thing, but I've got other things on my mind. I slow for the Hwy 58 exit, and Scarlett gives me a surprised look.

"The scenic route—at this hour?"

"I want to hear more of your thoughts on this. When we get to the mansion, RH will dominate the conversation like he always does... Besides, I want to talk about us a little—do you mind?"

"No." Scarlett leans across the console and grabs my hand. "What woman in her right mind wouldn't want to ride on back roads in the wee hours of the morning, with a man who—"

"Isn't in his right mind?"

"Stop saying that!"

"Well, it's true, Scarlett. I'm not even certain I *saw* the night nurse in the graveyard. When the cop and I walked back to get my album, I checked the gravel on the path where I was attacked. Only one set of footprints, showed—mine."

"You got a good look at her at Betty's. I'm pretty sure you didn't imagine that, did you?"

"Yeah, guess you're right. One thing I know for certain."

"What's that?" Scarlett said.

"I'm starving!"

"No 24-hour fast food joints between here and the mansion. The perils of traveling back roads."

I check my watch. "Yeah, but if we kill fifteen minutes, Bubba's in Snow Hill will be open for breakfast. Best tenderloin biscuits in the state, and I really am starving!"

"That does sound good." Scarlett sits up, adjusts her holster and leans back into the seat. "I thought you came to terms with RH?"

"I have, and after tonight I'm more determined than ever to let the police handle this. But if what you're saying is true, and this person is willing to go after a cop, everyone I'm around is in danger, including, you."

"Please tell me you're not going back to Miss Minnie's place?"

"Do I have a choice?"

Scarlett's face turns beet red, "Are you serious? What if I hadn't been there tonight?"

"I thought you said you didn't think she wanted to kill me?"

"That's not what I said. I said she may have killed Betty just to hurt you. She's crazy and unpredictable. I don't think she has a set of rules to operate by. If anything, she's opportunistic. There may come a time when killing you makes more sense to her."

"OK, OK, but I have to know my family is—"

"Mr. Fisher has that place surrounded by guards and the police make regular patrols by there. If there's a safe place for you, it's the mansion.

Geez!"

Between my stupid statements and this slow-driving road, Scarlett is not a happy cop. At the top of the hill I spot something sure to improve her disposition. Bubba's of Snow Hill's flashing sign is a welcome distraction from the desolate stretch of highway and contentious conversations just traversed .

"They're open!" I say. "Let's get a biscuit!"

"Don't take this the wrong way—but I have an image to maintain. No acts of affection in public. I'm still the sheriff."

"Fine! Cuff me, smack me around a little bit before we order and they'll think you're on official business!"

"Don't be like that."

"Well, don't treat me like an idiot. I'm not going to be kissing all over you in public."

"I'm sorry." Scarlett smiles. "I have an idea, let's act like a normal couple?"

"Scarlett, normal couples *don't* act. That's what makes them normal."

"Can it, or I *will* cuff you—and smack you around!" Scarlett winks. "Don't try me."

"You don't have the nerve—I'll eat crow if you do!"

Scarlett smirks but doesn't respond.

We walk from darkest night into a place lit by long florescent fixtures hung from the ceiling by thin metal chains. Cinderblock walls are painted a glaring appliance-white, made dingy by farmhands, loggers, and factory workers who lean against them to recover from a long nightshift or snatch a little rest before they begin the dawn-to-dusk jobs before them. Vinyl floor squares, glued to a concrete pad, are worn thin from the constant foot traffic to a panel of beverage-coolers at the back of the store. Women behind the serving line greet the regulars with a nod, then hand over their usual orders already prepared and stuffed into grease-stained white paper sacks.

When Scarlett walks up to the counter the women stand a little taller, become a little more professional, and beam at one of their own who has undoubtedly made it in a man's world. "Morning, Sheriff, pleasure to see you here. What you want? Got your man-friend with you?"

"No, a prisoner. I'll have a tenderloin biscuit." Scarlett looks at me. "And the prisoner will have?"

"Y'all got 'enny fried crow back there?" I call out.

"No, we don't fry crow. Got some fried fatback for ya—it's real crispy."

Some people think Southern or soul food is too rich and fattening. I'm not one of them and apparently neither is Scarlett. Despite her little joke, we both wind up with tenderloin biscuits smothered in gravy. Our food comes in styrofoam trays that we take outside to an old picnic table under a tree. Each savory bite melts in my mouth and for the moment, no conversation is as important as finishing our food before the crisp morning air turns it cold. Scarlett finishes her biscuit first, and looks up at the tree spread over us. "Magnolia, my favorite tree."

I shake my head, "Actually, this particular tree is a loblolly-bay tree. Most people think they're magnolias, but this species only grows in the South. North Carolina is about as far north as you'll find them."

Scarlett gives me a whimsical look and a wry smile. "I'm impressed. I had no idea you were a dendrologist."

Now you know a man loves a compliment, something women fail to offer far too often, if you ask me. I want to deserve Scarlett's compliment, but I have an honest streak. "Well, I hate to disappoint you, but I'm pretty sure I'm not a dendrologist. Sounds like somebody who studies water seeping through caves."

"No, no—it's someone who studies trees. You were passing along some serious information about them. I thought you must have some background—"

"Betty taught me what I know. She knew all *kinds* of things about plants and gardens. Poor Sarge could barely tell the difference between a pine tree and a river birch. I often wondered how they worked so well together, being so different and all."

Scarlett stands, "Do you feel like stretching your legs? I love this little downtown area. It reminds me of my hometown."

I stand to join her and we head out for downtown Snow Hill.

"Well, guess this makes you a walking contradiction," I say.

"How's that?"

"You look very cosmopolitan to me. I'm a little shocked that you come from a small town—"

"Nothing small about Hartsville, especially not the people! My dad always said that."

"Hartsville, South Carolina? I think I was there once. Nice enough place, but your dad *was* rich. Why not live in one of those playgrounds for the wealthy?"

"I think the operant words are, '*was* rich.' Things change, Cape. Besides, you know that home is where the heart is. I mean look around, couldn't you live here?"

We're standing on the bridge spanning Contentnea Creek and the beginning of the Snow Hill, proper. Radiation fog clings to the slow moving tea-green water passing under us. A palette of late fall-colored leaves frame the creek. We turn and look up Greene Street as it rises out of the mist and continues up the small incline that probably gives Snow Hill its name. In the pre-dawn darkness each street lamp is surrounded by a tight halo of light struggling to burn through the lifting fog.

"OK, I don't know how you managed to ask that question with this view, but who couldn't live here? It's beautiful, something like Norman Rockwell would put on canvas," I said.

"Exactly." Scarlett reaches for my hand and we stroll up the hill, passing by still-closed shops and trendy restaurants that opened here to avoid the competition and costs of bigger towns like, Goldsboro, Kinston, Greenville, and Wilson.

"Do you miss all the fabulous places you visited when you were an airline captain?"

"In some ways, I guess. But like you said, home is where the heart is— and this area is my heart. It took me a while to see that, but I finally figured it out. I'm a country boy."

"Is that why you came back?" Scarlett asks the question I've asked myself a thousand times.

"It's strange, no matter how I tried to convince myself that I hated this place, something kept pulling me back. Sort of like what a homing pigeon senses, I guess? As it turns out, coming back here was the worst and best thing I ever did."

"What was the best thing?"

"Finding Laura, and eventually Jana."

"And the worst?"

"Meeting, Mr. Gustavo Jobim, Walter Cronus Kress, and William Johnston."

"I should have known." Scarlett brushes a monarch moth off the bridge railing and we watch it fly toward the street light. "You don't think there was a little Divine Intervention that brought you back here?"

"Maybe something intuitive, but I don't know about divine intervention...plus I really missed Sarge, Betty, and especially, Miss Minnie."

"You and Betty were close. I thought her death would hit you harder. Yet, you've barely mentioned her."

"It bothers me how Betty died, but not that she died. I'm so glad I visited with her in time. She was like a school girl smitten by the thought of a once-in-a-lifetime date with the boy of her dreams. She can't wait to get to heaven! She believes she's going to see Sarge there."

"You don't?"

"When I was a kid I never even considered that question. My Grandfather believed *The Word*, lived *The Word*, taught *The Word* and died content in *The Word*. After my parents died when I was five, someone promised me I'd see them again. To me, at that age, I thought we were talking a few days, maybe a month or two. But as I grew up, I realized that would happen only after I lived an exemplary life and then died. Guess I lost interest after a while."

"So you believe in ghosts, but not God?"

"I guess—but you're a God-fearing woman?"

Scarlett shrugs her shoulders and interlocking her fingers in mine.

"I wouldn't say I've lived an exemplary life. I'm a sinner and I know I've fallen short of the Glory of God, but I also know my sins are covered by—"

"I know, I know—Jesus."

"That's right." Scarlett seems to struggle before going on. "But my father is a little like you."

"Agnostic?"

"No, he's just as dismissive of Jesus as you are."

"So agnostic, right?" I said.

"Oh no, he believes in Jesus. It's just that he plays for the other team."

"What?"

"They say people should never discuss religion or politics. I don't know who *they* are, but every now and then, *they* come up with some real good advice," she says.

"So, conversation over?"

A car coming at us flashes their lights, then dims them. Scarlett drops my hand and moves to the inside of the sidewalk.

"No, just the religious topic, if you don't mind?" Scarlett said. "I don't feel like explaining my family life."

"I understand, that's a topic I avoided most of my life, too. Before I forget, I do want to thank you for coming to Wilson, tonight. I'm surprised the cops didn't arrest me for being the last person to see Betty alive."

"Cops, do what they have to do. They know what they are dealing with in this case."

"Well, Darius Martin didn't seem to be on that page."

"Detective Martin had every right to view you as a person of interest. So would I if those murders had taken place in Slick Rock County." Scarlett said. "You have to remember, I tipped off Wilson that you might be in danger."

"Wonder who made that call? Cops said they didn't want to be identified."

"I don't know where they got that. I suspect the only reason they responded that way is because I'm an officer of the law."

We get to the top of the hill and have a seat on a bench across the street from the courthouse.

"You're convinced the night nurse caught a ride with me, aren't you?"

"Yes, the more I think about it, the more sense it makes. When I saw your tail light blink I didn't think any thing of it at first, I was busy. But after you left and things quieted down, it hit me. Bulbs generally blow when they become intermittent. I asked myself what else could cause a bulb to appear like it was malfunctioning? The only answer was that someone walked in front of it. My view was blocked for a second by someone, but the bulb was fine.

"When I went over to where your truck was parked, I noticed drops of water had peppered the ground. There were also some very small shoe prints without a shoe heel markings. Since neither you nor I had been at the back of your truck I put two and two together. She obviously popped your back door and hoped inside. I tried to call you."

"That phone does crazy things sometimes. Must have silenced itself again." I pull out my phone. "Wonder if Jana's tried to call me? If she has, I'll need to call her back. She'll be worried."

The screen shows three incoming calls from Scarlett and one outgoing call to an Orlando number I don't recognize. "Scarlett, I've got an outgoing call on here that I know I didn't make?"

Scarlett looks at my screen, "Is it a butt-dialed number?"

"Yeah, that's probably it. But wait a minute—how does a phone butt-dial if it's not in my pocket? It was in my console."

"Maybe it bumped up against something?"

"Yeah…it's possible."

"Unless," and we say at the exact same time, "the night nurse called!"

"Scarlett grabs the phone. What time did you get to Betty's?"

"Boy, you cops are all alike. I just spent a half-hour answering that same question the cops managed to ask in a dozen different ways. I got there at exactly 11:00 PM, I left at exactly 12:41 A.M."

"How can you be so sure?"

"Same question they asked."

"And your answer was?"

"I'm an airline captain. Prompt Arrivals and Departures are very important to us."

Scarlett adds what every traveler in America can agree with, "Too bad that attitude doesn't carry over to the T.S.A!"

"Agreed!"

Scarlett pushes a button on my phone, "The outgoing call was dialed at 11:30 P.M. Couldn't have been a butt-dial."

"Oh wait, Betty had me move my truck inside the garage because of the HOA rules."

"What time was that, exactly?"

"Well, the Arrival-Departure time-check habit goes out the window when we are just repositioning things I guess?"

"You have no idea?" Scarlett asks.

"No, but since you mentioned the time-line thing, how did the cops know I was at Maple Forest?"

"When you didn't answer. I called Betty and she said you were probably going by the graveyard."

I remember the phone ringing away at Betty's and Betty not answering it. Why would Betty break a habit of not answering the phone? I think about telling this to Scarlett then decide against it.

"Let's get to Greenville. Mr. Fisher is an early riser."

The Fisher mansion is beautiful no matter the time of day. Highlighted by the magenta rays of a rising sun, the mansion is nothing less than spectacular.

"Stunning, absolutely stunning," Scarlett gushes under her breath.

We roll to a stop at the bottom of the driveway, and I notice some additions to the place. In front of us is a ten-foot-high metal gate constructed of *faux* Roman spears painted black with gold-colored points spaced about 6" apart. A fence of identical material surrounds the mansion. Cameras are strategically placed along brick pillars that support the fence. An armed guard approaches, but rather than the pleasantries I exchanged with the guard at Ally's place, this tight-lipped security force takes its job seriously.

"State your business," the guard demands.

"I live here."

The guard looks though a photo galley on his iPad and points the screen at Scarlett.

"Good morning Mr. Thomas and Sheriff DuBois. Do you have business here or are you a guest of Mr. Thomas?"

"Guest of Mr. Thomas."

The guard speaks into a microphone clipped to his jacket. He nods at instructions from someone inside, then says "Welcome home, Mr. Thomas." He gives Scarlett a quick going-over, "Morning, Sheriff, welcome to Fisher mansion."

Before Scarlett can acknowledge his greeting, the guard turns his attention back to me. "Mr. Thomas, I need for you to pop the hatch so I can inspect the cargo area."

"I guess I don't need to give them instructions on how to inspect vehicles," I whisper to Scarlett as he the looks under my truck.

The guard stands, gives a thumbs-up toward the mansion and yells, "Clear!" I take that to mean we are good to go and start up the long driveway.

"Boy, this place has changed." I tell her.

"I told you. It's a fortress. Now do you understand why I want you to come back?"

"Hey, I'm a little slow, but it's starting to sink in. Who ordered all this security?"

"RH, as I understand it."

I let out a low whistle. "Not taking any chances, is he?"

"Nope, does that bother you?"

"No." I look at Scarlett. "But what does bother me is that RH is condescending and irksome. I guess that's a cop thing…"

"What's that supposed to mean?"

"I think you know."

Scarlett frowns, "No, I'd really like to know what you mean."

"About you, RH, or cops in general? Because I have an opinion on all three, separately and together—"

"Me. And if you tick me off, forget about the other two."

I park my truck and switch off the engine. "Well, Ms. DuBois, at the risk of ticking you off…"

Scarlett, a scowl on her face, sits straight up in the seat, crosses her arms, and does her best to intimidate me. It's a wasted effort, though. I got this.

"I think you are an incredibly fascinating woman. Only your beguiling wit and superior intelligence exceeds your extraordinary countenance. Never have I had the honor—and may I say sheer pleasure—of being in the company of such a rare creature. Despite your restrictions on displays of public affection and your command to *act*, rather than *be*, a normal couple. I believe we are teetering on the precipice of a deep and soulful relationship. In fact, one to be admired by the ages—and sages."

Scarlett presses her hands against her skull like she anticipates an explosion from deep inside.

"You have this knack, Cape, of turning me on and turning me off at the same time. It drives me crazy!"

"Sadly," I assay, turning both palms upward and shrugging my shoulders, "your lament echoes my storied past."

Scarlett leaps across the seat and kisses me deep and hard. I want more and embrace her tightly, but she squirms away. "No, the kiss is how I respond to being turned on. The cold shoulder is how I respond to being turned off. I don't want to be another lamenting woman from your storied past, understand?"

"I do, and I don't want to ever turn you off again. Ever."

Scarlett unbuckles her seat belt and grabs the door handle. "Did you really mean all those things you said about me?"

"Naw—total BS."

"Are you serious?"

I laugh and kiss Scarlett on the forehead, "Come on, let's introduce you to Mr. Fisher."

"Aaah! What a turn-off!"

Mr Fisher, is sitting in the breakfast nook, accepts a pour of coffee from Louise, but in a surprise move, sees me, stands with a wide smile, and grabs my hand. "Welcome home, son."

I smile and pull Scarlett up beside me. "Mr. Fisher, I'd like you meet Sheriff Scarlett DuBois."

His eyes twinkle as he folds Scarlett's hands into his. "I am very well acquainted with this beautiful young lady. As a matter of fact, I contributed quite heavily to her election campaign."

"You sure did, sir and I'll never forget you for your generosity," she responds giving Mr. Fisher a peck on his cheek.

"I so wish my girls could have lived—I know they would have insisted I back you as I did…" A far-away look comes into his eyes. Then he recovering , he takes Scarlett's arm. "Come, join me for breakfast," he says making a sweeping motion at the table.

"Oh we couldn't," Scarlett answers rubbing her belly. "We stopped at Bubba's and had a tenderloin biscuit…with gravy."

"Well, in that case," Mr. Fisher says, "You may not be hungry again until tomorrow!"

While Scarlett and Mr. Fisher share a laugh, I'm trying to get my head around the fact that Scarlett forgot to mention to me her apparent close association with Mr. Fisher.

Before I give this any more thought, RH Carter comes into the kitchen. "Well, I see the prodigal son has returned," he says.

If this jerk wasn't doing such a good job taking care of my family, I expect I could kill him. "Yep, thought I'd drop by the old mansion and give it little ghettofication."

RH gives me a funny look, leading me to believe he doesn't know much about real estate. "*Ghettofication?*"

"Yeah, you know where an unsavory character like me moves into the neighborhood and the property prices drop like anvils."

"Jeez-Louise, you back on that kick again!" RH says.

"What's that you need, Mr. RH?" Louise, interjects.

"Excuse us," Scarlett says, and guides me toward the foyer. "I thought you wanted him—"

"He started it! Do I look like a damn prodigal son to you?"

Scarlett holds up her thumb and index finger spaced very close together and puts them in my face, "Just a teeny-weeny-bit. Be nice now, please?"

"There's just something about that guy—one minute I kinda like him, next minute I want to kill him."

"I know—someone has that effect one me. But you have to let it go. Even you were impressed by the security he has around the place."

"I'll just ignore him." I turn to leave.

"Where're you going?" Scarlett said.

"To get my phone out of my truck."

"Oh, I thought—"

"Don't worry, I'm staying. You're right, it's the safest place I can be."

I practice my deep-breathing-calm-down exercises and everything else I can think of to cool off on the short walk to my truck. Nothing works, I grab my phone and try to choke it. The phone immediately starts dialing. As I'm trying to end this butt dial, a very familiar voice yells, "Who is this?"

"Wong numbah, calling numbah-one son," I say in a very bad Chinese accent.

I press the disconnect button, then dial Scarlett's number. "How may I help you, Mr. Thomas?"

"Come outside, quick!"

"I'll be right there, what's wrong?"

"Just meet me at my truck."

Scarlett jogs out of the front door and races toward my truck, "What's wrong?"

"When I picked up my phone, it rang the Orlando number from last night. Someone answered before I could hang up. But I recognize the voice!"

"The butt-dial call?"

"Yes."

Who was it?"

"...RH Carter."

"You have his number—didn't it show up on your screen?"

"He must have another phone. This one was listed 'Private'. It was RH, Scarlett. I'm *certain*."

"But, could you be mistaken?"

"Maybe…"

"And maybe your dislike for RH clouds your judgement sometimes…? Cape, what I'm about to tell you may make things worse between you two."

"How's that?"

"During the Gustavo Jobim trial, RH came in to support the family. Jobim's lawyer got a change of venue—to Slick Rock County. I met RH, …And we dated."

"Is that when you got to know Mr. Fisher so well?"

"Yes."

Everyone is entitled to their life before someone new comes into it. I've often dealt with situations like that. Even so, it seems like Scarlett should have told me about Mr. Fisher and RH before now.

"That's cool," I say, my face carefully set.

Scarlett gives me another one-eyed-arched-eyebrow looks— "No, I don't think it is. You're mad, aren't you?"

"A little surprised—that's all."

"Are you sure?"

"Yeah, no big deal." I look at my phone. "Hey, just so I can ease my mind about RH, did he just get a call before I called you?"

"Yes, he did. Said it was a wrong number—A Chinese asking for his son."

"OK. Guess I was mistaken—it couldn't have been RH at that Orlando number."

Scarlett gives me a condescending smile. "See, everyone is *not* out to get you."

"Yeah…Lucky me."

CHAPTER TWENTY-TWO

Scarlett gets a guided tour

We walk back into the mansion, RH motions for Scarlett to join him and Mr. Fisher at the table. I tag along under the mistaken assumption that I'm welcome, too.

"Cape, if you don't mind, I'd like to update Scarlett on what's been happening since I've seen her last. If you have a few minutes later, though, I'd like you to meet someone who is very special to me."

"So, I guess you and RH visit a lot?" I said under my breath to Scarlett.

"Only official business, Cape, don't be like this."

I smile to save face. "Since I'm not worthy of an update, allow me to update you." RH rolls his eyes and I consider blackening both of them. Despite RH's clear lack of interest, I continue for Mr. Fisher's benefit.

"I was attacked last night. A common fantasy in this haywire brain of mine, I know, but last night's attack was certain." I glare at RH. "Want to know why I'm so certain that I was attacked, Mr. Roll-Your-Eyes?"

RH clenches his jaw and tries to stare me down, but it's a badly failed attempt to shut me up.

"Because my friend Betty is dead. Probably killed by the same person who killed Ally and Celine.   After knowing I possess this esoteric information , you no doubt see that you need me to join your little update group. But I'm out of the detective business. I'm not playing cop like you guys anymore.

"What I am going to do is focus on getting my AeroMax job back. I figure a globetrotting target like an airline pilot, will make things more difficult for the killer. And with any luck, my move just may save my family!" I nod to the group, "I'll be in my room."

"We *want* you to get well," RH says. "Jake's orders to us were to ensure that you have less stress. That's why I leave you out of the briefing, not as an insult to you."

"Really, RH? Because it sure seems like an insult! And a condescending one at that. You're trying to make me look like an idiot so Scarlett will think you're Joe Cool."

"What?" RH takes a step toward me. "Cape, come back here!"

I turn away and flip the bird over my shoulder. "Less stress *this*, Flatfoot!"

"What a hothead! I ought to kick—"

"Calm down, RH! Cape, is not well." Mr. Fisher turns to Scarlett. "Sheriff, is what Cape said true? Was his friend really killed, or did he imagine that, too?"

I think about responding to Mr. Fisher's asinine question, but instead speed up my retreat. Halfway up the second flight of stairs, Louise comes running by me holding her stomach.

"Hey, Mr. Thomas."

"Hello, Louise. How you—?"

"Ain't got time to talk...comin' outta both ends." Shortly after Louise slams the bathroom door, I hear noises that confirm she'll be in the bathroom a while.

I top the landing and the first thing I see is Louise's keys dangling from her cleaning cart. The temptation and opportunity are too great—I may never get both again. Even if this gets me tossed from the mansion, I have to know if the locked room is connected to the attacks on me. I grab the keys and hustle up to the third-floor passion room.

It's a no-brainer that the new deadbolt on the door will have a matching new key. After four tries, the fourth shiny key turns the lock and I step inside to search for clues. Even though I have no idea what clues I am searching for.

As before, the room is covered in dust. Remembering Louise's trick to cover my tracks, I dash back down to her cleaning cart and grab her dust mop. I tiptoe around the bed, making sure I don't step on the bra and panties turned yellow by age. The cigarettes in the ashtray are coated with dust, too, but I can still make out the brand, Tareyton, discontinued years ago. With two fingers I pick the note-card propped against the ashtray so I don't disturb the dust on it. *Darling, only a few more weeks and we'll have it all...and this hellhole will be just a bitter memory. Love always, [Splat]*

The name of the note's author is nothing more than a blob of ink diluted by a water stain, perhaps caused by a drop of water from one of the highball glasses? I replace the card in the exact position I found it, then step over the stylish bra and panties that show the owner of the lingerie was a very shapely woman. The man's boxer's look to be a size small—not a big bruiser. Knowing this may help identify the lovers, but I don't see other obvious clues lying about, so I move on.

No matter how lightly I step, my tracks leave distinct prints. At the rear of the bedroom stands a small dressing table. I ease open drawer after drawer hoping to find a picture, card, or something that reveals the identity of the room's former occupants. No clues here, though. The room must've been emptied years ago before it was sealed up. I move on to the closet, but it's also empty. Strange...Even so, I notice the clothes rod is not seated properly in its notch. I lift the rod to replace it in the notch and, as I do, the entire back wall of the closet slides open.

Sunlight pouring through the window is blinding. For a second I think I'm in an adjoining bedroom, but as my eyes adjust, I notice there are no doors, not even a closet in this room. I move over to the window and look down on the driveway. From where I stand on the third floor, the room has to be almost dead center of the mansion.

On a long table under the window are six stacks of hundred dollar bills. Two of the stacks appear to be equal is height. The third stack is shorter, perhaps half the height of the other two. The fourth stack dwarfs the fifth stack and only a couple of hundreds top the sixth stack. The balance of the sixth stack is one- and five-dollar bills with a few tens and twenties in the mix. The order, neatness, and lack of dust on this section of the table suggests recent use.

Another table, in the center of the room, covered in dust, but it holds boxes of loose currency filled with 20's, 50's, and 100's. Along the sides of the walls are different-colored duffle bags stacked to the ceiling that look to be packed full. I walk over and unclip one of the bags, denominations of currency like those on the table spill out. On a tall metal cart beside the table is a printing press with engraving plates of various denominations. Stacks of blank paper that look to be the same texture of legal currency surround the press. Do these stacks of paper await their illegal transformation? None of the equipment looks to have been used in years, though.

I grab a handful of bills from the table and some samples from the different-colored duffle bags. Though, I'm sure what the purpose of the blanks is, I snatch up a couple of them just for later proof. After sorting the sample bills, I cram them into different pockets. I back out the room, careful to walk in my earlier footprints. Once in the closet, I lock the rod in place and the wall closes. From the closet I continue to backtrack and cover my tracks with the dust mop until I'm out in the hall again.

I hear Louise flushing her discomfort away and know I won't be caught. Perfect timing! Louise's footsteps signal that she's walking back to her cleaning cart. I move away from the passion room and race down to the second floor to stand in front of another room I have to see. Unlike the passion room, the first key I try fits the lock.

"What you doin'!"

Like a kid with his hand in the cookie jar, I turn and face an angry Louise.

"I want to see Laura's room."

"Well, you don't have to be so sneaky about it." Louise pushes me aside and opens the door. "All you had to do was ask!"

I bow my head to show proper contrition. "I'm sorry, Louise, but after the chewing out you gave me over the other room, I thought you might not allow it."

"The other room is a completely different matter. You didn't go back in there, did you?"

I hate lying to her, but manage a pretty convincing response. "No." I point up toward the third floor. "See for yourself."

"Well, I just may do that. You welcome to touch things in here, but be sure to put them back where you found them. Mr. Fisher likes for everything to be as it was. Now, go on in and have your moment, but if you been in that other room I'm going tell Mr. Fisher. It ain't right to go snooping round other people's property."

"You're right—I—." No need to add to my lie, so I shut up.

Louise cracks the door and steps aside, "I'm goin' be just down the hall there. You go on in when you get ready." Louise hangs the keys back on her cart and stands behind it. "And don't you break nothin' in there. I know how clumsy men can be."

My heart is racing, because whatever lies behind this door belonged to my soulmate and the mother of my only child. For the first time in my life, I'll be in the most intimate setting Laura Fisher ever knew. I turn to Louise, "Thanks for doing this…I can't tell you what it means to me."

Louise smiles and looks deep into my eyes, "Some people share a lifetime together and never have that look you have on your face, Mr. Thomas. Me and Miss Laura were close. When she used to talk about you, she had that same look on her face." Louise palms my face and gives me a surprise peck on the cheek. "You take all the time you need."

Louise turns to walk away, but I touch her arm so she turns to face me. "Thanks for telling me that—I've often wondered." Louise nods and goes on.

Once inside, I lean against the door and close my eyes. Scents from within the room send me back to the night long ago when we sat in front of the outdoor fireplace at my Grandfather's old house. I didn't notice Laura's scent that night, but I remember it now. I inhale deeply, push the door open and step inside.

The room before me is not the frilly, *frou-frou* room I imagined Laura would have had back in the day. Even by today's standards this room is stylish. An Art Deco vanity table and mirror draw my attention. On top of the vanity are several crystal perfume bottles, that is the source of the seductive scent permeating the room. An Italian Art Deco rosewood armoire with mirrors on both doors is on a wall behind me. I walk over and open the doors.

But inside are no treasured outfits or that perfect little black dress women search for and never find. Instead, the luxurious armoire contains working clothes. I pull out one of the lab coats and pride fills me when I read the name tag, Laura Hale Fisher M. D. So Bianca lied! Laura *was* a doctor and I'd bet my last nickel she was a *great* doctor, too. And the coat still holds a vague scent of Laura. I press the coat to my chest and try to imagine how Laura would feel in my arms.

I do a mock bow to Milady Lab Coat and say, "Shall we?" Miss Coat bows slightly, and we foxtrot around the room, gliding across the floor in the rhythm of star-struck lovers. Around and around we go until we stop in front of a tall chest of drawers. "Madame, what secrets are you hiding here?"

I hear her laugh and imagine her saying, "Oh wouldn't you like to know, Mr. Thomas."

The coat seems to come alive as if it is urging me to explore the rest of the room. I close my eyes hoping Laura will materialize as she did on my deck that night at my house—but she doesn't and I replace the coat.

Back at the tall mahogany chest with sterling silver pulls next to the door to the bathroom, I admire its unusual shape and narrow drawers.

Still laughing at our spontaneous dance, I pullout one of the drawers. Bras of all colors and styles are in one of the drawers and another is filled with panties. I feel like a Peeping Tom and bang the drawer shut.

In life, they say, timing is everything. A few years one way or the other and Laura's life and mine would have been so different. Even without her immense wealth, a doctor and an airline captain would certainly have been a power couple.

Whatever the reason—my resurgence of lost-love emotions, or maybe the little foxtrot move, I'm feeling dizzy, so I make a beeline for a small antique chest at the foot of Laura's bed. Though I doubt Laura ever used it for this purpose, I sit there and gather my thoughts. The room continues to spin so I grab my head to hold myself in place.

"Dad, are you OK?"

Jana is sitting beside me and pulls me close. Her scent is the scent as her mother's, something I've never realized until now. Nice that they're subtly related that way, even today. Though I never got to know Laura over the years, I'm overcome with thankfulness to her for giving our daughter life. I hug Jana, squeezing her tight. "Just a little light-headed, honey."

"You want me to call Jake?"

"No, I don't need a doctor—just a little winded from dancing with your mother—"

"Oh, no!" The look on Jana's face is the same one I got when I gave the kids cap pistols and water cannons. "Dad I have to call Jake! Something is wrong—"

"Pretending!—I was just *pretending* to dance with her." I hold Jana back from me a little so she can see that I'm not crazy. "I held up the coat and saw it even has her name on it. With that, I really felt her presence. I danced around the room with the coat, and I know that sounds weird—but we're connected." I start laughing, "Hell, call Jake—maybe I am crazy."

Jana takes the coat out of the closet and slips it on. "You're not crazy. I talk to this coat sometimes, too." She holds her arms out. "Dance with me, Dad."

There's no music, but we don't need it. Like the winning pair on *Dancing with the Stars* we glide around the room in perfect harmony. I hum "—out together dancing cheek to cheek..," thinking about Jana and how timing has affected her life, too. "You know, I wish Laura and you and I could have been a family living together for all your—"

"Dad, it's—"

"Jana, let me finish. This is something I need to get off my chest and something we've been—forgive the pun, dancing around since I came home."

Our dance slows. Jana closes her eyes and puts her head on my shoulder.

"In some ways—a lot of ways really, from the grave, your mother has made up for not being in your life." I tell her.

Jana nods. "That's true, and she did other things for me beside the entries in her diary. I haven't told you or anyone else this..." Jana walks over to the lingerie chest. "She left me birthday cards in the bottom drawer for every year that she lived, though unfortunately, none are left. It was her way of giving me advice based on the number of years she lived, I guess. She even assumed I would have children—pretty neat, huh?"

"Well, that *is* neat, but I was referring to the fact that she left you a stinking fortune!"

What starts out as a wink and a smile turns in to belly laughs. When we stop laughing and Jana says, "Well, there *is* that..."

"On a more serious note, what really bothers me are the things we never got to do. I mean, look at us dancing—I love it. It just rips me apart that I wasn't there to take you to a father-daughter dance, for instance." I kiss the top of her head. "I missed your dance recitals, your tea parties, your prom. But my biggest regret is not being there to protect you from that creep who abused you!"

Jana lowers her head and sobs begin to rack her body, "I used to blame myself for making him hurt—"

"No, no, no." I wrap my arms around Jana again and hold her tight, "I'll kill him if I ever see him!"

"Dad, the Bible says we have to forgive, though we may not forget. I've forgiven him. I want you to forgive him, too. He will always be a part of our lives, until we forgive and forget about him, OK?"

"I can't, Jana."

"Dad, all of my life wasn't horrible. Mr. and Mrs. Smith were there for me, in their own way. Just because you weren't, doesn't mean you failed as a parent. You didn't know about me."

"I should have known about you. Why didn't this God of yours let me know about you sooner? Answer me that!"

"Dad, think about this. Just seconds after you found out I was your daughter, you took a bullet that was meant for me. God put you in my life at the exact moment I needed my dad most. Don't you see?"

"You credit God." I look around the room. "I think it was Laura."

"I so wanted you to be my dad. I had a feeling, but when Michele read the diary and confirmed it was you, it felt like I was in a fairy tale come true, my knight in shining armor had come to save me—but then Gustavo aimed the gun at me!

You were my super hero, flying through the air...then came the explosion and the blood. The EMT's had to pry the gun from your hand...I was sure you were dead. It was like I found what I had been looking for my whole life—but—," Jana snaps her fingers, "you were gone! What you did for me was true love, Dad. *John* 15:13 says 'Greater love hath no man than this, that a man lay down his life for his friends.'"

Jana sits on the bed. "You see? I don't need a dance or tea party with you to know that you love me with all of your heart."

As earlier, we regard one another. This time, no belly laughing, just tears. "Well, there *is* that," I say

Jana wipes her tears and sits up, "I have amazing parents. I can never repay Mom for what she did, and I can never pay you for saving my life."

"All this religious stuff—"

"That's the *Gospel*, Dad."

"OK, but how did *you* get it?"

"Mr. and Mrs. Smith took me to church, but even before that I knew I was not alone."

"I don't understand?"

"When they were taking you to the hospital, this song I've always heard when times get tough started in my head."

"What's the song?"

"*Hush, little baby, don't say a word, Mama's gonna buy you a mockingbird.* Jana sings.

"*And if that mockingbird don't sing, mama's gonna buy you a diamond ring,*" I answer her.

"*And if that diamond ring turns to brass, Mama's gonna buy you a looking glass.*" She adds.

"*And if that looking glass gets broke, Mama's going buy you a billy goat!*" I finish with a laugh.

"So you know the song, too, Dad?"

"I do—from when I was a little kid."

CHAPTER TWENTY-THREE

Cape meets Salome

I close my eyes and hug Jana. When I open them, I am staring into a very familiar pair of coppery eyes. I shove Jana onto the bed and dive at the night nurse. This time my aim is true—I drive my shoulder under her chin and slam her to the floor. Like a cat, she slips from under me, pops up on all fours, and scurries to the corner of the room. Slick move, but this time she won't get away. I reset like a sprinter in blocks and prepare to crush her. The full weight of RH Carter comes crashing down on me in my kneeling position. I can't move a muscle. RH twists my arms behind my back and forces me to my knees. Jake, Scarlett, and Louise grab RH and pull him off of me.

"What the hell is the matter with you?" RH yells.

"It's her, the night nurse! I'd know those eyes anywhere."

Scarlett extends her hand to the night nurse, helping her stand. "Cape Thomas, meet Dr. Salome Matkusa." Scarlett says, "RH's fiancée."

"No, no, this woman is the night nurse who tried to kill—"

"Stop it, dammit!" RH grabs me by the collar and snatches me to my feet, looking around at the others. "I'm tired of everyone coddling this nut case. Has anyone else ever seen this *night nurse* besides, Cape? Have you seen her, Jake? You were at the hospital when he was," RH does the air-quotes thing, "supposedly attacked!"

"There was a selfie." Jake stammers

"Photo-shopped," RH replies. "I'd bet money on it!"

"Well, in that case." Jake says looking at me, "I guess I haven't."

RH turns to Scarlett, "How about you?"

"I can't say what she looks like, but I believe there's an attacker. We all need to calm down. Cape isn't in the habit of wrestling women. This seems to be a case of mistaken identity—"

"Obviously! And whether you admit it or not, you know this guy is wacko. You can do *so* much better, Scarlett!" RH says.

"How about the foot—ouch!" Before I finish posing my question Scarlett digs her nails into my forearm.

"How about what, Dad?" Jana said.

Scarlett's glaring at me.

"How about for the sake of compassion, we do as Scarlett suggests and chalk this up to a case of mistaken identity?" I hold my hand out to, Salome, "RH, is right, my dear, I'm wacky."

Salome rolls her head around and stretches her neck from side to side to make sure it's in working order. "The color of my eyes is very rare. Only about 1% of the world's population has amber eyes. If you have seen, *or imagined you have seen*, someone with eyes like mine, I see how you may mistake me for that person. I forgive you, Mr. Thomas."

"Thank you—I appreciate that. Now if y'all will excuse us I need to get the sheriff back to Slick Rock."

Scarlett smiles at everyone. I figure she is about to tell them good-bye and head back to work, but instead she hits me with a question. "Does this mean I'm not going to get a guided tour of the mansion?"

"It certainly does not, young lady." Mr Fisher says. "Cape, why don't you show her around?"

"I'll take her, Mr. Fisher. Don't nobody in the worl' know this house better'n me." Louise says and grabs Scarlett's and my arms.

I think about begging off, but I'm curious why Scarlett tried to peel the skin off my arm.

Jake embraces Jana and RH embraces Salome, then the couples follow Mr. Fisher until RH turns and snaps, "Watch your step, Chief. You put your hands on Salome—"

"Darling, that isn't necessary. I'm sure Mr. Thomas and I will get along just fine. Isn't that right, Mr. Thomas?"

Before I can answer, Salome turns to the others and asks, "May I have a moment with Mr. Thomas—alone?" Everyone nods and Salome guides me back into the bedroom.

"I wanted to tell you that, I'm sorry about your friends' deaths."

"You mean, Betty and Ethan?"

"Who? I was speaking of Ally Kress and Celine Seabolt. Have others of your friends died, Mr. Thomas?"

"Yeah, as a matter of fact, they did, over in Wilson. I thought you might have…heard?" From the corner of my eye I can see Scarlett in the hallway, straining to hear our conversation.

"No, Mr. Thomas, but I've only been to Wilson once."

It's a long-shot, but I give it a whirl. "Just curious, when was that?"

Salome looks me dead in the eye, without the hint of a smile, and says,

"Last night, Mr. Thomas—why?"

Did I just hear" last night" or am I imagining this conversation, too? Doesn't matter, I see Scarlett standing in the doorway. Jigs up, witchy-woman—now Scarlett knows!

Salome joins the others in the hall. I lean against the wall, cross my arms, and wait for Scarlett to slap cuffs on this evil-doer. Instead, Scarlett gives her a knowing smile and nods. When Salome returns the gesture, I'm confused as crap.

This woman is toying with me and Scarlett knows it. Yet, for some reason she sides with Salome. I stay calm, though that's hard when everyone is turning on you. Jana breaks from the pack."Dad, it's OK," she says, kissing me on the cheek.

I forget about the potential Salome-Scarlett conspiracy. I care only how my little girl feels. "I'm sorry I ruined our moment, forgive me?"

"I love you, Dad. Nothing will ever change that."

As the others leave, Louise turns to me and whispers. "That amber-eye woman's trouble—don't trust her."

"Why do you say that? Did you hear what she said?"

"I ain't hear nothing—but she ain't right in the head."

"What do you know about her, Louise?"

"I know she's here to make trouble. And speaking of trouble, sounds like you and the Sheriff got some of that, too…"

"It's just his jealousy." Scarlett says from the stairwell. "Cape has just learned RH and I dated a few times."

Funny how she can hear Louise and me whispering, yet couldn't hear Salome. "And you forgot to tell me you knew Mr. Fisher so well, too." I add.

"I told you at the farm that I was checking on you because the family requested it. I didn't know I needed to go into all the details on *how* I know your family!"

"Well, if I knew your family intimately, I'd tell—"

"*Intimately*? You can't possibly know if RH and—"

Louise holds her hands up. "Y'all actin' like fools."

"Excuse me." Scarlett says, and pointing at me. "Cape is acting like a fool—not me."

"Wrong! The correct terminology," I clarify, "according to your *boyfriend*, is that I'm acting like a wacko!"

Louise drags Scarlett and me together. "We ain't got time for this! I'm not supposed to talk about guests, but somethin' evil about Salome. Her being here don't bode well for this house."

"No kidding." I agree.

Louise ignores my comment, and launches into her proofs.

"First, Salome keeps asking me questions about the twins' mother, Miss Cali. We ain't suppose to talk about that. Second, every question Salome asks she already knows the answer. Third, she's two-faced, say one thing to your face and another behind your back. You know what I mean, Mr. Thomas." Louise grabs her stomach, "I got to go. I swear, ever since that woman got here my stomach ain't been right. My auntie thinks she put a hex on me!"

Louise hustles to the bathroom, again, and Scarlett and I continue our hushed conversation.

"I agree with Louise. That woman is up to something! I know I'm a nut case, fantasizing all kinds of things, but that Salome attacked me."

"Well, she does have unusual eyes, but she explained why you may have thought that..."

"But Scarlett, she admitted she was in Wilson last night. I saw you reading her lips, you know she's up to something—yet you side with her!"

"I'm no lip-reader and I wasn't *siding with her*. I was being civil. You should try it sometime! Feels great."

"You know what *civil* means?"

"Yes, I do."

"Not the Merriam-Webster definition. Some folks think 'civil' is just another word for butt-kissing— politically-correct bull-hockey."

"Who thinks like that?" Scarlett said.

"Sarge—and me. That's who!"

Scarlett does an exaggerated eye-roll much like RH displayed earlier. Something they choreographed to make me look even more foolish.

"Proving Salome isn't your night nurse will be easy." Scarlett said. "All we have to do is compare her shoe print to the mold I lifted from the creek."

"That's what I was going to suggest until you raked the skin from my arm—"

"I don't want RH to know that I have that print."

"Why's that?"

"You said you wanted out of the investigation business, so for that reason I'd rather not answer your question."

"Fair enough, but for the record, if something comes up that concerns the safety of my family or me I expect some type of briefing from you."

"Every time I make a move to keep you safe or bring you into the loop, it backfires." Scarlett said. "That, or you accuse me of siding with the enemy...or should I say *sleeping* with the enemy?"

"You mean things like telling RH about your trail cams at Miss

Minnie's?

"Of course! See what I mean?"

"I was just guessing you told RH about the trail cameras, but you did, didn't you?"

"I did." She admits. "I even offered to share the location with him and set him up to receive a live feed. He declined."

"Good, I don't want RH to know about my comings and goings. And you shouldn't have told him."

"How exactly does putting another pair of eyes on your location hurt you?"

"It hurts me—because sometimes it seems like you're *for* them and against me."

"Cape, I'm not out to hurt you." Scarlett runs her fingers through her hair and leans her head back. "No matter how I try to help, you take it the wrong way."

"I know, you're trying to help, but sometimes I sense that you aren't. I guess that's my wacko episodes. But why would Salome tell me she was in Wilson last night but give no explanation of why?"

"English isn't her first language, so maybe you misunderstood her," Scarlett says giving my hand a squeeze. "And the next time you have a wacko episode—just *know* I'm on your side, OK?"

"You're probably right about Salome. I'll try to keep my fears down to a minimum." I say. "Thanks for understanding."

Louise comes back down the hallway sweating like a gym-rat working out in a sauna. "If y'all want to tour this place, you need to come on. I got to lie down."

"That's fine, Louise. We can do it some other time," Scarlett says.

"Well, I don't need a tour," I reassure her, "but I got a few questions about the *passion room*."

Louise sighs, then sits down on a small tufted leather bench in the hall. "That'd be a good name for it, too."

"What happened there, Louise?"

Louise looks up and down the hallway, then stands. "I'm feeling some better. Let's go to the observation room. We can talk there."

As we pass by, I consider pointing out the passion room to Scarlett, but think better of it. For some reason, Louise tiptoes up the stairs, so Scarlett and I follow suit. No one speaks a word until we are inside the observation room.

"Wow!" Scarlett says, a lot like my own reaction to its panoramic view.

"Mr. Fisher owns the land for as far as you can see." I said. "Isn't that right, Louise?"

"That's for sure, and I'll tell you all about it one of these days." Louise mops the sweat dripping off her face with a paper towel. "But right now I ain't in the mood to chit-chat about nothing but that woman. My auntie won't around her no more'n a minute and knew she was trouble. And when she knows, you need to listen."

"Who is your auntie?"

"Oh, you know her. You stay at her place."

"Miss Minnie?"

"That's right, and she wants me to warn you."

"About what?"

"You got trouble coming, Mr. Thomas."

"Too late, the trouble already found me last night."

Louise's eyes widened, "Anybody in this family die last night?"

"Not, that I know of," I say.

"Then that ain't the trouble she's talking 'bout. Hear for yourself what she say." Louise digs her phone from her apron pocket and gives it to, Scarlett.

Scarlett puts it on speaker and plays the message: "*Child, I had me a vision, about Mister Willard's boy. He 'scapes the Angel of Death once but might not agin—someone in the family gonna die. Can't make it all out, but I know this much: Something evil cloaked in good headed this way.*"

"What time was the call?" I ask.

Scarlett looks at the time on the message. "Before the attack at Miss Minnie's place."

"I called the sheriff department and told them to go check on Mr. Thomas. They said, you already on the scene, Sheriff," Louise says. "I didn't worry too much after that."

"I signed out to check the cameras," Scarlett said. "Is Miss Minnie an early riser, Louise? I'd like to ask her more about this vision of hers."

"She is. Matter of fact, she called right after you and Mr. Thomas showed up here this morning. She said to get out of here."

"Why?" I ask.

"Miss Minnie said, more people going' die, maybe 'fore the sun goes down. I'm scared, Sheriff."

We look outside at the waning morning sun.

"I think you'll be safe here, Louise," Scarlett says. "I need to talk to Miss Minnie."

"I'm going with you." I say. "Do you know where she lives?"

Scarlett nods and turns to Louise. "I'd send a deputy by here, but with all these guards it's a waste of manpower. You want to ride with us, Louise?"

"Naw, you right—can't nobody get at me in here. I'm goin' lie down for a minute then clean up the kitchen. Tell Aunt Minnie I need something for my stomach, if you don't mind?"

"Pepto Bismol work for you?" Scarlett asks.

Louise rubs her stomach. "Don't need that kind of medicine. That woman put something evil on me. Aunt Minnie will know what I need."

"I believe the passion room has something to do with all this," I say. "What happened there?"

Louise looks out the window toward Greenville. "When I started working here, you couldn't see the town from this house. So much has changed. Over all these years one thing has never changed. My first orders when I came here to work were never unlock the door that led to what you call the passion room."

"Why do you have a key to the room, then?"

Louise turns and locks eyes with me. "Unlike you, Mr. Thomas, I respect people's privacy and wishes. I 'spect Mr. Fisher gave me a key because one day he knows I *will* need it—that day ain't come yet, but it may."

"You mean the day you caught me in that room is the first time you went inside?"

"Not exactly. When I first got here Mr. Fisher would check on the room from time to time, but that room was shut for years."

"When you say, 'not exactly', what does that mean?" I ask.

"Only other time I saw in that room was the time I saw Miss Bianca coming out of it."

Bianca in the passion room—that's settles it for me. There's no doubt, for me anyway, of who is responsible for the money-laundering and counterfeiting operation in the secret room.

"You do know a deadbolt was added since I was in the room, right?" I said.

"Is that right? I hardly ever look at that door to tell you the truth." Louise answers.

"Really? Aren't you the only staff who works the third floor?"

"Yes, Mr Thomas. Why do you ask?"

"Just curious."

"Oh, now that you mention it." Louise says, "I did show the locksmith up here, same as I did when the lock was changed after Bianca was caught coming out of there."

"What's in there?" Scarlett says. "You guys act like it's the vault for the Fisher family fortune or something."

Louise can't hide her guilt—she's seen the money room, and from the look she's giving me—she knows I've seen it, too.

"Am I right?" Scarlett probes.

Louise and I respond at once, but with different answers. "No, ma'am, nothing like that!"

"You're kidding, right?" I say.

"Well, what's in there, then?"

"Just a big dusty room, with a twist."

"What kind of twist?"

I explain the general disarray of the room and the clothing on the floor while Scarlett looks like a Girl Scout listening to a ghost story around a campfire.

"Sounds like someone was caught in a tryst?" Scarlett said

"That's what I figure." I said, "I'm pretty sure it was his second wife, Maria. I know she was fooling—"

"She fooled around all right, but that room was locked before she got here." Louise says. "Mr. Fisher hired her as what they called an *au pair* for Miss Laura. I called her a nanny right up until she married Mr. Fisher and became the lady of the house."

"Well, that blows my theory and makes the note card even more puzzling," I said.

"What did the card say?" Scarlett asks.

"It was short, and if memory serves the words were: '*Darling, only a few more weeks and we'll have it all…and this hellhole will be just a bitter memory. Love Always*'.

I couldn't read the name, because the note was written with a fountain pen, and it looked like a big water droplet from one of the highball glasses dripped on it and smudged the name."

"Do you think it's a crime scene, Cape? Sounds like they were discovered in the throes of passion?" Scarlett said. "I could get a warrant. I really need to see that room since a murder may have occurred there."

"I don't think it's that kind of crime scene…" I know, depending on the statute of limitations for counterfeiting, that the room *is* a crime scene. Problem is Bianca, the likely culprit, is dead and Mr. Fisher might get the blame. I can't let that happen.

"So, no signs of violence?" Scarlett said.

"No, nothing like that."

"Maybe whatever happened in there was just too painful for Mr. Fisher and he sealed it off," Scarlett said. "So the activity may've been strange, but nothing illegal."

"Do you know the story of Mr. Fisher and RH's family?" I ask.

"Yes, that came out at the trial of Gustavo Jobim. Apparently, Mr.

Fisher fought like crazy to have the prosecution keep that out of the trial, but to no avail. Everyone in Slick Rock County knows Mr. Fisher's wife slept with another man, and that hers was a planned pregnancy."

"Well, I guess the passion room was the breeding room, then."

"That must be it." Scarlett agrees. "I could see him closing the room off after that. Maybe we should just forget about the room?"

"Ha! I never thought I'd hear a cop advocating for *not* snooping around…"

"Cape, this case is already so convoluted, do we really need a forty or fifty-year-old rabbit to chase? Let's stop whoever is trying to murder your family and then we can solve the tryst case, OK?"

"How about the message on the card?" I said, "According to Mr. Fisher, everything went as planned and each couple left with a child. But that card leads me to think things weren't as harmonious as Mr. Fisher has portrayed. Wouldn't that be relevant to our case?"

Scarlett, gives me a tired look. "I'm going to focus on the evidence at hand. If you want to run down a fifty-year-old note, be my guest. Louise, can you direct me to the powder room?"

Louise, still staring out the window, says softly, "Bottom of the spiral staircase, the door straight ahead of you." Scarlett leaves closing the door, and I stand to follow her.

Louise says, "Mr. Thomas, you remember what I told you when you first got here?"

"I was drugged, not thinking straight that day—remind me, Louise."

Louise backs away from the window and motions for me to come closer. "I said, around this place, it's a good idea not to believe everything you hear, and only half of what you see."

"You also said you didn't mean anything by it—it was just an old Southern saying…"

Louise stands on her tiptoes and whispers, "If you don't want to destroy this family, you'll do well to believe only half of what you see around here."

"Half of what I see? And that would be…" I whisper into Louise's ear, "those things behind the closet wall, and in the passion room?"

"*Especially* those things, Mr. Thomas."

I take a last look at Louise before I close the door and join Scarlett. The look on Louise's face is high anxiety. No longer is the Fisher family fortune a secret.

Mr. Fisher is at his desk in the library as we pass by. Scarlett stops and prepares to speak, but I push her gently down the hall. "We've visited enough," I tell her. "Let's get to Miss Minnie's." She nods and we escape unobserved.

Since Scarlett knows the way to Jimmy's house, she slides in behind the steering wheel of my truck and buckles her seatbelt. "What did you mean when you told Louise, 'half of what I see, and that would be?'"

"You heard that, but you didn't hear Salome admit being in Wilson?"

"Don't change the subject. Why were you two whispering?"

"I'll tell you all about it later. It fits into chasing fifty-year-old clues category."

"Fine, but as soon as this is over, I want an explanation."

"You'll have one, I promise."

"I hope Mr. Fisher doesn't think it was rude of me to leave without saying goodbye." Scarlett says.

"I don't think he'll mind. He seems pretty enamored of you."

"Still jealous?"

"Of Mr. Fisher?"

"RH."

If I've learned anything in life, it is to not to rush my answer, especially if said answer is to someone you care about. "No matter what I say, Scarlett, it will come out wrong."

"Why do you think that?"

"I have a knack for mis-speaking and turning you on and off in a single sentence—you said so yourself."

"Try me."

"I had no idea how connected you were to Mr. Fisher or that you dated RH. Some of my reaction to that news, admittedly, was jealousy. RH is on top of his game, but I can't get back on mine." The scar along my temple stings a little as a constant reminder of what I'm about to say. "RH is right, Scarlett. Even if I was at 100%, you *can* do a lot better than me."

Scarlett hits the turns signal and checks the side mirror. "I should have told you about my connection to your family. The jealousy you felt, in some ways, was justified. How about we put that behind us and see how things unfold?"

"Well, sounds like we've landed on some common ground." I said.

"So it does, Mr. Thomas, so it does."

She merges like a boss into late-fall traffic returning from the Outer Banks via I-587. As she changes lanes, I change the topic. "What do you think about this vision-thing of Miss Minnie's?"

"I was born and raised in Hartsville, the upland of South Carolina, but my mother was straight out of Beaufort, S.C. I spent a lot of time there and I'm familiar with the Gullah culture."

"You know Miss Minnie doesn't claim to be Gullah. I used to think she was a witchdoctor when I was a kid."

"There is something different about her, that's true!"

"Miss Minnie's 'special,' same as my mother and grandmother."

"What does that mean?"

"They see, or saw, in the case of Mother and Grandmother, things before they happened. They also may have had connections to dead people."

"You actually believe that!"

"I saw Laura. Don't get me wrong—we didn't talk, but I know she led me to Jana. Nothing you say will convince me otherwise."

"I remember hearing that at the trial, but you can't be serious…"

"Think what you want, Scarlett. Miss Minnie saved me when modern medicine couldn't, and she sees things that others can't."

"You're not joking, are you?"

"She promised me the sky and made sure I got the best seat in the house—I don't need any more proof than that."

"And that seat would be?"

"Left seat in the cockpit of a 747, baby."

Scarlett shakes her head and checks her rear view mirror. "I guess it goes without saying that you believe her…vision."

"Yep."

"But it's so vague—'evil cloaked in good': what's *that* mean?"

"Dunno. All I know is this, when whatever is supposed to happen… happens, it'll make sense. Miss Minnie is smart like that."

"That may be, but she can't see into the future."

I arch my eyebrows and roll my eyes at Scarlett.

"You actually believe she can, don't you?

"Yes, I do."

"And you don't think that's the least bit unscientific?"

"No, I don't."

Scarlett slows for the Slick Rock Hospital exit off I-587. "This isn't the way to Jimmy's house— is it?"

"No, but it's a direct route to the hospital," she explains.

"Why're we going there?"

"I've got a deranged passenger who needs help."

I look at Scarlett and smile, waiting for her to smile back: she doesn't. "You're kidding, right?"

Scarlett laughs and pulls over. "Unless I get a kiss real quick, you sir, will be in a padded cell wrapped in a straitjacket PDQ!"

I give her a quick peck on the lips, but she pulls me in for real humdinger. "I like this new common ground we've found!" I say.

Scarlett guns the Yukon and rejoins the traffic flow on I-587. "So do, I, mister."

Once we turn off the Black Creek-Fremont exit things become a little more familiar, even though I've never been to Jimmy's house. Scarlett guides the Yukon down the back roads that are undoubtedly part of her patrol area, then slows and turns onto a narrow paved driveway. A huge house sits alone atop a small rise. "That can't be Jimmy's house! It's worth a million bucks, at least."

"Twice that much, according to the tax records, but it's not surprising. You do know he's one of the most sought-after CPA's in the state, right?"

"Scarlett, he used to clean my yard. He was a drunk."

"Wasn't it you who said, 'People change'?"

"Yeah, but I didn't realize people could change," I point at his house, "*that much.*"

Jimmy, as luck has it, is actually there doing yard work. Something I've seen him do hundreds of time, but never in designer coveralls. "Morning, folks, just spraying for aphids before I head to the office. Is there a problem?"

"We came to see Miss Minnie. Is she around?" Scarlett asks.

"She's in her 'Granny Pod.' It's where she goes when she gets herself in a tizzy."

"What seems to be the problem?" Scarlett asked.

"She had one of her visions about people dying—most of the time they don't amount to much, but this one is different. I called Louise and she said you and Cape were OK, but Miss Minnie is still worked up."

"Betty, was killed last night, Jimmy" I explain, leaning across.

"*Sarge's* Betty?"

"Yes, and it seems like I delivered—"

"It's an ongoing case," Scarlett says. "Can't discuss details."

"Well, hell! It's not like anything I say will bring Betty back."

"That's true, but it may undermine law enforcement's ability to solve the case."

"Pretend you didn't hear that, Jimmy." I tell him. "Can you take us to Miss Minnie?"

"Got a board meeting in an hour and I need a shower. Just follow the walkway around the pool." Jimmy says, and pointing in the direction of the Granny Pod "You'll recognize it, Cape. It's a replica of her old home place. She doesn't like my place when she's 'focusing.' Says too much junk in the way blocking her visions."

"We just walk 'round your house, then?"

"Naw, front door's open. You'll see the pool out back—the Granny Pod's down at the bottom of the hill. And just one more thing... Miss Minnie has spells of 'mean-ness', I call them. I think it might be a little dementia setting in. She acts cranky, ignore her."

"Dementia has nothing to do with Miss Minnie's being cranky. Take it from one who knows!" I smile.

Jimmy's house looks like something from the cover of *Southern Living*. Walking through this beautiful home gets me to thinking. If Jimmy can overcome his problems—there's hope for me. I notice a picture on top of a Baby Grand piano that I had no idea Jimmy could play. It's a picture of Jimmy and me watching Grace work in the yard while we sip cocktails leaning up against my new Jaguar. I remember the moment but not the name of Grace's friend who took the picture. Scarlett notices the picture, too. "You make it sound like Jimmy only worked for you. Looks like you were friends, too..."

"You know, Scarlett, I was so busy thinking Jimmy was taking advantage of my hospitality that I forgot all the things he did for me, things I never paid him to do. Like the clean car you see here. I never washed it or took it in to be detailed. I guess in my mind my vehicles just managed to stay spotless."

I pick up the picture and notice how Jimmy is looking at me—like he's proud to know me. "Jimmy tried hard to be my friend. I don't know why, but I was a jerk then. I don't remember consciously thinking that he wasn't as good as me, but I behaved that way. God! And to think of all the little things he did to help me when I moved into Miss Minnie's place... You should'a left me on the bottom of that creek."

"If I'd known how you treated, Jimmy—you'd still be there, trust me."

"Huh?"

"Kidding—sort of."

We walk by the glimmering pool and a pool house just as fashionable as the main house. I'm stopped cold in my tracks when I see the Granny Pod. It's a full-scale model of the shotgun house on Miss Minnie's place. No wonder the beadboards Jimmy brought to finish up Miss Minnie's porch fit exactly.

We step onto the porch and I knock on the door. "Miss Minnie, you in there!"

"Who wants to know?"

"It's me, Cape."

"Who?"

"Mister Willard's boy."

"Come on in. Wipe them feet, I just swept up in here."

The house, while a replica of her old homeplace on the outside, is nothing like the original on the inside. The interior is tasteful—a cheerful country decor. "Boy, Miss Minnie, this is nice, but don't you miss your wood stove?"

"Boy—you crazy? Who goin' to miss all that work? Shoot! Jimmy put central heat and air-conditioning in here. Why I'm goin' miss a smoky old stove?"

"Nostalgia?" I venture.

"You can keep nostalgia—too much work in it for me!"

Until this moment Scarlett has been an observer. "I like your thinking, Miss Minnie." She steps up and takes Miss Minnie's hand. "We talked a time or two. I don't know if you remember—"

"I remember you just fine. Voted for you, too. Matter of fact, you the only politician I ever voted for who didn't let me down."

"Well, thank—"

"Ain't no need to thank me. Just keep doing your job, that's thanks enough. Wish all you politicians get that through you thick heads. Don't nobody care about being thanked. We just want you to do the job we hired you to do."

"Yes, ma'am," Scarlett says. "I still appreciate your vote."

Now it's my turn to enjoy the moment. One thing about Miss Minnie, if you don't want to know what's on her mind, probably best not to get around her.

"Both of you come over here and kneel down."

I have no idea what's in store for us, nor does Scarlett, I'm sure. We both kneel. "Bow your heads."

Miss Minnie puts a hand on each of our heads. "Lord Jesus, thank you for answering my prayers and keeping them safe, and I pray for the souls —what's the name of them peoples who died?"

"Betty Bishop," I say.

"And Ethan Warren." Scarlett adds.

"In Jesus' name I pray for the souls of Betty Bishop and Ethan Warren, Amen."

Scarlett stands up. "Miss Minnie, how did you know someone died?"

Miss Minnie finds her spit cup and unloads. "Had a vision. Couldn't figure it out to start with, at first I thought it's just one, now I know it's two. Won't stop there. At least one more going to die, maybe many as three."

"Do you know who is going to die?" Scarlett asks.

Miss Minnie pushes Scarlett away and pulls me in by my arm. "Come here, boy."

I move beside Miss Minnie and she gets between Scarlett and me. "I need to talk to Mister Willard's boy. Alone!"

"Now, Miss Minnie—"

Scarlett gives me a sign to calm down. "Miss Minnie, Louise said, she needs something to settle her stomach, I'll run by the drug store to get what she needs while you talk to Mr. Willard's boy."

I think of Jimmy's talk about spells of meanness. Scarlett is way ahead of me; she's one gracious person.

"Isn't that nice of the Sheriff, Miss Minnie?"

"I reckon. I want you to take me out to my place after we done talking. Can you do that for me?"

"Yes, ma'am."

"What do I need to get for Louise, Miss Minnie?" Scarlett asks.

"Tell her to drink some sassafras tea and mix a little slippery elm in with it."

"Do I get that at the drugstore?" Scarlett asked.

"What kind of question is that?" Miss Minnie said, "I can't believe I voted for you—twice!"

Scarlett nods with a musing smile and walks toward the door. "How about you pick me up at my office when you finish here. I'll have my deputy take me back to my cruiser. I'm upsetting Miss Minnie."

Scarlett presses the button on her collar and makes her request, "Any deputy 10-41 near Jimmy Swain's place?"

"I'm in the neighborhood, Sheriff. What you got?"

"Need a ride. I'll be out front."

"10-26, five minutes, Sheriff."

When Miss Minnie and I get to my truck, Scarlett is gone. "Miss Minnie, that's not like you," I say as I buckle her seatbelt. "Scarlett's nice —"

"Ain't got time for all this foolishness. Take me out to my place, right now. I want you to be my eyes."

Miss Minnie is always opinionated and outspoken, but I've never known her to be rude. "You were pretty hard on the sheriff, I thought you liked her?"

"Ain't got nothing to do with like. Something ain't right and I can't figure it out like I used to when I could see. Gets me all agitated and fretful when I can't *see* signs."

"Well, when things *focus* for you, I hope you'll apologize to the sheriff. Without her, I'd probably be in jail right now."

"Jail is a whole lot better than hell, Boy."

"What's that supposed to mean?"

Rather than answer, Miss Minnie closes her eyes and lays back on the headrest. I want an explanation, but I've known Minnie Reynaud long enough to know that my answer will come at a time and place of her choosing.

"They coming at you from all sides, Boy."

"They?"

"Yes."

"But popular consensus says Kress and Johnston aren't behind these attacks."

"Don't know no Kress an' Johnston. All I can tell you is they's more than one, and one ain't what they seem."

"Evil cloaked in good—"

"Hush, Boy. I can't concentrate with you jabbering."

Miss Minnie turns her head toward the window. If she wasn't blind I'd swear she sees the harvested fields and patches of woods sliding by her window. Less than a quarter mile from her driveway she sits up. "You go down to that place where you made that raft."

"You mean the Huck Finn place?"

"Such a foolish name for one of God's wondrous creations!"

"It's a great name! I don't know why people don't get it."

She holds up both hands, "Shh! You talk blocks my focusing!"

I feel like a kindergartner being chastised by my favorite teacher. Miss Minnie puts her window down and searches the woods with eyes that can't see.

"Stop! I want you to walk down that path. Keep your eyes on the ground. It's wet along the creek. I want you to walk that creek and tell me what you see."

"That's it?" You're not even going to say what I'm looking for?"

"You looking for signs! Are you daft?"

I love Miss Minnie, but today I've had enough of her. I can't wait to walk down to the Huck Finn place—alone! I get out and slam the door.

"Walk that creek good, too!" Miss Minnie yells as I break into a trot to get away.

The late autumn air is heavy with the syrupy scent of red and white oak acorns. Deer and wild turkeys mesmerized by the aromatic treats, forage through the woods around me and give me a sense of belonging. I break off the path and head toward the trail cams Scarlett set up.

I give the cameras a close going-over, but I don't see where the lenses have been painted over. In fact, they look fine. I leave the clearing and head for the creek. Animal tracks mingle with those made by Scarlett's work boots last night. Before I get back to the Huck Finn path, I notice another set that joins Scarlett's. Small shoe prints with slick bottoms, no heels.

Only one thing they can be, tracks made from the slippers the night nurse was wearing in the Maple Forest Cemetery. The boot and slipper tracks run parallel down the creek and never cross or intermingle. All the signs indicate that two people walked side by side down this creek-bank together, but that is unlikely. I notice a place where Scarlett's tracks face the creek, a place she must have stopped for a moment. A few yards behind her, the night nurse's tracks veer off to the Huck Finn path and intermingle with mine. The night nurse was probably stalking Scarlett, until she saw me, an unarmed target. Just as Scarlett surmised, the night nurse is driven by motive and opportunity. The place where I was attacked is a mass of intermingled tracks, as I expected. Only Scarlett's and my tracks come out of the creek. Again Scarlett's right. The night nurse entered the creek, apparently swam out, then got in my truck.

I dutifully report my finding to Miss Minnie. "What does it mean Miss Minnie?"

"I see good and I see evil. Can't put my finger on it. Don't trust nobody this day, Boy."

"What about Fami—?"

"Two faces!" Miss Minnie cries.

"Two faces?"

"Two faces, is coming for Louise! That's just the beginning—coming for you, too."

"How can I help, Louise?"

"You tell her to get her Bible out and keep the Word between her and this evil I'm seein'."

"What if the Bible doesn't work, Miss Minnie?"

"The Word always works, Boy."

CHAPTER TWENTY-FOUR

Louise on the run!

Slamming car doors wake Louise in her third-floor room. She gets over to the window just in time to see Jake and Jana strapping the kids into their car seats. RH, Salome, and Mr. Fisher wave to Jake and head down the driveway in Mr. Fisher's car. Jake hurries to the big Suburban, guns it and races to catch up with the lead car before they pass through the gate at the bottom of the hill.

Satisfied she is over her flu bug, Louise showers, dons a new uniform and heads downstairs. On the second-story landing she retrieves a freshly stocked cleaning cart, hangs her loop of keys on the cart handle, and starts her rounds just has she's done for the past forty years.

When she passes by the staircase balcony, something new catches her eye. "Why they got a rope tied to that railing?" Louise mumbles as she starts down the hallway. "Must be something too heavy to lug up the stairs, but why not use the freight elevator?"

Louise peeks over the railing to see. At first glance, the swaying rope is only a length of rope. When the knotted loops swing back under her feet, though, a deep-rooted memory from her youth punches her in the gut. She leans over and hauls the rope up hand over hand until she's staring at a noose, a *noose*!

Just like those the KKK crackers used to infuriate and terrorize the black community of her youth. "A damn noose don't scare me no more! If I—" Before she finishes the threat, Louise sees a solemn figure dressed in black standing in the foyer.

"Who you? What you want!"

Like the Grim Reaper, the intruder looks up and slowly points a boney finger at Louise.

"Me? You want me?" she asks in a strangled, croaking voice.

The Reaper nods, then slinks into a cat-like creep up the sweeping staircase. Louise runs back to the cart, pockets her keys, and aligns the wheels with the staircase below. "Don't come no closer. I'm calling the police, right now!"

Louise reaches in her pocket and remembers exactly where she left her phone…in the observation room so Scarlett could listen to Aunt Minnie's message. The Reaper, more than a quarter of the way up the staircase, doesn't take its eyes off the trembling prey.

Louise's sweating hands slip from the hardwood handle, but somehow she manages to keep the cart under control. "Git, now! I'll run your ass over with this cart. I *mean* it!"

The Reaper ignores the threat and continues a methodical advance. Louise's voice cracks, and her words scrape against parched vocal cords. "I'm 'bout to ruin your day. Git now!"

The Reaper pulls a dart from a quiver on its back. By feel alone, the deathly figure chambers a dart in the blowgun and lets it fly. Louise ducks, and the dart thuds into the front of the cart. "Ah, hell no! You ain't killing me, Devil." Louise shoves the cart down the stairs, then turns and runs like a woman half her age.

The Reaper, almost somersaults across the cart, but the handle snags a foot and jerks the intruder over the railing. Like the cat with nine lives, by clawing at the hardwood railing, the creature avoids tumbling to the marble foyer-floor below. Balanced on the outside railing, the hostile figure leaps at a diagonal for the balcony, flipping over the railing, and then slamming a knee into Louise's metal mop bucket that had fallen off the cart.

Even at top-speed, Louise is still more than a dozen feet from the end of the hallway. Down on one knee, the Reaper loads another dart, steadies an elbow on the injured knee and fires again. The shot is nowhere near dead-center of Louise's back, but it's a hit.

Louise feels the burn in the heel of her hand as the dart pierces skin and muscle. Undeterred, though, she stumbles ahead and makes it to the top of the third-story landing. The uneven padded step-sounds of her pursuer tells Louise her attacker is injured but still agile enough to get her. Only one option: on legs turning to rubber, Louise braces against the solid-core-door of the passion room. After what seems like an eternity, she finds her key, but since she hears steps padding along toward her on the third floor now, her hand shakes so the key bounces against the lock like a woodpecker after a borer.

She looks over her shoulder just in time to see the Reaper aiming for her head. Filled with adrenaline, Louise unlocks the door, flings herself inside and slams the door shut. She locks the deadbolt, snatches the dart from her hand and sucks at the wound. A bitter taste of the poison fills her mouth and she spits it onto the floor. Her preemptive wound-cleaning has helped some, but the remaining poison is spreading through her body like water over a broken dam.

Leaning against the door to steady her wobbling knees, a jarring crash from behind it knocks her to the floor. Even though the door is solid, it likely can't withstand the force of the Reaper's kicks. On all fours, Louise wills herself to the closet and uses the door handle to pull herself upright. Another powerful kick rattles the passion-room door, but it manages to stay on its hinges. Louise looks at her tracks across the dusty floor—if the door doesn't hold, she has only one hope of surviving.

She snatches the closet door open, lifts the clothes rod and waits for the wall to open. "Can't kill what you can't find, Devil!" Louise says with scorn, and hits the releases that snap the wall closed. "I'm in Lord Jesus, but how I goin' get somebody to notice me way up here, and I can't even stand! Ah, shoot!"

CHAPTER TWENTY-FIVE

Strange night in Slick Rock

It is almost lunchtime when Miss Minnie and I get back from the farm. With all the crazy talk she's been doing this morning, I'm having second thoughts about leaving her alone at Jimmy's place. His high-tech alarm system is good, but not as good as the armed guard we have at the mansion. "Miss Minnie, you've never been to the mansion, why don't you come and stay with me—just until Jimmy gets home?"

"I don't like being around other folks—you, included. See that you take care of Louise—the Sheriff-lady ain't much on doctoring."

"Yes, ma'am, I'll take care of her."

When I turn to leave Miss Minnie, she does something she rarely does —calls me by my name.

"Cape, come here."

"Yes, ma'am."

"You remember all the things I taught you?"

"Of course I do, Miss Minnie…most of 'em, anyway. Why?"

"You remember what I tol' you about running away?"

"Yes, ma'am: Run away—and find a better day."

Miss Minnie smiles like my answer has given her the greatest peace of mind she's ever had.

"Miss Minnie, you OK?"

"I am now."

Miss Minnie turns and pulls the door closed behind her. I head out to check on my patient, who I'm pretty sure Scarlett has already taken care of. When I turn on the Slick Rock exit, Scarlett calls.

"Miss Minnie was in such a bad mood I hated to bother her. Ask her how much slippery elm I need for Louise?"

"Louise, doesn't have her medicine, yet?" I said. "It's been almost six hours!"

"I'm a Sheriff, not a handmaiden!"

"Whoa, calm down. If I'd known you were so busy, I'd have taken the medicine to Louise before Miss Minnie and I went to her place."

"Sorry," Scarlett says. "It's been a hectic day. Now, how much slippery elm do I need?"

"Grab a handful—that should do it."

"A handful? I'm pretty sure that isn't an option."

"Are you buying? You can get it for free if you know where to look."

"I'm looking at it now—they sell it by the bottle, not the hand."

"You at the drugstore or the health-food store?"

"What difference does *that* make?"

"If Louise is like Miss Minnie, she'll use only the health-food brand, but both'd rather have fresh."

"Well, guess where I am?" Scarlett said.

"Drug store. Save your money—I got a local source. If you need a ride, I'm like two-seconds away. Then you take it to her at the mansion."

"Why would I do that?"

"To get back in the good graces of Miss Minnie, and as a bonus, get to spend a little time with me?"

"Guess I do need a ride—and Miss Minnie's vote back," she says.

"How about the bonus time with me?"

"That's of subjective value, Sir."

"Fine, I take back my ride offer."

Scarlett appears out of no where and pops my passenger door open. "Too late!"

"No, it's not!"

Scarlett leans across the console and plants a wet, juicy kiss on me.

"Thought we weren't supposed to show affection in public?"

"As Sheriff and a woman who has landed a great guy, the voters can understand that or vote me out of office—I don't care."

Hard not to smile on that one. Like I said, I love a compliment.

"Well, out of respect for your badge and office, I'll keep my pawing and fawning down to a minimum—but only 'til the election's over."

"Too bad, I was looking forward to some pawing and fawning."

"Great, I'll find us a back road!"

"I was kidding." Scarlett gives me a straighten-up-and-fly-right look. "Drive, we're on a mission of mercy."

I nod, turn toward the mansion, and Scarlett sounds off again.

"Health-food store is the other way."

"Some country gal you turned out to be!"

"What's that supposed to mean?"

"Only a city-slicker wouldn't know about slippery elm in the wild. Just so happens Mr. Fisher has some in his greenhouse, like most self-medicating country people."

"Good. Show me what it looks like and I'll save a fortune in OTC drug purchases in the future."

On the short drive back, we don't talk much until Scarlett slips her hand over mine. "I love that you and Miss Minnie speak the same language. Is she the reason you know so much about homeopathy remedies?"

"I don't really know that much about home remedies. I guess when I was coming up, I thought my grandfather was the smartest guy in the world. That night when the doctors sent me home with pneumonia was the first time my grandfather ever showed his love for me. He was a hard man, expressed no feelings at all. When we got to Miss Minnie's, he handed me over to her and said, 'Minnie, he's all the blood I have left in this world. Save him if you can.' Miss Minnie said, 'I can doctor on him, but its's in *His* hands now.'"

"Who cured you, God or Miss Minnie?"

"Miss Minnie gave the glory to God. But I gave the glory to Miss Minnie. Any time she told me about curing folks after that, I figured she knew what she was talking about."

"So you're an atheist?"

I smile. Between the atheist question and the why-I-never-married question I've got enough answers to fill a book. "I lost my parents when I was five. Someone promised that I would see them again. When that didn't happen, I had a little falling-out with, God."

"Yet your grandfather and Miss Minnie are believers. How do you square that?"

"I'm not one of those atheists who tries to shut down prayer in school or move the Ten commandments to courthouse basements. I figure live and let live is how life works best. Everyone is entitled to their own beliefs —Constitution guarantees that. My grandfather was also a big constitutionalist. I may not have picked up his faith, but I have no quibbles with his legal beliefs."

"Well, this world could use a few more atheists like you."

"And many would argue vehemently against that."

Our conversation rolls us right up to the mansion gate. The guard stops us and moves to the rear of my Yukon. "Back so soon, Sheriff?"

Before Scarlett can answer, I take our relationship a little deeper. "You know, the Sheriff is going to be around here quite a bit. Rather than log her in and out, why don't you put her on the family roster?"

"Will do, Mr. Thomas. Anything else?"

"Nope." Scarlett and I share a look. "I think that settles it."

About halfway up the long driveway, Scarlett points to the mansion. "Cape, is that a curtain blowing in the window or someone waving at us?" Even in the twilight, I see something white moving in the window. "Why would a window be opened this late in the year?" Scarlett said.

I gun the Yukon and we race up the driveway. Before I come to a sliding stop at the front door, Scarlett opens her door too early and falls to the ground, twisting her knee. I help her up and we bust through the door. The usually spotless house, is in total disarray. Louise's cart and contents are scattered across the foyer and a noose hanging from the bannister is impossible to miss. I hightail it to the stairs and Scarlett yells, "Stop!" Taking out her pistol, she goes ahead of me. "You follow me!"

As Scarlett does the police-slide-up-the-wall-approach, I follow along mimicking her technique, but in the process knock a painting off the wall. If we had an element of surprise, I just ruined it.

"Louise!" Scarlett yells. From up on the third floor we hear a muffled incoherent response. Scarlett breaks into a stiff-legged jog and I pass around her like a cop in hot pursuit. I run by the passion room and head straight for Louise's bedroom. Instead of following me, Scarlett stops in front of the passion room and yells for Louise. Now we make out Louise's cry for help. "She's in here," Scarlett says.

Scarlett holds me back and points at markings on the door that look like shoe prints.

I shrug and yell for Louise again.

From behind the door we hear a faint, "Help me! I'm dying."

Scarlett jams a shoulder into the solid-core door but bounces off.

I remember Louise's cart at the bottom of the steps and take off running. "There's a key on Louise's cart. I'll be right back."

I jerk the cart upright and look for the ring of keys, nothing. I throw towels and linens out of the way and still can't find the keys. I race back upstairs and yell to Scarlett, "She has the keys with her, we'll have to break the door down!"

"Good luck with that, the thing is made of solid oak."

I hit the door with my shoulder and immediately bounce back across the hallway. Scarlett and I sync up and run for the door again. The door creaks and gives a little, but we have to generate much more force.

I brace against the wall and get ready to give the door another go. "Wait," Scarlett says. "If she's in the clear, I can shoot around the lock and weaken the wood." Scarlett gets close to the door and yells her plan to Louise ending with, "Let me know when you are clear of the door!" A fading voice says, "Shoot, shoot it open."

BANG, BANG, BANG, BANG! Scarlett kicks at the lock and the door flies open. "Louise," We yell simultaneously. A muffled voice from behind the closet answers, "Yes."

I pop open the lever to the back wall. Scarlett holsters her pistol and drops to the floor beside Louise. "What happened?"

Louise struggles to sit up, and we pull her up against the wall. "A ninja shot me with a dart. I sucked most of the poison out, but I'm weak as water and it's hard to breathe. Help me stand."

I see a broom and a large pair of granny-panties tied to the handle. "Louise, were you waving this in the window?" I said.

"You damn right, I would have tied my bra on there too if I thought it woulda helped!" Louise unties the panties from the broom. "You turn your head while I put these on."

"Why didn't you yell?"

"I was too weak after I opened the window. My legs give out and I got short of breath."

"Tell me the details of what happened." Scarlett says, back on point. "And did you say something about a ninja?"

Louise starts jabbering like a radio DJ getting paid by the word.

"I'm making my rounds 'n I see this rope tied to the bannister. At first I think maybe Mr. Fisher hired some workmen to bring something heavy up the stairs. Then I look down and see a noose tied to the end, just like them old KKK boys used to use."

"What?" I said.

"That ain't the worst of it, Louise adds. "While I'm lookin' at this noose, a devil dressed in black from head to toe is lookin' up at me. So I say, what you want? It don't say nothin', just lifts an arm up real slow and point at me like the Angel of Death! Anyway, it starts comin' for me. I give fair warning but it blows a dart at me. That's when I let the devil have it!"

"Is that how the cart got in the foyer?" Scarlett said. "Did the the ninja throw you down the steps?"

"Naw... I pushed the cart down at it. Little thing near 'bout jumped that big old cart, but the handle caught it's foot and over the railing it go. I didn't hang around to see what happened after that. I was hoping I killed that devil, but next thing I know it's flipping over the bannister. So I take off runnin' that's when the dart hit me. I hear it trying to run, but it musta hurt itself, cause it couldn't catch me and that devil was plenty fast coming up them steps to start with."

"Where did the dart hit you?"

"In the fat of my hand. It went in and the tip came out the other side."

"Where is it?"

"I believe I put it in my apron pocket. I don't know, to tell you the truth. Got so scare when it kept trying to bust the door down that's all I could think about. Lord, I did some praying 'cause it was hitting that door 'bout as hard as y'all did!"

"What time did the ninja dart you?" I said.

"Maybe an hour ago, a little longer."

"How can Louise be in such good shape after only an hour? It took me almost three hours to recover and you had to help me breathe."

"We better get her an ambulance." Scarlett says.

"Don't do that. It'll worry my boy to death if he knows I had to go to the hospital." Louise said. "Help me to a chair. Once my legs get rested I'll be fine." I grab a chair from the passion room.

Scarlett looks around the room for the first time. The money is hard to miss, same with the printing plates. She eyes the wall-to-ceiling stack of duffle bags.

Scarlett takes out her flashlight and shines it on the floor, finding footprints—*So Cape's been in here before.* She moves the light to a dustier section of the room, discerning older, harder-to-see shoe prints with the initials J D on the heels—*Jon, Jonnie Boy was here, too. He dated Bianca and this had to be his intro to the money-laundering and counterfeiting scheme that got him killed.*

Scarlett shines the light on the floor in front of the table with the stacks of money. Multiple shoe prints are all around and it. She shines her light on Louise's shoes, just as she thought—*And here are your prints, Louise. You've been here before, too. Or have you?*

"Louise, when you came into the room—where you incapacitated immediately?"

"I don't know about that but I was zapped, n' plum fell out!"

"So you fell on the floor right off?"

"Yes, ma'am, and then I woke n' tied my drawers to that old stick you see there."

Scarlett shines her light back in front of the money table, it would take more than a few minutes to lay down that many tracks. *You've been her many times before, haven't you Louise?*

While Scarlett shines her light all over my and Louise's prints—Louise and I just stare at one another. Rather than question us about our footprints and the gobs of money in the room, Scarlett directs her attention to Louise.

"Describe your attacker for me. Was the attacker a man...or a woman?"

"Well, the attacker was as strong and as whip-fast as a young dude, but I still got the feelin' that, well, it was a woman. I know that sounds crazy, but...it was her that tole me. Her face was covered up except for her eyes — and, Sheriff, I won't *ever* forget those eyes."

"Same here, Louise." I agree.

"They were the coldest ice-blue- eyes, I ever—"

"You mean, amber... almost golden, right?" I say.

"No, Mr. Thomas. I stared right into her eyes, and they ice-cold-blue."

"Cape, don't interject your attacker's attributes into Louise's statement." Scarlett said. "What else do you remember about her?"

"She was in all black, head to toe, and moved like a cat."

"Why do you think it was a woman, did you see her face or perhaps her hands?" Scarlett said.

"No, only thing I can see was her eyes."

"And you're sure they were blue?"

"Yeah, Sheriff, 'xactly like yours."

We get Louise down stairs and into Raphael's pickup. She's pretty shaken up, so we don't head back inside until the pickup clears the gate and blends into traffic. I can't help but think of the fear I felt when the drug paralyzed me. "Boy, I hope Louise is OK."

"She'll be fine."

"What makes you so sure?"

"The hospital has much more than I had at Miss Minnie's and I managed to keep you alive, didn't I?"

"Yes, you did, and I especially liked your last treatment."

Scarlett ignores my invitation to engage in a little banter.

"The money room, is that what you and Louise were whispering about before we left for Miss Minnie's wasn't it?"

"Yes, and the reason I wanted to keep it a secret for two reasons: I don't want Louise to lose her job—"

"Are you serious? She's not going in there to clean, Cape."

"I know that, but you saw the dust on that place. If Louise was a thief there wouldn't be anything left in there but dust. Besides, did you notice some of the dates on the smaller bills?"

"No, I was trying to identify Louise's attacker—and I'll get my head around how much money is in that room later."

"Some of those bills were only a couple of years old."

"And why one's, five's, and ten's? Counterfeiters print large denomination—20's and higher?" Scarlett says.

"Do you think Louise is involved in the counterfeiting operation?"

"I know this, Cape. Unless people are pathological liars, they usually lie to hide the truth." Scarlett said. "Do you think Louise is a pathological liar?"

"Well, she did leave me hanging for a breakfast she promised me once, but no, I don't think she's a pathological liar."

"Yeah, me, either—but it's a little funny how she tried to shift the blame from Mr. Fisher, to Bianca."

"I know it's not good manners to speak ill of the dead, but if any wrong doing was going on in this house, Bianca gets my vote."

"I didn't know Bianca as well as I did Laura, so I can't speak for her veracity. But I don't see Mr. Fisher being involved in criminal activity, either. He has a stellar reputation as a straight-shooter. Plus, I'm not nearly as concerned about an old crime as I am that someone managed to breech security here at the mansion. Louise is lucky she survived that attack."

"So where do we go from here? I guess you need to show RH the money room first, right?"

Scarlett walks down the hall and checks the alarm system. "Someone forgot to set it when they left. You need to make sure the family takes this alarm-setting seriously in the future."

"How do you know so much about our alarm system?"

"I advise quite a few people on what types of alarms to buy, including Mr. Fisher. I'm a sheriff, Cape. It's part of what I do."

"Good, you can get me up to speed on this alarm. I'm sure there's an app for my phone?"

A worried look comes across Scarlett's face, probably because she doesn't want to spend time teaching a technologically challenged person about a sophisticated alarm system.

"Would it bother you if we don't tell RH or the authorities about Louise's attack—or the money room? Just for a while?"

"Because if they see the money room they may arrest the entire Fisher Family, including me and Louise?"

Not even close, you sweet naif. This has nothing to do with the Fisher family! That room solves every problem my family has ever had. I have to have that money to save my father.

"Yes, Cape, that's precisely why I we can't let the others know that, and I'd like to question Louise before we move ahead. I think there's a story about that room that only Louise knows."

"I agree you can always tell the task force after you talk to her."

265

"And I can use this time to feel Mr. Fisher out. Maybe he doesn't know anything about the counterfeiting, but then again, he could have been in cahoots with Bianca…"

"Not probable, but Mr. Fisher did say he loved Bianca. And thanks for not playing it by the book, Scarlett. If Mr. Fisher's arrested, I don't know what Jana will do. She loves him, me, all of us, like we're helpless children. Seeing him in a police car would kill her."

Scarlett rubs her left knee and blood seeps though her pants.

"What happened to you?"

"I must have cut it when I jumped from your truck. Do you have a Band-aid?"

I go to the bathroom to get one, plus a tube of Neosporin. Scarlett rolls up her pant leg while I get down on my knees and play doctor. "That's no cut, that's a gash! How did that happen without ripping your slacks?"

"I don't know, you saw me fall."

I did see Scarlett fall and I'm pretty sure her other knee hit the pavement not the one with the gash—but, as usual, I could be mistaken. "Right, but you may want to let a doctor have a look so it doesn't go septic."

"Oh, I'll be fine." Scarlett grimaces, "It's not as bad as it looks."

I nod. "Well, lucky for you I'm not your doctor—you'd be up for an amputation."

"Very lucky in that case—and yet another reason we can be glad you directed your considerable talents toward aviation and not medicine."

"You know, I have to hand it to you. Even your veiled insults come off as nice…irritating, but nice."

"Right back at you," she says.. "But I prefer to think of what I said as a backhanded compliment. I'm not into insults—veiled or otherwise."

I know wise men allow the lady to have the last word because if they do not, they know the next word spoken is the beginning of a new argument. I'm feeling a tad wise, so I change the subject.

"Explain this to me. How can Louise's and my recollections of our attacker vary so greatly? I know the person who attacked me had amber or copper-colored eyes. Louise is just as certain her attacker had blue."

"Eye-witness accounts often contradict one another, especially eye color. However, if the race is contradictory, then you have to think the accounts don't agree, and there may be two different perps."

"So you give Louise's description as much weight as you do mine?"

"Yes, why?"

"Well, we've established Louise isn't a pathological liar, but she'll stretch the truth. So how is it that her account gets the same consideration as mine?"

Scarlett gives me that look school teachers save for their most insolent students. "Our other eyewitness has... *issues,* too."

"Hmm, *issues?* Another veiled insult coming off as charming!"

"You complaining or complimenting me?"

"Definitely complimenting, RH and Darius Martin, would just call me a brain-damaged, wacko, and disregard any account I gave."

"That's because they're only cops, I'm a cop and a seasoned politician. Don't forget I've been elected sheriff twice." Scarlett says. "I have a couple of tricks I use to make sure that happens."

"I'm all ears; politics is becoming lucrative, so I may run for office, too, someday."

Scarlett holds up one finger and begins her list.

"One, you pretend ugly babies are precious, no matter how ugly they are: and two, always sweet-talk brain-damaged-wackos from wealthy families."

I reach over and fold down Scarlett's two fingers. "You may want to veil that insult some more."

"Why's that?"

"If word gets out about how you improve your electability, you'll still get the ugly baby vote, but your rich-wacko vote'll be shaky."

Scarlett kisses me passionately, and I'm thinking maybe we'll...

Like a mind reader, Scarlett dashes my hopes. "That's *not* what I'm thinking."

"Then why'd you kiss me?"

"I really need the rich-wacko vote," Scarlett purrs. "How'm I doin'?"

"Landslide!"

Scarlett grabs me by the hand and pulls me back upstairs. "Let's go back to the money room. I need to inventory the contents of those duffle bags—they could be nothing but counterfeits."

"No, I don't think so I looked in most of them. Most of the bags're silver certificates. If they aren't fake, they're worth a lot more than face-value." I hand Scarlett one of the silver certificate bills I confiscated. "What do you think?"

"When did you get this?"

"The first time I went into the room. I was going to show it to you...so much has happened since then I kind of forgot about it."

Scarlett rubs the bill between her thumb and index finger. "I think it's real."

"Do you think it's remotely possible that this is the way the Fisher Fortune was created?"

Scarlett shakes her head. "Mr. Fisher isn't the type of man to make money illegally—and we can't let him take the blame for Bianca's crimes."

"I hope you're right. I just couldn't feel the same about him."

In the passion room, Scarlett eyes the clothing on the floor.

"I don't think these are men's boxer shorts." Scarlett uses her penlight to pick up the shorts. "While these look a little like men's boxers," and she gives the garment a shake, "these four straps dropping out of the garment make this a 'closed girdle'. The straps hold up the woman's silk stockings. My mother actually wore this brand—Treo."

"So the couple getting it on in here…were *women*?" I ask.

"Looks that way," she says, nodding slowly. "And if I don't miss my guess, the money room also connects to…" Scarlett moves to the far wall and pulls on a small lamp mounted on the wall. A narrow pocket door slides away to reveal a very lavish bedroom. It doesn't take much investigating to see we are in Bianca's bedroom.

"Wow, secret doors. Just like in the movies!" I say.

As Scarlett slides the pocket door back into place, its alignment with the wallpaper pattern is plumb.

"So how do we get back inside the secret room?" I ask.

Scarlett resets the light fixture on the wall and the door slides back open.

"How did you know that?"

"Many of the big old homeplaces in these parts, have secret rooms and passageways. My brother and I used ours as a playroom, but during the War the entire family may have hidden in there for safety. Not having one would have meant death to wealthy owners in those days."

"Boy, you elitists sure live different from the rest of us."

Scarlett picks up a picture of Bianca on her nightstand. "She was always gorgeous. Did you get to know her well?"

"I knew her, but not well." I hate to lie, but I also don't kiss and tell. Before Scarlett probes for details, I change the subject. "Hey, I wonder if she was the 'other woman' in the passion room? But she would have been way too young. If this room connects to her room, though, she took part in the counterfeiting operation, right?"

Scarlett nods her head. "Can't see it any other way."

"You don't think Louise will tell anyone about what we found in there do you?" I said.

Scarlett turns back toward the money room and grabs her knee. "You know, I may run by and check on Louise before I call it a night. I'll get one of the doctors I know over there to look at my knee. It's throbbing now."

"Want me to ride with you?"

"That's sweet, but I'll be fine. Besides, I have to get up early to meet William Johnston at the Macedonia Prison Farm."

"Why do you talk to him? He's a real slime ball."

"Ah—because he's willing to *talk*! I don't think Kress and Johnston are behind these murders, but they can *solve* the case."

"I'm not optimistic 'bout that, but do give Johnston my worst regards."

Scarlett smiles, then locks me in an embrace and pushes her warmth against me. "Don't make it hard for me to do my job…"

"They killed Ally and Celine. They won't hesitate to kill us, if it proves advantageous—."

Scarlett puts her fingers over my lips. "How 'bout when I get back, we pick up with what you were thinking about earlier?"

The thought strikes me that a lot of men would be swayed by this temptress, but I don't happen to be one of them. "Scarlett, I hope you don't think I would even *consider* going back to my sleaze-bag ways—"

"You better say yes real quick, or that option goes away."

"Yes! Affirmative, Roger, Aye, Ja, Si, Oui, Evet, Hai, and just for your little police-officer ears, 10-4!"

"In the meantime maybe you can get," Scarlett points at the splintered passion-room door, "all this fixed up—we can't let anyone know about the money room."

"We've got all the time in the world; only Louise works the third floor…and after my little stay at Miss Minnie's I'm quite the handyman. No one will suspect a thing."

"And Cape, you're sure no one but you and Louise knows about the money?"

"Positive!"

Perfect…

CHAPTER TWENTY-SIX
Scarlett goes to Macedonia

Scarlett DuBois braced against the early morning temperature hovering around freezing. Condensation from her breath beaded the cold steering wheel in her hands. The gelid vinyl seat-cover penetrated her cotton slacks enough to give her the shivers. Not until tepid air began blowing from the vents could she relax against the seat to consider the challenges ahead.

Chances were good that Johnston knew as much, or more, about the ongoing murder investigations than she did...but did he? Her earlier discussions with Johnson convinced her that his *inside* source on the Taskforce was high up. Now she wasn't so certain. Johnston could be playing her, having no one on the Taskforce at all. She hated to admit it, but Johnston had a way of pulling information from her while divulging very little himself, an uncanny asset that put her at a disadvantage. Today, she reminded herself, do more listening than talking.

Thankfully, even though Johnston's duplicitous nature made finding the truth nearly impossible, speculation and facts were easy to separate. She had no doubt Johnston knew about the Fisher family fortune, but not its location or amount—score one for the home team.

He couldn't know about the telltale imprints of Jon's initialed shoe-prints left in the dust of the secret room. Not a big surprise that Jon was able to penetrate the Fisher mansion. After all, he squired Bianca to her Debutante Ball in Raleigh and was generally regarded as a lady's man. His bad-boy image intrigued Bianca from the moment they met, so their relationship had lasted until their deaths.

It was no surprise that Jon joined Bianca in her illegal activities. Even at twenty, Bianca had the potential to make the FBI's Most-Wanted list. But why wouldn't Johnston admit they had been dealing with Bianca? It wasn't as if Johnston had a gentlemanly bone in his body, or the decency not to trash the dead. There had to be a reason Johnston was shielding

Bianca. Or was his silence on the subject meant to make her suspect everyone, even Mr. Fisher and Cape Thomas?

Johnston, covert in his actions, was at least predictable; any move he made was beneficial to him and detrimental to his opponents—and she considered herself an opponent.

Scarlett made a mental note to bait Johnston with her knowledge of Bianca. Maybe that move would cause him to open up about his source on the Taskforce, or admit he didn't have one.

As her cruiser descended into the lowlands around Macedonia Prison Farm, convection fog rolled over the hood and lowered her visibility to near-zero. The last mile to the gatehouse was as much about feel as sight. A female guard came out of the gatehouse, and this time there was no snappy salute.

"Personal information on the first line and purpose for your visit in the remarks section."

Scarlett took the clipboard, filled out the first line and put *interrogation* in the remarks section.

"How long you think you might be here?"

Scarlett handed back the clipboard. "Depends on how cooperative the prisoner is, I guess."

On her walk to the visiting area a familiar voice came out of the fog.

"Good morning, Sheriff."

She turned to the voice and Johnston emerged from the fog like a ghost. "Follow me, I've found a private place we can talk."

Scarlett caught up to him, matching his stride.

"Where're we going?"

"Anywhere but inside the buildings, they're all bugged. We can visit on the exercise track since you're a law-enforcement officer."

The exercise yard was covered in discarded remnants from a nearby shingle factory, so Johnston led her to its graveled infield. "It's too quiet on that rubber track; let your feet shuffle in the gravel here." Johnston said. "Jams the listening devices."

"I don't remember you being so concerned about eavesdropping the last time I was here."

Johnston peered into the deep fog around them. "They've been putting a lot of heat on Walter and me. The press is hounding the warden for an interview with one of us. We've turned down all the requests, but that just makes the little vultures more certain that we're involved in the murders. You any closer to solving the case?"

"I'm sure you know more about the case than I do."

"I know this, Sheriff. The second part of our payments comes due soon. Unless you get us some money into the hands of those blood-suckers, your old man will die and the info he has on everyone will get out. Walter and I, along with other important people, will be looking at sentences that may as well be for life."

"How much money are we talking?"

"All your old man's assets were seized and your public servant's pay won't come close to what we need."

"How much?"

"A half million will keep your old man alive for six more months, but the bloodsuckers want their final payment after that."

"How much is the final payment?" Scarlett asked.

Johnston gave her a wicked grin. "Well, doesn't matter now, does it?"

"What do you mean?"

"Don't toy with me, Sheriff. I may be in prison but I know what goes on outside. Your questions are ones someone with money or access to money would ask. You found the money, didn't you!"

No need to hide the fact. One way or another she'd have to work with Johnston to get her dad to Samoa, far from prosecution.

"Yes."

"Where was it?" Johnston salivated.

"No way I'll tell you," Scarlett said. "People fair a little better around you if they have something over you."

Johnston sneered, "Got a little bit of your old man in you, don't you?"

"I've got a *lot* of my Dad in me!"

"Not that it makes any difference, but we'll have Fisher's money soon enough."

I don't think so. Scarlett smiled.

Johnston shuffled with some rancor in the gravel and mumbled, "Good to know you're being honest with me."

"And just how do you know that I am?" Scarlett replied, proud that she listened more than talked.

"Seems like your friend Louise is a little talkative now that she had a good dose of nitrous oxide."

"Louise?"

"When people insult my intelligence, it really pisses me off. I know the maid and Cape Thomas know about the room. And now we have access to Louise Bordeaux. If we get that information from her, so can someone else." Johnston crunched his feet vigorously in the gravel. "Sheriff, it's said that two people can keep a secret…if one of them is dead." He let's the words sink in. "Louise said a 'secret room' saved her life. Someone at the hospital knew she worked for Fisher. My people got to her—gassed her till she talked about a secret room with a bunch of different-colored duffle bags and printing machines." Johnston stirred the gravel again, but harder now. "Guess who came up with using color-coded duffle bags to separate the different types of currency, Sheriff?"

"Is your source at the hospital, a doctor or a nurse?"

"That's not important—answer my question."

"Oh, I'll take a wild guess and say, you." Scarlett said. "But I thought you'd never been in that room?"

"I devised the operation, no need for me to physically be there. That would be stupid."

"What else did Louise say?"

"She said there were millions of dollars, but there should be over a hundred million in cold hard cash in that room…unless that little bitch skimmed off the top."

"Bianca, you mean?"

Johnston cut his eye at Scarlett, and did a mock bow. "I'm impressed, Sheriff, but not surprised that you figured that out. To be honest, I thought you would have fingered the old man."

"Mr. Fisher is alive and well. That room has been abandoned for years, but if Fisher knew about it, that wouldn't be the case. Whoever ran the operation had to be in prison or dead. I went with dead, as in Bianca."

"Bravo for you." Johnston clapped his hands. "How big *is* that house, that the old man doesn't even know about an entire room?"

"Another room and another story keep Mr. Fisher from learning about the money room. Bianca had to take that into consideration before she set up the operation."

Johnston moved closer to Scarlett and whispered in her ear. "We have to secure that money. It needs to be moved to a place accessible only by you. Have you inventoried the resources there?"

"No, but there are lots of duffle bags. If they're full, Bianca didn't skim much off the top. Unless all the bags are full of counterfeit cash?"

"There is no counterfeit money in there. The plates were stored there, then all the cash was to be laundered. Most of the bills are silver certificates, and they're in the green bags; red bags are Federal Reserve notes; and blue bags for bleached one-dollar bills for the counterfeit operation in Mexico. How many green and red bags are there?" Johnston said.

"We didn't count them."

"Guess."

"Lots—green and red bags are stacked to the ceiling."

"Drag your feet, make noise." Johnston said. "We have to silence

Louise, and you know that Cape Thomas is a blabber mouth. They could jeopardize everything, including your father's life, which indirectly affects a lot of other lives, including mine, Walter's, and yours, Sheriff."

"Maybe I can talk to Louise, stall her in speaking openly until I can hide the money?"

"For the moment she is heavily sedated and will stay that way. At some point we won't be able to limit her visitors. Louise has to be silenced."

"No, I can talk to her. Tell her she has—"

Johnston kicked the gravel like a chicken scratching for worms. "You know, Sheriff, you want to be neutral and keep your hands clean. That works out just fine in fairly tales, but not so well in real life. To insure that you and your daddy make it to Samoa and live out your days in comfort, certain steps have to be taken. We no longer can depend on our other inside connection—I think they've been offered a better deal. They know the secret room is in the mansion. If they haven't found it, they're close."

"That's impossible, security is too tight," Scarlett scoffed

"You managed to breach it."

"Your connection at the hospital and the Taskforce is one and the same, right?"

"You're bright— surely it won't be hard to figure out who it is. They have to be eliminated, too." Johnston said. "We simply can't trust them anymore. Someone has gotten to them. Bringing someone else in is too risky, especially with the money that's involved. I'm afraid we have to go *all in* with you…and I'm not sure that's a good bet."

Scarlett looked calmly into Johnston's eyes and steady-shuffled her feet in the gravel. "You're right I want to keep my hands clean and everyone safe, if I can." She started to walk away, then turned and faced Johnston. "And you're right, I am bright. The person who you think is a threat is already working with me…and never consider me weak because I'm a woman. I have done and will do, what it takes to get the job done."

Johnston applauded her much longer than before. "Bravo, bravo, very impressive, Sheriff. What's your team's next move?"

Scarlett stared at Johnston until he blinked. "I think I'll get Cape Thomas to run by the hospital and *save* Louise, then have them meet me in a *very* private place."

Johnston smiled. "Two for one… I like your thinking, Sheriff."

My little stay at Miss Minnie's, with guidance from Jimmy, has turned me into a Beast of a handyman. Something no one has ever accused me of up to this point in my life. I take one of the doors off an obscure back room in the mansion and temporarily use it to seal up the passion room.

Bright and early the next morning, while Scarlett is on her way to Macedonia Prison Farm, I head over to the door plant in Pine Level and buy a reinforced steel door made to look exactly like the oak door Scarlett and I destroyed.

When I stand back to admire my work, it occurs to me that no one will be the wiser to what happened behind this new door. It also occurs to me that no one is getting into this room without a key or a search warrant, not even Mr. Fisher. Sometimes a plan comes together even when you have no plan!

Before I reward myself with a well-earned lunch, my phone rings. "Where are you?" Scarlett says.

"I just replaced the door on the on the passion room with a high-grade metal one worthy of Fort Knox. It must weigh 100 pounds!"

"Thanks for securing that, but we need to move the contents to my evidence room in Slick Rock."

"Why? No place is more secure than this—"

"Cape, I don't have time to explain now. Johnston just told me that Louise is in grave danger."

"What kind of danger?"

"The medication they gave her at the hospital must have made her talkative. She was babbling about a secret room, and now Johnston knows about it. I'm sure he has plans to kill her, even though he swears he won't. You have to get her out of there, now!"

"How can I get her out of a hospital? I'm not family."

"You wouldn't think that a man who has broken into half the FBO's around the world would have a problem walking a friend out of a hospital."

"Those FBO's weren't staffed at the time…I got it! I'll call a security expert."

"Who?"

"RH. All he has to do is flash a badge and—"

"No, whatever you do! Don't let RH know what you're up to."

"Why?"

"He can't be trusted. That's all I can tell you."

"He's with the Feds."

"There's a leak in the Taskforce reporting directly back to Johnston. It *has* to be, RH Carter."

"I *knew* it!"

"Cape, you have to move fast. Get Louise out of the hospital and take her to Miss Minnie's place in the country. I'll meet y'all there…and don't tell a soul where you're going. Not even Jana and especially Louise's

Rafael."

"I'm on it. I should be there in an hour."

"Perfect! We should arrive about the same time, and Cape—?"

"Yeah?"

"I never told you this, but you're stinking cute…and I love you."

Say what—? *Cute & Love—Wow, that happened fast!* Maybe so, but I'm ready for love. Probably not quite there yet, but falling in love with a gal like Scarlett isn't hard. I look at my watch and realize I'll have to fly to make the farm in an hour.

Like a jet on departure roll, I zip down the stairs. My takeoff roll is cut short by Detective Darius Martin standing staunch in the foyer.

"Hello, Mr. Thomas, the guard at the gate said you were the only one here. The door was opened so I thought I'd show myself in."

In my haste to replace the secret-room door I forgot to close the front door. And I think I'm fit to take over the alarm system…dumb!

"Can't say that it's nice to see you." I try to step around Darius Martin, but he covers a lot of real estate. "What brings you down here, anyway?"

"Oh, thought I'd get a little bar-be-que."

"Stick with the yellow-mustard-based sauce, the color suits you better. Bye!"

"I need only a minute of your time, Mr. Thomas."

"I'm not talking to you unless I'm lawyered up—got it?"

Darius Martin, still blocking the door, lifts his head, scratches under his chin, then slowly lowers his eyes to mine. "Mr. Thomas, I understand why you'd feel that way. I was pretty hard on you in Charlotte. But you were my prime suspect—*only* suspect, really."

"Well, I appreciate your honesty. Since that's the case, I'm calling my —"

"You're not a suspect—a person of interest, but not a suspect, Mr. Thomas." Martin says. "And this is not official business. I'm—"

"That being the case, if you'll excuse me. I really do need to be going."

I brush passed Darius Martin and turn to face him. "Since you showed yourself in, you can show yourself out. Bye!"

"Mr. Thomas—you're in danger."

"Hell, Detective, I've been in danger forever. Nice to see you figured that out."

"Mr. Thomas, are you aware that, Sheriff Scarlett DuBois is in constant contact with William Johnston and Walter Cronus Kress?"

I step back inside, slam the door, and square off with Martin. "As a matter of fact, I do know that. I even know what they discuss. Why the sudden interest in what's going on in this part of the world? Doesn't your jurisdiction end at Charlotte city limits?"

"It does, but my being a cop doesn't end there. The warden up at Macedonia Prison Farm is an old friend of mine. He's been able to capture bits and pieces of today's conversation between, Sheriff DuBois and William Johnston."

"I'm sure Scarlett is well versed in the lies and tricks the police use to get information out of people. So whatever you think you heard that may incriminate Scarlett, will surely be disproved once she makes her report to the appropriate people."

"That's part of the problem, Mr. Thomas. She checks in under the guise that she is questioning the prisoner, but about what? Johnston and Kress were tried and convicted—no case is ongoing against them."

Checking my watch, I see this conversation is taking up way too much time. I need to get to Miss Minnie's. "Look Detective, this sounds like police business, not mine. Now, I really have to go."

"Mr. Thomas, I can't prove it, because I don't have enough evidence, but I think Sheriff DuBois has plans to kill you."

"Boy, talk about a far-fetched…! I'm not one to kiss and tell, but I can assure you that Sheriff DuBoise has anything *but* plans like that."

"While y'all were kissing and telling, did she happen to mention her father is in cahoots with N.A.R.C.O. And if you aren't familiar with them perhaps you've heard of F.A.R.C. and E.L.N.?"

"Nope, doesn't ring a bell."

"FARC? Revolutionary Armed Forces of Columbia? ELN, National Liberation Army? They're evil. They pale in comparison to NARCO, however. If you're so close, shouldn't she have mentioned this to you?"

"She may have mentioned it. I can't say for sure. I'll ask her the next time I see her."

"And when will that be, Mr. Thomas?"

"None of your damn business!"

"We think Sheriff DuBois has discovered the funds in the Fisher family fortune. Does *that* ring a bell?"

"Float that question around Greenville! You'll get a thousand opinions. Trust me, that's just some folklore. An urban myth!"

"Mr. Thomas, I know you're trying to protect the Sheriff. She's not who you think she is, though, and there's a good chance she's involved with the murders of Ally Kress and Celine Seabolt."

"What a crock! No wonder you can't solve these murders. You're always chasing after the wrong person. You want to find out who killed Ally Kress and Celine Seabolt? Go put pressure on Water Cronus Kress and William Johnston. They hired the killer, I'll bet anything on it! You should be ashamed of yourself—Scarlett DuBois is twice the cop you'll ever be! Now unless you want to handcuff me to those stairs over there and pretend like I'm not under arrest, I have things to do and places to be…and since you are looking for dirty cops, why not give a real good look at RH Carter, huh? Word on the street is that he's the problem, not Scarlett."

"Why do you think so? RH Carter, is key to solving the case."

"That may be, but only because he's playing for both sides!"

"You mean, that's what Scarlett DuBois, told you?"

"Good day, Detective…and just to show there're no hard feelings on my part. I'm going to share Cape Thomas's five best places to eat eastern-style bar-be-que—the good stuff! Southern Smoke, Skylight, Wilbur's, Parker's and Grady's all get five stars from me."

"I appreciate your suggestions—mighty kind of you. Why don't you choose the place and I'll buy lunch?"

"Like I said, Detective, I'm in a hurry."

"If I could ask you just one more thing before you go…?"

"Make it a good one!"

"To your knowledge, has Sheriff DuBois ever been to the home of Ally Kress?"

"No."

"Are you sure?"

"Yes, she told me herself that she and Ally discussed meeting there during the Johnston and Kress trial, but she never went. As a matter of fact, she said she hadn't been to Charlotte since she was a kid." I look at my watch and see I'm really late…something that ticks off airline pilots. "Good day, Detective. You're in Greenville and it's noon, so give B's Barbeque a shot, always a winner!"

"Mr. Thomas, her cell phone records tell another story."

"Maybe she passed through Charlotte and didn't stop. You're chasing a dog-track lure, Detective—all it will do is lead you back to the starting point. Scarlett DuBois is a fine woman. Now—"

"We found hairs belonging to Scarlett DuBois in Allison Kress' home."

"You know, Martin I figured you for a lowlife when you handcuffed me to the bed and pretended I wasn't under arrest. But this ploy is even below you! I met with Scarlett before I left for Charlotte to talk with Ally. I'm sure that Scarlett sheds hair. Maybe I brought a few strands into the house with me, or maybe RH planted 'em there to frame Scarlett. Mystery solved!"

"Fine. But we found one of the Sheriff's hairs on Celine Seabolt's little pinkie and a trace of DuBois' DNA under her fingernail—you remember shaking hands with Ms. Seabolt?"

"I probably did, but I don't remember."

"The hands of Ally Kress and Celine Seabolt were washed clean, postmortem, according to the coroner. But somehow or another the killer didn't thoroughly clean the right pinkie of Ms. Seabolt. We think that happened because you came back unexpectedly and scared the killer off. As for the highball glass, cigarette, and ashtray with your DNA…the evidence doesn't fit the crime scene. Someone planted that evidence, and that person is Scarlett DuBois!"

"Martin, I've been lied to by the police before. I know your little tricks. You're a dirty cop just like RH Carter, who might be the killer! And if he's not I'm almost 100% certain that his fiancée attacked me in the hospital, at Miss Minnie's place, and in Wilson. You're not here because you're a caring cop. You're here trying to find the Fisher family fortune. Fool's Gold, Detective Martin, Fool's Gold! Now get out! Or I'll call cops who do have jurisdiction in this county."

CHAPTER TWENTY-SEVEN
Escaping with Louise

The usually full parking lot at Slick Rock General Hospital holds true to form except for one space near the farthest outreaches of Hades. I park in that spot and consider stocking up on provisions before the long trek to the main entrance. Even from this distance, I can make out my grim old Room 416. My phone rings and the name on the screen reminds me that there is no need to dwell in the past. I have a bright future ahead with a special someone.

"Always glad to hear from my favorite law-enforcement officer, especially after getting a visit from my least-favorite one."

"Darius Martin," Scarlett says. "Why's he in Greenville and what does he want?"

"Asking questions about you, and the Fisher family fortune…think he knows something?"

"Maybe—What kind of questions he ask?"

"I'll tell you all about it when I see you. But, just for clarity, you never visited Ally in Charlotte, did you?"

"No, we spoke of meeting a few times, but I never visited. Why?"

"Detective Martin asked if you were ever in Ally's home. Just wanted to make sure I told him the truth—you know how fierce cops get when they think you're lying."

"Did he tell you why he wanted to know?"

"Uh-oh—got a bad signal under this awning. I'll grab Louise and we'll see you on the farm."

"Cape, stop while you have a signal. Why is Darius Martin asking about me?"

I step out from under the awning and try to align myself with a cell tower camouflaged as a pine tree.

"He said they found your hair in Ally's home. I told him I saw you just before I visited Ally and must've carried it down there myself."

"Anything else?"

"Yeah, said your hair was on Celine and some—"

"That can't be, I was very—"

"Darius Martin is a liar. He told me that to turn me against you."

"Thank God it didn't work—did it?"

"Heck, no!"

"Did he say anything else?"

"Says you're planning to kill me. What a laugh!"

"Are you kidding?—I *love* you."

"That's what I told him—the guy is a total nut. How he made detective is a mystery, he's always after the wrong person. He thinks you murdered Celine— and Ally, too"

"You're kidding…"

"Nope."

"Well, I'll just give Mr. Martin a call. The nerve!"

"Don't blame you a bit, Scarlett." I said. "I have to go if I'm going to be on time."

"Cape, Jake is Louise's attending physician, and I don't know how to tell you this… He may be working with Johnston and Kress."

"How do you know?"

"Some information about Louise and the money room got back to Johnston, and it had to be from Jake. I'll tell you all about it when I see you. In the meantime, don't let Jake know what we're doing."

"Not a problem."

In one conversation my opinion of Jake is forever changed. That backstabber! I'm so mad at Jake that I walk into the sliding glass door without noticing it's closed. My loud thud causes the receptionist at the desk to look up from her computer.

"Well, hello, stranger!"

The receptionist is a friend of Traitor-Jake and I should know her name, but I can't grab her handle. "How you doin', *darling*?"

"I'm fine! I was just asking that good-looking son-in-law of yours today how you're doing. We've missed you around here."

"Well, I miss the people, especially you, but I'm in no hurry to be admitted again. Just visit friends, family."

"I know that's the truth. What can I help you with today?"

"Can you tell me Louise Bordeaux's room? I'm here to pick her up."

She scans her computer screen, then looks back up.

"You sure the name is Louise?"

"Yes, her son, Rafael, checked her in last night."

A nurse from the 4th floor whose name I can't remember, either—steps up to the screen. "I think he means 'Elouise' who works for Mr. Fisher. She was pricked by a dart."

"Right."

"She's in 317, but she isn't due to be discharged today, sugar. She's scheduled for more lab screenings in an hour."

The nurse and receptionist exchange a look they think I'm crazy—better get that cleared up before they call Traitor Jake.

"Thinking one thing and saying another." I point at my head and spin my finger around in circles. "Story of my life lately. Sorry. I meant to say, 'visit', not 'pick up'—a pickup's what I *came* here in. "

"Well, don't you worry. That happens to us all. After all you've been through, you can surely be forgiven. Why don't I let Dr. Draughon know you're here?" the 4th floor nurse says.

The receptionist nods and breaks out into a big smile. "I'll call him right now."

"NO! Uh, please, don't call him."

"Excuse me?"

"I just remembered, I had to tell him a fib."

"Gracious! Whatever for?"

"Jake asked me to take the grandkids to the park, but I told him I had some chores to do around the house."

She smiled. "Oh, I understand *eg-zactly* where you're coming from. My kids think I'm a 24-7 babysitter, too. You go right on up."

I open the door to Room 317 and am greeted by a weak, "Is that you, Dr. Salome?"

"No, Louise, It's me, Cape Thomas."

"Why you here?"

"To get you out of here."

"Why?"

"You're in danger. I need to get you to Miss Minnie's place where you'll be safe."

"I can't walk. Every time I start feeling better, Dr. Salome comes in and knocks me out with another shot."

"Salome...Jake's your doctor, right?"

"No, *she's* my doctor, I ain't see Dr. Jake. They say I been hallucinating, they want to run some test."

"Come on, Louise, things aren't what they seem. I have to get you out of here."

"I better wait here until Dr. Salome tells me I'm healthy 'nuff to leave. Besides, I don't feel so good, Mr. Thomas."

"Louise, Scarlett called me. Jake is your doctor but he's working with

Kress and Johnston. You remember them, don't you?"

"Yeah, they the people trying to kill, y'all."

"Well, you may be part of the 'y'all,' now. I've got to get you out of here. Once we're safe, we can sort out what's going on. Are you with me?"

"I can't walk."

"I'll take care of that. Be right back."

First shift is a lot different than third shift. The corridor is busy with nurses, attendants and doctors. No way I can steal a wheelchair and just waltz out of this place with Louise.

I walk the corridor until I find another bank of elevators. When I step inside one, I see this is the express elevator to the emergency room. Two nurses step in with me. "You do know this is for ER personnel only?"

I nod and push the red button marked ER.

"Do you work here?" one asks. "You look familiar."

"No, to tell you the truth, I'm trying to find a wheelchair for my favorite aunt."

"Why, all you have to do is ask, and someone will deliver one to her room."

"Ah, yes, but the chair is not *for* my aunt. I have a potted plant in my truck that I need to deliver to her."

"A potted plant?"

"Yeah, I know it sounds crazy…but my aunt wants to make sure I haven't killed that plant while she's been here in the hospital. It comes from a cutting of my great-great-grandmother made. My aunt thinks I'm hiding the fact that I've killed it., so I need to bring it by her room for a quick visit."

"That's a new one on me! How big is the plant? A medicine cart may work better for you…" I try to imagine Louise sitting atop a metal cart; pretty sure that won't work. "It's big. I think a wheelchair would work better."

"There's plenty of chairs in the storage area near the ER. I'll get you one."

"Why, thank you!"

As the nurses walk off, I hear one whisper to the other. "That's Doctor Draughon's, father-in-law." The other nurse laughs, "He's nuts and his whole clan is nuts. Who asks a potted plant to visit?"

The second nurse leans in close, whispering. "Lord, ain't that the truth? I hope that aunt he's visiting isn't on Dr. Draughon's side of the family. That man's too cute to go crazy!"

In spite of being snarky, the nurse is true to her word. Before I return to get Louise, I scout my potential escape route. I push the empty wheelchair toward the double doors in front of me. Beyond the doors a cacophony of urgency erupts and they burst open. A cadre of medical personnel rush by me, all eyes focused on the gurney they're huddled around. *This* is the situation to cover our escape.

I scramble to the correct elevator and sit in the chair on the ride back to the 3rd floor. Four nurses join me on the second floor and one asks if I need help. I assure her I'm fine and roll out at my stop like a boss. In Room 317, Louise is up and drinking water. "I got to flush these drugs out of my system." Louise chugs another cup of water like a shot of tequila. "Why we goin' to the country, again?"

"Scarlett says you're in danger. Jake and RH Carter may be involved. As soon as I make sure you're safe. I'll come back for Jana and the kids."

"How about, Mr. Fisher?"

"I have to leave him there; he'll never turn against RH. Scarlett will fill us in when we see her." I look at my watch. "Gotta roll." I push the chair in front of Louise. "Your chariot awaits."

No sooner do I get out of the door than Jake steps from the elevator. Lucky for us he's in deep conversation with a Dr. Salome Matkusa. I twirl the chair around and start back for the room. Before I get there, I hear Jake and the Salome's voices fading away as they head down the corridor in the opposite direction. I spin the chair around and run for the elevator. Louise yells, "You hurt me and Rafael is going whup yo' ass! Slow this thing down!"

"We gotta go before Jake comes back."

"Oh, you don't have to worry about that. Dr. Jake and Dr. Salome have them a long lunch every day. He won't be back for an hour or so."

"How do you know that, thought you haven't seen Jake, right?"

"Oh, they're the talk of the hospital. It's all the nurses talk about when they think I'm asleep."

"You mean they're having an affair?"

"That's the word," Louise says with a decisive nod.

I grip the handles of the wheel chair as if I'm choking Jake's neck.

We wait just down the hall from the ER until the next medical emergency comes crashing through. We don't have long to wait. All heads turn toward the trauma team attending the gurney coming out of the ambulance. I line Louise up with the exit and pull off a daring hospital escape. Every single person in the emergency room waiting area is engulfed in their own misery, only one attendant notices us and asks, "Want me to push that chair for you, sir?"

"No, son. But keep one handy for Dr. Jake Draughon."

"Why's that?"

"Because if I don't kill him, he'll ride in one for the rest of his damn life!"

"Hey, I know you, man. You were on the 4th floor for years! You're Dr. Draughon's father-in-law?" The attendant says.

"Not anymore. From now on, I'm his worst nightmare!"

I hit the door before the ambulance even pulls away. I roll Louise along the far side the ambulance, using it for cover, just in case Traitor Jake accidentally scans the parking lot. The pushing is easy on the smooth pavement. When we hit the section of the parking lot where gravel is mixes with asphalt, the chair gets a lot harder to push. "Think you can walk yet, Louise?"

"How far you parked from here?"

"Almost to the main road, why?"

"I ain't walkin' that far."

"Come on, Louise. It's uphill most of the way—I'm dying here."

"You doing just fine, keep pushin'."

By the time I reach my truck, my legs are burning like they've been heated with a blow torch. Even before I stop, Louise is standing up in the chair waiting to put her feet on the payment.

"Quick recovery." I note.

"Fresh air does a body *good*." Louise replies, giving me a big grin. "Don't you feel better after a good exercise like that?"

I pop the lock with my key fob and Louise hops into the passenger's seat. Even though the air is cool, I'm sweating like an Icelander in Florida. "I've felt better, to tell you the truth."

It takes me a good fifteen minutes to recover from my good exercise, just as we hit the Wilson exit for I-795. I hand my phone to Louise. "Call Rafael."

"Why? Rafael on a job site in Buxton."

"Does he work all the time? He should be in the hospital with you."

"He offered to stay, but Rafael is a lot better off at work than in a hospital."

"Well, he'll have to come back. I'm not leaving you alone at Miss Minnie's place."

While Louise and I are discussing the merits of a child caring for a sick parent. Jimmy calls. "Cape, where are you?"

"Passing the Sims exit. Just about to turn on to I-795, why?"

"It's Miss Minnie."

"She's OK, isn't she?"

"She's fine, physically, but something is all over her. She's got this notion that something bad is going to happen to you and Louise. I told her Louise will be fine at the mansion."

"Louise is with me, Jimmy."

"Really? Come to my house. Once she sees both of you, maybe Miss Minnie'll calm down."

I look at my watch. Checking in with Miss Minnie is not an option if I'm going to meet Scarlett on time. "Let me make a phone call see what I can do."

"Hurry, Cape. She's seen all kinds of signs, and to tell you the truth. I'm also starting to feel like something's not right."

"I'll call you right back. I need to talk to Scarlett"

"Scarlett, as in Sheriff Scarlett DuBois?"

"Yes."

"Sounds like you two may have more than a professional relationship…"

"You know, Jimmy,   you have a lot more talent than number-crunching. Don't mention this to anyone, but I think Scarlett and I are headed for something big. It's time I put down some roots."

"Well, I like the sound of that."

"I'll tell you all about it the next time I see you. And tell Miss Minnie we're late to meet Scarlett but we'll be by later."

Scarlett answers before the first ring plays back to me. "Where are you, Cape?"

"Just turned onto I-795 about thirty minutes from the farm. Miss Minnie is upset. I should run by and see her, but I'm already—"

"Don't do that. You didn't tell anyone we're meeting, did you?"

"Well, just Jimmy and Miss Minnie."

"I told you not to do that!"

"It's Jimmy and Miss Minnie! Who I trust with my life. I'll can tell them anything and they got my back!"

"I know, I know. I'm on edge. I don't know what or even who we're up against. Why is Miss Minnie upset?" Scarlett asks.

"Had another vision—feels something bad is going to happen."

"Cape, that may be true if you don't get to the farm—right now."

"What do you mean."

"It's probably nothing, but I get the feeling from Johnston that they are about to put their revenge plan into motion."

"You mean kill me and my family?"

"Yes."

"They've already killed Ally, Celine, Betty, and Ethan. The plan is in motion to add us, you think?"

"They didn't kill those four. I know who did, though."

"Who?"

"I'll explain when I see you. One more thing. I want you to throw your phone out of the window, right now!"

"So they can't track me?"

"Yes!"

"Can't I just take the battery out?"

"Cape Thomas, do you trust me?"

"With all my heart."

"Then throw the phone out...and hurry, I can't wait to see you!"

I open the sunroof and fling my phone toward the Kinston-Raleigh exit sign. Louise looks at me like I've just tossed away her first born. "Wasn't that your phone?"

"It was."

"If we run into trouble, won't we need it?"

"Don't worry, Louise. We're about to be surrounded by the cavalry."

"You mean the Sheriff?"

"Yes." I pat Louise's hand. "Trust me, we'll be just fine."

Scarlett turned on her blue lights and pressed the accelerator to the floor. Darius Martin must've found something more substantial than transferrable DNA if he's ready to bring charges or he wouldn't have opened up to Cape. Though the world would never understand or empathize with her, all she did in Charlotte was what was necessary to save her father. Any loving daughter would have done the same.

An inquiry crackled across her radio and interrupts her train of thought: "What's your 10-20, Sheriff? We need someone to respond to a disturbance at Skeeter Pointe Country Club."

"What's the problem?"

"Pokemon hunters and golfers having a turf battle on the 9th green."

"Sounds likes a problem in paradise. When the club comes up with a ruling, we'll enforce it. I'm taking the rest of the day off."

"Want to add a location to that, Sheriff, in case we need you?"

"Nope. I'll be back for second shift"

Scarlett eased her cruiser to a stop at the narrowest point along the path at Miss Minnie's. Two sets of fresh truck tracks in the dusty path meant everyone was in place. Perfect. Scarlett removed a harden-steel cable from her trunk and stretched it across the path. With the ease of a Tri-County lineman, she bolted the cable to trees on either side of the path and hung a "No Trespassing by order of Slick Rock County Sheriff's Department" sign on the cable. Just for good measure, she crisscrossed the path with yellow crime-scene tape. Though her weapon wouldn't be needed, Scarlett racked her 12-gauge tactical shotgun, chambering one of eight rounds from the magazine. She removed a small Kevlar case of five darts from her shirt pocket. Very carefully, she dipped the darts into a vial of curare poison, or *woorari* as the natives in Brazil call it, and blows them dry. With a steady hand, she loaded one dart into the blowgun and slipped the guard over the muzzle. Under her breath she whispered one word: *Showtime.*

Louise gets out of my Yukon and flitters around like a kid visiting Disney World for the first time. "Lawd, I can't believe how this place looks! Aunt Minnie had everything so neat. Can you believe how run down it is?"

"Yeah, the yard does look bad." I turn and beam at the house with its newly repaired roof and haint-blue porch. "But you have to admit the old house's roof and porch are coming together!"

Louise turns and walks to each side of the house. I move back so she can get a full view of the splendor. "Looks like jacklegs tacked some tin on the roof and splashed a little paint on the porch ceiling. Rafael would tear the whole thing down and start over! Ain't no way a quality builder like Rafael would put out a mess like this."

"Well, he doesn't exactly operate on shoestring budgets…"

Louise backs away from the house shaking her head. Then looks up sharp. "Lawd, don't *tell* me! You made this mess, didn't you?"

"Well, Jimmy, mostly…but I helped."

"Jimmy Swain?"

"Yes."

"What does he know about building? Y'all should have called Rafael. He wouldn't have charged Aunt Minnie a dime!"

"I didn't think about that." I look at the building with an objective eye. "It was a temporary fix. Uh, we wanted to stop the rain from getting in the house before we really spruced it up."

"Why'd you paint it then?"

Before I can construct another lame excuse, I look up in time to see Scarlett's cruiser kicking up a small cloud of dust as she makes her way to the house. My initial reaction is to go over and give her a kiss, but the look on Scarlett's face is not one to invite smooching—she's all business. Scarlett may be worried Louise will spread the word about our budding relationship. I make a mental note to keep it all business with Scarlett until we're alone.

"Glad to see you, Sheriff DuBois. What's up?"

"Did you secure the passion room?"

"Yep, and it looks very professional." I glare at Louise. "Not even Rafael can find fault with that repair job."

"Do you have a key?"

"Yep." I hold up the key and dangle it at her.

"You know, I've thought about that room. I'm pretty sure everyone responsible for it is dead now. Guess you better give me the key and I'll turn it over to the Taskforce." Scarlett says.

I toss the key to her

"You mean Bianca?"

"Yes, and my brother, Jon—Jonnie Boy."

"What's your brother got to do with that room?" I say.

"I saw his shoe prints in the dust." Scarlett looks at Louise, "And your shoe prints were in there, too, some much older than yesterday. Care to explain, Louise?"

Louise hangs her head and begins to sob. "Rafael is a good man. He needed a break to start his business, but the banks, they don't loan money 'less you got twice as much as you need...and that goes double if you black and had a little trouble. Especially back then."

"Ah, that's how Rafael got his start." I remember our earlier conversation. "And that's why you owe the Fisher mansion, and not Mr. Fisher?"

"Yes...and those piles of money that you saw in there, Sheriff. That's the money I made Rafael pay back. I messed up when I loaned money to some of my other family. They weren't as successful as Rafael. I been using my money and each week I pay back their debt. I'm no thief."

"Is that's why the short pile had all the small bills?" I ask.

"Yes. Some weeks I didn't have but a few dollars left over after paying my bills." Louise explains.

"Why are the money stacks in that order?" Scarlett presses her.

"I'm ashamed to admit it, but we came up poor. After my mama died, I had to take care of my brothers and sisters. I was only ten. I made sure they went to school, but I had to keep house to make money so we could eat. At first I did laundry for people and then Aunt Minnie took pity on us. She helped me some and tried to get me to go to school, but I had a lot of little mouths to feed. If I tried to get help from the state, they would have found out how young I was and broke up my family. Probably send all of us to foster homes and we never woulda been a family again. I couldn't allow that!"

"So you never went to school?" I said.

"No, I was big for my age. Everybody knew Mr. Fisher would hire people if they really wanted to work. Lot of people work for Mr. Fisher that he don't need. Anyway, I walked up to his house when I was 12 and told him I could cook and clean. He asked me how old I was and I told him 18. He gave me a job and when he learned the old house we were staying in didn't have power, Mr. Fisher let us live in a tenant house he owned. Long story, but now you see why I'll never leave him. Even now, he still loves one dish he showed me how to make, 'Crab Louise,' and won't let nobody make it but me."

Scarlett and I look at one another, then back at Louise.

"I see by that look on y'all face that you think I made a bad choice. Well, that ain't so. All of my brothers and sisters have jobs, and all of them have college educations."

"So rather than count the money, you used the same denominations and determined the payback by measuring the piles?" I ask, clarifying her story.

"Yes, at first—but Rafael made me take adult classes on managing money."

"How did you find the room?" Scarlett asks, going in a new direction.

"I was cleaning out the closet in Miss Bianca's room. I heard a noise behind me and knew it had to be coming from the passion room. So I snuck down the hall and, sure enough, the door to the room was open! Miss Bianca was in a hurry—I could hear her snatching things up in the money room. I hid on the other side of the bed where I could see into the closet.

As soon as I get down, Miss Bianca come out and lower the clothes bar that slides the wall back in place. I waited till she closed and locked the door, then I went over to the closet and lifted up the bar. I was going to tell Mr. Fisher about it when I got the money paid back. After Miss Bianca died, though, no one ever went back in the room again, so I figured I had plenty of time...and I did too." Louise points at me. "Until you showed up...then I figured the cat would get out the bag sooner rather than later—I was right."

"Sorry, Louise," I say.

"Did you know about my brother and Bianca?" Scarlett asks.

"Miss Bianca had so many *friends* I couldn't keep up with them—nobody else could, either."

"You created the story about the passion room to keep people out, didn't you?" Scarlett muses.

"No Sheriff. The story I told you about the room is true. Mr. Fisher put that room off limits just as I told you."

"Yet Bianca used it for cover."

"Miss Bianca never cared about what Mr. Fisher thought or said."

"I can vouch for that," I add. "But if Bianca used the room, why is the dust so thick?" I ask.

"Miss Bianca first used the dust mop like I did that day I caught you in there. Then she found the secret door from her bedroom to the money room—and nobody used it again until, you."

"What happened in the passion room? I *have* to ask," I smile

"All I know is what I was told."

"Do tell!"

"When I first started to work for Mr. Fisher, there was an old white woman, Hannah, who worked the main floor. She started me upstairs on the fourth floor for what she called "proper training." It was about a year before a guest or public visitor saw me. Miss Hannah was a professional housekeeper, from Ireland. When she said once that the Irish was the blacks of Europe, we kinda bonded!

"When I come off the third floor, she trained me for the second floor. That's the first time I ever saw or heard anything about the passion room. I was young and powerful-curious, so I worried Miss Hannah, to death about showing me the room. At first she would only tell me about it. Finally, one day she said, 'Come on, Louise, I got something I'm goin' to show you.' She opened the room and let me look. And all them years ago it looked just like it does today. I asked her what happened and she told me that's where Mr. Fisher caught Ms. Calis foolin' around."

"With RH's daddy, right?" I say, turning to Scarlett. "Guess you were wrong about the clothes belonging to women."

"No, she be right, Mr. Thomas." Louise says.

"Who was the woman?"

"Ms. Calis and RH's mama was in that room, and when Mr. Fisher caught them, Ms. Calis said, 'Why wouldn't I be with her? She's twice the man you'll ever be.'"

"Why didn't you tell us earlier?" I ask.

"Because of what happened to Miss Hannah when Mr. Jobim caught me and Miss Hannah coming out of the room. He said I was young and didn't know better."

"But Hannah?"

"I don't know 'cept what I saw from the window. Mr. Jobim put all Hannah's belongings in the back of the car and Hannah in the passenger seat. I never saw her again. The next day Mr. Jobim drive up with a new maid, Maria. She married Mr. Fisher and had Bianca not long after she got here, but you know that story, Mr. Thomas."

"So you never went in the room again until you saw Bianca in there?"

"No, I had all those mouths to feed and I didn't want what happen' to Hannah to happen to me."

"Did Hannah go back home?"

"Years, after Hannah left I ask' Mr. Fisher if he ever heard from Miss Hannah…" Louise's voice trailed off. "Mr. Fisher say, I don't recall anyone name' Hannah ever working for me, Louise. Do you remember anyone name Hannah?"

"I say, 'I don't know what you talking about, Mr. Fisher. Who is Hannah?'" Louise nods knowingly, "Now you know what I meant that day when you first come to the mansion and I told you, 'Don't believe nothing you hear and only half of what you see, Mr. Thomas.' Because even if you saw it— don't mean you *seen* it."

Scarlett looks down the path, then back at Louise and me. "Well, I thought you'd solve that mystery for me, but I see that the mystery of the Fisher fortune will never be solved. Not a mystery what happened to Hannah, though."

"What?" I ask.

Scarlett's lips curve into a sneer. "Darling, remember that two people can keep a secret, if one of them is dead. That's what Mr. Fisher knows and unfortunately that is what I believe, too."

"I don't understand…"

"I know you have this thing for me, Cape, because we had sex. Men are like that. They pretend women are the clingy ones, but that just isn't so. I've used sex my entire life to get what I want." Scarlett holds the key to the passion room near her face and jingles it. "You see, I thought the only way I would get this was to sleep with you again—or kill you. The thought of sleeping with you again bored me. I decided it would be more interesting to kill you."

"Scarlett, if you're joking." I look at Louise's mouth agape as she stares right at Scarlett. "It isn't funny."

"She ain't jokin' Mr. Thomas. She's the one who attacked me in the mansion. That was you, won't it, Sheriff?"

"Yes, it was, Louise." Scarlett coos, tracing her fingers across my face, then letting her hand rest on my shoulder. "Too, too bad for you, Cape. If I had gotten to Louise, she would have revealed the money room to me. You still would be a lonely, delusional, broken man—but alive to live however."

"But Scarlett, why did you save me after the 'night nurse' darted me, if you planned to kill me?"

"Night Nurse, Cape?…Really? You were wrong about Louise. She is a much better eyewitness than you. At least she identified her attacker."

"So the night nurse is…Salome! But she's a doctor, marrying RH."

"And a very smart one, too," Scarlett agrees. "RH, in spite of his position, is a salaried federal employee. Salome, like me, is a woman from a family that lost its fortune. She and I met years ago—at the Debutante Ball. After I stopped dating RH, and after I found out you would live, we decided she should hook-up with RH—for another reason. When she found out the potential payoff, she decided to play on the winning team, mine."

"Is RH part of this *winning team?*" I say, confused beyond belief.

"No, he has no idea, but now he will never experience marital bliss with Salome or me, so it doesn't matter, " she smiles.

"RH is smart, he'll figure out what's going on."

"RH is a tool and a fool."

"You won't get away with this, Scarlett, RH will see to that. Besides, if you and Salome split the money, won't Johnston and Kress kill you in a heartbeat?

"Salome will be getting a lot more than the money in that room, and Johnston and Kress have their own near-term mortality to prevent. Theirs is not as critical a problem as yours and Louise's, though."

"Scarlett, Detective Martin is on to you! And don't forget how dedicated he is to solving the five murders in his city."

"That's a bit of a problem, and I do have to shift suspicion from me. That may not be so hard since you've already admitted *you* probably brought my DNA with you to Charlotte."

Now I'm glad I didn't tell Scarlett about the DNA they found under Celine's fingernail, but Scarlett may be smart enough to cover her tracks, anyway—because of my big mouth. I decide to buy a little time by changing the topic.

"Yeah, you *can* probably do that, but you won't get away scot-free. Turns out Darius Martin is a very smart cop, much smarter than you. So you won't get away with killing Ally and Celine, but to satisfy my curiosity —Johnston and Kress *paid* you to kill them, didn't they?"

"Still blinded by your hatred for Johnston and Kress, aren't you? Actually, I killed Ally and Celine to keep Johnston and Kress in prison." Scarlett said. "But had they gotten out, they would have killed the women. Either way, both were going to die—so I guess you're right. Johnston and Kress were the motivating force for me."

"Why kill Betty? She was dying anyway!"

"Yes, when I had the rope around her neck I realized how sick she was. I took the rope off and the old gal begged me to finish it. I thought why not? The kindest cut," Scarlett says, smiling a real smile. "You see, Cape,

I'm not a horrible person."

"Yeah—you a real Angel of Mercy. And who is James Sauls?"

"Another notch in my belt, he's the stalker who chased you on the mansion grounds, and the hunter who shot the crossbow at you down in the woods."

"Why'd he do that?"

"Because, like you, he thought sex meant love, darling."

"And you killed him because he was probably a decent guy and once he found out you were an evil bitch, was going to the police?"

"I'll tell you it's a miracle! Praise the Lord. Cape Thomas, is completely healed. His brain works! Hallelujah!"

"The praying and Christian thing…that's all a lie, too?" I add to distract her from shooting Louise and me.

"Sho' is, honey. But without the Lord Jesus Christ you can't get elected in Slick Rock County." Scarlett reached into the back of the cruiser and snared the blowgun. "I'd really like to lay out my master plan for you, but I'm pressed for time. I need to lay out both of you first, no dithering around, then establish a time-line alibi. To tell you the truth, I thought yours was going to be a quick, clean kill, but Darius Martin's questions about my presence at Ally's means I have to change my plans—just a bit. I have to give your friend Detective Martin more proof that you were always the killer."

Talk about feeling stupid? Darius Martin did everything but hand me a lifeline, and I chose to side with this off-the-rocker-cracker.

"Let me guess." Scarlett muses, dart gun on standby, "Right about now you're feeling really stupid for not trusting Darius Martin?"

"Wow, you must be psychedelic."

"You mean psychic, don't you?" Scarlett says with a smug eyebrow-arch.

"Naw, I got it sooo right. You're a bad-trip, bitch!"

CHAPTER TWENTY-EIGHT
Scarlett takes care of business

Scarlett handcuffs me, hands in front, and ties Louise to a one of the four post I replaced on the front porch. "You stay here. I'll be back for you later. I need to pick up a few things in the secret room and you're my ticket to access it." Louise looks at a middle post near the steps. "Please, tie me to that post over yonder so I can sit on the steps, I'm weak as water."

Scarlett rolls her eyes, unties the rope, and jerks Louise over from the corner of the porch, but she stumbles and falls.

"Hey, don't hurt her!"

"Shut up!" Scarlett lashes Louise to the middle post and kicks me in the groin. I roll on the ground in pain and Scarlett kicks me in the back. "Get up and move!"

Louise looks at me, mouthing something as Scarlett shoves me down the path. I'm not too sure I read her lips correctly, but if I did, our problems may be lighter.

"Where we going?" I say.

"The place where I put you under my spell."

"The Huck Finn Place?"

"'Huck Finn Place,' what a joke! That's what you named the place as a kid, so I think you had problems with reality long before you were shot in the head."

"*Huck Finn* was a great story, nothing weird about liking it."

Scarlett shakes her head. "You also believe a ghost led you to your daughter and a witch doctor is your surrogate mother. That doesn't sound weird to you?"

"If you put it that way, I guess it does."

"So why would you think I'd fall in love with a person like you?"

"I thought I was stinkin' cute—and you said you loved me?"

"Just a little flattery and BS, like you slathered on all those flight attendants, darling."

"Look Scarlett, we *all* have emotional flaws…"

"No flaws here, Cape-O."

"In your eyes maybe, but you strike me as a woman with *daddy issues*. I'm betting the only kind of guy you could go for is some lying crook—like your old man."

Scarlett jerks me backwards by my collar and I fall across a stump at the edge of the path. "That's going to cost you, smart ass. I was going to kill you nice and easy, but nobody talks bad about my daddy!"

"How about I apologize and we go our separate ways?"

"Funny!" Scarlett says and stomps her foot down on my throat. "What did Louise say? I saw her mouthing something."

"Don't have a clue, but since we're back on questions… I got one for you. Why do you hate me? I haven't been mean to you…"

"You're like all the players who finally decide to settle down and do the family thing. You think you're such a fine catch that women will fall madly in love with you. But you didn't move my swoon-meter a bit. You arrogant…I'm-an-Airline-Captain—bastard!"

"Not the way I see myself, quite the contrary, actually. Cyril Connolly describes my former life perfectly: '*I have always disliked myself at any given moment; the total of such moments is my life.*'"

Scarlett pulls me back to my feet. "Oh, I bet that fake-sad quote had those dippy flight attendants swooning every time you 'confessed it' to them so they could 'heal' you."

"Look, I've never claimed to be perfect, but I never intentionally misled or hurt a woman—and I've known some great ones. I fell for you because I thought *you* fell into that category—stupid me."

"Yes, you *are* real stupid, Cape Thomas."

Nothing like being called stupid as one of the best ideas you've had in years pops into your head!

"Not as stupid as you might think, Scarlett. I've had my doubts about you for a while now. My conversation with Detective Martin pushed me to choose between trusting you and trusting him. I gave you that key because it's a duplicate to an empty room. I gave the original to the detective, and unless I miss my guess, he's processing the room for evidence as we speak."

"You dumbass! Without that money my father dies!" Scarlett shrieks, flying into and rage, kicking me square in the chest. The force of her rage sends me crashing into one of the trail cams she installed along the path. After sinking to the base of the tree, I try to clear my head. Scarlett grabs me by the shirt and pulls me up against the tree.

Grinding her teeth and snarling, she says, "Nice try! You had me going there for a second. Darius Martin has no jurisdiction in Slick Rock County! Besides, he's stupid, too. If I had the evidence he has against you, I'd already have charged you with murder."

"Seems like setting me up as the murderer would work against you, huh? I mean without me you'd never have found the secret room."

Before I stagger away from the tree, I notice all of the trail cams have blinking lights. And the lenses *haven't* been painted over as Scarlett said they were. "Hey cams! If these things still work—are you recording my pre-murder?" Please, somebody be listening.

"Oh shit!" Scarlett snatches the power cords from each camera and removes the SD cards. "Thanks for the reminder, Cape-O. They were live-feeding into my office." Scarlett laughs a genuine, hardy laugh at my expense. "Boy, you are touched in the head!"

"Yeah, that was kind of stupid—but remember, without me this wouldn't have worked out for you."

"Don't flatter yourself. Bianca laundered money with Johnston and Kress. They knew the operation was in the mansion and they suspected Louise knew where it was. If they hadn't gotten to her first in the hospital, she would have told everything. Besides, I never figured you as a way to access the Fisher family fortune."

"Why would they think Louise was involved? It's not like the money changed her life style one bit."

"Without old wealth or good credit, Rafael Bordeaux's rise in Greenville was suspicious to a banker like Walter Cronus Kress. That's also why you were never considered as a source to find the money-laundering room."

"Why attack me in Charlotte? That was you in the pickup truck, right?"

"Yes, the evidence I planted wasn't enough to establish probable cause. I needed more prints from you to convince Detective Martin that you were the killer."

"Prints on what, another glass and cigarette?"

"No, when I realized how dumb Detective Martin was, I knew I was going to have to wrap the case up into a neat package for him. I took a sterling silver cross off of Celine before I killed her. Once I immobilized you with the dart I was going to get your fingerprints on that cross and plant it back in Ally's home. Your prints on a personal item like that could only mean one thing, even to someone as slow as Darius Martin."

"So, you didn't anticipate me escaping?" I said.

"No, you got lucky, but your escape forced me to switch to plan B...

and I always have a plan, B. " Scarlett promises with a surly smile.

"The deputy who stopped me on I-40 wasn't part of your plan? That's why you had dinner with me rather than kill me?"

"Yes, I had to wait for an opportune time to get your prints, then plant more evidence. Being in Slick Rock County made it harder for me. As Sheriff I'm pretty much monitored 24-7 by dispatch."

"Sooner or later, Darius Martin would have been on to you, Scarlett."

"I know that. But by the time that happened, my father and I would be safely out of the country."

"So the sheriff's department isn't monitoring you now?" I said.

"I've built up some time-off for when I need a little personal space. We have a radio code for it. Today I invoked it because of a silly disturbance at Skeeter Pointe Country Club. It's a way of letting me go dark and get away from my problems for a while."

"That's nice, but you may have a problem you haven't anticipated."

"Nice try, Mr. Thomas, but I have all the bases covered."

I try my best to look relaxed and hope Scarlett is buying it. "You know Detective Martin asked me an interesting question before I blew him off."

"And what was—?"

"He asked when and where I was meeting you. I told him 'None of your business.'"

"So, that's good—not bad."

"Hmm, guess we'll see. When I left the hospital with Louise, an unmarked police car followed me to end of the path that leads here. I'm pretty sure Darius Martin was in that car."

"Liar! Only two sets of truck tracks were on the path—no car tracks."

Two set of tracks—who else is here?

My question is answered when we hit a streak of sugar sand on the path. I notice a wide sets of tire tracks, much wider than Scarlett's cruiser or my Yukon. Whoever is here with us is just up ahead. And—there's the glare off the hood of a 350 heavy-duty Ford pickup with very dark-tinted windows.

As Scarlett nods to the driver, a shadowy figure moves from side to side as if gathering something from the back seat. Salome steps out of the driver's side and goes around to open the passenger door. Jake, half-steps half-tumbles from the truck hogtied and blindfolded.

"Salome is having an affair with, Jake, you know that, right?" I say.

Rather than answer, Scarlett nods again to Salome, who reaches across the back seat and drags another man across, then out the door, bound exactly like Jake. Even with his blindfold, I recognize him from a photo on the wall outside Scarlett's office. Former sheriff, Calvin Oliver is not at this moment amused.

"So you're behind this, DuBois? I might have known!" Calvin says.

"Shut up!" Scarlett yells and kicks her former boss in his groin. "Remember that day you made me swallow the evidence?"

"I don't know what you're talking about, you crazy bitch. Don't try to make it about sexual harassment! You jumped on my bone like a hobo on a ham sandwich!"

"Think what you want," Scarlett says. "All I know is this: there's always a day of reckoning for a jackass like you...and that day is today!" Scarlett kicks Oliver so hard again, I feel his pain.

Traitor-Jake, blindfolded slides up against the truck and makes his way around the crumpled pile of humanity wallowing on the ground. "Sheriff, is that you?" Jake yells.

Scarlett ignores Jakes and begins to unhook a machine from the Ford pickup. I've seen plenty of machines like this before—a limb chipper like the ones tree-trimming crews use. When Scarlett finishes lowering the machine's landing gear, she stops to catch her breath. I figure this is a good a time to ask a nagging question.

"What's with the wood chipper?"

Scarlett places her hands on her hips and kneads the stiffness from her lower back.

"I hate William Johnston, but in some ways I'm beginning to understand and appreciate his diabolical mind. You think Louise 'borrowed' a little money from the stockpile in the secret room, but Johnston told me there should be as much as a $100,000,000 in that room. I counted the duffle bags. There's nowhere near that kind of money in there, probably less than half that amount. Johnston told me how my brother died. You see, the drug cartels across the border use machines like this to get people to talk. Apparently they are very effective. I think Louise may need a little persuasion to tell me where she hid the rest of the money. I'm going to arrest Rafael and bring him out here to the farm and give him a little demonstration on how the chipper works."

"You're going to threaten to run Rafael through it?" I said.

"No, that's where Jake comes in. I'm going to run *him* through it. That should loosen up Louise's tongue. When Louise takes me to her stash of hidden treasure I'll kill Louise and Rafael. I promise you, I know enough ways to obscure evidence that their deaths will remain unsolved for decades."

"How do you *obscure* Jake's death?"

"I don't, I pin his death on you."

"How's that?"

"Jake wronged your daughter. Surely a man, *temporarily imbalanced*,—I'm being kind to you—could be pushed over the edge to avenge his daughter?"

And that wouldn't be hard to prove, especially considering my loose-lip comments to the ER attendant. Me and my big mouth!

"Jake isn't having an affair is he?"

"No, of course not. Salome is a doctor, too. She knows many homeopathic procedures from her homeland Honduras. Jake is curious, he quizzes her during their lunch breaks. Salome and he share an interest, nothing's going on there except figments of imagination in other's minds...yours included."

"But her attacking me in the hospital to make me distrust my mind?—a little risky to do something like that in such a public place, wasn't it?" I ask.

"My thoughts exactly, but it turned out to be a brilliant move. Salome knew the place well from visiting Jake." Scarlett smiles. "Even if she hadn't escaped that night, no one would have believed your wild tale about a doctor trying to kill you. Once the family thought there was a threat, the odds of me, as law enforcement, getting involved were pretty good."

"Scarlett, if money is all you want, there's no need to hurt all of these people. I'll walk in the mansion and deliver every bag of money to your office—"

"You're an idiot again!"

"At least let Jake and Louise go. Use me for ransom—"

"Shut up! I'm not kidnapping you because no one would pay ransom." Scarlett says. "We have a great plan and it won't fail."

"If your plan is to frame me for murder that's not much of a plan. I can be a hot-head, but I'm not a psychopath, and there is zero evidence of that. Nor is there any evidence, other than some you planted, very badly I might add, to support that I killed anyone."

"Again, I know that. I'm just muddying the waters. By the time they get around to investigating me, I'll be long gone. Now get over here behind these controls!"

Scarlett backs me up to the knob and makes me squeeze each one, for good measure she flattens my hands onto the smooth control panel.

"Now I'll tell you the real plan," she whispers.

"Thank you!"

"You won't be tried for murder, you'll be dead. The evidence I planted will prove you killed Jake and they will surmise you had an unfortunate accident trying to hide your crime."

"So this is how it ends for me, too?" I said.

Scarlett is stony, then pulling a small case knife from her pocket, cuts me across the palms of my hands. "What the hell?"

"Rain may wash off some of your finger prints, but the blood and DNA on this machine will last long enough to confuse the investigation. Buys me more time to get away." Scarlett said.

"What about Sheriff Oliver?"

"He's a sacrifice to the cause feminism."

"Why?"

"He's a pig! That's all you need to know."

"How does Salome benefit from all this if she isn't in for a cut of the money?"

"RH, told her the story of how twins were born at the Fisher Mansion. Once she marries RH, whether RH refuses to recognize it or not, he will be a sole blood heir to the *real* Fisher family fortune, one worth far more than a billion dollars."

"Let me guess—then RH dies a mysterious death?"

"Very impressive, Cape, you're making a remarkable comeback."

"Doesn't take a genius to see there's a little hitch in your plan. RH Carter is *not* the sole heir—"

"He will be once Salome returns to the mansion and eliminates the other heirs."

"You bitch!"

CHAPTER TWENTY-NINE
Some Q' DownEast

Slamming the door, Darius Martin gets into the cruiser and flips open his notebook to Cape Thomas's address in Goldsboro. If Thomas wasn't such a hothead, he could verify the highball glass and ashtray were planted evidence, but Thomas was in Sheriff DuBois' corner. Same was true of former Slick Rock County Sheriff, Calvin Oliver. The little crap-eating grin Oliver wore during questioning about Scarlett DuBois suggested more than a working relationship.

"Always professional and very good at keeping evidence secured, that's who she is." A pat answer that suggested something sexual when Oliver grabbed his crotch and let loose a laugh.

Men like Calvin Oliver were the reason women and minorities seldom applied for openings on local police forces. In most cases, one percent ruined the reputation of the remaining ninety-nine percent of law enforcement officers who encouraged minorities and women to give law enforcement a try. Luckily, Darius had been recruited by such a lawman and was still mentored by him.

Today, in fact, is a perfect day to check in with his old friend. Picking lint from his blazer, Darius chuckles as he waits for his phone to connect. Even after all these years he doesn't want to disappoint his friend with a less-than-stellar professional appearance. Satisfied he turns his attention to the reason for the call. Nothing about the clues he's discovered so far is fitting together—a good indication that his theory is crapola. The only way to know for sure is to eliminate his first suspect, Cape Thomas. A difficult task, considering he and Thomas are, no longer on speaking terms.

"Well, well, a call from a big-city cop! What can I do for you?"

"You can turn this call into a visit—where can we meet?"

"My fiancée is out and about, and I don't expect her back for at least four hours. But I'm not using this time away from the old ball-and-chain driving to Charlotte."

"You don't have to. As it turns out, I'm on my way to Goldsboro—only a few minutes away on I-795."

"Well, if you're willing to buy lunch, I'm willing to invest a little drive time to Goldsboro."

"Only been through Goldsboro, never stopped. You got any suggestions for lunch?"

"Yeah, head to Wilbur's, grab us a table and a couple of iced teas. I'll be there before they bring you hushpuppies and barbecue chicken sauce."

"Wilbur's—that's the place on the way to the beach, right?"

"Yep, but take Hwy 70 Business, because the new by-pass will take you straight in to Kinston. If you miss the Goldsboro exit—call me and we'll do lunch at King's in Kinston."

Martin finds a parking spot near Wilbur's main entrance, steps out and stretches, when a powerful roaring noise sends him diving across the front seat and grabbing for his gun. An old guy parked next to him points to the sky. "You thought that F-15 had you, didn't you?"

"Damn sure did." Martin says. "Mighty loud—people around here don't complain about the noise?"

"Complain?" the man says, "People here say that's the *Sound of Freedom*, won't hear no complaints here 'bout our jets."

"Sound of Freedom," Martin nods. "I like that."

Inside the renowned eatery, Darius looks up and down the long, narrow room. "Sit at the counter if you want, or we have a two-topper left," a female voice from behind calls out.

Darius Martin slides into the two-topper and flops down. Like a circus performer, he pushes his broad shoulders against the ladder-back chair until it balances on the back legs. The red-and-white checkered plastic cloth reminds him of NASCAR-themed restaurants in Charlotte, but other than that, nothing about this place gives any proof of the culinary awards decorating the walls. A quick look around the room reveals a country decor worn down by decades of use. The knotty pine walls are stained dark from grease and age, and clash with Sixty-style floor tiles. Pig paraphernalia adorns every nook and cranny whole-hog, no pun intended, and other porcine decals are stuck at random on dusty-paned windows. Why would a business opt for decor caricaturing animals customers were about to eat?

"What you want to drink, Hon?"

"Tea, and a friend will be joining me."

"Awl-right, Hon, and I'll just bring you some chicken sauce and hushpuppies while you wait."

As the waitress pours the tea, Martin pushes the bowl of sauce and basket of hushpuppies to the far side of the table.

"Something wrong, Hon?"

"No, it's just that I've never had chicken sauce. Is it...soup?"

"No sir, it's a dipping sauce. Try just one! They're real good."

"I think I'll pass." Martin takes a sip of his tea and feels a rush. "Is this tea or syrup?"

"You want unsweet, Hon?"

"No, no, it's fine. I'll deal with it."

The waitress does an apologetic bow half to the side and manages a smile. "Want me to bring you somethin' else? We got salads and I can get you some water—with lemon in it?"

"No, my friend'll be here in a bit and we'll order, then."

"Let me know if you need anything, Sugar."

One more sip of tea and Martin understands why the waitress changed his moniker from Hon to sugar—she was the tea-maker for this joint! He picks up one of the crunchy hushpuppies and daubs it gingerly into the sauce. The combination of fresh ground cornmeal, chicken drippings, and various secret herbs and spices stimulates his tastebuds and kicks his saliva glands into high gear. He sips the tea, discovering that the overwhelming sweetness goes perfectly with the spicy sauce! He crunches away on the hushpuppies till he realizes he hasn't saved any for his old mentor!

"Oh, Miss."

"Yes, sir?"

"May I have some more sauce and hushpuppies?"

"You sure can, Hon." The waitress beams. "I'm glad you liked it! Want some more tea?"

"Please." Darius Martin has drained his glass. "Just curious—how much sugar is *in* the tea?"

"Oh, you don't wanna know, Hon!"

This guy needs to franchise the place, Martin decides. Hell, Charlotte would go crazy over a place like this! As thoughts of investing in a barbeque franchise for retirement fill Martin's mind, a familiar figure fills the empty chair across the table.

"Damn, Bud! You ate it all?"

"Don't worry, RH. I ordered us some more."

"Naw, that's OK. Let's get some que—get the feast started!"

Conversation doesn't begin until the last bites of barbeque on their plates are pushed onto their forks with a hushpuppy. Martin pushes his chair back from the table again, but this time decides to forego the balancing act. "I got to get Down East, more. Damn, that was good!"

RH Carter grins and nods. "True, but I know a hankering for good food didn't bring you way down here. What's up?"

"Cape Thomas."

"Is he still your prime suspect?"

"No, and here's why." Martin slides his chair under the table and leans in close. "My friend, the warden up in Macedonia…"

"Curtis Price?"

"Hell, you know Curtis better than me, what was I thinking? I understand you've been doing a little work up in Macedonia, too. How's that going?" Martin asks.

"Not well. Johnston is playing us, but despite the evidence, I don't think he's connected to these murders."

"Sheriff DuBois was up there yesterday. Curtis played me her tapes. Have you listened to them?" Martin said.

"I tried Johnston and Kress are plenty smart, but because of her tone of voice, you almost think DuBois is playing along with them rather than trying to get quality recordings. The background noises during crucial parts of their conversation also make the recordings useless. We're not going to get anything from jailhouse snitches, either. Every prisoner in there knows Johnston and Kress are filthy rich and plenty powerful. Hell, they've paid off half the population accounts just to make sure they stay safe. What changes your mind about Cape Thomas?"

"I took it as far as I could. Someone tried to set him up, but he never killed anyone. As a matter of fact, I think he was lucky to get out of Charlotte with his life."

"You talk to Cape about that?" RH said.

Darius Martin lets out a laugh so loud, he gets a glare from the next table

"He's so pissed at me, he won't even talk to me. He's your kin. Think you could pave—?"

"Forget that. Cape Thomas may dislike you, but he hates my guts." RH said.

"Speaking of guts, I got this gut-feeling I can't shake."

"About Cape, you mean?"

"Yes."

"Don't worry about him. If we can keep him in the mansion and off that crazy survivalist kick, he'll be fine." RH said.

"If I could get him to talk, I think I could put all the pieces together. I cornered him at the mansion, but he blew me off. Sort of led me to believe he and Sheriff DuBois have been getting busy, if you get me drift?"

"You know I dated her, too. Before I met, Salome." RH said.

"What's your opinion of her?"

"Nice gal, but I always got the feeling she wasn't nearly as interested in me as in my connection to the Fisher family. She wanted much more access to the place that I had clearance for. I mean, Mr. Fisher is my godfather and all, but I'm not family. I did talk him into supporting her for Slick Rock County Sheriff, though."

"So she's a gold-digger?"

"No, she comes from big money, too. She knew the Fisher girls back in the day, and maybe that's her connection. All I can tell you for sure and certain is, she never had one bit of interest in me until she found out I was connected to the family."

"Do you think that's why the sheriff has an interest in, Cape Thomas?"

"If it is, she chose wisely. Jana would give Cape the keys to the kingdom tomorrow if he wanted them. But, Cape isn't at all impressed with Fisher money."

"Why do you say that?"

"Cape Thomas loves the idea of family, flying, and friends. Pretty much in that order."

"Why is that?"

"You talk to any of his friends?" RH says with a smile.

"No, why?"

"They're an eclectic bunch! Cape's parents died when he was young, so certain friends he made became his family. Like this old lady, Miss Minnie. She's a witch doctor, saved his life—and became like a mother to him. Then there is some old veteran and his wife taught Cape to fly. He raves about them all the time. Another one is a guy who used to clean his yard." RH cups the back of his hand next to his mouth. "And get this, the yardman turns out to be a CPA who is now wealthy times ten."

"Any other friends who might be willing to help me get to him?"

"Nope. Only other person that is close to Cape is Scarlett DuBois, and I think he's fallen hard for her. Oh, I forgot—Cape and the mansion's main housekeeper, Louise, seem to be tight, too. You may make a little headway with her…"

"Duly noted—and what is it with the family-fortune thing?" Martin asks. "Thomas accused me of trying to steal it!"

"There's an old rumor that some kind of hidden treasure is in the

Fisher family, supposedly hidden in the mansion. If that treasure exists, and anyone knows its whereabouts, my money is on,Louise."

"Do you think there really is such a thing?" Martin asks.

RH strokes his chin in his best imitation of Mr. Fisher and laughs, "'No! Total poppycock!' to quote Mr. Fisher. But what do you want to ask Cape? I may be able to get Jana to intercede for you. We're tight—I'm the donor who saved her life."

"I found an ashtray and a highball glass at Ally Kress's house with Cape's prints and DNA on them. I asked Cape if he drank or smoked anything when he was visiting Ms. Seabolt. He was adamant that he hadn't, but that answer is what put him on my list. His statement was a flat-out lie. When I questioned him in the hospital, he told me a story about a break-in at his house in Goldsboro. He mentioned seeing an odd glass and ashtray there. Sheriff DuBois investigated the break-in, but according to her no glass and cigarette in an ashtray was found."

"If I had that kind of evidence and the suspect lied about it I think I'd arrested Cape?"

"Yeah, I was going to, but my gut says he's not lying. Turns out the glass and ashtray belonged to Ally Kress. Yet, Cape is certain that he saw it in his house in Goldsboro. If he's guilty, why admit to even seeing it? And he described it perfectly. So how did the two items get from Charlotte to Goldsboro and back to Charlotte?"

"Let's pretend it did." RH suggests. "I'm all ears."

"The only connection is the local investigating officer."

"Scarlett DuBois?"

"Yes, and here's the kicker. We not only found her DNA in the house, we found one of DuBois' hairs and DNA under Celine Seabolt's finger nail."

"You figure it got there when Celine fought for her life?"

"Can't say for sure, but here's something weird. Celine Seabolt's and Ally Kress's hands were washed *after* they were hanged. The other victims were shot at a distance—no DNA on them."

"Darius, have you talked to Scarlett?"

"On some other matters, but I did ask Cape Thomas if DuBois was ever in Ally Kress's home. He said DuBois was adamant that she was never there."

"Sounds like case solved to me."

"Well, but Cape Thomas said if Sheriff DuBois' DNA was there he likely brought it in. Turns out he may be correct. We did find some of Scarlett's hairs on his clothing and he's admitted to touching Celine's body. You know it's a stretch to think he could have transferred Scarlett's hair to Celine Seabolt's fingernail, but a good defense attorney could make a case for reasonable doubt. Especially if Cape Thomas tells Scarlett DuBois what I questioned him about."

"Right, and she'll say she forgot but she did visit Ally, just in case we find DNA where Thomas *didn't* go in the house."

"Exactly." Darius Martin said. "And if Cape Thomas is in love with Scarlett DuBois…"

"He'll certainly tell her." RH concludes

"Yep."

"He won't, though, if he finds out she's a murderer." Carter says, punching numbers into his phone like he's sparing with the device. "Jana, I need to talk to Cape—say what? How about the old shack?—sealed off, you say?" RH pressing the phone to his chest and whispers to the detective, "Cape is missing from the mansion and he's not at that shack of his. Jana had a neighbor check it—he says the path is blocked off."

"He was heading out when I met with him," Martin said. " He didn't say, but I got the feeling he was meeting Scarlett. You don't think we could cut her off before she meets him, do you?"

"There's a good chance."

"How do I get to Slick Rock County sheriff's office?" Martin asks.

"By putting my ass in your car—I'll drive!"

For the first part of the ride to Slick Rock there is no conversation passes between the old friends. Each man plays a mental chess game against a very worthy opponent. But five miles from Slick Rock, their ideas surface.

"I pushed Cape too hard in Charlotte." Martin says. "How we going to win his confidence back?"

"Don't know that we can—Cape Thomas thinks we're both bad cops." RH said.

"How do we detain the sheriff, then?"

"I'm all ears."

"I've got enough evidence to arrest her for suspicion of murder, but I don't want to do that until we know if she met with Cape or not… 'Course I can ask her about the report she made on the break-in at Cape's place in Goldsboro?"

"That'll take all of 30 minutes." RH says. "We need at least a couple of hours…"

"How about you ask for an immediate meeting now, under the pretext of giving her a full briefing from the Task Force?"

"Now, that just may work." RH says. "Let's play it by ear. I asked Jana to call me when Cape shows up—should be soon."

"But what if he's *already* called Sheriff DuBois, or worse—met with her?"

"Well, she is the only cop he trusts." RH muses. "So if he hasn't, he certainly will. And then she'll know your evidence against her."

"Yep. I didn't want to divulge it, but I had to get Cape talking."

RH let's off the gas and the car coasts into the parking lot of the Slick Rock County Sheriff's Department.

"I'd a played that card, too," RH admits.

The dispatcher at the sheriff's office gives a casual glance at Darius Martin's CPD badge, but sits straight up when RH flashes his FBI Identification. "Sheriff's not in right now, she's 24-7," the deputy says. "That's a made-up code. Means she's had it for today. She got a little perturbed over a dispute between some golfers and Pokemon hunters at the Skeeter Pointe Country Club. I 'spect she's havin' a spa moment, as she says."

"Ah, we've all been there." RH smiles. "Don't suppose you know which spa?"

"I don't know much about spas. I *do* know when the Sheriff is 24-7, she dudn' want to be disturbed. Unless this is an emergency?"

"No, no, nothing like that," RH assures him. "We just wanted to look over a report she made on a break-in at the home of a Mr. Cape Thomas, and I also need to give her a briefing. Don't suppose we could see that report while we wait?"

"I'm sure she wouldn't mind, but I'd rather wait until the Sheriff gets back. I just started a few weeks ago. Kind of hoping to make it to the FBI, like you. Don't want to set a roadblock in my way."

Darius Martin looks at the glass-paneled walls of Scarlett DuBois office and notices a bank of monitors along one wall. Over one of the monitors is printed: Cape Thomas.

"I thought about making the move to the FBI, when I was younger, and I wish you well." Darius said.

"I appreciate that. Y'all want something to drink? Got fresh coffee back there and there's a refreshment center in the break room. Well, really it's a drink machine and a box of snacks in a closet. Honor System. If you don't have change, I'll be glad to treat you?"

"That's mighty kind of you, but we just left Wilbur's…Don't believe I caught your name, son?" RH says.

The deputy comes from behind his desk and shakes RH's hand. "I'm Freddo Ellis, my friends call me Ellis-Ellis."

"Mind if I call you, Ellis?"

"Not at all."

RH hands Ellis his business card. "When you make that application to the FBI, let me know. I'll put in a good word."

"I probably shouldn't tell you this," Ellis says, proving to Carter that the card has once again worked its magic, "but I know the Sheriff would want to know if the FBI dropped by. She'll be back here for a shift change in a couple of hours. She's covering for a deputy dealing with a calving situation."

"Even if she's, 24-7?" RH inquires.

"Yes, sir. Only way some of the deputies can afford to work here is to have a job on the side. Most of their jobs are farm-related."

Darius Martin shrugs his shoulders and gives RH a quizzical look. "Calving?"

"Country version of maternity leave…" Ellis explains.

"Say Ellis, I couldn't help but notice that really comfortable couch in the Sheriff's office. Don't suppose we could sit in there and rest while we wait? Tough FBI guys never need breaks, but an old police detective like me could *sure* use one."

"I don't know, Detective, Sheriff's kind of funny about her office…"

RH notices Martin's finger pointing at the row of monitors on the wall. As soon as he sees, 'Cape Thomas,' over one of them, he turns toward the deputy.

"How about if I promise we won't mess with a thing and we'll keep our hands where you can see them?" RH points to the bank of monitors. "Don't need rest, but I could do with a little TV. "

"Those aren't TV's, Sir. That's the sheriff's little invention. She calls it the 'Hot-Spot Center.' We don't have a lot of crime in the county, but when we do, it tends to be in certain areas. Break-ins and such. Lots of cities and bigger counties have surveillance cameras all over the place, but not here in Slick Rock. Sheriff figured the cheapest way to stretch our budget is to install self-activating trail-cams around certain areas of the county.

Our small force can't be everywhere. The cameras are infrared, but lots of times we get a clear-enough picture the perps admit to the crime rather than makin' us do an investigation."

"That's a good idea," RH says. "Don't you think, Darius?"

"Brilliant!" Darius leans over and whispers to RH, "What the hell's a trail-cam?"

Before RH can answer a clear image of a handcuffed Cape

Thomas escorted by an angry Scarlett DuBois walks across the 'Cape Thomas' monitor.

"This thing got audio, Ellis?"

"Yes, Sir."

"Turn it up."

"That's as loud as it goes."

Darius Martin put his ear to the speaker just in time to hear Cape Thomas say: "If these things work—are you recording my pre-murder?"

"This thing record?"

"Stores on the sim card in the camera, Sir"

"Where's this taking place?" Martin asks.

Ellis moves from behind his desk and looks at the monitor. "That's the sheriff—what's she doin'?" Before the others can answer, the trail cams go dead. "She just unplugged the cameras—must be moving 'em somewhere else…"

"She's doing more than that. Take us there, right now!"

"I can't leave my desk. I'll call another deputy—"

"Don't touch that radio!" Martin screams.

"I can't leave without talking to the Sheriff!"

"You touch it and I'll charge you with accessory to murder!"

Ellis looks at RH. "Can he do that?"

"If he can't, I can! Let's ride, Ellis-Ellis!"

CHAPTER THIRTY
Pure Evil

Scarlett and Salome grab Calvin Oliver on either side and stand him up on the bed of the pickup. Scarlett hops down from the bed, and gathers some broken tree limbs from the edge of the field.

"Fire it up!" She yells

Salome looks at the chipper, then back at Scarlett. "I have no idea how to start that machine."

"You feed these branches in there when I tell you."

The wood chipper is a simple, efficient machine. Scarlett hits the switch and it fires off. She nods to Salome, who fills the throat of the machine with branches as a high-pitched, grinding whine drowns out Sheriff Oliver's pleas. He moves as far away from the machine as possible, but there is no safe haven for him. Scarlett and Salome wrestle him over to the throat of the machine, but he grabs the top of the feed bed and holds on for dear life. This is not going to be a fast, quick kill. Like lionesses, the two women prowl the sides of the conveyor belt pulling Calvin Oliver toward the spinning carbon blades. Oliver loses a little ground to the conveyor belt, he pulls like crazy to lift himself away from the blades.

As Calvin fights for his life I ease over beside the still blindfolded Jake. "We got to get out of here."

"Cape, what's going on?"

"You don't want to know, Jake."

A scream like I have never heard or ever want to hear again pierces the air. I look up just in time to see a cloud of red-mist fly from the chipper's discharge spout. "Oh God! It got my feet. Stop this damn machine, you crazy bitch. I can't hold on much longer!"

Calvin is not the only one running out of time. Our time looks short, too. "Jake jump up and down. Try to loosen your ropes!"

Jake hops up and down like a dork on a pogo stick. Other than enabling him to look like a fool, the jumping is ineffective. Before I come up with a better plan, I see two beautiful black hands, one holding a knife, protrude from under the truck. The empty hand points to Jake and motions for him to sit.

"Jake, sit down."

"Hell no, let's make a run for it, Cape!"

"Sit down, Louise is going to free you."

While Louise works on Jake, I keep my eyes on the chipper. Scarlett grabs a ball peen hammer from the pickup's toolbox and takes aim at Calvin Oliver's fingers. I kneel beside Jake as Louise cuts the rope from my handcuffs. When I look up, I fully expect to catch Scarlett and Salome bearing down on us, but instead the two psychos are still mesmerized by the chipper.

Louise rolls from under the truck and motions for us to follow her, so Jake and I oblige. One last look at our captors tells me both are still engrossed with the morbid spectacle they've devised. Scarlett raises the hammer high over her head and slams it on the pinkie of Calvin Oliver's left hand. Another balloon of red mist shoots from the machine. Grasping Oliver by the arms, she lowers him into the swirling carbon teeth and I hear her yell, "When it gnaws up that little bit of manhood of yours, I'm letting go—asshole!" Less than a minute later I hear a final blood-curdling scream from Calvin and the three of us run like none of us has ever run before.

Louise turns and looks at me. "I don't know these woods."

I move into the lead. "I do, follow me. I got an idea."

"I hope it's a good one, Cape." Jake says, as the chipper shuts off. "They've got nothing on their mind now but us."

I know Scarlett thinks I'll head to the Huck Finn Place, because I told her that was my escape route. Lucky for me I kept my deepest secret to myself.

"How much farther we got to go?" Louise said. "My legs are wore out from pulling that porch post down."

"You were able to rip down a support beam?" I asked. "How?"

"Shoddy workmanship, Mr. Cape—Oh, Lawd, I can't go much farther!"

I point to an old sawdust pile left in the woods from a logging operation years ago. "Just make it to that pile Louise."

"What is that?" Jake asks.

"Swiss Family Robinson Place!"

"Do what?" Louise said.

"Come on! I have a canoe buried at the top of the pile." We dig in the sawdust like hungry dogs after buried bones. As soon as the canoe bottom is visible, we flip it over and slide it to the bottom of the pile. "I'm pretty sure it'll handle all three of us." I reassure them. "If it doesn't, I'll swim along side."

"Are you nuts?" Jake ask.

I know that's a rhetorical question but I'm tired of explaining my mental capacity. This is where I stake my claim to a full recovery. "No, Jake. I'm *not* nuts! If I were, we wouldn't have the slightest possibility of escape. I hid this canoe the first day I was here. I didn't tell a soul about it, not even Jimmy."

"I didn't mean nuts like that, Cape. I meant nuts like why a canoe? Why the hell didn't you hide a speedboat?"

"I'm with him." Louise says. "Too pooped to paddle!"

"I'll paddle. Remember we'll be going with the current. The undergrowth is almost like a jungle a little ways downstream. Scarlett and Salome can't catch us once we get there." I say.

Jake points to the open area along the creek. "What's going to slow them down here?"

"That's the tricky part, but we've got a head start. Let's make the most of it!"

I steady the canoe while Jake helps Louise into it.

"No, Jake, Louise needs to rest. You take the front. I'll take the back. You know how to paddle, right?"

"Know how to paddle, are you kidding? You'll think you've got a 300 HP Yamaha on this thing—I'm not going into that chipper, Cape!"

"Louise, you keep a lookout behind us. I don't know for certain, but I'm betting Scarlett is a marksman."

"That ain't all that hussy is!" Louise grumbles.

Jake proves to be as good as he says, and soon the canoe is cutting through the water quicker than I anticipated. "We keep this pace up and we'll be long gone before they know we're missing. Stroke, Jake, stroke!"

"Oh Lawd!" Louise says. "We in trouble y'all!"

As the last fragments of Calvin Oliver's skull fly from the discharge spout, Scarlett closes her eyes and braces herself against the machine, sensing an orgasmic spasm washing over her. As it blooms, flowers and passes in pleasure, she opens her eyes only to realize her next victims are gone. "No! Where have they gone?"

Salome, just out of a trance of her own, spins around in circles looking for the escaped captives. "How can this be? They were handcuffed!"

"But not shackled, damnit!" Scarlett picks up the rope she used to tie

Cape Thomas to the chipper. "Cut clean! Did you pat Jake down before you put him in the truck?"

"Yes, and all he had was a wallet—I put it in the dash pocket. See for yourself!"

Scarlett gets down own her knees and crawls around the truck until she finds Louise's familiar foot prints. "They had help. I know where they're headed. Let's go!" The two women race through the open forest like wolves in hot pursuit of more prey.

They don't let up their torrid pace until they hit the Huck Finn Place. Scarlett dashes around the clearing looking for any sign of the trio, but nothing. "That lying bastard! This isn't his launching point, but the water *has* to be his escape route. Come on!"

Scarlett runs full speed along the creek bank until she sees the sawdust pile. "Look! Fresh tracks—and they have a boat. Narrow rut, must be a canoe. Even going with the current, they can't travel much faster than five or six mph. If we run we'll catch them—they can't have gotten too far."

The first bend in the creek yields their first glimpse of our canoe. Sitting high and pretty on open water. Scarlett gets down on one knee and steadied her pistol. Her first shot falls short and to the right. She adjusts, walking the bullets up the water until she hits Jake Draughon. When he slums forward, Scarlett jumps to her feet. "Come on, I got one of them. We'll put my raft in at the bridge downstream and head back toward them!"

"Why can't you kill them from here?" Salome said. "I don't like the water—I can't swim."

"They're out of range now, but they have no escape route from here to the bridge. This thick cutover runs right up to the bridge. They can't walk through that underbrush, it's too thick and the swamp on the other side is even worse, sinkholes and no telling what-all."

When Scarlett passes by Minnie Reynaud's home place, she sees the missing front porch post. So that's why Louise wanted to sit by the steps. "No damn good deed goes unpunished," Scarlett mumbles.

"I'm sorry—I didn't hear you?"

"Nothing. Here's the key unlock that cable and lock it back after I go through. We have a crime scene to tidy up. Don't want anyone stumbling on it before we get back."

The drive to the bridge is at full speed with her siren blaring, but inside the car the silence is broken only when they reach the bridge. "Take this shotgun." Scarlett says, shoving it to Salome.

"It won't do me any good, I don't know how to use one."

"You can carry it, can't you?"

"Yes."

"Then take it. I'll get the raft out."

Scarlett pulls the firing pin on the emergency two-man flotation device. "Always knew this would come in handy. Stupid county commissioners didn't see the wisdom in equipping my patrol cars with personal floatation devices. We're in hurricane country, for Christ's sake!" Scarlett stands back and looks at the fully-inflated device.

"This should work like a charm!" Scarlett says as she bolts on the electric motor. "Pop the hood and put my battery in here. We got fish to fry!"

When I turn to see what Louise is focused on, bullets start flying. Scarlett kneels, zeroing in on a moving target. Ahead of me is nothing but chaos. Louise lets out a yelp and Jake slumps over his paddle clutching his shoulder. "Keep him in the canoe, Louise!"

Louise pulls Jake into the bottom of the canoe.

"Is he dead?"

"No, bullet went through his arm." Louise said. "How you doing, Doctor Jake?"

Jake tries to sit up. "I think the bullet went close to an artery. I have to stop the bleeding."

I want to help Jake, but I know the only thing that will help us is more distance from Scarlett DuBois and her large-caliber pistol. "Louise—"

"Don't worry about us, Mr. Cape—I'll put a tourniquet on his wound. You just get us outta here!"

"Once we get around that bend up ahead, we should be fine. No open ground between us and the bridge. We'll flag down help once we get there."

Jake's moans are disconcerting, also reminding me what a jerk I am for thinking he was, 'Traitor' Jake. "Jake, how you doing, buddy?"

"I'm in capable hands." Jake looks at the neat bandage Louise has made from strips of his shirt. "Louise, have you had medical training?"

"I raised five children from the time I was ten years old. We couldn't afford doctors. What doctorin' I know I learned from Aunt Minnie."

"Good. She's a fascinating woman. Her IQ must be a gazillion. I saw her do things that were never taught in medical school." Jake said, struggling to take his attention off the bleeding and pain. "We get out of this alive, I'm taking her to some medical school as a featured speaker."

"Miss Minnie knows roots and herbs, but lots of her healing comes from the Master." Louise clarifies for him.

"I can imagine," Jake says. "Faith is powerful medicine and I want to explore that further, too."

"I thought you were an atheist?" I said.

"I'm not sold on the whole of religion, but I'm totally convinced there are powers beyond the scope of man. I saw that when Miss Minnie saved you. She tried a few concoctions and finally raked them on the floor. Her real juice came when she prayed over you all night."

"Why did you allow that, anyway?"

"Miss Minnie was so positive that God could save you. Her faith was unshakeable. I knew you weren't coming back," Jake said wryly. "And I hate to admit, but I only let her try so when she failed, she'd stop believing in her Spaghetti Monster in the sky. Boy, did that turn out differently than I expected."

"You never told me that."

"I've always had respect for holistic remedies, but Miss Minnie added faith-healing to that list...that's what got me in trouble with Doctor Matkusa. She knew many of the drugs used in her native Honduras. Interesting enough, one of them, the curare vine, is the source of the poison dart that almost killed you, Cape."

"I got a confession for you." I said. "I'm ashamed to tell you this, but I believed you were having an affair with her."

"You aren't the only one, and I can see why people thought that." Jake said. "I love Jana with all my heart, Cape. I'd never hurt her or my family." Jake puts his hand over the side of the canoe and lets the cool black water run between his fingers. "Since we got a little time to kill... agh, probably not the best choice of words... I was adopted, so I never had a family of my own. Jana and I share that. It's one of the reasons we grew close and fell in love so quickly. I'd never hurt Jana, Cape. That's something you can stake your life on."

I steer the canoe away from a broken tree top and rest the paddle on my lap. During this lull, I think about my relationship with Jake. Seems like we got the Doctor/Patient part down pat, but never developed the Father/Son-in-law part.

"Well, if I hadn't been so reckless in trying to kill off my grandkids on a regular basis, and if I'd stayed at the mansion sooner or later we'd a had this conversation."

"Cape, Jana, wasn't mad at you. She's over-protective of our kids...for obvious reasons."

"I know and I should've known better, but I've never raised a kid, much less grandkids."

"Oh, you won't doing a thing wrong with them young'uns, Mr.

Thomas. I was brought up like you. Teach'em right from wrong, as best you can, then give'em free rein." Louise says. "Children smarter than you think! In some ways they're much smarter than adults. You ever notice how if a child don't like someone…it's because that person is generally evil? Think about Sheriff DuBois. When she first walked in the mansion, Cape T and Laura hauled buggy to get up in my lap."

"Excuse me, Louise." I dig my paddle into the water and point the canoe at a new path I've never seen before."

"What you doin', Mr. Thomas?"

"I don't remember this path, but it may get us help quicker."

"Don't remember what?" Jake sits halfway up.

"That logging path. Last crew that cut this tract must have built it?

"Think we could use it to get to the highway?" Jake asks.

"It'd be a long walk—at least a mile or two. I don't think you're in good enough shape to—"

"Cape, I'm a little woozy from blood loss, but I can make a walk like that," he says.

"Glad to hear that, but we're a lot better off just floating down to the bridge and flagging down a car." I advise.

Jake settles back against his seat and leans up close to Louise. "You've got blood on you. Have you been shot, too?" Jake asks.

Louise stares past Jake and points down the creek. "Lord God Almighty! Look there!"

Around the bend but headed straight for us are Scarlett DuBois and Salome Matkusa making good speed against the strong current. "Where the heck, did they get an inflatable boat," I said. "with an electric motor?"

My question is rhetorical, but Louise obliges. "I don't know, but they sure closin' the distance mighty fast!"

"Turn around. We have to outrun them!"

Jake sits up, grabs the paddle from Louise and digs deep in the water with powerful smooth strokes. As I drag the back of the canoe, we complete the u-turn in record time. "Hurry, Cape. She's good with that pistol and she gettin' in range."

"Paddle Jake, paddle!"

"I'm doing all I can!"

"Give me that paddle." Louise grabs the paddle from Jake and she digs in with even deeper, smoother strokes. I look back and a tinge of excitement hits me. We're actually putting a little distant between our canoe and Scarlett's raft. When I face forward I notice the side of Louie's blouse is soaked in blood and two steady streams running down her paddle. No way she can hold out at this pace.

I dig my oar into the water and steer for the bank. "What ya' doing, Cape? They're bound to catch us now." Jake yells.

"Louise is hit, too, Jake."

"What?"

"She got a bullet, too." I said.

"How bad is it, Louise?"

"I'm feeling mighty weak, but I ain't quittin'."

Just before we slide under the limbs left by the riparian buffer trees I notice that Scarlett has slowed her pace, holding steady against the current. She knows we're in trouble but has no idea whether I stored firearms in the canoe. A great idea, but not something I thought to do.

"Why's she holding off?" Jake asked.

"She's not sure if we're armed, but she knows you two are wounded. Like any good predator, she's biding her time—waiting to attack when we're most vulnerable."

We beach the canoe on the new logging path and I help Jake and Louise out.

"Jake, I'm going to hang here and keep an eye on Scarlett. Stay on this path—it will take you to the highway. Do what you can to stop Louise's bleeding, but do it on the move. We don't have long before they come ashore."

Jake tears more strips of cloth from his shirt and ties off Louise's wound. "I got the bleeding stopped, but she needs to get to a hospital. That bullet has to be close to her heart."

"Can you make it to the road, Louise?"

"I'm feeling some better. Even got a little pep in my step!" Louise says. For ten yards, she takes strong strides, giving me hope we can all make it to the road. I turn to check on Scarlett. They are less than a 100 yards from shore and easing closer. "Come on, guys, we gotta go! She knows if we were armed we wouldn't let her get that close before we opened fire."

Louise grips Jake by the shoulder and leans heavily on him. I get on the other side of Louise and together Jake and I manage to pull her along. As valiantly as she tries, Louise only manages a few steps before she has to rest. Scarlett and Salome are less than eighty yards from shore when she unholsters her pistol.

"Louise, where's that knife you used to cut our ropes?"

"In my pocket." Louise pulls the knife out of her pocket and locks eyes with me. "But even a butcher knife ain't no match for a gun, Mr. Cape."

"I know, Louise." I take the butcher knife and slide it behind my belt. "Far as I go, Jake."

"Are you crazy?"

"Now, I thought we were done with the name-calling?"

"Come on, Cape. Stop joking around, we don't have time for this." Jake looks at Louise. "Tell him again how a knife is no match for a gun!"

"Jake, I've seen how those two women moved in the graveyard at Wilson. They're like ninjas! We can't outrun 'em, even if we were in good shape. Keep a steady pace and make sure you stay with Louise, no matter what. We owe her our lives, don't you ever forget that."

The landing is still vacant, but I see Scarlett and Salome huddling in the raft, no doubt planning their attack. I take a step toward the creek and realize this is probably the last conversation I'll ever have. Not every dying person is granted the gift of last words.

"Jake, you take care of our family. That goes for Mr. Fisher, too." I look at Louise and see tears of pain in her eyes. "Louise, you could have saved yourself back there at Miss Minnie's, instead you chose to save us, too. I don't know what the balance is on your debt to the Fisher mansion, but I'm cancelling your note."

"Cape, this is crazy, let's just keep walking…the three of us—"

"Shut up and listen, there's a secret room in the mansion. Louise will show it to you. There may be evidence in there that suggests Louise did something wrong. She didn't. You make sure the authorities understand that, got it?"

"Hell no, *you* make sure they do. This is suicide!"

"Jake, you have everything in life I've ever wanted, a good woman—a soulmate, and a beautiful family, and work that contributes. That story you told me about you and Jana. I want the happiness you two found to last forever." I hug Louise and give Jake a bear hug. "Don't let me down, son."

"Cape—may I call you, Dad?"

"I'd consider that an honor, Jake." I put my hands on their shoulders. "Louise, thanks again for saving our lives. I do hope I can return the favor."

"Me, too, Mr. Thomas, me too. Mind if I pray for you?"

"I'd like that, Louise. Better make it a quick one, though. Y'all need to get going and I need to take this fight to them while they're in the water."

Louise grabs the middle of my handcuffs, Jake puts his arms around us, and Louise prays: "Lord, please stand with this man today 'cause we know, Lord, if you stand with us, ain't nobody can stand against us. In Jesus' name, we pray."

Before we break huddle, Jakes says, "I still say this is suicide."

"I'll admit the odds aren't in my favor, but I have a fighting chance. I have a weapon. I can swim like an otter, and—thanks to Louise, I now have Jesus on my side."

Jake shakes his head. "In that case, sounds like you got'em right where you want'em, Captain Cape Thomas!" Jake snaps off a crisp though left-handed salute as he and Louise start down the path. I walk backwards, keeping my eyes on them until they round a bend in the path and I'm alone.

I look through the low-hanging limbs to see Scarlett and Salome no more than fifty yards from the landing. Scarlett yells, "Give it up, Cape! Bring them back and I won't run you through the chipper. A head shot for each of you, nice and clean. I promise."

"My granddaddy told me to never to negotiate with a liar."

"You're no match for us, and your partners there can't out run us!"

"We'll see about that, Scarlett."

I make a mad dash for the canoe and Scarlett starts firing. I land in the water and flip the canoe over, using it for cover. The first bullet zings through the aluminum skin and rattles against the insides. I swim under the canoe, hanging onto the gunwales and push it toward the sound of the gun. In rapid succession Scarlett fires four more rounds into the canoe. I pull the knife from my belt and bite down on the blade across my mouth. Filling my lungs with air, I sink under the water letting the current carry me under the raft, never having to make a ripple.

Once under the raft, I push the butcher knife low into the rubber side and rip a tear in it over two feet long. Scarlett fires down into the tea-black water. The bullets cut a white trail through the headwaters of the Northeast Cape Fear River but sink to the silty bottom. I come up for a quick gulp of air and catch a break. Scarlett is reloading and Salome screams, "I can't swim—take me to shore!"

My predatory instincts kick in, telling me to cut the weakest one away from the herd. Scarlett with a fresh clip of ammo, stands up and starts fires. I skim along the bottom of the river and see that the raft is obscured but its outline is visible. The current is moving us both along at the same speed but the raft is listing. Making adjustment for the current, I kick upward off the bottom with all my might surfacing beside the raft nearest Salome.

I grab her and a fresh supply of air at the same time. Before Salome can make a move on me, I plunge the knife into her neck. She grabs her throat with both hands, but I pull her down to the bottom with me. Like a gator storing a kill, I shove Salome into a tangle of limbs on the river bottom. Wide-eyed, she digs her fingernails into my flesh. Bubbles from her last breath are targets for Scarlett's next clip.

From the angle of the bullets I judge Scarlett's position in the sinking raft. I sink back to the bottom, plant my feet and shoot upward again. Scarlett is on the up end of the raft, facing away from me. She turns right into my outstretched hand. I grip her wrist and snatch her under the water with me. In the struggle she loses her long-barrel Ruger. The tip of my knife goes in just under her ribcage and Scarlett holds up both hand in surrender.

She's unarmed, I'm armed, and I have the advantage in the water. I motion for her to surface and she complies. I swim to the bank and wait for her there. Scarlett flops on her back and stares up at the sky. "I guess you really are a world-class swimmer...and did it while handcuffed, impressive."

I hold out my hands. "Unlock these cuffs." If for no other reason than I have the butcher knife pointed at her throat, Scarlett again complies. I take one of the cuffs and snap it around her wrist and click the other one around a stout tree limb she can't break.

"What are you doing?"

"I'm going to get your partner in crime. Her body won't last long down there."

Once I get Salome onto the bank I close her eyes. She looks to be in a peaceful slumber rather than stone-cold dead. "I guess, RH is in on this, too."

"No, RH is clean, Cape."

"But, you said—"

"I lied. The longer I could convince you that the cops were against you, the more control I had of the situation."

"Was it worth it, Scarlett?"

"I'd do anything for my Dad, his freedom."

"Why kill us? Why not just steal the money? You had the key..."

"Two people can keep a secret if one of them is dead, remember? Besides, Johnston already knew Louise had been talking. It was only a matter of time before he had his people get to Louise and find out where the money is."

My adrenaline rush wears off and I feel myself becoming hypothermic. Scarlett's blue lips are a good indication she's feeling the effect of the cold air, too. "Guess we better get a move on." I try to put the key in the cuff holding Scarlett to the limb but I'm shivering like crazy. Scarlett fishes a small waterproof case out of her cargo-pants pocket. I hear the case hit the ground, but don't figure out what it is. Scarlett stabs me in the back with one of the darts. I try to move back from it, but she holds on tight.

"Just sit right here and let me have that key," she orders.

I try to throw the key in the water, but Scarlett slaps it out of my hand and it lands on the water's edge. Scarlett rakes it in with her boot and unlocks her cuffs.

Too late…poison's working on me and I crumble at Scarlett's feet. She stokes my head. "Poor, Cape. I do wish I could stay and keep you alive. Maybe even have sex again, but I have to tie up two loose ends." Scarlett puts my butcher knife in her empty holster, and cups my face in her hands. Instead of slicing my throat as I fully expect, Scarlett kisses me hard and deep. She backs away, never breaking eye contact. "I see my kiss puzzles you, darling. It shouldn't be hard to figure out—that was the 'Kiss of Death.'" Scarlett turns and looks at Salome's lifeless body. "Good-bye, Cape. Killing you really got me off. I'm so horny right now."

CHAPTER THIRTY-ONE

Captured!

From the backseat Ellis points at a police cruiser parked by the creek. "Stop, that's the Sheriff's car."

"Is this the place the camera transmission was coming from?" Darius Martin asks.

"No, that's at Miss Minnie's place, about three miles down the road, but that's the Sheriff's car. If you want to talk to her, this'll be your best bet." The trio walks out on the bridge and scope out the creek in both directions. "I don't see her." RH Carter says.

Ellis walks over to the cruiser and notices the trunk is slightly ajar. "You don't suppose…"

When Darius Martin holds one finger to his pursed lips, Ellis and RH go into stealth mode. Martin motions to Ellis to flip open the trunk on his command. Martin and RH pull their guns and face the trunk

"Now!" Martin says, sweeping his gun around the empty space.

"Nothing! Maybe we better head to the farm."

"But her raft is missing." Ellis says after looking into the empty trunk.

"Raft?"

"Yeah, Detective. Sheriff got all the cruisers equipped with rafts after that carload of kids got swept down the river and drowned in the last hurricane. Sheriff said our department would be capable of handling water rescues and not have to wait for back-up the next time. We practice rescue drills once a month."

"Good thinking on her part." Darius Martin says. "You got any idea why she'd have her raft out today?"

"Not unless she's got an emergency, or a suspect on the run. If she called for back-up and I wasn't there to send help, guess that ends my job. Thanks to y'all." Ellis, a hunter and tracker, notices something the two veteran cops miss. "The way the grass is pressed down, it looks like something heavy slid across it. Had to be her raft, and two sets of tracks lead down to the river. She's headed upstream and someone's with her."

"Can we get a raft?" Darius asks.

"I can call another deputy. They'll have one."

"We don't have time for that. It there another way we can get up the river?"

"Normally, no, but my daddy's a logger and he shovel-logged this tract a few years ago. The old logging path he put in is about a mile up the road. If it hadn' washed out, we should be able to drive almost to the river. Be tough in your car even if the path is in decent shape."

"Why do we want to go down the path?" Darius Martin asks.

"Because it's the only opening between here and Miss Minnie's farm. We'll be able to see up the river almost to her place from the landing—if we can get to it in time."

Carter looks at Darius Martin's low-slung Chevy Impala parked behind the Sheriff's cruiser. "Damn, Darius why don't you drive a 4-wheel-drive truck, like every other grown-ass man in North Carolina?"

"Because I don't need one. Our roads are paved in Charlotte!"

"Well, make a note. Next time you come DownEast, leave your city-slicker-ways home."

"Just get in the car, RH." Martin says. "Lead me to that path, Ellis. I'll show you country-ass boys how we do it in the city."

"Straight ahead on the left, and you might make it to the river, even on this thing. My daddy builds good paths."

Five hundred yards down the path, the Impala bottoms out, and a pitiful sight fills their windshield. Jake sits Louise down and they both start waving like two shipwrecked souls flagging down a passing ship. "RH, thank God! Scarlett DuBois and Salome are trying to kill us. They may have already gotten Cape! He's standing them off at the river."

"Salome?" RH asks. "*My* Salome?"

"Yes, but I don't have time to explain."

"Salome, as in your fiancée?" Darius Martin asked.

"I guess, but that can't be right. She barely *knows*, Scarlett."

Darius Martin points his gun at, RH. "Ellis, take his gun."

"Darius, what the hell are you doing, man?"

"RH, I want to believe with all my heart you're innocent, but when you trained me, you said never ignore my gut, that's what keeps a cop alive. I know you've been doing undercover work with Johnston and Kress, same as Sheriff DuBois. If she's partnered up with your fiancée to kill people, that makes you suspect in my gut. Turn your gun over to Deputy Ellis."

"You're nuts! If what Jake says is true, you'll need back-up." RH says.

"And that includes me!"

"Ellis, can you get a backup unit?" Darius says.

"Yes, sir. Someone should be here in ten minutes."

"Get EMT out here, too. Louise has been shot," Jake adds.

Darius motions to Jake and Louise with his pistol. "Ellis, cuff RH. Folks, stay here. Help is on the way."

"I'm going with you." Jake says.

"No, I can't be—"

"I'm a doctor. Cape is my father-in-law. If he's not dead already, he may need me. I'm going!"

"Let's go then."

Detective Martin and Jake, neither versed in hunting or tracking, jog over tracks that would be an obvious warning sign to hunter-tracker Ellis-Ellis. In addition to the heavy tracks Jake has put down carrying Louise, there is a second, lighter set of tracks that veer sharply off the path. From her hiding position off the trail, Scarlett DuBois watches Jake and Detective Martin run by. With the grace of a panther, she flows back into predator mode and begins stalking her prey down to the river.

I died once from a gunshot to the head and doctors managed to bring me back to life. Dying slowly from poison is a whole different deal. Sights and sounds surrounding me are vivid. Dazzling colors of leaves and the chirping bird-calls seem to be in harmony. In this time I rue the days I rushed through life never stopping to appreciate the beauty of Earth, our only home place.

Like the icy fingers of the Angel of Death a growing cold of the paralysis creeps over me, seeps into me. I can no longer even shiver to help maintain body heat. Soon my organs will begin to shut down. The thought of suffocating terrifies me and I fight to suck air into my lungs. The best I can do is a few choppy breaths. I push with all my might to will my dying legs to get me close to the water. Drowning will be a much quicker death than agonizingly progressive suffocation.

My legs quiver and I manage to make it to the incline of the riverbank. If I can just lift my legs high enough, the weight will be enough to roll me into the river and down to the deep.

Darkness gathering on my periphery vision signals that my time is near. One final try and my weight pushes me down the embankment. I wiggle for the last few inches and mercifully my head is under the cold water. I open my mouth and let the water rush in.

Light fades and darkness surrounds me I have never felt more alone or terrified. Somehow even with water filling my lungs and rushing into my ears, I hear *That if thou shalt confess with thy mouth the Lord Jesus and shalt believe in thine heart that God hath raised him from the dead, thou shalt be saved.* I know that scripture, Romans 10:9. *Say it and believe!* "Lord Jesus!"

My surroundings, once dark and foreboding, turn light and open with air. No longer burdened by my body, I float on a breeze that lifts me higher and higher. I've never felt more alive, so whatever awaits me, I'm ready for it. At about tree-top level, I look back on my body, and I hear: *Hush, little baby, don't say a word, Mama's gonna buy you a mockingbird.* In the distance I can see a white Mansion against a blue sky—this scene is so familiar!

Far off in the distance I hear my name being shouted, "Cape!" The voice is loud, sharp, and urgent. I see Jake and Darius Martin racing down the path heading straight for my body.

Unseen by Jake and Darius, Scarlett is loping after them only yards behind, sizing up the situation and planning her attack.

They grab my body out of the water, Jake turns me on my side and water flows from my body. Detective Martin is on his knees with bowed head and closed eyes.

I turn back to the river and on the other side I see Mother, Father and Grandfather. They are happy to see me and I'm happy to see them. My mother gets down on her knees and prepares to catch me when I leap. Jesus is standing on the other side , too, dressed in a robe of light. Again, I am drawn to the warmth in his eyes and smile on his face: *"Ask and it shall be given you; seek, and ye shall find; knock, and it shall be opened unto you."* Jesus opens his arms and my mother is all smiles, ready to fill her arms with her bundle of joy. Only a few stepping stones and I'm home.

I look back at Jake and Darius, both bent over me now. Jake does compressions and Darius gives me mouth-to-mouth. Scarlett is no more than fifty feet from them now, with her butcher knife at the ready. Jake and Darius are sitting ducks.

"Jesus, you said ask and it shall be given." I say. "Send me back, please."

Traveling at warp speed through a kaleidoscope that connects Heaven to Earth I crash into my body and all its misery. It feels like an elephant is doing jumping-jacks on my chest.

"That's it! That's it! Come on, damn you. Breathe!" Jake screams.

My lungs burn as air heated by the fires of Hell fills them.

"Come on, Dad. Breathe!" Jake urges me.

I jerk my head away from Darius and try to warn them about Scarlett. "B—"

"Don't try to talk. I'll keep you breathing until the poison wears off.

You're going to be fine."

"Anything I can do, Doc?" Darius Martin asks.

"You may have to take over in a little bit. My arm is bleeding again."

"Be—" I struggle to talk.

"Relax, you're back." Jake smiles down.

"Be-Hind-You-damnit!"

Jake turns and Scarlett stabs him with the butcher knife. Before Darius Martin can draw his weapon, Scarlett stabs him in the neck with her second dart. Instinctively, Martin grabs his neck, but Scarlett bum-rushes him into the river, pulling him deep to the riverbed.

Jake puts his hand on the knife handle and pauses. "I think she got an artery."

A rush of bubbles stirs the waters in front of us. Jake and I know the bubbles are the last breaths of Darius Martin. If not for me being so stupid, he would still be alive.

"Run, Jake. Save yourself."

"I can't." Jake said. "She got me good. No way I can run."

A miracle breaks the surface of the water. Darius Martin and Sheriff Scarlett DuBois, her arms pinned behind her, stands and stumble up out of the river. Without a word Darius puts Scarlett's arm behind a tree and handcuffs her.

"What the hell?" Jake gasps. "How did you do that? I thought you were a goner."

"When I saw she wanted me in the water, that suited me just fine. I'm an ex-Navy Seal." Martin explains. "But I feel the poison spreading—what do I need to do, Doc?"

"You have to stay respirated, or you'll die. The poison wears off fairly quickly, but you won't be able to breathe in a few minutes, if that long. Lie down beside Cape here and I'll keep both of you going."

Darius looks at the knife in Jake's chest. "Want me to pull that out?"

"No, I may bleed out before help arrives."

Darius sits up. "Naw, I can't let that happen. She ain't goin' nowhere. I'm going for help." Darius tumbles over onto me and starts gasping for air. "How long before I can't breathe, Doc?"

"Minutes, five minutes, tops."

"Cape, can you breathe on your own? I need to concentrate on Darius."

I gasp for air yet only get half of what I need to answer. "Help—him."

"Jake, I was med student, I can help." Scarlett said. "Handcuff me to Cape. You won't be able to keep both of them going. I know, I kept Cape alive."

Jake moves over to Darius to get the key.

"No, Jake, don't trust her!" I say.

"Why? What harm can it do?" Scarlett says. "It's not like I can kill all of you and get away. The jig's up. I want to help."

"The hell! Don't let her!" I say, running completely out of breath. I suck in a little more air and finish the thought. "She killed four people in Charlotte and—."

As Jake fumbles around for the key, Darius shakes his head, gasping "No. Don't let her go!"

I try to move over to Darius, but I feel like I'm made of lead. Jake grabs me and pulls me beside Darius and alternates respirating us. I turn my head away. "Sit me up…I think I can help Darius. You take care of yourself."

"Cape, you know I'm not a bad person—"

"Shut up!" The energy it takes to yell at Scarlett zaps me. I slump over and Jake pulls me out of his way.

Somehow Jake manages to keep Darius and me alive, but the color drains from his face and his breathing becomes shallow.

"Cape, those times you saw Jesus…was He real?"

I remember back to the warmth and love in the eyes of the man on the other side. Finally able to breathe a little, I sit up and face Jake. "Done a lot of thinking about it—yeah, Jesus is the real deal."

Jake respirates Darius one more time, leans back against a tree, and motions for me to help his slowly recovering patient.

"Set me free," Scarlett begs again. "I can help. Look at Jake—he's dying! I'll admit to everything if you let me get enough money out of the mansion to pay my father's ransom."

Out on the highway sirens turn on to the path and grow louder and nearer.

"Jake, they're here. Hang in there!" I yell.

"His car is blocking the path," Scarlett says. "They can't get here on foot in less than ten minutes. Uncuff me. I can keep Jake alive."

"Shut up, Scarlett!"

"I'm not going to make it, Cape," Jake says. "

"Think of Jana, think of the kids— "

"No, Cape, you don't understand I'm dying…how do I get to know Jesus…or is it too late for me 'cause I never loved Him?"

"Doesn't matter if you love Jesus…He loves you."

"Tell me what to do—"

"Confess with your voice that Jesus is Lord and you believe that He rose from the dead."

"That's it?"

"Pretty much—"

Jake leans forward and slowly sinks onto Detective Martin's chest.

I roll Jake over and start to respirate him, but one look at his face is all I need to know that Jake Draughon is dead. I continue respirating Darius until he breathes a little on his own and an EMT is pushing me out of the way to take over.

"You callous son-of-a-bitch...! You let the father of your grandchildren die!" Scarlett hisses as Deputy Ellis stands her up, "You don't deserve to wear the uniform," Ellis says, "or this! ripping the badge from her jacket. Then he shoves Scarlett over to RH Carter who cuffs her hands behind her back.

Ah—*Something evil cloaked in good...* just like Miss Minnie said, I think, then lean back against the sturdy bark of a tall pine, awaiting my turn with the EMS guys.

CHAPTER THIRTY-TWO
Crime and Punishment

Leaves that have managed to hang on until the last day of fall succumb to a bitter north wind blowing across Slick Rock. As soon as I step outside, I realize the blazer I've chosen is too lightweight, not capable of withstanding today's weather. Rather than return to the mansion for a warmer jacket, I opt to face Mother Nature, whose sudden freeze is only an ice cube in comparison to Jana's deep frost. Besides, my meeting with the engraver who will add Jake's name to his sepulcher at Forest Lawn shouldn't take long. I'm not looking forward to the finality of this task, but someone has to do it. Even though Jake has been dead two years today, Jana refuses to accept his death, so I volunteer to do what must be done.

Bare poplars lining the driveway quake in the wind and stir my pent-up remorse. I stop in the place Jake caused me to fall into a mud puddle. That seems funny now. Hard to believe that someone as young and full of life as Jake is no longer with us. A pang of guilt shoots through my heart and I remember how I took advantage of his good nature to escape from the mansion. Had I listened to RH and the rest of the family, there's a good chance Jake would still be alive. This thorny regret may also be on Jana's mind, though she never mentions it.

Jana is standing under the portico in her housecoat. I step out and give her a sweeping two-hand wave, but she turns and goes back inside. I stop at the now-unmanned gatehouse and begin a text to her—our primary form of communication now. But I erase my message before sending and head to Forest Lawn.

The engraver's truck is parked next to the mausoleum, so I pull in behind it and walk up to the cab. The driver hops out and shakes my hand. "I'm Cal Bowden, just wanted to tell you, I'm sorry for your loss, Mr. Thomas. Doc's death was personal to me. I mean we weren't best buds or nothing, but he saved my little boy's life. I won't ever forget that…and there's no charge for the engraving."

"You don't have to do that, Cal. We don't mind pay—"

"I know Mr. Fisher can buy the county if he has a mind to, but I couldn't afford insurance when my boy got sick. Doc Jake knew that and never charged me a dime for curing my boy. The hospital charged plenty, but Doc cut my expenses anyway he could. Said if he could find any natur-o-pathic, reckon I said that right, remedies he'd see I got those rather than the expensive prescription stuff. I asked him how he knew about such things. He said an old lady right here is the county and some foreign-named Doctor schooled him pretty good in all that.

"I don't believe Doc was no religious man, but one time when my boy was going through a rough patch, I asked him what else I could do, since it looked like the best medical science had to offer failed us. He said, 'Pray for a miracle, some times they happen.' I ain't never forgot that, neither. Since the Good Lord seen fit to send us a miracle, me and my family go to church every Sunday."

Cal's story would be good for Jana to hear, too. I consider asking Cal to stop by the mansion, but discard the notion—don't know how Jana would treat Cal right now.

"I'm glad you told me that story. Jake *was* a fine man. I had no idea he was so altruistic."

"Doc was the best al-true-risk-it there ever was, Mr. Thomas, the very best." Cal looks at his watch. "I reckon I better get to work. Please tell Doc's widow and young'uns, me and mine is sorry for their loss."

"I will."

"Oh, and one more thing, my old lady's pregnant. If it's a boy, we're going name him Jake…you know, after Doc. I wanted to name him Doc, but the old lady said that sounded like a cartoon character. I said, well, a young'un named, Doc might fancy they could be a doctor one day." Cal shakes his head. "But she's a mite headstrong. I'm pretty sure our boy will be named Jake."

"I pray it's a healthy baby boy, Cal. Jake would be honored."

For some reason I can't bring myself to leave as I watch Cal add Jake's name to the stone. I don't know that I've ever witnessed a labor of love before, but I'm overwhelmed by the caring way Cal works on the marble.

The shadow of a man coming up behind me reaches all the way to Jake's sepulcher and stops. Things like this used to spook me, but no more because the threat to my family is over. The enormity of the shadow announces my visitor.

"Good morning, Detective!"

"Got eyes in the back of your head, now?"

"Nope, I only know one person who sports a shadow the size of a Mack truck. What brings you back to Slick Rock?"

"Well, I'm driving along, just my Mack-truck shadow and me, on my way to the beach. And I see Slick Rock is close. So I think, maybe I'll just drop by and see, Cape Thomas for a minute. He's always quick with a compliment—or was that shadow remark an insult?"

"Definitely a compliment, Detective, and I always have a minute for the man who saved my life."

"Feeling's mutual, Cape."

"Darius, glad we made it to a first-name basis."

Darius Martin spreads his tremendous arms and pulls me into his chest for a man hug. "I appreciate that. I thought maybe you still had hard feelings...for how I treated you in Charlotte?"

"Got over those feelings the moment you saved my life." I peek over to see how Cal is progressing and Darius follows my gaze. "Shame such a good life had to end like that."

I've had that thought so many times I never want to broach the subject again. "True. So why're you here, Darius?"

"I know that Jake's dying is eating you alive. It didn't help that Scarlett accused you at the trial of letting Jake die—and then every time a microphone was stuck in her face. It bothered me, too, but she wasn't going to keep her word or get help for him."

"I know that, and I know I didn't have the medical expertise to save Jake." I look at Darius. "I'm just happy that I had the CPR skills to keep you going until help arrived."

"You did good, Cape."

"So they say."

"Is your daughter handling Jake's death any better?"

"We don't talk that much—it'd be a lot easier for her if I'd died and Jake had lived."

"It's natural to feel that way—I lost friends when I was in the Seals. You always feel guilty that you lived and they died."

Cal, stands and regards his work. "All done here, Mr. Thomas." Then he points to Darius. "Seen you on T.V. Glad you caught her, Detective. Good job."

"Thank you, but I had a lot of help."

"Ain't what folks round here say," Cal says. "I'll be seeing y'all."

Cal grabs both our hands.

His callused grip is like a vice, and even Darius winces.

"God Bless and keep y'all safe!"

We watch as Cal secures his tools and drives off.

"So, how do *you* cope with the guilt, Darius?"

"Unfortunately, some vets don't. That's one reason for the high number of veteran suicides. I volunteer to work with vets who are struggling."

"What do you do?"

"Once they realize that I'm one of them, they listen. I tell 'em how I see it. Our buddies died doing their jobs to make sure we didn't die. Same as we do for them, when somehow we survive and they don't. Every day now I promise to make the most of the life my buddies died to give me. We owe 'em that—along with our deep gratitude and our continuing memory of their sacrifice."

I think of Jake and his decision to leave his safe place and come back for me. "Something happened out there that day. I can't get it off my mind."

"What's that?"

"Promise you won't repeat this to anyone? If it gets out they'll ground me for good."

"Whatever you tell me stays our secret," Darius promises.

"Before you and Jake brought me back. I was up in the air hovering above the trees looking down at my body. Coolest flying I've ever done. I saw you guys coming down the path. I also saw something you didn't see."

"What was that?"

"I saw Scarlett following behind you. I wanted to warn you, to let you know that I was just fine being dead."

"But you did warn us."

"Too late for Jake, and without your Seal training you would have died, too. Scarlett DuBois, is a worthy adversary, even for a Navy Seal."

"So did you see the bright light and all that?" Darius said.

That question is the very reason I don't speak of what happened to me. "Forget it. I know, it sounds crazy."

"I didn't mean it like that. Cape, this isn't the only time I've heard a story like this. It's amazing how similar they are, but I'd like to hear yours."

"Darius, when I was a child, my grandfather read me stories from the Bible. I've done a lot of thinking about this and a lot of reading the Bible lately. There're a couple of verses that explain what happened to me. John 14:2-3. I can't quote them exactly, but they go something like—"

"In my Father's house are many mansions: if it were not so, I would have told you I go to prepare a place for you. And if I go and prepare a place for you, I will come again, and receive you unto myself; that where I am, there ye may be also."

"Pretty impressive, Detective."

Darius has his eyes closed and seems to be quoting from photographic memory. I have no doubt he quoted the verses verbatim.

"Not really," Darius smiles. "My father is a Baptist minister."

"When you and Jake got to my body, you prayed over me, didn't you?"

"You saw that?"

"Yes, and knowing that, and hearing that your Dad is a minister, I guess I can share this. What was your prayer, by the way?"

"I prayed for God to bring you back and keep us all safe."

I tell Darius about seeing my family and how happy I was to be back with them. "Then Jesus said, 'Ask and it shall be given you; seek, and ye shall find; knock, and it shall be opened unto you.'"

"And you asked to come back," Darius says. "didn't you?"

"Yes. But why did Jesus grant my request and only answer part of your prayer? Why didn't He save Jake? Or at least let him live long enough to get saved?"

Darius gives me the funniest look. Like somehow or another I missed the big picture.

"Jake's, last words *were*, 'Jesus is Lord.' As he fell against my chest, I heard him whisper that. It was a happy moment for me!"

"What?"

"That's right, I was there, remember?" Darius bows his head and looks to be offering a prayer—I can't be sure.

"Cape, I'm going to tell you like I tell the vets when they ask that same question. All I know for sure and certain is that God doesn't make mistakes."

That statement gives me a lot of food for thought.

"Boy, that takes a load off. I made a vow to Jake, a lot like that promise you make to your fellow vets. A world-class brain surgeon gave his life to save me," I say. "The least I can do is be a first-class airline pilot with the life I was given."

"How's that going for you?"

"I take my check ride at week's end. I start back as a co-pilot, but I can't complain. I've been out of flying a while. My first flight is with a Captain who is the best stick-and-rudder man I've seen."

"Is that so?"

"Yep, trained him myself."

Darius moves closer to Jake's sepulcher to admire Cal's work. I walk beside him.

"I appreciate you opening up, Cape."

Darius runs his hand over the lettering. "That fellow does good work, smooth as glass."

I tap Darius on the shoulder, he turns and faces me. "You weren't just passing through Slick Rock, were you?"

"No, RH was worried about you. He felt like I could help and I wanted to try—I owe you that."

"You have, and maybe you could stop by and see RH? He pretends, but I know it's hard for him, too."

"Funny, you say that. I'm taking him to Southern Smoke for some *Que* today."

"Thought DownEast didn't set well with you?"

"This place is growing on me, especially the bar-be-que."

"It's the best!"

Darius puts his country-ham size hand on my shoulders and locks his eyes on mine. "I feel like there's something you're not telling me. You sure you're OK?"

"I am now, but a few months ago, I visited the Huck Finn place. I left a note in my truck—I was ready to end it."

"What stopped you?"

"I looked down in that stream and it reminded me of the one you cross to get to, Jesus. I knew if I did what I'd planned, I'd never make it to that mansion on the other side."

Darius gives me a big bear hug and puts his business card in my blazer pocket. "Cape, if you ever need to talk, you call me. We've been in battle together, now. That makes us brothers in arms."

"It's an honor to be your brother. I got a jump seat for you any time you decide to fly Aeromax Airlines. You just tell them to give Cape Thomas a call."

Darius looks at my sepulcher across from Jake's. "You mean, *Captain* Cape Thomas, don't you?"

"That's exactly what I mean."

What I used to enjoy most, spending time with my family, is now limited and strained. For that reason, I practically live in Atlanta while I train with AeroMax. About the only time I make it back to the mansion is when I'm called to testify for the prosecution in Scarlett's appeals trial. In between I try to forget about her, but sometimes when I'm testifying I look at Scarlett, who always has a pleasant smile on her face, and wonder what might have been.

Those thoughts are quickly vanquished when I think of how, Ally, Celine, Betty and the others died at the hands of this cold-blooded killer. The trial is pretty cut and dry, because of the overwhelming evidence, plus testimony from Darius and me seals Scarlett's fate.

Even though it is expected, her verdict hits me hard. Scarlett rises before the judge, who decrees: "Scarlett DuBois, a jury of your peers has found you guilty of first-degree murder. I order that you be transported to Central Prison, where you will be executed by lethal injection."

No emotion shows on Scarlett's face, but when our eyes meet I see the warmth that drew me to Scarlett in the first place. When the deputies lead her away from the defense table, Scarlett turns to me and pleads, "Cape, please forgive me?"

I turn and leave the courtroom without a word, but my gut is tied in knots. Although I know she deserves to die, I feel relief that it will be years before that happens.

Two years after Scarlett is sentenced and after more than a few glitches in my training, I move back to the flight deck as a first officer. My first day back is going well and I feel right at home in the cockpit. That is, until I mistakenly sit in the left seat, the captain's seat. I unbuckle, move to the co-pilot seat, and peruse the preflight checklist. Penni, a flight attendant from my distant past, pokes her head inside the cockpit door. "Good to see you back in a 747, Cape."

"Thank you, darlin'. Good to be back."

Shane walks up behind Penni. "Excuse me, ma'am. Would you mind telling the elderly gentlemen that's he's in my seat?"

"But, you're the captain?" Penni says.

"No, ma'am, you're mistaken. Any time the older gentleman is on the flight deck he's the captain. Please convey my order." Shane bends down and whispers to her, "You may have to yell, I understand older people don't hear so hot."

"Cape, this young whippersnapper says you're in his seat."

I stand and shake Shane's hand. "My hearing is just fine, Captain. Probably a good idea to let me ride shotgun a while—training didn't go as smoothly as I'd hoped. The company wants to make sure my 747 flying skills haven't atrophied—"

"Well, that's because the suits weren't riding with you when you rolled a 737 on a maintenance flight. Just like the suits weren't there when you skimmed an Aerostar across the water to get into Bader Field in Atlantic City with a tail wind. And last but not least a 25,000-hour 747 captain doesn't fly right seat on my flight deck."

Every event Shane recalls is true, and as much as I want to, I can't deny them.

"It was wrong of me to do stupid things like that, Shane. I endangered people's lives, *your* life, I—"

"No, no—you took seat-of-the-pants flying to a new level. I'll never be half the pilot—"

"Shane, truth is I was stupid, and seat-of-the pants-flying is doing things half-assed. The company has a system for a reason, to keep passengers safe, get it?"

Shane's face turns six shades of red. Captains are never dressed down by first officers and I know I've overstepped my bounds. Shane leaves the cockpit to cool off and I hear Penni whisper, "That's not the Cape Thomas I remember."

"Yeah, me either, Penni," Shane says. "Cape Thomas has balls of steel —this imposter's are made of cotton-candy!"

Shane returns to the flight deck, adjusts his seat, and slides under the controls. "Let's go over the checklist."

"Ready when you are, Sir." I answer.

Because most of the captains on the line know or have at least heard of me, there are no more scenes like Shane and I had when I'm teamed with them. They do their jobs as captains, and I do my job as first officer.

I want to be back in the left seat so bad it consumes me! For the next year, when I'm not flying the line I spend all my extra time honing my skills flying aerobatics and gliders. Even in gliders, I fly only to the tolerances Sarge demanded. At times I feel and hear Sarge beside me, pushing me to focus and to better my best because one day my passengers may need all the acumen a guy like Sullenburger provided on the Hudson that cold day in January 2009.

Rather than commute back and forth to the mansion, I rent a small apartment near the airport in Atlanta. When I have a spare moment, or someone asks, I show off the pictures of my family stored on my phone. Truth is, Jana and I haven't spoken in months. I call every night, but rather than talk to me, Jana hands the phone over to the kids. When we finish talking, she has them pray for me before they go to bed. I always end my conversation with "Tell your mom I love her, too..." They say they do, but she never answers back.

My old nemesis Darius Martin has become my best friend, and his calls provide encouragement that keeps me going. I know some-thing's up when he calls one day and asks if my offer of a jump seat is still valid. Two things I've learned about, Darius Martin: he doesn't like to fly; and he's a terrible actor. I check my schedule and see I'm flying with Shane on my next trip. Which is unusual since Shane requested not to be paired with me since our dust-up.

"You still got pull, don't you, Cape?" Darius said.

"Well, the captain determines jump-seat assignments, but as it turns out I'm flying with a captain who may see things my way. Come down to Atlanta—you can stay with me. If the jump seat doesn't work out ,I'll use my employee discount to cover your ticket."

The flight goes off without a hitch and when we land at RDU, Shane, who's been a butthole the entire trip, orders me to taxi to the gate. I see firetrucks along our route and figure a retiring captain or a fallen hero is on board one of the planes taxiing to the gates behind us. To my surprise, the trucks spray an arc of water over our plane. "What's going on, we got a hero on board?"

Shane shrugs with a big old jackass-eating-briars grin. "I guess someone did something really cool." Before I can ask more questions, Shane parks the plane at the gate. "Follow me, Cape." Going down the spiral staircase, I catch a glimpse of one of my old flight attendants, Linda Jessup, the doctor's wife. She's dressed in an AeroMax uniform and looks every bit as beautiful as she did when she actually worked for AeroMax. Darius Martin, a one-way passenger who shouldn't be onboard, nor should he be in first-class, waves to me. I turn to thank Shane for getting Darius the upgrade. That's when I notice the first-class section is *packed* with people from my flying past. I wade into the crowd hugging and kissing friends I haven't seen in years.

At the back of the cabin is my old girlfriend, Grace, who got me fired from AeroMax, not intentionally but to save her marriage that didn't work out. She, too, is dressed in an AeroMax uniform and looks exactly the way she looked when I first laid eyes on her as a new hire. She hugs me, fitting into my arms like the last piece of a Jigsaw puzzle. Before I can express that feeling, the crowd starts to part as a tall, gray-haired gentleman comes down the aisle to me. "Mr. Thomas, I haven't had the pleasure of meeting you, I'm Ross Force, CEO of AeroMax Airlines."

"Yes, Sir. I recognize you from the posters and billboards...and may I say you've done a fine job since you took over the company."

"Thank you, Mr. Thomas. I'm a fan of your's, too. In truth, you have a lot of fans and admirers in management. We've been monitoring your progress and I'm impressed with the way you do things by the book." Mr. Force, reaches into his pocket and pulls out a set of gold wings. "Please remove your silver wings, Mr. Thomas."

"Yes, Sir."

Ross Force pins me in gold and steps back so a publicity photographer can get a shot of us both.

"I speak for the entire company when I say—" Ross pauses for effect, "Welcome back, Captain Cape Thomas!"

From out of nowhere comes Jana and the kids, with Mr. Fisher. The look on Jana's face tells me we have no more tension. Our relationship is solid. "Dad, I'm so proud of you and I want you to teach Cape T and Laura your old-school ways."

"You mean hunting, fishing, and general mayhem?"

"Yes, but with conditions." Jana says beaming.

"Oh, brother…!"

"Dad, you have to teach them all the old-school ways at Miss Minnie's place. The same place you learned them."

"Did you check with Miss Minnie on that? Last time I was there, I kinda screwed things up."

Jana moves to the side and Miss Minnie and Jimmy stand before me. "I want you to have this, Boy." Miss Minnie says, and hands me the deed to her farm.

"But you could sell the farm. The money from the sale—"

"Ain't no profit left in that place, especially after the half-ass remodeling y'all did out there. Jimmy said I'm better to give it away and declare the loss. And Jimmy is successful, not some gypsy vagabond like you turned out to be." Miss Minnie said.

"Now, Miss Minnie," Jimmy says. "you don't want me to tell about all the crying you did when we almost lost your favorite gypsy vagabond, do you?"

"Won't crying, I don't know where you got that idea. All I know is that I like my new house you built me better than I like that old shack in the middle of nowhere." Miss Minnie said.

"But, you always said that place connected you to your roots and it was our path to the sea." I recalled for her. "And you were right, because without that escape route I would have died."

"Look, boy. We don't need any escape route no more, and I'm just goin' be upfront with you. No way I'm tradin' Shangri-La for Shoddy-Da!"

"Miss Minnie, without you there, that place means nothing to me. You made it special," I say. "Everything I know about nature I learned from you."

"And I plan on bein' there to teach them babies about the Good Lord and that what He provides is all we need," Miss Minnie says, shaking her finger up in my face. "I'm also plannin' on joinin' up with the saints there, and when I'm done, that's goin' be my final resting place."

"OK, but I'm confused. I thought you didn't want to be in the middle of nowhere?"

"Ain't nothing changed—don't never listen! I said I didn't want to *live* in the middle of nowhere—resting eternally ain't the same thing. And one more thing, don't you mess up that place no more with your jack-leg carpentry!"

"I won't Miss Minnie. I'll hire Raphael to do all the work, and let's hope it's a hundred years 'fore you have that meeting with the saints."

I turn back to Jana. "I'm so happy you and the kids are here! But why the change of heart?"

"Because I had time to sort things out and I realized, without the skills you learned from Miss Minnie you wouldn't be here. This world is changing, Dad. I don't want my children to be defenseless. Teach them the things Miss Minnie taught you! You're the only father they have now."

"Any chance of you joining us?" I said.

"I was hoping you'd ask."

Every idea I've had about paradise is blasted wide open. It's not a tropical island or the land of milk and honey. Paradise is being surrounded by people you love and who love you back.

"I want to start right away." I said.

"You're the boss, Dad!"

When I finish saying my good-byes to everyone, Shane heads back to the cockpit to finish paperwork, and only Grace and I are left on the plane.

"I'm only going to be in town for a few days." Grace says. "I'd like to see you…"

"I thought you'd have married by now?"

Grace reaches for my hand. "Never got over you. I should have never gone back to my ex."

Funny how honesty begets honesty.

"The fault wasn't yours, Grace. I failed myself and, more importantly, I failed you."

Grace hugs me and I hug her right back.

"I got a chance to talk to Detective Martin on the flight," she says. "He tells me that you had a life-changing experience?"

"You mean my near-death experience?"

"No, I mean your encounter with Jesus. Remember when you made fun of me for believing?"

"Yeah, that was wrong. People have a right to their beliefs—without being harassed."

"Boy, you have changed."

"Trying, but I'm still a sinner."

"We all are."

I nod. "May I see you tomorrow?"

"Let's go right now, Cape. I don't want to waste one more day—Let's start our lives anew. No looking back—"

"I can't. I made a promise to someone—"

"Lady-friend?"

"It's not like that, Grace."

Grace hands me a business card. "OK. But if you're ever in Denver, look me up. Good-bye, Cape"

Grace bolts from the plane and Shane joins me in the doorway. We watch together as she runs down the jet bridge. "Got to hand it to you, Captain. You're the only guy I know who would turn that woman down. The one you're meeting must be a looker!"

"It's not what you think, Shane."

"Right." Shane gives me an exaggerated wink and nod. "Anything you say, Captain Casanova."

"People change." I unpin the gold wings from my jacket and hand them to Shane.

"What the hell, Cape?"

"Give them back to, Mr. Force. Tell him I appreciate the promotion, but I've got a better offer."

"Why? I know what you went through to get these back."

"Shane, what's important is who we love and who loves us. That's the true measure of life." I said. "I didn't realize that until I found out how Sarge really felt about me."

"I know he was hard on you. That's no secret, but I'm sure he cared about you."

"Actually, he loved me, but if Betty hadn't told me about his feelings I would never have known that. What a loss that would've been for me... When I die, I don't want you standing over my grave wondering how I felt about you. I love you. You've always been more than a friend and a coworker to me—more like a son. When you made the heavies, I never told you, but I was proud."

Shane looks at me like I've sprouted a third eye and grown horns.

"I know what I'm saying doesn't make sense to you, now. But when I'm gone...it will."

"Damn, Cape!" Shane wipes at his eyes. "This A/C system on here must be contaminated, it's full of irritants."

"I'll make a note of that on my final inspection."

"Don't go, Cape. I'm not ready to lose my mentor. Besides, I…I need you around to straighten me out when I do something stupid, like try and abdicate my captain's position to some doddering, unqualified old geezer."

"One day, that old geezer will be you," I smile, extending my hand. "I'll keep an extra rocking chair on my porch for you when that day comes."

"You can't quit, you love flying!"

"I'll never give up flying. First thing I'll do at Miss Minnie's place is put in a runway. I think I'll start teaching kids how to fly. There's a shortage of pilots, you know. And now that I'm part of a rich family, I guess I can do it for free. You know, like Sarge used to do. I expect to see you out there helping on a regular basis."

Shane snaps to attention and fires off a crisp salute. "I'll be there every chance I get."

"I appreciate that. Keep'em safe, Shane."

I brace against the cold wind howling over the tarmac and make my final walk-around of the plane. When I finish, I back off and stare at the 747's beautiful aerodynamic lines silhouetted against the gray winter sky. What a way to make a living—what a wonderful life I've had.

"Godspeed, old girl."

I give her a salute, snappier than the one Shane afforded me. "Captain Cape Thomas, signing off for the last time from AeroMax Airlines."

I consider chasing after Grace. Instead, I reach into my pocket and pull out a note I received only a few weeks earlier:

Cape: I suppose you've heard about me dropping my appeals and asking the state to carry out my sentence as quickly as possible. They have obliged. Even though I don't have any family or friends that claim me, I know I won't die alone. I owe you that. The talk you had with Jake just before he died put me on the road to salvation. Even so, I'm scared and it would mean so much to see a familiar face before I die. If you can't make it, please forgive me. Love, Scarlett.

Central Prison, in Raleigh, with its recent make-over, looks nowhere near its 133 years of age. The brick buildings could easily be mistaken for a hospital or state offices, if they weren't surrounded by razor-sharp concertina wire.

After my little stint in the Charlotte jail, I promised myself I'd never get close to the penal system again. Scarlett's request, however, trumps that notion. If I were in her place, I'd want someone there by me, too, in my time of need.

Despite the fact that Scarlett killed people I loved, and almost killed me I know there is good in her. There is no way to justify what Scarlett did, but the Bible says we must forgive. I don't know that I'm there yet, but I made a promise...and I tend to keep my promises.

Scudding clouds, racing off ahead of an approaching warm front scrape the tops of the parking lot lights. Bare limbs of oaks bordering the prison property are in a pugilistic battle fueled by the wind. I step out of my truck and take in all nature has to offer. I have no idea what privileges a condemned prisoner like Scarlett is afforded, but I hope it includes one last look at the natural wonders outside her prison walls.

The guards in the Visitor's Center have me step through a metal detector and pat me down for any weapon or contraband I may try to slip in to the condemned prisoner. From there, I'm escorted to the Central Prison Mailroom where I'm told to sign an attendance book. At another location, family members of victims and the press, are processed in and sign an attendance book, too. Eventually we all wind up in an area called, The Observation Room.

Five rows of plastic chairs each reserved for the condemned one's family and attorneys sit next to the observation window. My latent Baptist training emerges and I look for a seat way in the back. A guard corrects my seating choice, guiding me to the front row next to the execution-chamber window. No words are spoken, but I hear others as they fill the seats behind me.

In the Preparation Room, Scarlett, wearing only her underwear and an incontinence brief, is being readied for execution. She is placed on a gurney and her head is elevated to an approximate 45-degree angle. Her arms and legs are secured by leather cuffs. Canvas straps and adhesives across her torso hold her firmly against the gurney. A roll of gauze is placed into each palm, and she is asked to clench her hands and they are taped shut.

Once various monitoring devices and catheters are attached, a plain white sheet is placed over her. Only her head and arms are exposed. When fully prepared for execution, the Warden asks if she has any final words to be released to the public once the execution is over. According to the press release, Scarlett asked at this time for forgiveness and offered prayers to the victims' families.

From the Preparation Room, two guards roll Scarlett into the Death Chamber. She is only a few feet away from me when she makes eye contact. Her lips part into a weak smile and she mouths *Thanks*. I have never faced a condemned prisoner before and I don't know how I'm supposed to react. I nod, but don't smile. Scarlett has on no makeup and, other than showing some fine lines around her eyes, looks like a woman nearer 30 than 50.

The Warden nods his head and one of the execution team members attaches a cable to the cardiac-monitoring device in the observation room. Another nod and the privacy curtain behind Scarlett is closed. Her eyes are open wide. I'm sure she's been briefed that this is the beginning of the execution process. Her chest rises and falls rapidly and she starts to mouth the Lord's Prayer. Scarlett did wrong, but I know Jesus is on the other side of the river ready to embrace His lost sheep. I join Scarlett in the Lord's Prayer with the fervor of a snake-handling preacher on Sand Mountain.

The Warden returns to the Death Chamber and makes a call from the red phone on the wall. When he hangs up he barely dips his head and the sedative begins to flow into Scarlett's veins. A single tear forms in the corner of her eye and I watch as it slowly traces her high cheekbone and drops softly onto her hair.

It seems like an hour, but it takes only 14 minutes and 12 seconds for the poison that follows the sedatives to stop her heart. A physician examines her and declares her dead. A curtain is drawn across the observation room and we are escorted back to the Visitors Center. After signing some papers, I leave the Visitors Center hoping my sadness will stay there. But no. Instead, it settles in my heart and, I fear, it will becomes a permanent part of me like some low-grade poison running through my own veins.

I concentrate on my driving. Not until I leave the heavy Raleigh traffic, driving east, does my mind ease somewhat. After I park in front of Miss Minnie's old house, I'm drawn back to the time I spent here with Scarlett —good times, but sad to recall now.

I grab up two pieces of scrap lumber laying on the porch and nail them into a cross. No one claimed Scarlett's body, so I filled out the necessary paperwork to have her brought back here. I can't bear the thought of her being buried in an unmarked grave on prison grounds. Scarlett prayed for forgiveness, and I believe she will be granted that, but not by me, not now anyway.

I walk the path to the Huck Finn place and stop in the stretch of sugar-sand Scarlett loved. The soil is soft, pressing the cross into the ground where she will be buried takes little physical effort—looking at the finished product is much harder. I hit my knees to pray that I can forgive, but images of those Scarlett murdered fill my mind: Leonardo—Lenny, so young with so much to live for; his grandmother, an immigrant struggling to make it in a foreign land and beginning to succeed; Donna Sue Hobart, an innocent woman who died for doing her job; James Sauls, a man whose only crime was falling in love; Celine Seabolt, cut down in the prime of her life—and Ally, a woman full of love and willing to nurse a broken man back to health.

And Betty, sweet, sweet, Betty, and her young aide, Ethan Warren... Deep sobs rack my body. Though I know I'm supposed to forgive—I can't. Giving Scarlett a decent place for her eternal rest is all I am capable of for now.

Only one place in the whole world can comfort me. I continue down the path to the Huck Finn place, wandering in my heart to happier days. I slow to look at the place Scarlett put up the game cameras to monitor my whereabouts. As it turns out, tracking my steps is not the purpose they served. Rather than betray me, those cameras saved my life.

When the creek comes into view, I grab up two sweet-gum balls and press different colored leaves into each of the spiked seed pods. Not exactly perfect sailing vessels, but adequate for the contest I devised as a kid. Before they hit the water I choose the red-tinted maple leaf to beat the yellow poplar leaf over the hundred-foot run to the waterfall downstream. The poplar leaf gets a little jump on the maple. I trot down to the waterfall, anticipating a photo-finish as the gum balls jockey for position on the turbulent backstretch. About a foot from the finish line, my phone rings.

"Hey, Dad, the kids and I are here to see you—where are you?"

"At the Huck Finn place—the fishing hole I told you about."

"So we just follow the path down?"

"Yeah, but I'll meet you in the field and guide you to this place."

Across the field I see Jana and the kids, dressed in bib overalls and wearing straw hats. Each has a cane pole over their shoulders and they break out in a wild sprint when they see me.

What a sight! I'm going to love my new job.

The End

Hi, just wanted to thank you for taking time to read my book. I'd appreciate you doing a review for me or sharing a link on Facebook and Twitter. Take care and stay safe.

Ted Miller Brogden

Meet the author:

Ted Miller Brogden is an instrument rated pilot, certified diver, internationally published author, and practicing raconteur. He spends most of his time in eastern North Carolina and points South, but his favorite cities are New York and New Orleans.

When asked his simplified view of life, Brogden says, "I've always tried to face life like an oyster does—when given grit, give back a pearl."

Other Books by Ted Miller Brogden:
Jigsaw
The Last Kincaid

www.ingramcontent.com/pod-product-compliance
Lightning Source LLC
Chambersburg PA
CBHW021440240626
47153CB00001B/230